Praise for *Jack*

"For Marilynne Robinson's devotees, John Ames Boughton, the titular Jack of the fourth volume of her award-winning Gilead novels, is one of the most eagerly awaited literary figures since Godot . . . Robinson is acclaimed for her numinous accounts of faith, forgiveness and hope, but read in this electrifying year of national crisis, the Gilead books are unified as well by her unsparing indictment of the American history of racism and inequality, and Christianity's uneven will to fight them . . . I am looking forward to a fifth volume that will fill in their saga, and I hope it will be called *Della*."

—Elaine Showalter, *The New York Times Book Review*

"*Jack* is not only a personal story of 'apophatic loneliness.' It opens out into a social and political history of painful significance and relevance . . . The question that haunts [Robinson's] work—can people change?—is one to be asked of societies as much as of individuals. It is a theological question too. Like the great American writers she is so steeped in—Hawthorne, Whitman, Melville, Dickinson, Twain—there is a profound issue of freedom at the core of her novels. *Can* we change our lives?"

—Hermione Lee, *The New York Review of Books*

"*Jack* is a love story; it contains miracles . . . Robinson is pulling light from darkness, life from death. It is a remarkable fact of her genius that every page or paragraph of *Jack* could stand for the whole book. Every time Jack says something, he seems to say it all. The problems of the novel, both moral and theological, are so perfectly paradoxical that all we can do is circle around, waiting for them to eat themselves, turn into their opposites, or cancel each other out. And then, impossibly, there is Della."

—Anne Enright, *London Review of Books*

"As each new book appears, the world that Marilynne Robinson first created in *Gilead* becomes more textured and complex . . . What emerges at the end of *Jack* is the extent of Marilynne Robinson's command. She shares with George Eliot an interest in large questions and also a fascination with a wildness in the soul, with a sensuality and a spiritual striving that cannot be easily calmed, and can be captured only by the rarest talent."

—Colm Tóibín, *4Columns*

"Each of [Robinson's] novels has celebrated the fact that the ineffable is inseparable from the quotidian, and rendered the ineffable, quotidian world back to us, peculiar, luminous, and precise . . . There are passages when Jack's eye glimmers so clearly on the moment, when his dream logic feels so apt, that the whole world Robinson has illuminated with such care and attention reappears, and we are returned to the prophetic everyday."

—Jordan Kisner, *The Atlantic*

"*Jack* fits beautifully into the subtle weave of Robinson's Gilead books; that said, it could perfectly well be read on its own. It is a meditation on faith: not only faith in God but the faith human beings can place in each other, faith that will stand no matter what. Faith, indeed, that the world might improve and be redeemed."

—Erica Wagner, *Financial Times*

"With the sublime *Jack*, [Marilynne Robinson] resumes and deepens her quest, extending it to the contemplation of race . . . Robinson masterfully allows her protagonists to do the heavy lifting of the storytelling and employs deceptively simple dialogue as her primary tool. But make no mistake—there is richness and depth at every turn."

—De'Shawn Charles Winslow, *O, The Oprah Magazine*

"Every time Robinson tells this story, it is both a better story and truer."   —Nikhil Krishnan, *The Telegraph*

"Not just a meditation on faith and human suffering but a singular portrait of the divine."   —Leah Greenblatt, *Entertainment Weekly*

"*Jack* achieves something of a singular beauty . . . It's a powerfully moving book, and a reminder that no visit to Robinson's Gilead—even when it never sets foot in that town—is a wasted visit."
                                    —Alex McLevy, *The A.V. Club*

"In *Jack*, Robinson meets racial inequality head-on . . . *Jack* is not a novel that offers answers to the urgent moral question of American racism. Nor should it . . . [Robinson] traces a relationship from its complicated inception to its immensely troubled and moving maturity, and, in so doing, asks American readers to consider both the cruelties of our country's racist recent history and the utter potential, for white Americans in particular, of accepting that we are intrinsically able to do harm. That acceptance brings Jack closer to both love and grace. For our country—who knows?—it could well do the same."   —Lily Meyer, NPR

Alec Soth / Magnum Photos

Marilynne Robinson

JACK

Marilynne Robinson is the author of *Gilead*, winner of the 2005 Pulitzer Prize for Fiction and the National Book Critics Circle Award; *Home* (2008), winner of the Orange Prize and the Los Angeles Times Book Prize; and *Lila* (2014), winner of the National Book Critics Circle Award. Her first novel, *Housekeeping* (1980), won the PEN/Hemingway Award. Robinson's nonfiction books include *The Givenness of Things* (2015), *When I Was a Child I Read Books* (2012), *Absence of Mind* (2010), *The Death of Adam* (1998), and *Mother Country* (1989). She is the recipient of a 2012 National Humanities Medal, awarded by President Barack Obama, for "her grace and intelligence in writing." Marilynne Robinson lives in Iowa City, Iowa.

ALSO BY MARILYNNE ROBINSON

FICTION

Housekeeping

Gilead

Home

Lila

NONFICTION

*Mother Country: Britain, the Welfare State
and Nuclear Pollution*

The Death of Adam: Essays on Modern Thought

*Absence of Mind: The Dispelling of Inwardness
from the Modern Myth of the Self*

When I Was a Child I Read Books

The Givenness of Things

What Are We Doing Here?

JACK

Marilynne Robinson

PICADOR

FARRAR, STRAUS AND GIROUX

New York

Picador
120 Broadway, New York 10271

Grateful acknowledgment is made for permission to reprint the following material:
Lyrics from "I Wish I Didn't Love You So" © 1947 Sony/ATV Harmony. Sony/ATV
Harmony. All rights administered by Sony/ATV Music Publishing, 424 Church Street,
Nashville, TN 37219. All rights reserved. Used by permission.
Excerpt from "Acquainted with the Night," by Robert Frost, from the book
The Poetry of Robert Frost, edited by Edward Connery Lathem.
Copyright © 1928, 1969 by Henry Holt and Company. Copyright © 1956
by Robert Frost. Reprinted by permission of Henry Holt and Company.
All rights reserved.

The Library of Congress has cataloged the
Farrar, Straus and Giroux hardcover edition as follows:
Names: Robinson, Marilynne, author.
Title: Jack / Marilynne Robinson.
Description: First edition. | New York : Farrar, Straus and Giroux, 2020.
Identifiers: LCCN 2020012453 | ISBN 9780374279301 (hardcover)
Subjects: GSAFD: Christian fiction.
Classification: LCC PS3568.O3125 J33 2020 | DDC 813/.54—dc23
LC record available at https://lccn.loc.gov/2020012453

Picador Paperback ISBN: 978-1-250-83291-7

Designed by Gretchen Achilles

1   3   5   7   9   10   8   6   4   2

To Ellen Levine

My friend and agent for forty years

JACK

He was walking along almost beside her, two steps behind. She did not look back. She said, "I'm not talking to you."

"I completely understand."

"If you did completely understand, you wouldn't be following me."

He said, "When a fellow takes a girl out to dinner, he has to see her home."

"No, he doesn't have to. Not if she tells him to go away and leave her alone."

"I can't help the way I was brought up," he said. But he crossed the street and walked along beside her, across the street. When they were a block from where she lived, he came across the street again. He said, "I do want to apologize."

"I don't want to hear it. And don't bother trying to explain."

"Thank you. I mean I'd rather not try to explain. If that's all right."

"Nothing is all right. All right has no place in this conversation." Still, her voice was soft.

"I understand, of course. But I can't quite resign myself."

She said, "I have never been so embarrassed. Never in my life."

He said, "Well, you haven't known me very long."

She stopped. "Now it's a joke. It's funny."

He said, "There's a problem I have. The wrong things make me laugh. I think I spoke to you about that."

"And where did you come from, anyway? I was just walking along, and there you were behind me."

"Yes. I'm sorry if I frightened you."

"No, you didn't. I knew it was you. No thief could be that sneaky. You must have been hiding behind a tree. Something ridiculous."

"Well," he said, "in any case, I have seen you safely to your door." He took out his wallet and extracted a five-dollar bill.

"Now, what is this! Giving me money here on my doorstep? What are people supposed to think about that? You want to ruin my life!"

He put the money and the wallet back. "Very thoughtless of me. I just wanted you to know I wasn't ducking out on the check. I know that's what you must think. You see, I did have the money. That was my point."

She shook her head. "Me scraping around in the bottom of my handbag trying to put together enough quarters and dimes to pay for those pork chops we didn't eat. I left owing the man twenty cents."

"Well, I'll get the money to you. Discreetly. In a book or something. I have those books of yours." He said, "I thought it was a very nice evening, till the last part. One bad hour out of three. One small personal loan, promptly repaid. Maybe tomorrow."

She said, "I think you expect me to keep putting up with you!"

"Not really. People don't, generally. I won't blame you. I know

4

how it is." He said, "Your voice is soft even when you're angry. That's unusual."

"I guess I wasn't brought up to quarrel in the street."

"I actually meant another kind of soft." He said, "I have a few minutes. If you want to talk this over in private."

"Did you just invite yourself in? Well, there's nothing to talk over. You go home, or wherever it is you go. I'm done with this, whatever it is. You're just trouble."

He nodded. "I've never denied it. Seldom denied it, anyway."

"I'll grant you that."

They stood there a full minute.

He said, "I've been looking forward to this evening. I don't quite want it to end."

"Mad as I am at you."

He nodded. "That's why I can't quite walk away. I won't see you again. But you're here now—"

She said, "I just would not have believed you would embarrass me like that. I still can't believe it."

"Really, it seemed like the best thing, at the time."

"I thought you were a gentleman. More or less, anyway."

"Very often I am. In most circumstances. Dyed-in-the-wool, much of the time."

"Well, here's my door. You can leave now."

"That's true. I will. I'm just finding it a little difficult. Give me a couple of minutes. When you go inside, I'll probably leave."

"If some white people come along, you'll be gone soon enough."

He took a step back. "What? Do you think that's what happened?"

"I saw them, Jack. Those men. I'm not blind. And I'm not stupid."

He said, "I don't know why you are even talking to me."

"That's what I'd like to know, myself."

"They were just trying to collect some debts. They can be pretty rough about it. I can't risk, you know, an altercation. The last one almost got me thirty days. So that would have embarrassed you, maybe more."

"You are something!"

"Maybe," he said, "but I'm not— I'm so glad you told me. I could have left you here thinking— I wouldn't want you to—"

"The truth isn't so much better, you know. Really—"

"Yes, it is. Sure it is."

"So now I'm supposed to forgive you because what you did isn't the absolutely worst thing you could have done."

"Well, the case could be made, couldn't it? I mean, I feel much better now that we've cleared that up. If I'd walked away ten minutes ago, think how different it would have been. And then I really never would have seen you again."

"Who said you will now?"

He nodded. "I can't help thinking the odds are better."

"Maybe, if I decide to believe you. Maybe not."

"You really ought to believe me," he said. "What harm would it do? You can still hang up on me if I call. Return my letters. Nothing would be different. Except you wouldn't have to have such unpleasant thoughts about how you've spent a few hours over a couple of weeks. That splendid evening we meant to have. You could forgive me that much."

"Forgive myself," she said. "For being so foolish."

"You could think of it that way, too."

She turned and looked at him. "Don't laugh at this, any of this, ever," she said. "I think you want to. And if you're trying to be ingratiating, it isn't working."

"It doesn't work. How well I know. It is some spontaneous, chemical thing that happens. Contact between Jack Boughton and—air. Like phosphorus, you know. No actual flame, of course. Foxfire, more like that. A rosy heat of embarrassment around any ordinary thing. No way to hide it. I suppose entropy should have a nimbus—"

"Stop talking," she said.

"It's nerves."

"I know it is."

"Pay no attention."

"You're breaking my heart."

He laughed. "I'm just talking to keep you here listening. I certainly don't mean to break your heart."

"No, you're telling me the truth now. It's a pity. I have never heard of a white man who got so little good out of being a white man."

"It has its uses, even for me. I am assumed to know how many bubbles there are in a bar of soap. I've had the honor of helping to make civic dignitaries of some very unlikely chaps. I've—"

"Don't," she said. "Don't, don't. I have to talk about the Declaration of Independence on Monday. There is nothing funny about that."

"True. Not a thing." He said, "I really am going to say something true, Miss Della. So listen. This doesn't happen every day." Then he said, "It's ridiculous that a preacher's daughter, a high-school teacher, a young woman with excellent prospects in life, would be hanging around with a confirmed, inveterate bum. So I won't bother you anymore. You won't be seeing me again." He took a step away.

She looked at him. "You're telling me goodbye! Why do you

7

get to do that? I told you goodbye and you've kept me here listening to your nonsense so long I'd almost forgotten I said it."

"Sorry," he said. "I see your point. But I was trying to do what a gentleman would do. If a gentleman could actually be in my situation here. I could cost you everything, and there's no good I could ever do you. Well, that's obvious. I'm saying goodbye so you'll know I understand how things are. I'm actually making you a promise, and I'll stick to it. You'll be impressed."

She said, "Those books you borrowed."

"They'll be on your porch step tomorrow. Or soon after. With that money I owe you."

"I don't want them back. No, maybe I do. I suppose you wrote in them."

"Pencil only. I'll erase it."

"No, don't do that. I'll do it."

"Yes, I can see that there might be satisfactions involved."

"Well," she said, "I told you goodbye. You told me goodbye. Now walk away."

"And you go inside."

"As soon as you're gone."

They laughed.

After a minute, he said, "You just watch. I can do this." And he lifted his hat to her and strolled off with his hands in his pockets. If he did look back, it was after she had closed the door behind her.

A week later, when she came home from school, she found her *Hamlet* lying on the porch step. There were two dollars in it, and there was something written in pencil on the inside cover.

Had I a blessing, even one,
Its grace would light on you alone.
Had I a single living prayer
It would attend you, mild as air.
Had my heart an unbroken string

ring sing sting cling thing

Oh, I am ill at these numbers!
IOU a dollar. And a book.

Long Farewell!

Embarrassing. Absolutely the last person in the world. Unbelievable. After almost a year. He snuffed out his cigarette against the headstone. A little carefully, it was only half gone. And what was the point. The smell of smoke must have been what made her stop and look around, look up at him. If he tried to slip back out of sight, that would only frighten her more, so there was nothing left to do but speak to her. Della. There she was, standing in the road on the verge of the lamplight, looking up at him. He could see in her stillness the kind of hesitation that meant she was held there by uncertainty, about whether she did know him or was only seeing a resemblance, and, in any case, whether to walk away, suppressing the impulse to run away if whoever he was, even he himself, seemed threatening or strange. Well, let's be honest, he was strange, loitering in a cemetery in the dark of night, no doubt about it. But she might be pausing there actually hoping she did know him, ready for anything at all like reassurance, so he lifted his hat and said, "Good evening.

Miss Miles, if I'm not mistaken." She put her hand to her face as if to compose herself.

"Yes," she said. "Good evening." There were tears in her voice.

So he said, "Jack Boughton."

She laughed, tears in her laughter. "Of course. I mean, I thought I recognized you. It's so dark I couldn't be sure. Looking into the dark makes it darker. Harder to see anything. I didn't realize they locked the gates. I just didn't think of it."

"Yes. It depends where you're standing, how dark it is. It's relative. My eyes are adjusted to it. So I guess that makes light relative, doesn't it." Embarrassing. He meant to sound intelligent, since he hadn't shaved that morning and his tie was rolled up in his pocket.

She nodded, and looked down the road ahead of her, still deciding.

How had he recognized her? He had spent actual months noticing women who were in any way like her, until he thought he had lost the memory of her in all that seeming resemblance. A coat like hers, a hat like hers. Sometimes the sound of a voice made him think he might see her if he turned. A bad idea. Her laughing meant she must be with someone. She might not want to show that she knew him. He would walk on, a little slower than the crowd, with the thought that as she passed she would speak to him if she wanted to, ignore him if she wanted to. Once or twice he stopped to look in a store window to let her reflection go by, and there were only the usual strangers, that endless stream of them. Cautious as he was, sometimes women took his notice as a familiarity they did not welcome. A useful reminder. A look like that would smart, he thought, coming from her. Still, all this waiting, if that's what it was, helped him stay sober and usually reminded him to shave. It might really be her, sometime, and if he tipped his hat, shaven and sober, she would be more likely to smile.

But there she was, in the cemetery, of all places, and at night, and ready to be a little glad to see him. "Yes," he said, "I've noticed that. About darkness." Join me in it, even things up. I am the Prince of Darkness. He couldn't say that. It was a joke he made to himself. He would walk down to where she was, in the lamplight. No. Any policeman who came by might take it into his head to say the word "solicitation," since he was disreputable and she was black. Since they were together at night in the cemetery. Better to keep his distance. And he knew he always looked better from a distance, even a little gentlemanly. He had his jacket on. His tie was in his pocket. He said, "You really shouldn't be here," a ridiculous thing to say, since there she was. Then, as if by way of explanation, "There are some pretty strange people here at night." When there he was among the tombstones himself, taking a little comfort from the fact that she could not see him well, to notice the difference between whatever she thought of him in her moment of apparent relief and how he actually was. Not *what* he actually was, his first thought. Spending a night in a cemetery, weather permitting, was no crime, nothing that should be taken to define him. It was illegal, but there was no harm in it. Generally speaking. Sometimes he rented his room at the boardinghouse to another fellow for a few days if money was tight.

He said, "I'll look after you, if you'd like. Keep an eye on you, I mean. Until they open the gates." He would watch out for her, of course, whatever she said. It would seem like lurking if he didn't ask. Then she would leave, and he would follow, and she would probably know he was following her and try to run away from him, or hide in the tombstones, or stop and plead with him, maybe offer him her purse. Humiliating in every case. Catastrophic if a cop happened along.

"It was so stupid of me not to realize they would lock those gates. So stupid." She sat down on a bench in the lamplight with her back to him, which struck him as possibly trusting. "I'd be grateful for the company, Mr. Boughton," she said softly.

That was pleasant enough. "Happy to oblige." He came a few steps down the hill, keeping his distance from her, putting himself in her sight if she turned just a little, and sat down on the mound of a grave. "I'm not here normally," he said. "At this hour."

"I just came here to see it. People kept telling me how beautiful it is."

"It is pretty fine, I guess. As cemeteries go."

He would try to talk with her. What was there to say? She had been holding flowers in her hand. They were beside her on the bench. "Who are the flowers for?"

"Oh, they're for Mrs. Clark. All wilted now."

"Half the people in here are Mrs. Clark. Or Mr. Clark. Most of the people in this town. William Clark, father of nations."

"I know. That would be my excuse for wandering around if anybody asked. I'd be trying to find the right Mrs. Clark. I'd say my mother used to work for her. She was such a kind lady. We still miss her."

"Clever. Except that the Clarks are pretty well huddled together. You find one, you've found them all. I could show you where. For future reference." Complete nonsense.

"No need. It was just something I made up." She shook her head. "I'm going to embarrass my family. My father always said it's a baited trap. Don't go near it. And here I am."

"A baited trap."

She shrugged. "Anywhere you're not supposed to be."

He shouldn't have asked. She was talking to herself more than to him, and he knew it. Murmuring, almost. The crickets were louder. She reminded him of every one of his sisters in that prim coat that made her back look so narrow, her shoulders so small and square. He thought he had seen his sister hang her head that way, one of them. All of them. No, he was elsewhere at the time. But he could imagine them, standing close, saying nothing. No need to speak. No mention of his name.

"Well," he said, "I guess you should be glad that I'm the one you came across here. A respectable man would have every problem I have, trying to be protective. More problems, because he wouldn't know the place so well as I do. You'd probably be more at ease with someone like that. But I can slip you out of here, no one the wiser. It's just a matter of waiting till morning. A respectable man wouldn't be here at this time of night, I realize that. I'm speaking hypothetically, more or less. I just mean that I see your problem, and I'm happy to be of assistance. Very happy." That was nerves.

He thought he might have made her uneasy, since the realization was beginning to settle in that she really was there, not so unlike the thought he had had of her, and she might have heard a trace of familiarity in his voice, which would be worrisome to her in the circumstances.

She said, "I am grateful for your company, Mr. Boughton. Truly." Then silence, except for the wind in the leaves.

So he said, "I'll be the problem you have if you have one. If you stick to your story, you'll be all right. The guard isn't a bad fellow. You just don't want to be found in here with, you know, a man. I mean, that's how it would look. No offense."

"No, of course not."

"I'll go up the hill a ways. I can watch out for you from up there. All the regulars in here have probably passed out by now, or might as well have. But just in case."

"No," she said, "I'd rather you sat beside me here on this bench. You can't be comfortable where you are. The grass is damp." She may have wanted him to be where she could see him, to keep an eye on *him*.

"That doesn't matter."

"Well, of course it does."

"For a few minutes, then. I don't know the time. Sometimes a guard comes through here about midnight."

"It has to be past midnight."

"I'd say about ten thirty, if I had to guess."

"Oh! I've been walking around in here for hours. It seems like half my life. I went to one gate, then to another one, then all along the fence." He did not say time is relative. The few classes he had actually gone to had been interesting enough, but he had to remember how few they were.

She said, "This place is so big, you wonder who all they're expecting."

He laughed. "Everybody, sooner or later. About three hundred acres, they say."

"Nobody I know is coming here. They couldn't carry me in here if they wanted to, either. I'd climb out of the box."

It seemed she had forgotten about asking him to sit beside her, and he was relieved.

She said, "Isn't it sinful, anyway, putting up these big monuments to yourself? These rich old men, with their dying breath, saying, 'An obelisk will do. Something simple. The Washington Monument, but a little smaller.'"

14

"No doubt."

"Obelisks standing around by the dozen, groves of them. It's ridiculous."

"I can only agree." He thought he might have seen that word in print somewhere.

"When you think what could have been done with that money. Oh, just listen to me! I'm so tired I'm quarreling with dead people."

"It is a shame, though. You're absolutely right." Then he said, "My grave is in Iowa. You'd approve. It's about the width of a cot. It will have a little stone pillow with my name on it. Iowans aren't much for ostentation." And he said, "Maybe a grave isn't really yours until you're in it. You can never be sure where you'll end up. But I plan to make sure. I carry the address in my pocket. It's the least I can do, really. They're expecting me." He should have kept that cigarette.

She glanced toward him. Then she stood up. She gathered her flowers into a hasty sort of bouquet, wilted as they were. "I thank you for your kindness, Mr. Boughton. I feel better, now that I've rested a little."

So this is how it ends, he thought. Five minutes into a conversation he'd never hoped for. After years of days that were suffered and forgotten, no more memorable than any particular stone in his shoe, here, in a cemetery, in the middle of the night, he was caught off guard by an actual turn of events, something that mattered, a meeting that would empty his best thoughts of their pleasure. Those dreams of his had been the pleasant substance of long stretches of time, privileged because they were incommunicable and of no possible interest to anyone, certainly never to be exposed to the chill air of consequence. But she, Della, was gathering herself up in that purposeful way proud women have when they are removing themselves from whatever has brought on that absolute *no* of theirs. Forever after, the thought of her would be painful, because it had been pleasant. Strange how that is.

Just at the farthest edge of the circle of light she paused, looking at the darkness beyond it. So he said, "You would be safer if you'd let me watch out for you."

She said, "I wish you would get up off that grave and let me see you, then. It's strange talking to someone you can't see."

All right. He took off his hat and ran his hand through his hair. "I'll be a minute," he said. "I'm putting on my tie."

She laughed and looked around at him. "You really are, aren't you."

"Indeed I am!" He was happy suddenly, because she had laughed. Feelings ought to be part of a tissue, a fabric. An emotion shouldn't be an isolated thing that hits you like a sucker punch. There should be other satisfactions in life, to maintain perspective, proportion. Things to look forward to, for example, so one casual encounter in a cemetery wouldn't feel like the Day of Judgment. He had let himself have too few emotions, so there wasn't much for him to work with. But here he was, abruptly happy enough that he would have trouble concealing it. He came down the slope sidelong because the grass was damp and slippery, but almost as if there were a joke in the way he did it. I'm imitating youth, he thought. No, this feels like youth, an infusion of something like agility. Embarrassing. He had to be wary. If he made a fool of himself, he'd be drinking again.

"This is quite a surprise," he said, standing in the road, in the light. "For both of us, no doubt."

She said nothing, studying his face forthrightly, as she would certainly never have studied anyone in circumstances her manners had prepared her for. He let her look, not even lowering his eyes. He was waiting to see what she would make of him, as they say. And then he would be what she made of him. He might sit down beside her, after all, cross his legs and fold his arms and be affable. At worst he'd go find that half cigarette he had dropped in the grass, which was damp, not wet. Once she was out of sight. He was pretty sure there were still three matches in the book in his pocket. And she would walk away, if she decided to. Her choice. The darkness of her eyes made her gaze seem calm, unreadable, possibly kind. He knew what she saw, the scar under his eye, which was still dark, the shadow of beard, his hair grazing his collar. And then his age, that relaxation of the flesh, like the fatigue that had caused his jacket sleeves to take the shape of his elbows and his pockets to sag a little. Age and bad habits. While she read what his face would tell her about who he really was, she would be remembering that other time, when for an hour or two she had thought better of him.

She said, "Why don't we sit down?"

And he said, "Why not?" And as he sat down he plucked at the knees of his trousers, as if they had a crease, and laughed, and said, "My father always did that."

"Mine, too."

"I guess it's polite, somehow."

"It means you're on your best behavior."

"Which in fact I am."

"I know."

"Which can fall a little short sometimes."

"I know that well enough."

He said, "I really would like to apologize."

"Please don't."

"I've been assured that it's good for the soul."

"No doubt. But your soul is your business, Mr. Boughton. I'd be happy to talk about something else."

So she was still angry. Maybe angrier than she had been at the time. That might be a good sign. At least it meant that she'd been thinking about him.

He said, "I'm sorry I brought it up. You're right. Why should I trouble you with my regrets?"

She took a deep breath. "I'm not going to get into this with you, Mr. Boughton."

Why did he persist? She was reconsidering, taking her purse and her bouquet into her lap. Could that be what he wanted her to do? It wouldn't be self-defeat, precisely, because at best there would be only these few hours, tense and probationary, and then whatever he might want to rescue from them afterward for the purposes of memory. That other time, when the old offense was fresh, she had seemed to regret it for his sake as much as her own. He had seen kindness weary before. It could still surprise him a little.

He nodded and stood up. "You'd rather I left you alone. I'll do that. I'll be in shouting distance. In case you need me."

"No," she said. "If we could just talk a little."

"Like two polite strangers who happen to be spending a night in a cemetery."

"Yes, that's right."

"Okay." So he sat down again. "Well," he said, "what brings you here this evening, Miss Miles?"

"Pure foolishness. That's all it was." And she shook her head.

Then she said nothing, and he said nothing, and the crickets chanted, or were they tree toads. It had seemed to him sometimes that, however deep it was, the darkness in a leafy place took on a cast, a tincture, of green. The air smelled green, of course, so the shading he thought he saw in the darkness might have been suggested by that wistfulness the breeze brought with it, earth so briefly not earth. All the people are grass. QED. Flowers of the field. The pool of lamplight kept the dark at a distance. Shunned and sullen, he thought. Injured. He did not look at her, because then she would look at him. He had noticed that men in his line of worklessness, which did involve recourse to drink, were marked, sooner or later, by a crease across the forehead, but he did not touch his brow. It was nerves that made it feel that way, tense. If they sat there side by side till dawn, that would be reasonably pleasant.

She said, "I owe you an apology. I haven't been polite."

"True enough," he said. "So."

"So?"

"So, pay up."

She laughed. "Please accept my apology."

"Consider it done. Now," he said, "you accept mine."

She shrugged. "I don't really want to do that."

"Fair's fair, isn't it?"

"No, it isn't, not all the time. Besides, I promised myself I wouldn't."

"You promised yourself? That practically doesn't count. I break promises to myself all the time, and we're still on speaking terms, myself and I. When there's nobody around to hear us, anyway."

"Do you think I'm going to tell anyone else what you did? I can't believe I'm sitting here talking with you, now that I think about it."

"Well," he said, "so you thought you'd see me again, and you wanted to make sure you didn't give in to your better nature and let me make amends. You had to steel yourself against the possibility. Now here you are, glad to see me, whether you like it or not. We'll be here for hours. I'll be charming——"

"You're really not very charming. You should know that by now. You might as well stop trying."

He drew a breath. "All I'm trying to do is to keep some kind of conversation going. That's what you said you wanted. I acknowledge my limitations. No need to be harsh."

She shook her head. "Oh, I'm sorry. I am. Forget I said that. It's just that I've been so mad at you for such a long time."

He said what he thought. "I'm honored."

She looked at him, and he let her. The dark quiet of her face still soothed him, like a touch. She said, "I don't remember that scar."

He nodded. "It wasn't there." And then he said, "Thank you."

She looked away. "Let's not talk for a while. We can just be quiet."

"As you wish."

They were quiet, and then she whispered, "Did you hear that? Did you hear voices? Is somebody coming?"

"I didn't hear anything. But we could walk up the hill, out of the light, just to be safe."

"I guess we ought to do that. We could see farther up the road from there."

They were whispering. High-heeled shoes, of course. The ground was soft and uneven. They were trying to hurry. He thought of taking her arm, then decided he would not. They walked up beyond the farthest effect of the light and stood there, and watched a man in work clothes and a cap stroll past, singing to himself. Smoke, smoke, smoke that cigarette. "Maybe I could talk to him," she said, and he heard her shift a little, the beginning of an intention. When the man was gone, she said, "Why are *you* here?"

"I don't know. Why not?"

"Just about anybody in the world could give you a hundred good reasons why not."

"You want a better answer. All right. It's my birthday."

"I suppose I could believe that. It wouldn't explain anything."

"Not exactly *my* birthday. One I choose to commemorate, when I remember it. I have to be in the right frame of mind. Sober, for one thing."

"I guess that's sad, if it's true."

"Yes. Actually, I want to feel the sadness of it. I don't, always. So I come here. And then sometimes I just come here. For the quiet."

She nodded. Pensive, he thought. Even a little downcast. Turning his strange sadness over in her mind. So he said, "I had every intention of paying you back," and regretted it.

She looked at him. "Are you really trying to talk to me about money? Do you think I've given one thought to that money?"

"I just wanted to say that I know you could interpret what happened as a kind of theft, if you didn't know I meant to get it back to you. So I wanted to say that. I've wanted to for a long time. And this is my chance. I don't expect another one."

"Ah, Jack!" she said. Jack.

A minute passed. She said, "Laugh if you want to. I'm working on a poem. That's why I came here."

He didn't laugh, but he did want to.

She said, "I know what you're thinking."

"Farthest thing from my mind."

"What is?"

"That there is no real shortage of poems inspired by graveyards.

Of course," he said, "human mortality—that's another matter. Hardly touched on."

"It's another kind of poem. A prose poem, really. Not about death, either."

"I hope I'll have a look at it, when it's finished."

She shook her head. "There's not a chance in this world."

"I know. I was being polite."

"I don't know why I told you about it. I knew you'd laugh."

"I didn't." She glanced at him. "All right. I came close. It's a problem I have, even in moments of great solemnity. Which are rare, fortunately."

She said, "Maybe. Maybe they are."

"It comes upon us like an armed man. My father always said that when one of his flock fell off a barn roof or down a well or something. In a moment, in the twinkling of an eye. Some poor codger hauled onto the cosmic stage, no chance to rehearse his lines. It's good I never considered the clerical life. Not for a minute, actually. Too much on my mind as it is." She was quiet, and then she glanced at him, as if she were considering asking him one of those questions that are moved by compassion, questions women ask. So he said, "A poet. I don't mean to sound surprised. It's just never a thing you expect. Of anybody. Not even an English teacher."

"No, not a poet. Someone who tries a line or two now and then."

He nodded. "I've tried my hand from time to time."

"Yes, I liked the little poem you wrote in my sister's *Hamlet*. Those lines."

"Hmm. That was your sister's book, was it. Well, she'll probably like it, too. It has had a fair success with women. Two and a half couplets! I'd finish it if I could, but it doesn't really seem to be necessary." That would keep compassion from threatening for a while. Still, her quiet had become silence, a thing he had to regret. And he had a lively fear of regret. So he said, "Praise means a lot more, coming from someone with your education."

Silence.

"That was a ridiculous thing to say, I mean, it sounded ridiculous. But there's some truth in it. Obviously."

Silence.

So he said, "I suppose you thought I wrote it for you."

"Why should that matter. I never gave it a thought."

"No, you wouldn't have. I did, though. Write it for you. Then I thought it might have seemed—forward. In retrospect. Since you don't know me. And don't intend to."

"I liked it," she said. "My sister will, too. Let's leave it there."

"Thank you."

She laughed. "You do get yourself in trouble."

"Easy as breathing. Now *you* talk. There are too many hazards in it for me."

"All right. Let me see."

"Nothing profound."

"Don't worry."

"I'm a simple man who was brought up by a complicated man. So I have mannerisms and so on. Vocabulary. People can be misled."

"I'm not."

He laughed. "Not even a little? That's discouraging."

"You think too much about yourself. Putting on that necktie! No wonder you're all nerves."

"You are very frank, Miss Miles."

"I'm in a graveyard on a dark night passing the time with someone I'll never see again. Whose opinion doesn't mean a thing to me. If I can't be frank now, when in the world can I be? I can't even see your face."

"Yes, the moon must have gone down. The half moon. It's nice. If you like it, I guess. And I'm glad I'm here in the moonless dark to offer you my arm on this very uneven ground. You need not think of it as the arm of any particular gentleman. Kindly intent, disembodied. Civility in the abstract." He was surprised to feel her hand in the crook of his elbow.

She said, "Thank you." After a while, she said, "Have you ever noticed that if you strike a match in a dark room, it seems to spread quite a lot of light. But if you strike one in a room that is already light, it seems to make no difference?"

"Uh-oh. A sermon illustration."

She took away her hand.

He said, "Just joking. No, I haven't noticed. I'll make it a point to notice in the future. I'm sure you're right."

Silence.

He said, "Come to think of it, a moral could be drawn. More rejoicing in heaven over the sinner who repents and so on. Than for the righteous, poor souls. My father's favorite topic. So it was probably inevitable that I would take it wrong. You know how it is. You're a preacher's kid."

She said, "I was asking a different kind of question. I just think it's interesting. If you add light to light, there should be more of it. As much more as if you add light to darkness. But I don't think there is."

"A conundrum."

They walked on through the deep grass, shoulder to shoulder in the dark, breathing together. Humans, making their slight, bland sounds, breaths and whispery footsteps, while creatures all around them rasped and twittered as if their lives depended on it. He said, "Are you cold?"

"Not very."

"We're not just wandering. I know where we are. I want to show you something."

"Show me? I can hardly see a thing."

"Do you have any matches? No, you wouldn't. Foolish of me to ask. Well, I have a couple."

They walked a little farther, and then he said, "Come here," and took her elbow to help her down a slope. "Come a little closer. Now look at this." He struck a match, and a chalk-white face appeared in its light, then dimmed and vanished.

"Who is it?"

"No idea." He struck another match, and again the face bloomed out of the darkness, shadows cast up by the flame so the curves of its cheeks darkened the hollows of its eyes. Usually he would touch its plump stone shoulder, long enough to think that the warmth that passed from his hand might equal the cold that passed into it. But Della was there. His little rituals would seem strange to her. It wasn't comfort that he took from them.

She said, "A cherub."

"That's the idea, I suppose. The place is full of them. I like this one best. Do you mind walking back again? To the place where you found me? I am a little embarrassed to admit it, but I left a blanket roll there. In case I ended up spending the night. Which does happen. You could wrap up in it. You might find it a little—objectionable. Damp. It's always damp. You know how that is. Or you don't. Fair warning. Or I could use it, and you could borrow my jacket, which is probably better. But not as warm. Or we could just keep walking."

She said, "Let's keep walking."

"Yes. You're miserable."

"My own fault."

"Mine, too. I wanted to show her to you, to see what you'd think. So I took you all that way just to have a look at her."

"I wish I knew what to think. I've seen prettier babies."

He nodded. "That's all right. She looks a little better by daylight. But the rain hasn't been kind to her. She's pretty well lost an ear. She's been here a long time. Just short of eighty years, according to the inscription. There isn't a single word for that look of hers, is there. 'Terrified' isn't quite right."

"Maybe. 'Startled' might be better."

"There was moss on her lip a few weeks ago. It enhanced her metaphorical value, but it looked—uncomfortable. I used a toothbrush I brought here with me to clean her up a little." That gentle hand, lifted away, then resting on his arm again, another considered act. "You might want to add the moss back in, for effect."

"You should be the one writing a poem."

He shook his head. "Not much rhymes with terror. 'The Infant and the Armed Man.' What do you think?"

"I think 'terror' is the wrong word. You said it was yourself."

"Yes. Strange. Error is just an equivocation. But you add that *t* and you have another thing entirely." She was quiet, so he said, "Sorry, too much time on my hands. I think about things, very trivial things. To pass the time."

She nodded. "I do that, too. When I can't sleep."

"Another insomniac!"

"Not really. I think I would be one if I could walk out at night, under the moon, everything so quiet. I sit out on the porch step sometimes, in the dark."

"Well, I could wander by your house one night and find you there and squire you through the city." He said, "'Nocturnal.' I like that word. It sounds like the change there is when the streets are empty and the houses are dark, which is a much deeper thing than just, you know, the absence of light. I could show you. You hear your own footsteps, as if they mattered. I promise I'd have you at your door again when the first bird sings. Owls wouldn't count."

She nodded. "We'll never do that."

He said, "Sad, isn't it?"

They walked on for a while. Then she said, "'The bird of dawning singeth all night long.' Why is that so pretty?"

"So blessed is the time." He said, "Maybe. I know that bird. I don't consider it a friend. It's saying, Back to purgatory, Boughton."

She stopped where she was, quiet for a minute. Then she said, softly, "It's going to wake me up tomorrow. I have to get to school so early, I might as well just stay awake the rest of the night, anyway. Oh, what am I talking about? I'll barely have time to go home! I won't be able to pick up the tests I graded. I'll be walking home at dawn with my hair all in a mess. My shoes ruined. It's probably going to rain."

"They don't open the gates at dawn. Maybe half past seven. When the gardeners come."

"Walking along the street early in the morning, in the wrong part of town, all in a mess. What's anybody going to think."

"I'll see you home or wherever. Discreetly. From across the street."

"Oh, good. You're going to protect me."

"I'm tougher than I look."

"No doubt. Pretty much anybody is."

He laughed.

She said, "I shouldn't have said that. I know you're trying to be kind. I'm glad I'm not here by myself, I really am."

"Thanks."

"That was mean, what I said."

"It was a little bit funny, though."

"I got myself into this. I shouldn't be taking it out on you."

"That's true enough."

But she stood there, her hands in her coat pockets and her head lowered. So he said, "We should talk about something. To pass the time."

"I thought when I got this job I'd never ask for another thing. Sumner High School."

"It's a handsome building. I've walked past it a few times."

"I used to have pictures of it that I cut out of magazines. I dreamed about teaching here. When I got that letter, I thought I knew how my whole life would go. And I've just thrown it away."

"Maybe not."

"If they decide to make this into something compromising, I'm finished."

"Well," he said, "we've got tonight to get through, in any case. You could slip your shoes off. Keep them a little drier. They're not doing you any good, anyway, there's not much to them. A few straps." She looked at him, so he said, "If that was a rude suggestion, I'm sorry. This is quite a novel situation, even for me." And he laughed.

"No, it might be best. Better than walking home barefoot tomorrow."

"That was my thought. There are paths through the graves. The acorns haven't fallen yet. The hickory nuts."

She put her hand on a headstone and pulled off her shoes.

"Well, there. I guess this will be all right. It's ridiculous. Ridiculous."

I promise I won't think less of you. That is what he almost said. But he caught himself.

He laughed. "Sorry. Anyway, I can barely see you at all. You could, you know, take off—"

"Don't, please."

"Take off your hat. And borrow mine. That's all I was going to say! Since yours wouldn't keep off the rain."

Silence. All right, then.

Finally she said, "Did you ever wonder why no one except Hamlet seems sorry that the old King Hamlet is dead? He's hardly cold in his grave."

"I'm afraid I can't claim to know the play well, Miss Miles. My father cut it up with scissors and taped the pieces into a loose-leaf scrapbook, so we could act it out. So they could. What was left of it didn't make much sense. It wouldn't have, anyway. Our Ophelia, my sister Glory, was six or seven. She'd give all her flowers to the ghost— She was always wandering in on the wrong scenes, even after she should have been dead. Sharing out the popcorn. My father wouldn't say a word to her about it. He said it was an improvement. She sang 'Jesus Loves Me' in her mad scene because the actual song didn't survive the scissors. So my sense of it all is likely to be misinformed. I was interested to read the thing whole. That's why I borrowed your book."

Then he said, "I believe this is the kind of conversation you were hoping for? Scenes of domestic life?"

She said, "It's strange no one thinks Hamlet should be king. It seems as though there were stories behind the play we only get glimpses of. But nothing is done to hide them, either, I mean the gaps they leave."

"Yes, now that you mention it. One time our Ophelia got into the tub with all her clothes on, to rehearse her death scene. My brother Teddy caught her at it, and they talked about the dangers of playing at drowning in a bathtub. He said she didn't have to rehearse, because no one sees it happen. Otherwise somebody would have told Ophelia to get out of the water, probably her brother. She said, They did see! Somebody just stood there and watched me drown! Mermaid-like to muddy death, you know—she had a point, it would have taken a while. She came down the stairs trailing bathwater, shouting, Who let me drown! They decided it had to have been Gertrude, since she knew all about it. And nothing made sense, anyway, so no harm done."

She said, "My father never had much time to spend at home. He's sort of a leader in the community, I guess. He gets called away constantly. He spends lots of time with lots of people, trying to sort things out for them. It comes with serving a big church in a city. Especially a colored church, I think. He always made us show him our homework and our report cards, but he says he has a thousand children to look after, and that's true. We understood that. And then there are always people in the house, uncles and cousins and strangers of one kind and another. It's not such a peaceful life."

"One time my father was late to a funeral because Teddy and I had a game that went into extra innings. The widow dressed him down a little, I guess. He told her and anyone who ever reminded him of it that it was an exceptional game. We almost won."

She stopped, her head lowered. "Oh."

"Let me guess. Your father's favorite daughter is wandering the night with a disreputable white man. Barefoot. In a cemetery. If she's caught at it, the scandal will echo down the ages, into the farthest reaches of Tennessee, all its strange particulars scrutinized. Forever. And he was once so proud of you."

"It's not a joke."

"I wasn't joking."

"I'd like to sit down."

"We'll find a bench."

"No, here. Just for a minute." And she sank down on the grass. "Let me think."

"There's not much to think about, except how much worse your clothes are going to look if you keep sitting there in the damp like that. I'm trying to spare you added regret. We lost souls have to wander till the cock crows, nothing to be done. Maybe keep ourselves a little presentable if we can." He held out his hand to her and she took it and he helped her up. He didn't hold her hand a second longer than he should have.

She said, "You shouldn't call yourself that. 'Disreputable.'"

"I'm looking at the situation the way your father would. Loitering at night in a cemetery. Just that one fact would finish me off. Then there's all the rest. Actual years of it, I'm afraid. Hardly a day goes by."

"Well, what would your father say if he saw you here in the middle of the night, arm in arm with a colored gal?"

"He'd say, Thank God he's not alone. He'd thank Jesus with his eyes closed. He's not a man of the world, my father, and he might start fretting about particulars. But that would be his first thought. And we aren't arm in arm. Not that that would make any difference."

"It wouldn't make a bit of difference." She put her hand in the crook of his elbow. "Oh!"

"What?"

"I forgot my shoes! I left them back there, wherever we were!

I'll probably never find them. Everything just gets worse and worse."

"Well, maybe, but I have them right here, your shoes. I picked them up."

She shook her head. "I'm walking along barefoot in the dark and you're carrying my shoes. And I don't even know you. This is the strangest situation I've ever been in in my life. You better give them to me."

He did, and then he said, "I'm going to take my shoes off, too. That might make things less awkward, I believe."

"Why would it?"

"We can just try it out. We'll see. I could be right. There." He slipped off his shoes, pocketed his socks. His feet, where they showed beyond his trouser cuffs, had a dim lunar pallor even in all that dark. They looked very naked, not quite his and startlingly his. Sometimes he thought of the naked man who lived in his clothes, that bare, forked animal. He had dreamed a thousand times that he was somewhere public, wearing less than decency allowed. That was the feeling. Utter vulnerability. Then again, the cold of the grass was sharp and pleasing, like river water.

She said, "You were right. This is better." And laughed, which pleased him. And then they walked for a while, she holding his arm, her head at his shoulder, quiet. They were feeling that same odd cold together, and hearing the same night sounds, stranger to her than to him, he thought. He was introducing her to them, really. It was one thing to hear them from a porch or through a window screen, another to step into darkness itself where they were native and undistracted, making the dark spacious by the here and there of their rasping and chirruping. There was a soft clash of leaves when the wind stirred. Maybe another time when he was benighted he had imagined her walking beside him, more felt than seen, pensive as she was. By turning toward her he might dispel the illusion that she was there in the way of the dream, a soul, perhaps his own soul, in the now untroubled trust of her noiseless steps. The air smelled freshly come from somewhere new, if there was such a place.

She said, "Maybe everything else is strange."

Well, this happened to be a thing his soul had said to him any number of times, wordlessly, it was true, but with a similar inflection, like an echo, like the shadow of a sound. She, the actual Della, might not have spoken at all, since the thought was so familiar to him. So he did look at her, her head lowered pensively, and he asked her what she had said. "Your voice is very soft."

"Oh, nothing."

That meant she chose not to say it again, whatever it was. "Nothing" was a finger to the lips, a confidence she had thought better of. A confidence. Then she realized she should not be so much at ease with him. She decided to be reticent about the kinds of thoughts she didn't usually allow herself, after almost speaking them. If she had said those words, it meant she liked the night well enough, and he felt a tentative kind of pride in the thought. The night and the place were his own, more or less, and she was his guest in them, now that she had begun to seem a little more at ease.

She said, "It just seems to me sometimes as though—if we were the only ones left after the world ended, and we made the rules—they might work just as well—"

He laughed. "There's a thought. Jack Boughton makes the rules! Too bad there wouldn't be a few other people around to, you know, feel their force. Not that I carry grudges. Still. The first rule would be that everyone had to mind me. And the second would be that they could not hide their chagrin."

Silence.

She meant to be taken seriously. He'd known that, and still, he'd made his joke. So he said, "An interesting idea, certainly." They were strangers killing time. Remember that. Somehow he had been imagining something else, an almost wordless peace between them, a night like a ghostly presence witnessing this most improbable meeting, quiet and more quiet until she was gone and he had days to himself to remember her and nothing to regret. But she was serious, no doubt to keep their circumstance from taking on another character than detachment, from sliding into distrust or old anger. Might as well make the most of it.

She said, "I didn't mean you and me. I meant any two strangers."

"So long as one of them wasn't Rasputin. I'm sorry. You mean strangers in the abstract. I'm sure they exist somewhere, for purposes of argument. None in my immediate acquaintance. Strangers in the abstract always turn out to be fairly drearily particular on acquaintance. Under the slightest scrutiny, really. A glance will destroy the illusion. In my experience."

She shook her head, and said nothing. And why would she bother, when he kept on talking, and seemed to want to make a joke out of everything, and make the same sort of display of himself he made even when he was alone, toying with words, a sort of fidgeting of the brain. When her very hand on his arm meant that he could know a few of her thoughts if he were calm and a little tactful. "Sorry."

"No. That's all right. I understand what you mean about people. But they see more and know more and think about more than they would ever have any practical use for. I see that all the time. Even in children. They have their ideas about what is true or fair. About what matters. In the abstract."

"Agreed. Yes. But could we have a slightly larger population left after Doomsday? If there could be two, there could be two dozen, I suppose. I know I'm being literal-minded. But I try to imagine these two castaways absorbing the terrible fact, and then one of them saying to the other one, in this void, in this empty world—You know what we need around here? Some rules! When they had completely outlived any need for them? The one good thing about it all. Emily Post, Deuteronomy, the entire regime gone. It's not as if they'd want to murder, being just the two of them. They wouldn't need to steal, since there'd be no one around to own anything. They could forget about adultery."

"I think they'd talk about how things should have been. While there was still a chance. That's what I mean."

He nodded. "Interesting. But—sorry to be so literal—shouldn't we know how the world ended? That would be on their minds, I think."

"All right. It was struck by a meteor."

"Not our fault, then."

"No and yes. Like the Flood."

"Hmm. I see. So it's still that kind of universe."

"Yes. Probably. But we couldn't be sure. The meteor might have been just a meteor."

"If you say so. My father would say that a sparrow isn't just a sparrow. Because its fall means something, cosmically speaking. I'm not sure what. He is certain of it, though."

"My father would say that, too."

"So, consider the sparrows your meteor brought down, the lilies it pulverized. How could it be just a meteor?"

"If the people thought they knew how to understand it. I mean, if they believed that it meant something, they'd assume there were rules, and they'd probably think they were the rules they were already used to. Only they'd be a whole lot more serious about keeping to them. Some of them. For a while. Which wouldn't be interesting."

"And if they decided it didn't mean anything—"

"That's hard for me to imagine. I can't really think about that. But if they didn't know one way or the other, they'd be like we are. I mean like people are. That's more interesting."

"Maybe. But meaninglessness also has its pleasures. As an idea."

She shook her head. "I've tried to imagine it and I just can't. That doesn't mean it isn't possible."

He said, "That's kind of you. To leave a little space for nihilism. Most people don't."

"I know."

"At least my father didn't."

"Mine either."

"How could we know whether the nihilists were right? A voice from nowhere that had never spoken before and would never speak again—'It was just a meteor! Calm down! Interpretation is not appropriate!' That would keep the conversation going for the next two thousand years."

She said, "Meaninglessness would come as a terrible blow to most people. It would be full of significance for them. So it wouldn't be meaningless. That's where I always end up. Once you ask if there is meaning, the only answer is yes. You can't get away from it."

They walked along through the ranks and clusters of the dead. Forever hoisting their stony sails, waiting for that final wind to rise. Here lies Wanda Schmidt, her breathless, perpetual "Remember me!" spelled out as Beloved Mother. He actually felt he knew some of them, in their posthumous and monumental persons, that is, and he could not stroll past them without the little courtesy of a nod. Yes, I am here this evening with a lady on my arm. Quite a surprise, I agree.

He said, "Let me guess. Long arguments over Sunday dinner."

"Endless. We'd go around the table. We were supposed to be able to think and express our thoughts, my father said. Girls, too."

"I suppose predestination came up?"

"Not much. We're Methodists."

"I forgot. Yes. We also had those dinners. Was the Almighty free to limit what He could know. If He wasn't free to, He wasn't omnipotent. If He did limit what He could know, He wasn't omniscient. Unless He could know what He didn't know. In which case—and so on."

"Why would He want to limit what He could know?"

"Well, my father suffered considerably over the doctrine of foreknowledge. He was uneasy with the thought that there might be dark certainty in the universe somewhere, sentence passed, doom sealed, and a soul at his very dinner table lost irretrievably before it had even stopped outgrowing its shoes, so to speak. If the Lord chose not to know, then—that eased the Reverend's mind. Though it would in no way alter the facts of the case. Once, I pointed this out to him, and he just looked at me, tears in his eyes. Everyone else left the table. No more arguments for weeks after that."

"Were you that bad? I mean, that he was afraid for your soul?"

"Pretty bad. Let's talk about something else."

Quiet.

So he said, "Pious people do worry about me. This makes

37

conversation difficult. I can only assure you, as we two strangers wander through this solemn night, that I have not quite fulfilled my early promise. In case you're worried about that."

"No," she said. "No."

Then, even while he thought better of it, he asked her, "Why not?"

"There are just some people you trust."

"You could think of me as a thief if you wanted to."

"So I must not want to."

"Would it be better to be alone, or to be alone with a thief? I think that's an interesting question."

"I think you're trying to worry me. Anyway, it would depend on the thief."

"Right. And you and I have things in common. Fine families and so on." He said, "If there'd been only one thief at the crucifixion, whichever one it was, good or bad, it would have made a big difference, don't you think? In the story? As it is, we have the complex nature of criminality to consider. In the crucial moment. That's also very interesting."

"Well," she said, "maybe you flatter yourself. If you really were a criminal, I think you'd have cost me more than three dollars. And some irritation. And my copy of *Oak and Ivy*, which you'd better bring back, by the way. It's a hard book to find. My father gave it to me. His mother gave it to him. It was signed."

"What can I say? More to regret. I meant to bring it back with *Hamlet*. But one page has a sort of coffee stain on it. Not coffee, actually. It will be on your doorstep immediately. Such as it is."

"Did you write in it?"

"Hardly at all."

"How can you do that? How can you just write in somebody else's book?"

"In pencil."

"You know what I mean."

"My father said that I never quite learned to distinguish mine and thine. He had the Latin for it."

She laughed. "I love your father. You never talk about your mother."

"Yes. I don't." She was quiet. So he said, "My father thought my deficiencies might be physiological. He hoped they were. He laid them to my difficult birth."

"Predestination."

"Strictly speaking, no."

"Well, I won't follow you into the swamps of Presbyterianism."

"It's all pretty straightforward. Salvation by grace alone. It just begins earlier for us than for other people. In the deep womb of time, in fact. By His secret will and purpose."

"Then why was your father so worried? If it was true, what could he have done about it, anyway?"

"He saw signs of reprobation in me, hard as he tried not to. Reasonably enough. I kept him pretty well supplied with them. Of course, I knew about, you know, those signs. From his sermons. We all did. I may have been listening more carefully than the others. Or listening differently. He who has ears to hear, and so on. It wasn't so much the situation that he hoped to change. He just wanted a less drastic understanding of it. So he comforted himself with my difficult birth, which could not have disfigured my eternal soul, that most elusive thing. However it might have depraved the rest of me." Naked came I from my mother's womb.

"Well," she said, "this is all very interesting. But don't quote Scripture ironically. It makes me very uneasy when you do that."

"I am the Prince of Darkness."

"No, you're a talkative man with holes in his socks."

"You saw them?"

"No, I just knew they were there."

After a minute, he said, "I'll try not to be ironic if you take back what you just said. I am not talkative."

"All right."

"These are special circumstances."

"Yes, they are."

"I hardly say a word for weeks on end. Months."

"I couldn't know that."

"That's because you make me nervous. I talk when I'm nervous. Sometimes."

"You say you're a thief, you say you're disreputable, you say you're the Prince of Darkness, and you object to the word 'talkative.'"

He said, "It's a matter of personal dignity." She laughed.

"It is."

"I understand. I know what you mean. I would feel the same way, I suppose."

"Well, you hardly talk at all. You leave it to me. Then you draw conclusions."

Quiet.

So he said, "That sounded harsher than I meant it to. That was the wrong word. I didn't mean to be harsh at all. I just meant to say I appreciate it when you talk."

After a minute, she said, "You know what I think? I think Polonius misreads that letter, the vile phrase. I think Hamlet wrote 'beatified.' Not 'beautified.' But there's no way to know."

"True. Yes. High-minded conversation. Nothing more about socks or shirt buttons. Fraying of the cuffs. Holes in the pockets. Those three dollars."

Silence.

"Besides," he said, "Hamlet didn't write the letter. I mean, there was no letter. There's only what Polonius says it says."

"Shakespeare could have wanted the audience to know Polonius gets it wrong. He gets things wrong all the time. But I said there's no way to know."

"Yes. That isn't quite the same." That sounded cross.

Silence.

He had let himself feel concealed by the darkness, as if only a rough sketch of him, so to speak, the general outline of a presentable man, would be walking along beside her. But she knew what he was and nothing was concealed, and there was the night to get through, an ordeal now. She took her hand from his arm.

She said, "Have you ever thought of using a word like 'listening,' or 'murmuring,' in that couplet? Instead of a one-syllable word?"

"Yes," he said. "I have."

Silence. Then she said, "I offended you. I'm sorry."

These sensitivities of his. He might have said goodbye and walked away if they had not been together in a cemetery in the middle of the night. He was at least too much a gentleman to leave her there, or even to suggest that he might leave her there, or to remind her that she was indebted to his good nature in keeping her company, though the thought did occur to him. Easy enough to disappear among the headstones. The looming obelisks. That thought occurred, too. He had a way of anticipating memories he particularly did not want to have. That memory would be as unbearable as things ever are when there is nothing else to do but live with them. So he said, "I'm not offended. I don't want to be. I'll get over it in a minute." Then he said, "I'm going to ruin this."

That made her pause. "How, exactly?"

"The way I ruin things. It's a little different every time. I actually surprise myself. Except that it's inevitable. That's always the same, I suppose. One thing I can count on."

"I suppose I'm the one who ruined it, if it's ruined. I'm really sorry. It's been nice, considering everything. Walking barefoot in the dark. I wouldn't expect to enjoy that."

"All right," he said. "I'm all right. For a minute there I was plunged back into the land of the living. Terrible experience! Did you say 'enjoy'?"

"Yes, I did."

"Well, that helps."

"And we are not in the land of the living. We're ghosts among the ghosts. They'd be jealous. The two of us out here in the sweet air, just talking for the pleasure of it." She took his arm.

"Yes, two spirits. Invisible. Nothing else to say about us. I mean, in terms of our measuring up to expectations. Until the Last Judgment, anyway. The outward man perisheth and so on. Then again, if the outward man needs a haircut, that's a problem that can be solved, in theory. The inward man—renewed day by day—the same blasted nuisance every time. Sometimes I wish I were just a suit of clothes and a decent shave. Uninhabited, so to speak."

Quiet.

He said, "That must have sounded strange."

"Not really. My father had a word or two to say about the immortal soul. Poor, vulnerable thing that it is."

After a while, she said, "Remember, I mentioned that there

seemed to be stories behind *Hamlet*? That weren't told and weren't hidden? A letter behind the one Polonius reads would go along with that idea, wouldn't it?"

"I guess so. And why would Horatio have been around for months without letting Hamlet know he was there?"

"Yes. And Henry the Eighth said he'd broken biblical law when he married his brother's widow. The audience would know that. Claudius does exactly the same, worse, and only Hamlet is bothered by it. Isn't that odd?"

He laughed. "I can't keep up. I hung around college for a while and let my brother take my classes for me. If the subject of English kings came up, he never mentioned it. You should be talking to Teddy."

Her cheek brushed his shoulder. "You'll do."

Quiet. That would be embarrassment. Well, uneasiness at forgetting for a moment just who was walking beside her. Next she would mention Timbuktu. The dark side of the moon.

She said, "I believe we have souls. I think that's true."

He could deal with that. "Interesting," he said. "Yes, I suppose I agree. A pretty thought, in any case. Basically. Depending." Reprobation. Then he thought, You be my soul. But at least he didn't say it. "Are there things you don't believe, Miss Miles? I mean, that your father said you ought to believe? Are you at peace with the tenets of Methodism?"

"I like my church. I don't really like tenets, I suppose."

"The communion of saints? The forgiveness of sins?"

"Well, I do like those. I'm not so sure what they mean, though." She was quiet, and then she said, "I wonder sometimes if there would be such a thing as sin if God didn't exist."

"I'm certain of it."

"Why?"

"I don't know. I suppose sinning is doing harm. Agreed? And everything is vulnerable to harm, one way or another. Everybody is vulnerable. It's kind of horrible when you think about it. All that breakage, without so much as an intention behind it half the time. All that tantalizing fragility." He laughed. "Maybe it wouldn't be called sin. And I suppose there wouldn't be such a thing as forgiveness. Which would be a relief, frankly." Then he said, "In my opinion," wishing he hadn't laughed, and *really* wishing he hadn't mentioned tantalizing fragility. When did he first notice that in himself, that little fascination with damage and its consequences? He might alarm her. He might even mean to alarm her. Doing damage to this fragile night because it was such an isolated thing, an accident, with a look of meaning about it and no meaning at all. She held his arm and he guided her steps, skirting the places where the shadows of the burr oaks would have been and their acorns would have fallen for so many years. Any spirit looking on might have thought they had come there from days or years of dear friendship, passing through the graveyard on their way to the kind of futures people have ordinarily, heartbreak or marriage or something, when in fact they were not only strangers but estranged, she talking with him only to make the time pass, the long few hours.

Finally she said, "Sometimes I do wonder. If we were the only ones left after the world ended, and we made the rules, they really might work just as well. For us, at least."

"Us. So you think we could agree? We could come up with a new set of commandments, between the two of us? We'll still remember the Sabbath, I suppose."

She shrugged. "It would be pretty hard to forget it."

"I've tried," he said. "I've made the experiment."

"No luck?"

"I've forgotten one or two. They're hard to forget—no liquor, no cigarettes. All those bells. I've tried to plan ahead, to get through the day, but it's not really in my nature. If I've got 'em, I smoke 'em. Et cetera. Anyway, that's remembering. You just start a little early."

She said, "No, we'd have to keep the Sabbath. My father couldn't survive without it."

"Hmm. I thought the world had ended."

"In a manner of speaking."

"I have to object, Miss Miles. If we're going to keep honoring our fathers and our mothers, you know there won't be any new rules. So we have to let the world really come to an end. Hypothetically. If this is going to be interesting."

"I guess I don't want to imagine the world with them gone. It seems like tempting fate."

"All right. Tempting fate. So even fate can be lured away from its intentions."

It was true enough, though. The old gent gone, and the pious worry that fretted the edge of every thought he had almost gone as well. You will hurt yourself, why do you make things hard for yourself? You must take care of yourself, say your prayers, Jack. His prayers! What would they be? If I die before I wake. If I wake before I die. Much less likely. But he thought he might go home one last time. Last but one. Pull himself together and get on a bus.

She said, "Hypothetically, then. Let's say the world has ended, and we don't have to be loyal to the way things were before. What would we do that was different?"

He laughed. "Not a thing! We'd do just what we're doing now. If I could get you to go along with me."

"When morning comes, I mean."

"Oh. So there'd still be morning?"

45

"Yes, there would. The evening and the morning. We ended the world. Not the solar system."

"All right, I guess. But I'm beginning to wonder if ending the world was worth the trouble."

"How can you know? You won't try it out. You keep raising objections."

She said, "You have to relax a little bit. We won't do any harm just talking about it."

"Is your father out of the picture?"

"Hypothetically."

"Mine, too, I suppose."

"Well yes, he is."

"Then what?"

"You first."

"Why me?"

"Because I think maybe you've already thought about things this way. More than I have, at least. I don't think I wondered about it much until tonight. You know, wondered about it in so many words."

"I'll give it a try, I guess. What kind of rules are we talking about? Thou shalt not steal or The years of a man's life are three-score years and ten?"

"I guess you're right, stealing would be more like gleaning. But the years of a man's life—most people haven't lived that long, ever, so far as I know. That's just the best you can hope for. Generally. So it can't actually be a rule. My father had a great-aunt who lived to a hundred and one."

"My great-grandmother died at ninety-two. My father used to say, 'We who are young will never see so much nor live so long.' She came over in steerage and blamed us all for it for the rest of her life. We didn't justify the bother."

"How old is your father?"

"Sixty-five on the fourth of January. Threescore years and five. There is that exceptional-strength clause. He could make it to fourscore without casting any shadow on Moses. I'm sure he's aware of that."

"Is he exceptionally strong?"

"No. Not at all. But he is exceptionally determined." He said, "He's waiting for me."

Quiet. He could see her just well enough to know she had lowered her head, thinking about what he had said, what she might say, considering it all gently, since they were deep into night by then. He said, "I know. I should go home." Then he laughed. "I'm afraid that might put an end to him."

"Really? You really think that?"

"He lives on hope," he said. "He does. He's always been that way. So I show up, confirm his worst fears, tip my hat, and leave again. I couldn't stay there. He might not want me to, anyway. Then what would he have to hope for?"

"You have brothers and sisters. They come home, don't they?"

"Yes, well, we hope for things unseen. Me, in this case."

"You said you'd stop talking that way."

"Sorry. It's true, though. I will go home. COD. I have that address in my pocket. But I have to time it right. I have to outlast him. That may be my primary object in life!" He laughed. "He's not going to make it easy for me, I know that." He thought he must have sounded strange, but she didn't take her hand away. She was considering.

She said, "It's interesting to think about that. Things unseen. The reality is always different."

"Worse."

"Different. Unlike. Not necessarily worse or better."

He said, "I'm at my best unseen. The Prince of Darkness. The Prince of Absence, for that matter. You won't answer this, but just to clarify the point—the way you thought of me for the last few months—if you did think of me, but assuming you did. I know that isn't something I ought to assume. Never mind."

"Did I remember you as—what?"

"Oh, more presentable, I suppose."

"I never gave it a thought."

"Of course you didn't. And I'd have expected you to be a little taller."

"I'm barefoot, remember."

"True. But you actually weren't sure who I was, back there, when you first saw me."

"Oh, I knew who you were."

"But you thought about running."

"It crossed my mind."

"I see."

They were quiet. Then she said, "Maybe I'm remembering you now, since I can't really see you."

"All right, I suppose. Which me are you remembering? Do I have that scar?"

"The scar is there. I'm sorry about it. Other than that, it's just your—atmosphere."

"Cheap aftershave. Not that I've shaved. It spilled down my sleeve. Weeks ago. And cigarette smoke. And so on. A little atmosphere has to be expected, I guess. Sorry."

"You know I didn't mean that."

"Then what? My spirit?"

"You said we're like spirits."

"I should have said ghosts. Ectoplasm."

"They're spirits."

"Mine isn't."

"Mine is."

"If you say so."

"I do."

"Does it matter?"

"You seem to think so."

"True enough." He said, "You're very sure of yourself. At ease in your skin. While I—"

She stopped. "You actually said that."

"What? Well, yes, I suppose I did. I'm—not really sorry. That would probably give the wrong impression. It's a thing people say, isn't it? Or they say the opposite. Depending on cases. I've offended you. I'm terribly sorry. It's true, though, isn't it?"

"No. Much of the time it isn't true. When I find myself trapped in a white cemetery, it definitely isn't true."

He said, "You may not believe this, but I have had something of the same experience. A number of times."

She laughed. "I'm sorry, but I actually do believe you."

"Yes. Here's an example. I got a draft notice. I was so surprised they'd found me that I thought it must be an omen. Time to pull myself together, learn discipline and so on. So I sobered up, made a kind of habit of breakfast, that sort of thing. It was all I thought about for a week at least. I showed up at the post office, five minutes early. When my turn came, the fellow just glanced up from his notebook and said something I thought was—unnecessarily dismissive."

"What did he say?"

"He said, 'Next.' He made a gesture with his pencil, also dismissive. I decided I should consider the whole episode an omen, a sign, you know, that my past would be my future. Though he might just have known me from somewhere."

"Well, that's very sad."

"Yes. Humiliating. I don't know why I told you about it. In general I lie. I tell people I lied my way out of the army, and they always believe me. A bad heart, I say. Flat feet. Religious objections." Then he said, "But I wanted you to know I was capable of honorable intentions. That's why I told you."

"I knew that already."

"You did?" He laughed. "What a waste! I should have saved it for a better time."

She said, "There won't be a better time."

Quiet. Or was it silence. Usually he knew.

There was a bench, and they sat down. She pulled her legs up beside her, so she could partly cover them with the skirts of her coat. This meant that her shoulder was against his. If he put his arm on the back of the bench behind her, both of them would be more comfortable. He thought of suggesting it. They weren't friends. They were acquaintances, which was a different thing in their case than in others. She had thought of running when she saw him. If they were friends, he could say they would both be warmer if he put his arm, so to speak, around her. He could make a little joke about it, call her girlfriend, and she would say, Don't you wish, that sort of thing, and settle against him. He didn't move, and his arm and shoulder and then his neck became stiff with the effort of not moving, maybe with the thought of not moving. After a while, he felt her head tip toward his shoulder. She startled awake. "Still dark," she said. "Still night." A little while again and he felt her cheek on his shoulder, her hair against his cheek. His shoulder ached. He had a thought of a kind he had often: If he lived a more orderly life, he could at least keep track of his debts, keep them at bay a little. He was a bad risk, which meant that his creditors wasted no time in applying extreme measures. He was usually putting a little aside to stave off the more terrible threats, when people were thoughtful enough to give him even a dire warning, which meant there was usually some pocket money to be shaken loose by whoever decided Jack owed him something, or owed it to a friend of his. He suspected sometimes this might all be a joke everyone else was in on. It was hard to imagine any kind of future, living where he did, as he did. If he just gave up drinking entirely, that would save him some money and any amount of trouble and embarrassment. He would stay out of bars altogether. Then he would get a job of some kind. Then he would happen by Della's, and she would be sitting on the stoop all alone, listening to the wind and watching the fireflies, and he would think he had that book in his pocket, *Oak and Ivy*, and then his reverend father would be standing there with the book in his hands, brand-new, with ribbons in it like a Bible, saying, "The love of a good woman! Yes!" Jack's cheek had fallen against her hair, well, really, her hat, but when he woke, he did not move. He thought she might be awake, but she didn't move either. Well, he thought, this is pleasant enough. Why should he trouble himself with thoughts of reformation when mere chance could bring him to this moment, without effort or forethought on his part, without the miseries of anticipation. Yes, that blasted little hat. It was made of something stiff, scratchy, and it seemed to have beads on it. It had tipped away from her hair on one side. It would have been the simplest thing in the world just to slip it off, but she might be awake, and he was only more nervous about seeming familiar when she had been so trusting. Not intentionally, of course, but in fact, which is what matters. Aside from that, it hadn't begun to rain and no one had come by to bother them. He thought they must have been sitting there an hour at least. He was in the habit of noticing good hours, otherwise swept up in days about which there was not really much good to be said. A quarter hour, if it came to that.

She said, very softly, "You know, you shouldn't talk to me the way you do." And a shock of discomfort passed through him, part shame, part alarm, part irritation, part a kind of panicky bewilderment and reappraisal. The memories he had been storing up for future use, maybe refining a little, were all turning to regret and embarrassment even before he knew what unpardonable thing about them would be hectoring him on his deathbed, in all probability. His lips were suddenly very dry, so he said only, "Sorry."

"We're just out walking together. You're not obliged to tell me every worst thing you ever did."

He laughed with relief. "I haven't! Word of honor! But it is very kind of you to think so, Miss Miles."

She said, "When the world ended, nothing would matter but what you wanted to matter." She was talking into the darkness. "No more dragging around all the things you regret. Just regretting them would snuff them out." She made a gesture with her hand, like a bubble bursting. "That's one new rule."

"You don't seem like someone who would have much to regret. I mean, I have sisters like you. I told you. Four of them. They teach and play piano and remember everybody's birthday and send thank-you notes. When I was a kid, I thought it was an amazing thing to watch. One after another, passing from childishness to impeccability. A long time ago, of course, but people like that don't change. I suppose my sisters think they have regrets. That they know the meaning of the word."

"Well, I do know the meaning of the word."

"I'm not asking for a confession or anything."

"Good." She sat up, and stood up. "I hear that man singing."

They were both stiff and cold from their hour of rest, pleasantly miserable, walking up the hill to the deeper darkness, laughing a little, quietly, at their awkwardness. She was leaning on his arm. Tell St. Peter at the Golden Gate that you hate to make him wait. She said, "I guess he doesn't know another song."

"I suspect he sings like that to give us disreputable types a chance to avoid him."

"Very thoughtful."

"People can be like that. I've noticed, from time to time."

They waited together, very still and quiet, till the man passed by. As is our custom, Jack thought. How quickly things can become understood sometimes. "Did you happen upon the lake in your wanderings? You must have. It's pretty hard to miss. They call it a pond."

"I saw it."

"It's really best on a night like this, when you can't see it. You just hear it breathing, and you feel the breaths on your skin. On a still night, of course. Which this one is, at the moment."

"Yes, I saw those little chapels, I suppose they're tombs, but with stained-glass windows and everything, overlooking the lake, as if there would be anyone there to see it."

"Besides me."

"And me. I sat there on the step of one for a while, admiring the willows. Very poetic." She laughed. "That was when I still expected I'd find my way out of here sometime."

Jack said, "That is absolutely my favorite tomb. The one that looks like a gingerbread house? I have passed many a not unpleasant hour on that step."

"A gingerbread house—it looks like a witch is going to open the door and invite you in."

"True. No luck yet."

She shook her head. "Jack Boughton, how you talk."

"I mean there might be a plate of cookies involved. I believe that's how the story goes, isn't it? You'd take one or two, and then you'd just walk away: Tragedy averted."

"I don't think so. Dealing with a witch wouldn't be that simple."

"You speak from experience, I suppose?"

"I believe I do."

"Maybe I know that witch."

"You don't. You have your own witches."

"No doubt. I didn't mean to encroach."

"That's all right."

"We could walk over there, anyway."

"We've been walking that way for a while. We must almost be there by now."

"Well, that's true. I was thinking about the lake, and the willows, and the delectable tomb. Thinking you might want to rest awhile. I guess I wasn't quite aware of where I was taking you. Not everyone likes to spend midnight on the very porch of extinction, so to speak. The threshold of Judgment, if you prefer. No one with an interest in symbolism, at least. I should have asked." He laughed, and she was quiet. He wished he could take back every word he had said. "Did you notice? Its gargoyles are cherubs. The water pours out of the jars they're holding. A nice touch, I think. Gargoyles can be pretty grotesque." Still quiet.

Then she said, "I've been to so many funerals, so many burials. My father always said, 'That pale horse is carrying a child home to his Father's house.' Quoting somebody. Tombs don't really bother me."

"Me either, in all seriousness. I was attempting a kind of

joke." This wasn't really true. It was true that he was interested in the *way* they bothered him.

That man again, singing. "I—*wish* I didn't love you so. My love for you should have faded *long* ago." They were very quiet. "I—*wish* I didn't need your kiss."

Jack said, "He says it like he means it," and then regretted speaking at all because she seemed intent on the song and then on the silence that followed it.

Finally she said, "You can't sing that song without sounding like you mean it. You can't even say the words."

"It's a good song."

"It's a terrible song. I hate that word 'wish.' It sounds like somebody's dying breath! Like it's taking the wind right out of you."

"Yes. But it's still a pretty good song."

Then she said, "I did a foolish thing. I tried to use it in class. Expressive language that you'd hear right on the radio. Perfectly ordinary language. I thought it might help them like poetry better if I used that kind of example."

"I guess it didn't work."

"Well, they got embarrassed. Some of them started whispering and laughing behind their hands. Notes passed. At their age, I don't know how I could have expected anything else."

"They suspected you of romantic longings, I suppose?"

"I tried to talk my way out of it, whatever it was they suspected. Are the words of the song spoken words, or are they just thoughts in someone's mind? How do you feel when you wish for something? I was going to talk about that word 'so.' Most of the time you would say 'so much,' 'so well.' Something that finishes the thought. But just saying 'so' like that. It could mean a hundred things. All at the same time."

"Tenderly. Hopelessly."

"I was going to ask them whether they would be sorry or glad to have feelings like that. I don't know what I thought I was doing."

"Deeply. Utterly. Irrationally. Passionately. Futilely."

"Tenderly."

So after a minute, he asked her, "What would you say? Sorry or glad?"

She was quiet. Then she said, "I don't know. Those things can be hard to tell apart sometimes."

"Where tenderness is involved, definitely."

"Definitely."

He brought her up a hill. "Our lovely little tomb," he said. "And a fine view of the lake." He actually carried a handkerchief, as his father had told them all to do. Excellent advice. He used it to wipe down the steps, and then he shook it out and folded it. Too damp to put in a pocket. No place else to put it. "Please," he said, "make yourself comfortable."

She sat down on one side of the top step. "Now you sit down, too. There's room. I can move over a little more."

"I actually forgot—I thought we'd have more spacious accommodations, I really did. This is the first time I've brought a guest." "Masher" is the word his father would have used. A man who contrives to make himself familiar. A masher would be thinking, "Clever of me."

She said, "That's fine. But you can't keep standing there. We could go find a bench if you want to."

He said, "We're a little bit out of the rain here, if it rains." She moved over some more, pulling her coat around her. He sat down on the second step, rested his folded arms on his knees, and looked at where the lake was. They were quiet.

Then she said, "It's best when we talk. For passing the time."

"Yes. I was about to mention that."

They were quiet. The lake was darker than the darkness, visible because it was absolutely invisible. Like the sky on a night that was moonless and clear, a strong, present black. On one such night he had thrown a rock at a streetlamp, just to see the sky he knew was up there. He hadn't even been especially drunk. He had been asserting a fundamental human privilege, as he explained to the cop. The cop had said, "Drunk and disorderly," predictably enough. Was that a year ago? Five years ago? It all ran together.

He said, "The word 'lake' is related to the word 'lack.' An absence. No kidding, I looked it up. Long hours in the public library, out of the weather. The intellect can share its wealth without diminution. Somebody said that, if I remember correctly. So I always feel a little at ease in a library. I can take the best they have and no one is the worse for it. I mean, you know, things to think about. Not actual books. Well, I do get attached to certain things, books, but I bring them back sooner or later." Then he said, "I owe you one Paul Dunbar. With interest by now, I suppose."

She said, "Finish that couplet and leave the book on the porch and we'll be even."

"Spoken like a teacher."

After a minute, she said, "I'll probably be doing that for the rest of my life, no matter what happens. Talking like that. You start thinking in a certain way, thinking you have something to say to people. That they ought to listen to."

"Like a preacher."

"Worse. A preacher still has an air about him, even if his last church chased him out and barred the door behind him. He can still cite texts. People never quite ignore that."

"Things might turn out all right. You might be talking to adolescents about couplets for decades to come. An excellent life. I mean that. Really."

"Well, it is. Especially since I seem to be looking back on it."

"Well," he said, "you listen to this, now. Diligent effort has gone into this—what do you call it?—recitation. It sounds better if you shout it, but, you know, neither the time nor the place. I have to remember how it begins. Yes. 'Before their eyes in sudden view appear / The secrets of the hoary deep; a dark / Illimitable ocean, without bound, / Without dimension, where length, breadth, and height, / And time, and place, are lost; where eldest Night / And Chaos, ancestors of Nature, hold / Eternal anarchy, amidst the noise / Of endless wars, and by confusion stand.' John Milton. The greatest Presbyterian poet, my father said."

"He wasn't Presbyterian."

"True, but he wasn't anything else, either. My father found everything he wrote highly persuasive, which meant he must be Presbyterian, whether he knew it or not. He'd say he was joking, but if anybody pressed the issue, he'd get a little cranky." Then he said, "My point was, though, that I memorized that to impress an English teacher with whom I was briefly in love. I was fourteen at the time. I never did recite it. It has never been my nature to do what I ought to, for my own sake, even. She'd probably have thought better of me. But I remember it sometimes, and it pleases me that it's still in my brain. Along with not much else. So you never know what effect you might have had."

"And I never will know. I might never be in that room again. Never even have a chance to say goodbye to them. I'm beginning to realize I liked them better than I thought I did."

"Well, that's something."

"My last memory will be them laughing at me over that song."

"Things might turn out all right. I suppose there's something about sitting here in the dark that makes it seem unlikely. But you never know." He laughed. "And I'll never know. The end of this strange tale, I mean. How things work out. It will worry me. So. I will worry so."

They were quiet.

She said, "I'll set a book in the window."

"Which window?"

"The one by the front door."

"All right. Will it mean good news or bad news?"

"Good news."

"All right. Don't forget."

"I promise."

He said, "What if it's a while before you know for sure? What if they deliberate or something? It could take weeks. No book in the window—"

"I'll put a plant in the window. A sprig of ivy. So you'll know I still don't know."

"Without the book."

"With the book, if things seem to be going well enough."

"Otherwise, just the sprig."

"Yes."

He nodded. "That woman—is it Lorraine?—she might see the book there and think that's a strange place for it to be and put it away, or walk off with it."

"I'll be careful to use one she's already read."

"All right. I suppose that could work."

"I'll make sure it works."

"That will be kind of you."

"It's kind of you to worry."

"So."

"Yes," she said. They were quiet. Then she said, "'So' is a word they would use after the world ended. Or maybe they wouldn't need it anymore. Because they'd know what it means. Everything would just be what you think it would be."

"It's so dark," he said. "The night is so long. We'd step across a threshold of some kind. Utter darkness and endless time. That would be the way of things. No more 'so.'"

"Sometimes I feel like we've just been living on hints. Seeing the world through a keyhole. That's how it would seem to us when we looked back."

He nodded. "That's how it seems to me now."

She had leaned down, cupping her poor toes in her hands, cheek on her knee, facing him in the dark. There was an odd loveliness about it. Why did he think she seemed content? He believed her eyes were closed. Had my heart an unbroken string, your touch would set it trembling. He had almost penciled that into her book, then thought better of it. It wasn't a very good line. Trembling doesn't really have three syllables. And touch. What might she find suggested in that word. I will ruin this, he thought. I almost did, writing in those words, before I even imagined it would happen. I never would have imagined. If he touched her face now, ever so lightly, things would be different afterward. That's how the world is, touch anything, change everything. Caution is needed. Which meant that question was already in his mind—what would be left if the fragile were tested, pushed nearer the edge of the shelf, if that tension were sprung and the fragile thing, the essence of it, lost. This strange night lost, fallen into shivers and shards of embarrassment and distrust and regret. It crossed his mind that if he touched her dark cheek in the dark night, an elegant curve, bodiless as geometry, objectively speaking, if he followed the curve of it with just the tip of a finger, there would be a delicacy in the experiment she would understand if he could explain it to her. Pure touch, almost undistracted. He said, "Talk about something." Too abrupt. "Let's talk," he said, "about something."

She lifted her head. "I guess I was asleep. I was dreaming."

"Sorry."

"Don't be. It was a pretty ordinary dream. I couldn't find something I needed, I didn't even know what it was. I was all worked up about it. Now I'm here in the dark, sitting on the steps of a tomb beside a strange man I can't quite see. That's more like a dream."

"Hmm. It sounds like a very bad dream."

"Yes, but it doesn't feel like one. It's the feeling you have that makes a dream bad. I just realized that."

He nodded. "Interesting." Then he said, "You know, I actually sort of enjoy my life. I know I shouldn't. It could stand a lot of improvement. But maybe it's the feeling you have that makes a life bad. Or makes it all right enough most of the time." He said, "I aspire to utter harmlessness. It's a contest I have with myself. I have no real aptitude for harmlessness, which makes it interesting." He said, "Spiders and flies are completely safe around me. Mice. Vermin generally. I've learned there is a kind of pleasure in considering all the things and people I've never harmed. Never even made them notice me there, appraising their vulnerabilities. Which, I'll admit, is something I do." Then he said, "Sometimes." What a stupid thing to have said to her. "Let's change the subject."

"Yes. All right. This step is really hard."

"Cold."

"Damp."

"I'm sorry I woke you up. There's nothing like sleep for passing the time."

She said, "You should come to my place for Thanksgiving."

He laughed. "What have I done to deserve that?"

"Thanksgiving isn't something a person has to deserve. That's the whole point of it. Anyway, you've been about as harmless as you could possibly be. I appreciate that. It's not a thing I take for granted." Resting her head on her knees, looking at where he was, smiling. He knew that from her voice.

He said, "You could introduce me to your dad. 'The Prince of Darkness, Papa. I found him in a cemetery. He says he's harmless. The bruised reed he will not break, probably. Though he might be the one who bruised it.'"

"Don't joke like that. Anyway, I'm not going home this year. I mean, you should come to my place. You know, where you leave any books you decide to return?"

"I know it well."

"Just knock on the door this time. Stop being so sneaky."

He said, "You don't know what you're asking. Can the leopard change his spots? Besides, I always lose track of Thanksgiving. It moves around. It's not for people with disorderly lives."

She shrugged. "You might make an effort, just this once."

"I can't promise anything."

She said, "Oh, I know that."

So here I am, he thought. And here she was, Della, the woman he had recruited into his daydreams to make up for a paucity of meaning and event he sometimes found oppressive. No harm done. She was safe in his daydreams. Cherished, really. He had returned often enough to that one regrettable night, or that one almost regrettable hour in an otherwise wonderful night, to have put things right in his imagination, though not, of course, in his memory. A lingering farewell. Good night rather than goodbye. That was something.

Her sleeve stirred against him. The plum-colored cloth of her coat. He had once asked himself which colors yield to darkness first, and which of them float in it for a while. Twilight has nothing black about it, so black would be absorbed much more gradually than plum. She was clothed in twilight. That is the kind of thought I'll have when this is over and she is gone. Those ridiculous poems I never write down. In fact, she will be a respectable woman with a job and a street address, reading her newspaper over breakfast in the morning light. I'll walk by, and she won't see me. Or she might be on a train to Memphis, rehearsing the words she will say to her mother, her father, accepting disgrace because it would be easier, would require fewer words, after all the excuses and apologies she'd have made already. Never mentioning me, wishing she never had seen me, putting this night out of mind altogether.

Chilly as he was, his shirt dampened. He could not protect her at all. This sham, squiring her through the tombstones, when the fact was that, if she had just spoken to the guard while she still looked respectable and her flowers had not wilted completely, if she had told the man her wistful little lie, he would have opened a gate for her, after the usual sermon about personal responsibility and the like, of course, which was hard to begrudge him, since it was simply an added small compensation for walking around all night. Jack had been too surprised at seeing her there to think this through, and then he had been so pleased to fall into the role of gentleman, which in fact overtook him as often as he had a clean shirt on but was vastly more inescapable with this particular lady on his arm, and in the darkness that so kindly hid the marks of an ungentlemanly life. He actually could have rescued her by telling her to sit on that bench and wait for the guard, standing well back to keep an eye on her, for what that was worth. Then she'd have had the walk home in the dark, which would be bad but probably not as bad as the same walk home by daylight. He had his excuses. Surprise itself accounted for most of it. But excuses only meant that he had done harm he did not intend, which was another proof that he did harm inevitably, intentions be damned.

He said, "I actually believe in predestination. I'm serious."

"I don't."

"Well, of course you don't. Destiny has made you a Methodist."

"So you were just talking to yourself?"

"An old habit."

"You said you were harmless, even though you have no gift for it. Does that mean you're fated to be something you're not? That doesn't make much sense."

"I said I act harmless. Insofar as in me lies. That doesn't mean I succeed in being harmless. I don't usually guess right about what harmlessness would require in a particular situation. And so on. It doesn't even mean that I won't give up on the whole business sometime. Won't just relax and let myself be the rotter I am."

She was quiet.

He said, "Now I've scared you. You see what I mean. That's the last thing in the world I meant to do."

"You don't scare me, especially. You're just like everybody else. You seem to think other people aren't doing the same thing you are, more or less. I don't go around revealing my innermost thoughts, I can tell you that. The minute I did, you'd be scared of me."

He laughed.

"Don't laugh!"

He said, "I apologize. That was terribly insensitive."

They laughed.

She said, "I actually am full of rage. Wrath. I think I feel a little like God must feel the second before He just gives up and rains brimstone. I've heard people blame Him for that! I don't blame Him. I can imagine the satisfaction. I have to wonder when that last exasperation will come and I burst into flames. Nothing in particular, everything in general, plus one more thing, maybe one very tiny thing. Whoosh."

"Really?"

"Do I sound like I'm joking?"

"Not a bit. You've actually scared me."

"Don't worry too much. All my life I've been a perfect Christian lady. It's nothing I can help, I guess. Something to be grateful for, really. It makes my mother happy. I plan to keep on with it."

They were quiet for a while, and then she said, "Sometimes I shut myself in my room and throw myself down on my bed and I just let it run through me. All that wrath. In every bone in my body. Then it seems to sort of wear itself out and I can go for a walk or something. But it never goes away." And then she said, "You're very quiet."

"Yes. I'm just thinking of the major exasperations I've added to the list. I'll spend the next month adding up the minor ones. The ones that seem minor to me. I'm no judge, of course."

She said, "I don't think of it as a list. It's more like a mass, a weight. You know, when a cloud gets very heavy, and it begins to have its own life. It begins stirring inside itself, growling, making lightning. Maybe it was only one raindrop that changed it from a plain old gray cloud no one would ever notice. Just a handful of droplets would make the difference. Somebody's breath rising up, somebody saying something mean, telling some vicious tale." Her voice was very soft.

He said, "From now on I'm going to be so careful."

"Bring me my book."

"Oh, lady! I will do it as soon as humanly possible!"

She laughed. "I don't really believe that. It doesn't much matter. You've probably made a mess of it, anyway." She turned her face away from him. "I'm sorry," she said. "I shouldn't have told you all that. I can't talk about being mad without—being mad. But I'm all right now."

"Well, I guess we have one thing in common."

"What? What do we have in common?"

He was quiet. He had meant something so anodyne he was a little relieved at not having to go on. We are not as we appear. The Christian lady and the harmless man. The Prince of Darkness and the vial of divine wrath. There was some truth in it.

A night can seem endless, he thought. Insects going about their lives, very intent. Why all the chirping? His father saw him once with a mayonnaise jar with some grass in it and a caterpillar, holes punched in the lid in the approved style. He actually did plan to put water in, too, to watch for bubbles, since he had been wondering if caterpillars actually breathed. But he hadn't made the experiment yet. His father stood there with his hands in his pockets, looking off at the trees. "The creatures do want their lives," he remarked. "The ugliest little one of them. People don't notice it sometimes, but it's true." Yes, it is. Such lives. All that purpose. Always on their way somewhere. You had to admire.

Maybe a chirp meant "I exist!" and then "I exist!," as if it could matter. But it must, since they all do it.

There wasn't much wrong with her book. It shouldn't have spent so much time in his pocket. They call it foxing, when a book gets that worn look. He'd almost thought of selling it once. Really he was just making conversation with the clerk in a bookstore, one day when he felt like talking to someone. He hadn't really meant to sell it, and the clerk hadn't come up with a decent price, which was fortunate, considering. For a while he thought he might wander past her doorstep sometime, so he had kept it with him. But after he got that cut, that scar, he knew he never would. Here she was, and he didn't have a word to say to her.

Finally she said, "What are you thinking about?"

"I'm thinking about bugs."

"The gangster? The bunny?"

"Insects. Did you ever watch a spider swim? They're surprisingly good at it. I mean, I was surprised."

She shook her head. "I guess I never noticed." He thought, A spider isn't an insect. He didn't actually say that it was one, but that's how it must have sounded. She said, "You're the first person I ever spoke to about that. That rage. You're the only one. You'll probably be the last one, too."

What is it people say? "Would you like to talk about it? You might feel better—"

"No, I wouldn't. And I don't. I'm sorry. It's nothing to do with you. I suppose it's just the night and the tombstones." She stood up, and she began walking down the hill toward the lake. He watched her go until he could discern her, just. A gentle disturbance in the darkness, a warmer darkness where she was. That plum coat. She might be walking away from him, weary of him.

He thought he might as well follow. What could it matter? At the first hint that he was not welcome, he would step away. Actually, it would be the second hint, if her walking away was the first. A little injury to his pride, no matter. But she must have heard his footsteps in the grass, because she paused till he was beside her, and she put her hand in the crook of his arm. They came to the edge of the water, shockingly cold and stony, and stood there together for a while, anyway, and then she said, "You have to be a little bit kind to yourself."

"Why?"

"Because I said so. Because you're skin and bone. Because you're keeping a birthday in a graveyard."

"That was a joke."

"No, it wasn't. If I think of you sometime, I don't want to think of you here."

He said, "I won't be here. I have that address in my pocket. Instructions, and some telephone numbers. Mention of a modest reward. They'll see to it. My family. They're very reliable." She was silent, so he reconsidered what she had said. "Oh, I see. You mean I should reform my life. This has been suggested to me on other occasions. Just this morning, in fact. I asked a fellow for a light. Such a small thing to ask, but it didn't go very well. He kept the whole match to himself. That kind of day, I thought. A day of atonement. But you want me to change my life so that, if you do happen to think of me sometime—"

"I want you to be alive. That's all. Nothing complicated."

He laughed. "Not for you, maybe." Then he said, "My father was right. He told me once, The creatures want their lives. Every one of them. When this creature has an empty belly, he finds something to put in it. So, no need to worry." If you walk along the docks, you can almost always find a place where the dishwasher didn't show up.

She just shook her head.

So he said, "You caught me a little off guard there. At first I thought that was a remarkable thing to say. I don't believe I have ever heard anyone say that, so explicitly. Then I realized that I feel the same about you. I mean, that I'm glad you're alive. And hope you stay that way, and so on. I suppose the sentiment is fairly commonplace. Most people feel that way about most people, I believe. Which is a good thing. There can be disappointments, of course. I hadn't thought about it in so many words, but I see your point. Thank you, in fact." Nerves.

She laughed.

But he felt he should say, "You really don't know what you're asking." Changing his life meant changing himself. Could it be some misbegotten loyalty that made him so intractably Jack Boughton, when so many better options must be available?

She said, "I'm asking it, anyway."

"Then I'll try."

She shook her head. "Not good enough."

"Well, you have to understand certain things. Let's see."

"I'm listening."

"That may be the problem."

"Be serious."

"I'll try."

She shook her head.

"All right," he said. "I have not actually chosen this life. The path of least resistance is not a choice, in the usual sense of the word. I know it appears to be one. But when the resistance you encounter on every other path seems, you know, indomitable, then there you are. I'm sure I have been too easily discouraged. Still, I know whereof I speak, more or less."

She said, "That won't do. The path of least resistance put that scar on your face."

"It's done worse, believe me. But there is the path of less resistance. No improvement. That one cracked a rib."

"Don't tell me. It's none of my business. I don't want to hear about it."

"I was kidding."

"You weren't kidding. At least be honest about that." She stepped away from him, turned away from him. "Oh."

Two ribs. Not that it mattered. Finally he said, "You happen to have spent a few hours with a bum, Miss Miles. I'm sure this is an unusual experience for you. For most people, really. Anyone in my family, certainly." She was standing there with her back to him. It had to be morning sooner or later, and then it would be over, anyway. "This sort of life has its costs, I agree. But I'm basically harmless. Most of us are. If we're incorrigible, that might just be a sign of—contentment." He might have said "—resignation." They aren't unrelated. He was telling her to stop talking to him as if she had a claim on him, from taking that proprietary tone, of the fortunate to the less fortunate, the reputable to the disreputable. No, he wasn't really talking to her. The Methodists ran very good soup kitchens, and she'd have been in one of them, smiling and ladling, from the minute she was old enough to know the word "charity." He wasn't quite a regular, and this was St. Louis, but the thought that she might have seen him there sometime, in the bald light, bowl in hand, shocked him. He had given himself another of those unbearable memories, a stark vision of something that had not happened but was so very possible that he had to retrieve his handkerchief and

70

wipe his brow. A memory like that is half an impulse. He would make himself avoid everything Methodist—AME, Wesleyan, and United. There were things he sometimes imagined in his foolish moments he might say to anyone who seemed to take offense at him. To that man who shook out the flame on his match rather than giving Jack the use of it. Or to a brother or sister, if one of them ever found him. But to hear the words aloud, and spoken to her, was startling. He said, "Yes, I should try to do better."

"I didn't mean that."

Well, neither did he. It was probably best just to be quiet and wait until the conversation changed, as conversations will when no one is saying anything. Given a little time they change like weather, clouds passing, a breeze coming up. No way to predict, but something else is usually something better. He wished he had a cigarette. It was that shame he could never talk himself out of. Candor was no help at all. He walked along the verge of the water, just a few steps away from her, but far enough to make a point of some kind. After a few minutes she came and stood beside him, in the dark and the quiet, the water at their feet making its soft, idle sounds, sifting pebbles. She was in every way still. No words, just stillness, like a presence in a dream.

Finally he said, "You don't mean to judge me."

She said, "I don't."

"You probably ought to."

"Why should I?"

"Well, if things go wrong for you—the slide into haplessness can be quick. You can find yourself looking at the world from the wrong side before you know what's happened. I think people look at me and they see that. They call me preacher and so on. Professor. It usually means they want to give me a little trouble. I bother them, because they don't think I'm the sort who ends up like this. I know there might be more to it. Of course there is. I'm just saying it can happen. It's nothing you should be anywhere near. Take my word for it."

Stillness. A presence in a dream always seems to mean something. It has threat or guilt or grief like an atmosphere around it. Her stillness felt strangely like assurance. It felt very like loyalty, if he was not mistaken. It was as if she had said, We ended the world, don't you remember? Now it's just the two of us.

He was reminded of something. "Easier than air with air, if Spirits embrace, / Total they mix, union of pure with pure." Not that. That was not part of the assignment. The teacher had sent him home with a note. He put it in one of the Edinburgh books, those old theology books no one ever looked at, out of respect for their authority, for what his father called their finespun argumentation.

What she actually said was "You are living like someone who has died already."

Well, there was a good deal of truth in that. He had wondered from time to time whether he'd actually scared himself to death, or half to death, anyway. Harmlessness. A banner with a strange device. He said, "I'm almost never here, Miss Miles. I don't normally pass my nights in the cemetery, believe me. You might have gotten that impression because you happen to have come across me here. That's completely understandable. I mean, that you would not quite realize what a remarkable coincidence we're dealing with. That our lives should intersect—I would have almost as good grounds for supposing that you spent your nights here, if you think about it—not really, of course. I didn't mean that about our lives. But, logically speaking, you see what I mean." Listen to that fool go on.

She said, "The cemetery is part of it, I suppose. Maybe."

"So you're saying what? I'm a ghost of myself? The mere shadow of a man—and then the moon went down."

"Yes."

"No. That's pretty disheartening. I have to object."

She said, very softly, "I don't think it's disheartening. I think it's kind of—beautiful."

"Did you say 'beautiful'?"

She nodded. "Beautiful. In a way."

He laughed. "Well, that's a surprise."

She said, "Something happened that made you decide you'd had all the life you could stand. So you ended it there. Except you have to stay alive, for your father." Her voice came very close to that annoying lilt of realization you hear when people go spiraling off into some supposed insight. They become inaccessible to common sense, to distraction, even. She said, "You don't feel like part of the world anymore. Maybe you're more like most people than you think."

"I can't quite persuade myself that I'm like most people. And I certainly can't persuade anyone else that I am. If you find any of this beautiful, it's all right with me. Which is not to say you should. I must have misled you somehow. I'm pretty sure I've told you that I lie. I lied as a lisping child. So whatever you think I've told you probably isn't true. If it's actually what I said."

She nodded. "That's interesting."

"No, it isn't. It's a damned nuisance, most of the time."

Quiet.

She said, "I think most people feel a difference between their real lives and the lives they have in the world. But they ignore their souls, or hide them, so they can keep things together, keep an ordinary life together. You don't do that. In your own way, you're kind of—pure."

He sighed. "No no no no no. Your poetical impulses have overwhelmed your good sense. Miss Miles, I can't let that happen. Within five minutes I'll have come up with a way to disillusion you, and we'll both be unhappy."

She nodded. "That's how you defend yourself. That's how you keep yourself at a distance. Anyway, we're both unhappy as it is, so I'm not putting particular confidence in my illusions. If that's what they are." She said, "I'm just trying to tell you that there are reasons why you should, you know, keep body and soul together."

"To beautify, no, beatify, this tedious world. I can't tell you what multitudes are unmoved."

"Well, there's Jesus," she said, which startled him.

He said, "A gentleman I am at considerable pains to avoid." He thought, Sweet Jesus, don't let her try to convert me.

"I'm sorry. I know how that sounded. I really just meant that there is—anyone, any human being, and then that person's actual life, everything they didn't mean or couldn't say or wished for or grieved over. That's reality. So someone who would know the world that way, some spirit, seems kind of inevitable. I think. Why should so much reality, most of it, count for nothing? That's how it seems to me."

"That spirit would not always be impressed, depending on cases."

She shook her head. "I just think there has to be a Jesus, to say 'beautiful' about things no one else would ever see. The precious things should be looked to, whatever becomes of the rest of it. I hope that doesn't sound harsh."

Who could object? But she was very serious. How to put an end to this without offending her in a way he would have to regret? "Not harsh at all," he said. Something worse, something he lacked a word for.

74

Quiet. The black of the sky was dimming with light, so the black shapes of trees and the black of the water were beginning to stand out against it, beneath it. Morning birds had begun to stir. The figure beside him seemed veiled now, neither quite hidden nor quite visible. He could not bring himself to look at her directly, and she did not look at him, both of them as still as if the kindly dark were not receding from them. What would be the one sufficient thing to say, before the flood of light swept over them, now that their world was ending? Amen, he thought. He was undisgraced and she was unoffended, a devout hope more or less fulfilled.

They walked back up the hill to the tomb. Their shoes were there by the door in a neat domestic row, her handbag propped against them. The two of them sat down together, he to pull on his miserable socks, she to smooth hair that would not be smoothed, to reset hairpins and resettle her hat. She found a lipstick in her bag. Their attempts at repairing their dishevelments were embarrassed. We have waked up together, he thought. Like Adam and Eve. Daylight will make everything worse. He knew the stubble of beard made him look haggard, worse with his hat on, even though when he took it off his hair looked thin. He stood up, his back to her, as if that solved anything. He heard her walk past him and saw her go down to the deepest grass and bend to wet her hands in the dew. She washed her face with it and looked up at him, laughing, her face shining. She said, "I saw that in a book. They were getting ready to enter Purgatory."

He said, "Then I guess I'd better do it, too. I know for a fact that Purgatory has standards."

He went down to where she was, but then, standing there, scarred and stubbled, he felt that flinch of nerves, a tightening of the neck and shoulder, that made him tilt his head back and to the side, just a little, but enough to make him look supercilious, his sisters said, or as if he was about to take a punch, his brothers said. Daylight was Purgatory. It was terrible, being a thing to be looked at. He had always thought so, even before he had his history written all over him. She looked very young, with the sun sparkling in that furze of hair that had escaped all her smoothing and pinning. No one could say a word against her, think a harsh thought, surely, considering the mildness of her eyes, her gentle face. What could he ever have had to do with her? The question offended even him a little. What would her father think, or anyone who cared about her? He had to get her out of here, back to the right kind of life, in which he would of course have no place at all. So they should be quiet. "No more laughing," he said. "Someone will hear."

She said, "Yes, that was stupid of me," and nodded.

Not stupid, actually very pleasing. Her laughter meant, Look at me, Jack! Look at my face all splashed with light!

But he said, "We have a problem we have to deal with now. We really can't be seen together. We have to leave separately, when they open the gates. You first. If you need me, I'll be close enough to hear you call," and he walked away, more abruptly than he meant to. He didn't even look back. He put himself behind a big monument he had forgotten to show her, a stone pelican on it, weather-pitted, but with a beautifully, painfully arched neck, and he waited, looking out from its wings once or twice to see where she was. Still at the tomb. She'd taken something from her bag, a little notebook and a pencil. He thought he should walk back there to tell her he was sorry if he had seemed rude just then, leaving her like that, which would have been very foolish. He did want to say some sort of goodbye. That would have been unwise and might have seemed familiar. His palms dampened at the thought of how close he had come to risking it.

Then the guard came along on a lower path, not close enough to have to see her, shouting, "Morning, folks! Time to start the day! Better git while the gittin's good! Don't wanna hafta get the cops in here!" She stayed where she was. Men seemed to come out of nowhere, resurrected from their sleep, shambling, rumpled, rubbing their eyes. He thought, This must look very strange to her, though, on reflection, the remarkable thing was that it didn't look strange to him. She was waiting for them to pass. Then she put her notebook away and adjusted her hat again and brushed at her coat, nerving herself. She glanced around, gave no sign that she had seen him, tottered down the grassy slope in her high-heeled shoes, and took her place on the path of feckless humankind. When she was at a good distance, he followed along behind her.

She would walk out first, alone, and when she had had time enough to be gone, then he would leave. That was the plan. He loitered among the graves as convincingly as he could, as if he had dropped something and was looking for it, and then he heard her voice and the guard's voice. He had to see what was happening. Whatever it was, it was going on too long. He stepped into the road, and he saw. The naked man that lived inside his clothes began covering himself with sweat, sticking his shirt to his back. It wasn't only shame. Yes, it was. She held her head to the side, looking at the ground, waiting for the guard to stop talking to her, nodding now and then. Oh, sweet Jesus, the guard actually put his hand on her. He took hold of her arm. He shook it a little so that she would look up at him, look at that face under the billed cap, all intent with his little claim to public authority, and she would listen to him and say whatever he wanted her to say, "Yes, sir, I'm sorry, sir, I won't ever again." It was too soon, but Jack decided to saunter, he, that naked man, down to the gate and put himself a little behind the guard so that he would look away from her, so that she could walk away. He tried to whistle and failed, but he put his hands in his pockets and strolled pretty convincingly down to where they were, giving no sign that he knew her, of course.

And the guard did turn to him. "Don't you get smart with me!"

People said this to Jack fairly often, absolute strangers he had no thought of getting smart with. So it wasn't really a bad beginning. He said, "Good morning," a slight catch in his voice. He believed he was smiling. Leave, Della!

"You! I am sick of the sight of you, buster! I should have called the cops on you a hundred times before now! This time I'm going to do it! Don't think I don't know what's been going on here. Sleeping off a drunk is one thing, but bringing along a colored gal—we've got *dead* people in here!" He fixed Jack with a stare, decency much offended. Jesus, don't let me laugh. She was still lingering, watching. He felt like telling her, "Not *literally* a hundred times," since that would have made a very bad impression. Probably no more than a dozen times. What a foolish thing to worry about. Why was she standing there watching? He put himself through this humiliation so that she could walk away, and she was seeing him look at his shoes and sweat and plead, more or less, for another chance, sir. If she stayed any longer, he would have to punch the guard to give her an opening to get away, which would mean prison for him, and maybe for her, too, if there were any witnesses. He couldn't look up from his shoes to be sure. Dear Jesus, don't let me punch the guard. Then she left.

Three steps and gone. He felt a little surge of what was probably joy, nicely timed, because he was able to agree feelingly with every remonstrance—that's what the old gent called them—that the guard rehearsed for him. Yes, certainly, he would consider his life. He really would. He knew it was a shameful thing to burden society, to contribute nothing. He felt this intensely. And yes, he was still young enough to turn it all around. At some point he had doffed his hat.

Joy is an earnest emotion, and visible. The guard must have seen a light in his eyes, realization, yes, there could be a good and respectable life ahead of him. In fact, it was relief that she was gone and he had not been driven to violence, which never went well for him. The bruised reed he did not break. Not for lack of trying. Don't talk like that. The guard allowed that he had, at one time, pretty well given up on himself, remarkable as this might seem now. Bad friends! They're the worst thing that can happen to a fellow! Jack almost put in a word for bad enemies, then thought better of it. The guard checked Jack's face for any sign he might be less than serious. Then he said, "I've given you fair warning, bud. Now move along. I don't want to see you around here again, understand?" He was already distracted. There was another bum shambling down the road in need of castigation. Jack thought, My lucky day. He'd had to leave his bedroll and could not possibly go back for it, testy as the guard had been, but that might just make him change his life.

A nd so it was. After he had shaved and washed up and slept a few hours and put on the shirt he kept in decent shape, he actually stepped into the shoe store with the yellowing HELP WANTED sign and offered his services. The old woman at the counter said, "Nobody wants to work here. I don't want to work here. The pay is terrible and there aren't any customers. If you want the job, you're welcome to it. At least it'll keep you out of the weather. That's about all I can say for it."

Clearly this would not be too abrupt a change in his way of life to be sustainable. "Jack Boughton," he said, thinking, reasonably enough, that the information might be of interest to her.

"That's fine, Slick," she said. "Hang up your hat." Then she went back to staring resentfully out the window, jilted by the passing world, a woman left waiting at the altar of commerce. "Every damn person on earth needs shoes," she muttered, as if that fact proved there was malice behind all the public indifference. "Shoes are shoes," she said, as if to fend off the suggestion that the same six pairs had been posed in that window while far too many seasons passed. "By the way, those knots in your shoelaces look bad. Get yourself some new ones. I'll take 'em out of your wages," she said, and laughed.

At some point she had said, in that half growl of hers, something that included "Beverly." He wasn't sure whether it was a first name or a last name. It might seem rude to use it in either case. So in his mind she was "the woman."

All right. The absence of customers meant fewer people to deal with. No one would think to look for him there. The question was what he should do with himself, how to create some slight impression that he was of use, in case anyone happened to look in the window. He suggested that he might take down the HELP WANTED sign, but the woman shook her head. "I'd just have to make another one." So he might not last long enough to work off the shoelaces. He had thought, over the years, that by indenturing himself he would sometime observe practicality at close range, to glean the lessons and rituals of productive life.

St. Louis was a vast hive of enterprise, grocers and barbers and barkeeps doing whatever they did well enough to be there from one day to the next, one year to the next. His wanderings in the city had all confirmed this. Yet he had managed to find his way to a business that resembled busyness so little it surprised him every morning to find the door unlocked and the lights on. And when he walked in each morning, she seemed a little surprised. "You again!" she said once, and it took him a second to be sure she meant it as a joke, so that was bad, and worse was the fact that she noticed his hesitation and apologized. Actually she said, "Kidding." He'd flinched, that reflex of rigid pride and low expectations that had sent him out other doors, walked him away from personal items—a few books, two hats—he could not afford to lose and could not make himself go back for, since they exposed his instant of confusion, always out of proportion to the near-nothing that was at stake. His pride! How could that blasted thing have survived the thousand embarrassments it had cost him? Well, the woman apologized again—"Kidding"—and he had nodded and hung up his hat. And he reminded himself to move the hat rack nearer the door, where he might notice it if he sometime found himself making a sudden exit.

After a week the woman handed him an envelope with money in it. This seemed a bit more like charity than like honest gain, since he had waited on only two customers, neither of whom had bought anything. If some abrupt advantage emerged from the incomprehensible operations of the universe, it was a modest return on their random exactions, the disruptions and defeats. Or so he told himself, though it was clear that the woman had almost as stark use for the money as he had. He might actually be the burden under which their little bark foundered. For weeks he still strolled around by the docks after hours to see if there were dishes to wash, floors to sweep, avoiding places where he'd had trouble before. He imagined the woman might sometime need a loan just to keep him employed, and that he would provide it. He bought two packs of cigarettes, one for her.

And he did not drink! He was not even tempted to drink. He had fallen back on the old habit of imagining that Della might pass him on the street. The shoe store did not serve colored, but Della was so much on his mind that when the bells above the door jangled he was a little slow to look up and see someone who was not her walking in. When he left the cemetery, he had looked down the street in the direction she would have gone, and she was nowhere in sight. After the five minutes, six at most, he had spent accepting the guard's reproofs. This alarmed him; he couldn't imagine what it might mean, so after he had slept and shaved and put in what was left of his first day at the shoe store, and loitered until he was sure she'd be home and there'd be less risk of encountering her on the sidewalk, he walked across town, past her door. There was a book in the window, the cover toward the street. It was her sister's *Hamlet*.

An actual jolt of relief passed through him. It was as if he'd touched a power line. He had to wonder what he looked like in that half second when every nerve in his startled body was galvanized with joy, probably, though the particulars of the sensation were lost in the force of it. But the street was empty. Thank you, Jesus. He walked on, and then back past her door again, to make the experience milder by anticipation of it, by familiarity. This was indeed the effect, slight but marked enough that he had to persuade himself not to walk past a third time, which would inevitably involve a fourth. What a fool. Know thyself, Boughton. When he had gone a mile or so toward home, he began to doubt he had looked carefully enough to be sure there was not also a sprig of ivy. He knew the peril of relief, which was so welcome sometimes that he gave in to it impulsively and lost his grasp of the reality of the situation. He walked back toward her house half a mile, thought better of it, and went home to his rooming house. At worst, things were not terrible. He could sleep.

Della had said he was more like most people than he realized, so, when after a week or two business had improved enough that the word "business" began to seem appropriate to what went on behind that window, he felt he could actually attribute it to his being there, diluting the balefulness of the woman's endlessly fresh disappointment. Adding a degree of human warmth, possibly. Passersby no doubt saw them eating their sandwiches together from the little basket she always brought, even sharing a newspaper during the slowest hours. His mere presence might have broken a spell of some kind, disrupted the primal fear that loneliness is contagious, which puts the seal on isolation. So he had concluded. And there they were, chatting for the world to see. When customers came in, there was all that genuflecting to get through. The cost of doing this particular business. He could tell himself there was a kind of gallantry in it. Or he could think of it as an act of reverence, toward souls who would otherwise never enjoy even the outward sign of any such thing. His father would like that.

Della was speaking to him sometimes in his thoughts, or she was quiet, simply there at the edge of his vision. In her gentle way she was making everything easier. What would she find becoming in him? That was what he did. And by putting himself in the way of survival, not to put too fine a point on it, he was doing as she had asked him to do, so forthrightly. Can these bones live? Oh, Lord, you know. But for you, Miss Miles, I am eating this sandwich, for you I am smiling at this stranger, for you I am trying to sleep. He could not imagine an occasion when she might acknowledge any of this. No matter. Their lives were parallel lines that would not meet, he knew that, he would see to that. But they defined each other, somehow. Equidistance was like silence. It had to be carefully sustained to exist at all. He actually allowed himself thoughts like these, making an imaginary something out of literally nothing, finding a kind of reassurance in his successfully forbidding himself to walk down her street, past her door. Silence was one fragile thing he had almost never broken. Distance was another.

It had turned cold. It wasn't quite the dry, windy cold they had at home. When he first came to St. Louis, he thought the place looked like a corner of Eden where the bad news had not arrived quite yet. All that shiny vegetation, fat with life, untried by weather. At home the winter brought with it a high-minded rigor, every distraction swept away, cold light pouring through bare trees. He still felt as though an unwelcome demand came with autumn, then winter. A habit of dread persisted from his early education, from those years before he had mastered truancy. He had made an early start on a wasted life.

There were always the back porch steps and the kitchen door and the yellow painted table with mismatched chairs around it, and what always seemed at first the too-bright light and the too-warm air, smelling like steam from the rattling radiators and the mittens drying on them, and like cinnamon or yeast, or, if he came in late, like whatever supper had been, his plate of it warm in the oven. He could feel the relief in the house, but they had learned not to ask where he had been, what he had been up to. Even Teddy. They were grateful that he was in out of the cold. His mother would come into the kitchen to put his supper on the table and pour his milk.

"You never talk about your mother."

"Yes. I don't."

That tremor in her hands. He could have said, "I found a little creek where the ice wasn't solid yet, panes of ice, clear as glass." He could even say he liked the sound they made under his boots, how they shattered when he threw them down. She knew about his interest in fragile things, and would have liked to hear that for once no harm was done. But she was fragile, so he could not bring himself to comfort her. Half the time he would roll up whatever he could of his supper in a piece of bread and be out the door again. Better the cold. Better the dark. Why was that? He knew how she felt when he left. He felt it himself. Dear Jesus, keep me harmless. He knew what that meant. Keep me alone.

So, the library. He read *Hamlet* a number of times and developed certain opinions. It might really be about the love between Claudius and Gertrude, which struck him as very deep, and which might really make all the crimes and sins and so on unimportant, comparatively speaking. That would be extreme, but where else could you even think such a thing except in a book, or a dream? It was a profound friendship, the only one in the play. Hamlet is mistaken when he goes on about reechy kisses. He is the loneliest man in the world, so he can't see what it is that has pushed him aside, made nothing of him, let alone of custom, religion, morality, and the rest. A letter would be one way to tell Della that he had been thinking about things she thought about, and also that he was fit and well, as per her instructions. It would be a delicate business, making the case to a minister's daughter that morals might be eclipsed in some cases by other considerations, hypothetically. For the purposes of the play, which might be about the difference between love and loneliness, and how people on either side can't understand people on the other. He knew if he wrote it he might be tempted to mail it. Then he would have to wonder if the risk of offending her was part of the impulse. She would answer, or not. He would dread opening her letter if she sent one. Things were much better left as they were.

Days passed, weeks passed. He bought a new shirt and a new razor. The woman said, "Hey, Slick, time for a haircut." She had a point. And he bought shoe polish, at a discount, which meant she waved off the coins he offered her. He had trouble sleeping, because the chill in the air made him remember things. So he walked at night, though not the way he used to when he had nowhere to be in the morning. St. Louis was quite a town. He wondered if Della had ever seen Eads Bridge from down by the water. It looked like the walls of Troy. Gigantic, tawny stones, soaring arches. Of course, the stones themselves would be as ancient as the stones at Troy, and the fossils in both of them older, by the measure of the little lives that had fallen into whatever it was, clay by the color of it. And the eons they had spent evolving so they could end up there. The next time he imagined walking with Della by the bridge he would know many striking and impressive things.

Too much sleeplessness and he would be looking haggard. So no walking around for a while. To distract himself, he made plans and acted on them. The haircut, first of all. There was a roll of brown wrapping paper at the store. He took a piece of it and used it to wrap Della's book, so he could carry it in his pocket without further risk of foxing. His shoes were polished, and polished again. All this was easy enough. Then Mrs. Beverly said, "Store's closed tomorrow. Of course," and handed him an envelope with five dollars in it. After work he stopped in front of a florist shop to look at the roses in the window. Half price. The clerk said if he didn't sell them before the holiday he'd have to throw them away. So Jack walked home with an enormous red bouquet, roses in full bloom but still passable. He set them on his dresser, in a bucket, since that was all he could find that was big enough to hold them, and they looked so preposterous in that room, against the faded wallpaper roses, that he set them on the floor in a corner. Then for some reason he thought there would be no harm in getting himself a little bottle of something. He bought a larger bottle than he meant to. Rum. A couple of swallows would help him sleep.

He woke up feeling pretty damaged. He looked around for the bottle to see how much he had actually drunk and found it in a dresser drawer, exactly half empty, the lid tightly screwed on. He knew he became oddly prudent when he was too drunk to remember the reasoning behind his decisions. But he could guess. Half tonight and half tomorrow, and then everything would be resolved. Every possibility extinguished. He would not even glance in his thoughts at the worst of them. It was a relief that he would never know for certain what he'd have had to regret.

So when he woke up again and it was evening, he didn't put on his new shirt and he didn't shave. If he just showed up at her door looking like he always did, not as though he thought she might ask him in, but with the book to give her and some sort of apology to offer, then he'd have kept a promise. She might not have remembered everything she'd said, but of course she'd be glad to have her book. Some of the roses were dropping petals. Some were all right. It would be a sort of joke to offer them to her, a part of the apology. But, dear Jesus, he couldn't even decide to leave his room. A swallow of rum, just enough to dull him to what he was doing, and then he made the better roses into a bunch and put on his tie and jacket and hat and went out into the night, without the roses, but he came back for them. Yes, he had the book.

The first time he walked past, he saw lights on, so she was probably at home. He was almost disappointed. Just leaving the book and the roses on the step might be the perfect thing, in the circumstances. A nice gesture, and she wouldn't have him to deal with. Of course, he could do that in any case. The second time he passed her door, she, or someone, had turned on the porch light. This made him wish he had shaved. It made his scar itch. He walked far past her street, almost as if he had decided to give up on the whole thing. Then he went back again, thinking it might be late enough that if he did knock no one would answer. Then he could leave the book, possibly the roses. But then he dropped them into the bushes by her stoop. He would look ridiculous, standing there with a bouquet like a suitor, as if he thought he could ingratiate himself, showing up at her door in the middle of the night. Late as he knew it must be, disreputable as he knew he must look, displeased as he assumed she would be, he did finally knock on her door, because he just wanted to see her face.

She opened the door. That flinch. He saw tears in her eyes. She said, "So you remembered to come, after all. In the middle of the night. Liquor on your breath." She said, "It's after midnight. That makes you a day late."

This was bad enough. He hardly knew her, and he'd almost made her cry. But at least he knew now that she had been expecting him, a remarkable thing. He handed her the little package with her book in it and said, "I happened to be in the neighborhood," which was what he had planned to say if she seemed not to have remembered that invitation, or not to have meant it. He said, "My apologies. I mean that quite sincerely," and tipped his hat, which he would have removed except for that fear of trying to seem ingratiating. He did look at her face, no harm in that. He might as well take what pleasure he could before the regret really set in.

So he left her porch and set out on the long walk home or somewhere. It struck him how foolish he'd been to tell himself he was living for her sake, and how lost he was already without anything at all to tell himself. But he heard her footsteps. She had come after him, and she put her hand in the crook of his arm. "I kept a drumstick for you, Mr. Boughton, and some stuffing, and a piece of pie. Lorraine took the rest over to the church. But there's plenty here." She said, "I just don't want you to walk away looking so sad."

A parlor, very warm after the street. A drab couch on a bright rug, a little bookcase with books stacked on both sides of it, an upright piano with a lace scarf and a crowd of family pictures, one of them Jesus. He sat down on the couch with his hat beside him, and she went into the kitchen to make up a plate for him. He heard the front door open and close and felt the cold from it. That woman, Lorraine, said, "I suppose you know there's an old white man asleep on the sofa. I suppose you can explain that."

And Della said, "Oh, leave him be. He's just so weary."

He woke up thinking that a pillowcase is a pleasant thing. This one was perfect, a little crisp with laundering but very soft with use. He was lying crouched on a sofa with his head on a pillow and a blanket over him. What! He sat up, bewildered, in a lamplit room, a black woman in a housecoat and slippers watching him from an armchair in the corner. Lenore. No, Lorraine. His hat was in arm's reach. He said, "I should be going. Thanks for everything. Very much," and picked it up.

She said, "You're not leaving yet. You can't go sneaking out of the house before the sun comes up."

"I see," he said, for some reason. He wanted to ask where Della was, but decided against it. He thought he might make an attempt at conversation. "I understand you teach with Miss Miles."

"Algebra." She dropped the word like a trump card, and that was the end of conversation. After a few minutes, she did say, "The washroom is there across the hall from the kitchen. You better clean up. She's going to make you pancakes."

This last she said in that tone of incredulous rebuke people use to announce a wholly unmerited kindness. He said, "Thank you," on the grounds that the phrase seemed generally inoffensive, and went to find the bathroom. He pulled the cord, the light came on, and there he was, unshaven and scarred and haggard, in a little room that smelled like lavender. In the cabinet there were bottles and jars and curlers and pins, but no razor. He did find a wide-tooth comb. Tooth powder, which he put on the tip of his finger. It seemed very wrong to him that he should be looking at these things, touching them. But he did allow for a certain desperation in himself that had to be dealt with. He could hear Della in the kitchen. He washed his face again, gargled the water he could hold in his cupped hand, pulled the cord again, and stood there in the dark, feeling the overbearing innocence of strangers' domesticity. He absolutely should not be there. He could not help having noticed the painted cup on the windowsill with its bouquet of artificial violets. In the dark he was still aware of it, the kind of tentative claim on a rented space people make without even thinking about it. He could slip the flowers in his pocket and no one would notice for weeks, probably. The flowers would be there, in quiet effect, until someone noticed they were gone. He pinched off just one little bloom. Then he made himself step out into the hall. And there was Della, turning from the stove to smile at him. Sweet Jesus, more domesticity. She was wearing an apron—a sky-blue dress he thought he had seen before and a yellow apron with flowers on it. The little room was very bright, probably cheerful to a less nocturnal eye, to someone not wearing the clothes he had slept in.

He said, "I should be going. You've been very kind. I—" He was about to say something complicated about wanting to return her book and regretting any inconvenience. Then he said, "I can't be late to work," which sounded so much like a lie that the truth of it startled him.

She said, "It's five o'clock in the morning. I think you have time for a little breakfast."

The hiss of pancake batter on a hot skillet, coffee percolating. Here he was, within three feet of a woman so lovely in his thoughts that he was afraid of her.

She laughed. "So here I am, cooking breakfast for the Prince of Darkness. How does he like his eggs?"

"Over easy." Is that what people say? It sounded strange. I'm such a fool.

She said, "If you just sit down at the table—" Which meant, If you'll just step out of the doorway— She was standing in front of him with a plate in each hand. He took one of them and let her pass. There was a small table by a window, and two chairs. Lorraine was in one of them. Della nodded at the other one, that he should sit down, which left her standing. He said, "You—" and she laughed.

"We don't have company very often. There's another chair in the kitchen. Eat your breakfast."

"Company," Lorraine said. "You know, people around here have a name for him. They call him That White Man. It's short for That White Man That Keeps Walking Up and Down the Street All the Time."

Flinch. Della put her hand on his shoulder so he wouldn't stand up. "Do you really want him to leave now, Lorraine? Is that the idea now? It wasn't five minutes ago."

"I never wanted him here in the first place. Nobody asked me."

"No reason to be unkind. This wasn't his idea, either, remember."

"He might as well leave and be done with it. The whole neighborhood is going to know he spent the night no matter what."

He wanted to find his handkerchief to wipe his face. When he blushed, he sweated. Of course people noticed him, walking past her house however many times it was. He actually hadn't thought of that. Fool. But it would look a little abject to be mopping his brow with that monogrammed rag he had in his pocket. It wasn't even his monogram.

"Then let him eat his pancakes. If it doesn't matter when he leaves, anyway, he can leave in an hour."

Lorraine said, "This is just ridiculous. I sat up the whole night so I could keep an eye on him. Now I just want him gone. I'm going to go get some sleep, and he better be gone when I wake up. If anything goes wrong, it's your problem!" She said this last as her chair scraped back, and she left the room.

Della said, "She's a really nice woman, most of the time." She sat down across from him, her head in her hands.

He said, "This is all very embarrassing. You should have waked me up."

"And sent you out into the dark and the cold. I know. Not that it would have solved anything."

He couldn't stay and he couldn't leave. So there he was. The story of his life.

"If the world had ended that night," she said, "I could let you fall asleep on my sofa and give you breakfast in the morning, and no one would say a word about it. They might say it was nice. How could I wake you up so you'd be walking home in the cold? In the middle of the night." An earnest question.

"I've done that. Any number of times. I'm not exactly fragile."

She shook her head. "Nobody wants to wake up like that. You didn't even have your dinner."

"My fault."

She nodded. "True enough. I'll forgive you for it if you eat your breakfast."

"Seriously, though. It might be better if I left now. In an hour more people will be awake. It might be getting light by then."

"Yes, I think it would be better to wait two hours, so you won't seem to be sneaking away."

He laughed. "I believe I always seem to be sneaking away. My boss calls me Slick. She hadn't known me five minutes before she started calling me that."

She looked at him. "I can see what she means. It's kind of a compliment."

"No, it isn't. But she's all right. We talk a little baseball."

"Good," she said. She had taken her hands away from her face. "You're all right, then."

Solicitude. So he said, "Sure I am. I guess you better find

93

yourself another stray." That sounded rude. It was the flinch speaking.

"Oh."

He said, "All I mean is that I'm trouble. I might do you real harm, never meaning to."

She said, "I know that."

"I can't leave and I can't stay."

"Then you might as well stay."

"For those two hours you gave me. Maybe an hour and a half by now."

She said, "I make food for you and you don't touch it."

"I just thought I should talk to you first. I'm sorry about last night."

"I know that."

"It was hard for me to give up that book. I should have brought it back weeks ago. Months."

"I'll lend you another book."

He laughed. "I'd appreciate that. And I want you to know I didn't figure out some nefarious scheme to come across you in the cemetery. That was so—unexpected. I'm sure you must wonder about it."

"No, I've never wondered."

"All right, then. I was grievously at fault—no, let me make my confession. If you had just spoken to the guard, he'd have let you out. He'd have unlocked a gate for you. You probably didn't have to go through the whole night there."

"Do you think I didn't know that?"

Well.

She said, "I bring problems on myself. Some of them are worth it." She looked at him calmly, candidly.

He said, "You loosened my tie."

She nodded. "I unbuttoned your collar."

He felt himself blush. After a minute, he said, "You know, the world didn't end that night. Nice idea, but nothing came of it."

"I noticed."

"I'm just saying what your father would say. Don't take in strays."

"My father would never say that."

"Mine either."

"They always talk as though the world has ended. Turn the other cheek. Welcome the stranger. All right. Then they say, Well, you do have to exercise a little common sense."

"Yes, you do."

She looked at him. "You don't."

He laughed. "I'm a special case. For me, turning the other cheek is only prudent. Everyone on earth is a stranger, and I'm another one, so that rule doesn't really apply. No one to do the welcoming."

He had turned in his chair to stretch out his legs and cross them at the ankles. He put his hands in his pockets. Slick. He did want those pancakes, and courtesy obliged him to eat them, but there was something just a little mendicant about it. He couldn't quite pass from the thought to the deed.

She stood up and took his plate. "Nobody likes cold eggs."

"I actually—"

"I suppose you like them better cold? Jack Boughton, it's a shame how you lie." The plate in one hand, she went to the sofa table and picked up his hat. "Now I have a hostage," she said, and took it with her into the kitchen.

It was true, he wouldn't leave without it. If it had been sitting there much longer, reminding him by its battered raffishness of who he actually was, or who he usually was, anyway, he'd have been out the door. There was no gentlemanly way to take it away from her. Well, he could hear pancake batter hitting the skillet, so leaving was out of the question, hat or no hat.

He thought he might go out to the sidewalk to see if he could find a couple of roses in the bushes. It would seem a little miraculous to her to find roses on the table, slightly elegant, even if they were wilting. They would be something to give her, and then he could accept breakfast without being abject about it. She would see the roses and be pleased and probably laugh. But then he thought how bizarre it would seem to anyone who saw That White Man groping around in the shrubbery before dawn, only stranger if he did happen to find a rose or two. And then he realized that anyone passing her doorstep in the morning would see those roses and wonder what to make of them, and they would add interest to whatever stories might be circulating about lovely Della, who only meant to be kind. He felt his doom, that old companion who knew the worst about him long before he knew it himself, settle into him, however that happened. But it did. So when Della came into the room again, he could hardly look at her. This time she had a plate for herself, too, which made things better.

"Excellent," he said.

A moment passed, and then she laughed. "I guess somebody'd better say grace."

"All right." He folded his hands and bowed his head. He heard himself saying, "'Down to the grave will I take thee, / Out from the noise of the strife; / Then shalt thou see me and know me— / Death, then, no longer, but life.'" He looked at her. "I don't know why that came to mind. I hope I wasn't— I sometimes think the Lord might enjoy a few lines of poetry. I apologize—"

She said, "I know why it came to mind. You were thinking of that night the world didn't end."

"I guess I was. Sunrise was a disappointment, but not really a surprise. Otherwise, it was about perfect, I thought." Should he say he didn't write those lines? Well, of course she would know Paul Dunbar wrote them. He said, "Paul Dunbar," so she would know he wasn't trying to take credit for them.

She nodded. "'I am the mother of sorrows, / I am the ender of grief.' I like that poem."

Then they sat there eating together, sharing the syrup, stirring their coffee. He was the one who remembered that there was coffee, and he went into the kitchen and found the cups and saucers and filled them, and realized there would be less chance of a spill if he had filled them at the table, but he was very careful.

How had he found the nerve? She smiled at him and said thank you, as if it were just a pleasant, ordinary thing. She opened a little porcelain box with sugar cubes in it and dropped two in his cup and two in hers. After a while, Lorraine, in her robe and slippers, came down the hall and stood there a minute, looking at them. "Awfully quiet," she said.

Della laughed. "Have we been keeping you awake?"

"Yes, you have. It's almost seven. The sun will be up." She said, "The two of you just sitting there!" She could find no words. It was a little strange, that they had hardly spoken at all for a long time, he had no idea how long.

"I really should go now."

"Yes, I'll get your hat. It's a quarter past six, by the way."

He had seen his hat on top of the icebox, looking as alien as a thing could look. She brushed at the brim a little before she handed it to him.

He said, "I'm afraid it's beyond help." Then, "I have a confession to make."

"You wrote in my book."

"Actually, no," which wasn't entirely true. "Something else. This is a little embarrassing. I meant to bring you flowers last night, but at the last minute I lost my courage. I got them cheap, they were wilting. So I threw them into the bushes there by the steps."

"What kind of flowers?"

"Roses."

"What color?"

"Red. But my point is that they might look fairly scandalous— proof that you had a gentleman caller in the middle of the night. There are probably petals all over the place. I'd pick them up— but I guess that wouldn't be wise in the circumstances."

She said, "You have strewn my steps with rose petals. That's poetic."

"Thank you," he said. "And for the pancakes. And the good night's sleep."

She said, "Just trying to keep you alive."

"You don't have to do that. Try, I mean. You keep me alive already. Just the thought of you. I didn't mean that." It was much more than he meant to say. So he stepped out the door and put on his hat and then lifted it to her, that odd little gallantry, skipped down the steps, and walked away. He did turn once, and he saw her stooping gracefully in the faint morning twilight, gathering roses.

After two weeks a letter came for him, for Mr. Jack Boughton. The desk clerk read the name out slowly and squinted at him, then read the name again, as if studying the discrepancy between the written name and Jack's person. When Jack reached for it, he held it away from him. He said, "We used to have a Boughton here, but he's two weeks behind on his rent. As of yesterday. So I guess that means he doesn't live here anymore."

Jack had paid his rent. He had stayed sober, kept his job, bought a new razor and a decent aftershave. This may have been what threw him off. Normally he had to grant that he had made himself vulnerable to what might be called ridicule. He had no idea how many times he had been talked into paying his rent more than once. Then, before he knew it, he was all out of money, and after a few days the clerk was letting him off again, after threatening to throw his little hoard of shirts and socks and pilferings, his effects, as they say, out into the street. It was a kind of joke, he believed, when he was too fuddled to take a harsher view. There were always dishes to wash. So his life was not much affected, all in all. He drew a kind of resignation around himself, as if it were dignity.

Now he had, so to speak, waked up sober. The preposterous fellow with dirty yellow hair just the color of the tobacco stains on his fingers and greasy yellow-tinted spectacles was treating him like a fool. Jack grabbed his arm and took the letter out of his hand, which, he thought with some satisfaction, was probably normal in the circumstances.

On the flap of the envelope were written *D. Miles* and her address. So he put it in his pocket. He tipped his hat to the clerk, just to keep him off balance, and strode into the street and down the street until he was out of sight of him. I strode, he thought, still pleased with himself. But why would Della have written to him? The fact was that he had written his address on the back cover of her book, in tiny letters along the spine. She might never have seen it was there in faint pencil. He had sharpened one of Mrs. Beverly's pencils, then rubbed the point of it against a newspaper until it was so fine it cut into the paper if he was not very careful. He had gone out on the pavement to look up at the number of the house he had lived in, slept in, for at least two years. It was a long time since he had thought of himself as having an address. He had written, in the tiniest hand he could manage, *11N15th*. And she had found it and known what it must be, and sent him a letter. He had hardly dared hope.

He would have to sit down somewhere to read it. Somewhere private. It did not say, "Stop walking past my house," because he had stopped, with some effort. Of course, two weeks was not long enough to demonstrate his resolve, which was considerable, though she couldn't know that. She was not asking him to return anything he had pocketed. That one tiny flower.

The door to Mrs. Beverly's shop opened. The bell rang. He had gone to work, never having decided to. This must be what most people do, the explanation of the city, day after day itself. Mrs. B. said, "Morning, Slick. I'm going to need help with some shelving." She was a short woman afflicted with a fear of heights, rueful at the thought of climbing a stepladder.

"Glad to oblige." So the letter would wait in his pocket until noon. He put the stepladder against the wall of shelves in the back room, climbed up, and pulled down a dusty box. Brogans, he decided. One was brown and one was oxblood. He put the box aside, on the assumption that there must be another box like it, mutatis mutandis. Six boxes were saddle oxfords, but the seventh held a brogan and an oxford, a size twelve and a size eleven, not that this mattered, except that it made him check through the shoes that apparently matched. Among the oxfords he found a box containing a nine and a twelve. None of the other boxes contained a twelve and a nine. He put that box aside also. The next box contained one shoe, a nine, a wing tip. He set it aside. Ten boxes were matching pairs. In the eleventh he found two Christmas ornaments in bunched newspaper. Plain red balls with nothing particular about them to explain their being shelved here. The box said tasseled loafers, white, eleven. He noticed that the ornaments were a matched pair as to size and color. When he noticed that he had noticed this, it brought tears to his eyes. The wall of identical boxes began to look to him like something weirdly insoluble, like an algebra test in a dream. When Mrs. B. brought him his sandwich, he was actually sitting on the floor among these unaccountable boxes, dozens of them.

She nodded and said, "Bad inventory can do a lot of damage. I wouldn't take it too much to heart."

"Yes," he said. "My thought was that if we could make them into pairs, they'd be easier to sell. Possible, at least."

"I appreciate that. Might as well burn them, otherwise."

He imagined a reeking, smoldering heap. Surely she wouldn't. Why did he seem to know exactly what a burning shoe would smell like? He realized he was suffering a little slippage, losing ground to self-doubt. Sweet Jesus, he thought, just a plain sandwich, the usual ingredients. And so it was, peanut butter and jelly. He realized he had suppressed an impulse to tell Mrs. B. that this confusion was not his fault.

She said, "I don't know, Slick. You could be doing me a world of good." Then she began tidying up, putting lids on boxes. Indiscriminately.

It was the letter. He was on a knife edge—rebuffed, maybe. Or assured a little that no harm had been done. What to make of it, her, himself? Possibilities were pleasant on one side, drastic on the other. It was not in the nature of a letter to settle anywhere in between. He had to wash his hands before he could touch it. Whatever it said, he would keep it. He would read it once, and then it would be among his effects. Teddy would say, "There was a girl," and they would make it so much more than it was. So much less.

He wiped his fingers on the cleanest part of a towel they kept for buffing shoes and opened the letter. It said, "Dear Mr. Boughton, My aunt Delia is here visiting for the week. I would like you to meet her. Could you come for coffee at any time on Saturday or Sunday afternoon? Or any weekday evening? If you could come by for a few minutes, I would be very grateful." Then, "Yours truly."

This was worse than the worst he could have imagined. An aunt. Aunts never just drop by. Aunts weigh in. He had to go, even though he knew what the lady would say. It is better form, no doubt, to say face-to-face, "How do you do. Lovely weather. Don't come near my niece again." Very much meaning, where aunts come, uncles follow. Diplomacy is war by other means. He would show up, sober, looking as decent as he could without expense or trouble, take his scolding, and take his leave. "It has been a pleasure." Della's good name depended in some part on his presenting himself as a gentleman. He could not very well tell this aunt about the iron resolve that had kept him off her street for fifteen days, or that for weeks, before the one, inauspicious night, he had kept his distance as scrupulously as any aunt could wish. That hint at an address he had incised in her book was only meant as an assurance to himself that a cobweb of connection still existed between them. He'd have penciled in a nice little couplet, if he could have thought of one, something sad and formal, an adieu. So very sad and formal she would see the humor of it and laugh. That failing, he put his address, a sort of "I exist!" Thinking that, if she ever noticed it, it might also make her laugh. Well, he did imagine she might sometime stroll past, out of curiosity, and he might just then be stepping out his door, and there would be pleasantries, and they might walk a few blocks together. This sort of fantasy was lively enough that he knew he would never again fall behind on his rent. He would not have inscribed that tiny message if he had imagined at the end of it all having an aunt to deal with. He was so used to the sensation of being caught at some trifling, stupid thing, which always became a reflection on the whole of his character and his prospects—irrefutably, since the very triviality of it all would probably, sweet Jesus, make him laugh. But this was worse. This was not just anyone, self-deputized by an inch or two of standing in the world. This was a personage who would take some few minutes, at least, of his acute embarrassment back to Memphis, as an anecdote to be pondered, chuckled at, dismissed, that Della herself might smile at and shrug off when they teased her about it.

If he did not obey this summons, that would seem to signal disrespect, as if his acquaintance with Della meant nothing to him, whatever it might mean to her. Or it would suggest shame or guilt, and that would cast doubt on Della's insistence that their poor, strange shred of a relationship was entirely honorable. When, Christ knows, it was utterly, lyrically, gallantly honorable, whatever the neighbors were saying. A shabby fellow with a furtive air can be as gallant as the next man, depending on circumstances. The thought passed through his mind, actually unsettled his hair, that if he made a bad impression, one that cast doubt on her good judgment, her great, ministerial, aunt-delegating family might whisk her away to Memphis, away from Sumner and the dreams she thought had been fulfilled. He knew that if he dwelt on the possibility, he would be doomed, and she would, too.

The invitation was written to make excuses impossible. Come any time at all. It gave fair warning. My family have sent an emissary to look you over. He had never imagined that his name would be spoken to or among her family. He was hardly a beau, a suitor. And he had long felt at home, so to speak, among the anonymous, whose behavior might arouse some small interest in the criminal justice system, but no more than a "Get lost" from family and friends, assuming they took that much notice. He could probably take it as a compliment, an elevation of status, that an aunt would have come from Memphis, presumably to dismiss him with a ceremonious cup of coffee. He must be careful not to say, "I do stay away from her. I stay away from her every day. Hour by hour." He had learned that determination is suspect, more so as more effort is involved in it.

He would carry a folded newspaper to suggest he was a man with interests, with a foot in the larger world. A man with no lesser worries than the emergence of a stable peace in Europe. He would have bought it, the last journalistic word, not some fractious waif of time left on a park bench with the puzzle half finished. Aside from that, a shave, a haircut, that familiar walk, Aunt Delia.

It is odd, what families do to their children—Faith, Hope, Grace, Glory, the names of his good, plain sisters like an ascending scale of spiritual attainment, a veritable anthem, culminating in, as they said sometimes, the least of these, Glory, who fretted at her own childishness, the hand-me-down, tag-along existence of the eighth of eight children. He himself, who aspired to harmlessness, was named for a man who was named for a man remembered, if he was, for antique passions and heroics involving gunfire. He was afraid that Delia or Della might mention a cousin named Dahlia, and he would laugh. Sweet Jesus, do not let me laugh inappropriately.

He wrote back on Tuesday, saying that he would come to her house at two o'clock on Saturday, allowing himself some time to consider the situation, though he knew this was not wise. There was the mustering of a somewhat presentable self, which might take two days. That brought him to Thursday. He would spend Friday at work and then the library and then in his room trying to sleep. He would spend Saturday morning looking for someone selling something edible on the street, though he knew he would not be hungry. At one o'clock he would shave again, brush his hat, straighten his tie. And there his imagination failed.

He wrote several more letters and did not send them. He had done nothing to bring about that meeting in the cemetery. His being there at all was fairly unusual. It had honestly never occurred to him that Della might be there, too. And it was certainly not his intention to fall asleep on that couch. He was not drunk that night, though he had been recently, which was probably a factor. He crossed that out.

He had never been good at explaining things he did. It was just alarming to him to consider how much sense they always made at the time, or in any case, how unavoidable they seemed. He suspected he drank to give himself a way of accounting for the vast difference between any present situation and the intentions that brought him to it. By Friday he had covered every page in the little notebook he had bought so he could write that first letter. And then it was Saturday.

The aunt was bespectacled, shorter than Della and not as dark. She was one of those people whose flesh cleaves to her bones so neatly that he could not guess her age within ten years. She offered her hand, "Mr. Boughton. It's very good of you to come," and gestured toward the sofa. "Sit down, please." She sat down in the armchair. She looked at him without seeming at all to be looking him over, though of course she was doing just that. At any moment old Slick might emerge, Slick, the terror of every good aunt. She said, "Della has told me about you. She speaks very well of you."

"She's very kind."

"Yes, she is," Delia said. "Very kind."

There was a silence. He thought she might be waiting for him to say that Della had spoken about her, too, which was the kind of polite lie he was prone to, a garden gate opening on a minefield, more often than not.

"Well," she said, "I'm sure Della mentioned a cup of coffee—"

"Please don't go to any trouble." He stood up when she did.

She said, "It's no trouble! I'll only be a minute!" Kindly and officious, that little fluster of making welcome. So he took the minute to step over and look at the pictures on the piano. Slender young men and sturdy old men in dark suits and clerical collars, women and children in church clothes. And that picture of Jesus, the same one his father kept in his study. They were a sound, substantial family, clearly. If anyone could be safe anywhere, it would be in the embrace of a family like this one, he thought. Like his own family. And here he was, the shabby outsider, self-orphaned, wondering why all this seemed oppressive to him, why attention in the person of this unexceptional aunt should make him feel something so like guilt, when the idea was to seem capable of respectability, to shore up whatever Della might have said about him for Della's sake, though it bothered him to think she had told them anything at all.

Delia came back into the room. "Do sit down." She might

have said, "Sit down, dear," without the slightest change in the tone of her voice. "I wanted a few minutes to talk with you."

"Yes, ma'am, I understand."

"You know that Della is a wonderful young woman."

"Yes, I do."

"Even as a little child she was just as bright as a button. Always in a corner somewhere reading a book. She was already reading before she started school! Always talking about being a teacher. Then she read about Sumner High School, and she started dreaming about coming here to St. Louis."

"Yes, she told me that."

"Yes, well, of course she did. It has meant so much to her. Her daddy wanted to keep her closer to home. We all did. But her heart was set on coming here." There was a silence, and then she said, "I think that coffee must be done by now."

This kindly woman was struggling to get from the part of the conversation where they agreed that Della was a precious soul to the part where she told Jack to leave her alone. How to proceed gently enough to be rid of him without avoidable injury to him. He might just tell her he knew what she wanted to say, he appreciated the truth of it, had concluded on his own that his friendship with Della should be ended for her sake, and that he had come that afternoon to let her family know he understood and respected—for that matter, shared—their concern.

But she brought him his coffee, two cookies on the saucer, a tremor in her hand, a narrow bracelet loose on her wrist, and he realized he had decided not to put an end to this interesting struggle of hers. She sat down in the armchair again, and after a few minutes she said, "Della's father asked me to look in on her. We do worry. I wouldn't say she's headstrong. She isn't willful.

She's just impatient with—certain limits. She acts sometimes like they don't even exist. Smart as she is, I think she may not quite realize what the consequences can be for a woman in her situation, how much she can lose if there's even talk. I mention these things to her, and she just, you know, hangs her head and waits till I'm done."

Lovely Della, hanging her head, weighing things, keeping her thoughts to herself.

Delia said, "Of course I'm here to ask you to stop seeing her. I'm sure you know that. She knows it, too. She told me if I insulted you she'd never speak to me again! So I'm trying very hard not to do that. You can probably tell. And I did want to meet you. I know she's spoken to you about many things, maybe things she's never said to anyone else. She told me that once you two talked together the whole night. She told me how kind you were to her. How respectful." This was true. Still, he blushed. He could feel his brow dampen.

"I want to assure you—"

"No need. She's assured me already."

After a minute, he said, "Let me assure you of this. I know I should stay away from her. I'm an unsavory character. No, that makes me sound interesting. I'm a bum, without aspirations or illusions. My father is a preacher, and I know she sees that in me, the manners and so on, and it makes her more—at ease with me than she might be with another bum. But I've been honest with her." He checked his memory and decided this was true enough. If he hadn't mentioned the stint in prison, he had never found the right moment. Or looked for it, particularly. This also was not the right moment.

She said, "You don't owe me any account of yourself. I believe you when you say you'll stay away from her. That's what I needed to know. So I can speak to her father for her."

He said, "May I ask who brought me to her father's attention? Lenore?"

She nodded. "Lorraine. She's very protective of Della."

He laughed. "I bring that out in people."

She said, "Well, dear, maybe you do. And maybe you're a little too hard on yourself. I'm glad we've had a chance to talk. I feel much better now." She glanced at the clock. It was five minutes before three. She stood up and took his coffee cup and handed him his hat and newspaper and began the little fluster of polite farewell. "Thank you so much for stopping by." She was trying to be not too abrupt about getting him out of the house when the front door opened and Della walked in. In a burst of afternoon light, as it happened. "Mr. Boughton," she said softly, and made a brief study of his face. Her aunt looked at her with unconcealed exasperation. And there he stood, hat in hand, wondering what could possibly be expected of him. He said, "Miss Miles." And then there was a silence. Della took a step toward him, so that she was standing almost beside him, and he could actually feel her loyalty to him like a sort of heatless warmth emanating from her. He had to leave, but he couldn't move. Delia was looking at them with her head cocked and her hands on her hips. She said, "Mr. Boughton was just leaving." So he took a step, then another one, and turned to thank the aunt again, who was by then ushering him toward the door. When they were out on the steps, she said, "You'd be the great-grandson, I guess. This might not be as painless as I hoped, but it will be all right. We don't forget our friends, even very old friends." He'd meant to clarify that, if it ever seemed to matter.

He'd decided he should reconsider his life again. He was sitting on a bench by the river watching ducks and gulls and pigeons and the occasional squirrel. They were watching him, eyeing him, as if he owed them something. He had never departed by more than a cigarette butt from his refusal to be coerced, but there they were, like expectation gone sour, every time he came to the bench he thought of as his, the one just beyond the shadow of the great bridge, season and hour obliging. Now that he had Mrs. Beverly to consider, he came only on Sundays. He stayed from the time the clangor of bells, that dread summons, stopped shuddering in the air, to the arrival of the droves of kempt and restless children, running through and beyond the procession of strolling parents, then rejoining it, the adults with that fleeting atmosphere of church about them, of having been schooled again as to some aspect of the meaning of life. He was wearing his tie, and his shoes were polished. Some impulse to blend in. His father would say, You are not good for your own sake. That probably isn't even possible. You are good as a courtesy to everyone around you. Keeping a promise or breaking it, telling the truth or lying, matters to those around you. So there is good you can do and can always do again. You do not have to believe you are good in order to act well in any specific case. You never lose that option.

He said this from the pulpit, but he was saying it to Jack, who, to distract him from the parsing of some recent mischief, had almost confided to him that he had certain doubts about his soul. This near-confession was probably meant to stir his father to the kind of gentle exasperation that meant he'd be brooding about him for a week and preaching to him on Sunday, another boyish prank, really, even though what he had told his father was true enough. The whole congregation would have understood when he said good manners were an excellent beginning, a kind of discipline that could lead to actual virtue, given time. Jack could be terribly polite. Everyone in that sanctuary who was old enough to be capable of the slightest cynicism would be thinking, Butter would not melt in that boy's mouth! He was great at setting teeth on edge. They also understood that a minister had to find hope where he could, like anybody else. Jack would sometimes stand beside his father, grinning, shaking hands as the flock filed out, much more than charming, and his father's irritation and embarrassment would register as a tremor in the arm he put around him. It was in some part as a courtesy to his father that Jack began to slip out of the house before dawn on Sundays. If he were honest, the attractions of being anywhere else, in the chill and the dark, were also a consideration.

Be that as it may. He could think of the hours he had spent with Della without particular regret, not counting that time he had ducked out on her at the restaurant. He felt that he owed this to his father's sermons on the value of good manners, even without reference to whatever meaning they might have or lack in any particular circumstance. This was a truth arrived at by argument too precarious to be rescued by a truly emphatic conclusion involving a fist flourished in the air, yet too essentially wistful to be discredited by a guffaw or two in the choir. From all his father's careful instruction this was the one teaching Jack took away. So, on that precious day, when he saw a lady drop an armful of papers on the pavement in a rainstorm, he had crossed the street to help her gather them up. The wind had sent a few of them scudding off, and he had handed her his umbrella and ran a few steps to catch them. There was laughter involved. She had said, "Thank you, Reverend," out of respect for that dark suit he was honest enough to sell once it had dried out so he could stop deceiving people in that particular way. He knew he would not make it home for the funeral, and besides, he scrupled. His reluctance to toy with what were sometimes people's better impulses had brought that word to mind. There was little enough to be gained from it in any case. There was an unseemliness in asking a fellow for a dime or a smoke while wearing a suit like that one. Being unshaven was no help. Once or twice he heard out a tirade on the corruptions of the clergy by someone who took his actual, ordinary life for his secret life—a preacher on the bad side of town, abject with drink and general dissolution. That suit made a hypocrite of him. Still, when the lady to whom he had been so courteous said, Thank you, Reverend, it was as if she thought she knew him, as if her opinion of him were favorable beyond the fact of his having lent her an umbrella—which he would have to have back, since the gentle candor of her expression made him certain he had to be rid of that suit, which was depreciating by the minute. So he took the umbrella from her hand and walked her to her door, enjoying the gallantry of the gesture, nicely balanced between apparent and real. He had gotten his umbrella back without quite taking it from her. And when they reached her door, she had asked him in. "The rain might be letting up a little," she said, "if you have time for a cup of tea—" This was a little bold of her. He thought one of his sisters, Glory maybe, would invite a stranger in off the street on the recommendation of a clerical look and a minor kindness, never thinking to ask whether he had, for example, been released from prison lately. In a couple dozen months he had acquired habits he knew he might never outlive. Even then, taking a chair at a small table by a window, surrounded by the modest good order and general teacherliness of her apartment, he kept searching his memory for a word that rhymed with "scruple." Quadruple. He was calming himself, which meant he was nervous. Jesus was there among the pictures on the upright piano, the only one in color. "Quintuple" doesn't rhyme. How can that be? Sweet Jesus, don't let me say anything strange.

She brought tea in an old-fashioned china pot with a chip in its spout. She gave him a cup and saucer that somehow commemorated Memphis. Sunday things, because he was a minister. He couldn't see what her cup commemorated, but it was small and ornate like his. Like the cups that lined a narrow shelf in the kitchen at home at once pointedly and futilely out of his reach. Those little handles break off so easily, and they can't really be glued on again. His sisters tried and tried. Hope, the musical sister, had hands like hers, slender and somehow lively. He said, "Do you play?"

"Not really. Not very well. Do you?"

"'Onward, Christian Soldiers.'" She laughed. Actually, the only part of prison he missed, besides a predictable lunch, was playing piano for chapel services, which were sometimes funerals. He had worked up barrelhouse versions of some very solemn hymns.

She said, "The piano belongs to the woman I share this place with. Her mother left it to her. She doesn't really play much either."

He had said, for some reason, "I often regret—" and thought it best not to continue.

She nodded. "They had a terrible time getting me to practice. I told them I wanted to be a poet!"

That was interesting. "Did you ever stop wanting to be a poet?"

She shrugged. "I haven't stopped yet. I suppose someday I will. I don't have much to show for it. My grandmother met Paul Dunbar once. I guess that gave me the idea. I have a book he signed for her. It was her treasure. Now it's my treasure."

He had said, "That's very nice," and he had thought, Don't show it to me. Don't put it down anywhere near me. That old fellow dozing on the bench with his umbrella hooked over the back of it, and his cane, too, would have been waked up when the rain began and hobbled off somewhere, cursing himself for his own trusting nature, most likely. Then came that difficult algebra—did the exasperation Jack had caused cancel out the kindness he had done under the inspiration of a handsome umbrella? A kindness done to this particular lady because he was ready to enjoy the courtesy so newly and fortuitously possible for him? She did have a sweet face, a warm laugh. And he hoped he'd have helped her gather her papers, in any case. But the umbrella made a performance of it. As he hurried back to her, she lifted it a little to include him under it. Then he held it over her and walked her to her door. She had called him Reverend and offered him tea, and he had stepped over a threshold into a world where there would of course be a hymnal open on the piano, the odds and ends of a grandmother's china, no doubt a hundred trifling things not at all worth stealing that he could slip into his pocket, given the chance. She said, "I'll show you that book." He had almost said, Please don't. But in a moment there it was, open in her two hands to the page with the signature. Then she put it down on the table in front of the sofa and came back to her chair. "I'm always afraid I'll spill something on it."

He had said, "It pays to be careful." Then he said, "I've been reading some poetry lately." This was actually true. He went to the library most days. There was usually no one in the poetry section, so he could sit there till the place closed, trying to imagine what to do with himself now that all the world lay before him, so to speak. A kindly old librarian noticed him, always with a book open in front of him, of course. She brought him cookies on a napkin with a fraying embroidered flower on it and said, "You'll be sure to wipe your fingers," which he did, and he put the napkin on the front desk as he left. Then one time she set a copy of *Paterson* on the table in front of him, smiled to recommend it, and vanished, a little arthritically, into the stacks. He seemed to bring out the angelic in old ladies. And it was a very great book! It made it seem a profound thing to sit on a bench watching the river, the ships, the gulls, which was another way he had of killing time. He loved that book, and out of respect for that lady did not steal it, only put it behind shelved books where no one else would find it. He had said, "Have you read *Paterson?* W. C. Williams?" An actual question, since he wanted her to have read it. "No. I've heard of it. My tastes are pretty traditional."

"You have to read it. You'll see what I mean." He had said, "When I'm down by the river—that bridge seems like some huge ancient thing that has just leapt out of the earth, all mass and clay and fossils, on its way somewhere—everything seems like a metaphor, you don't need to know for what. After you read that book."

She was laughing at him, her eyes shining. "I'll get me a copy tomorrow, promise. And you have to read W. H. Auden."

"He's on my list!" It was a kind of pact! They laughed, and then they were quiet, and then he had said, "I should be going, now that the rain has eased up." It hadn't. "There's never time enough, in my line of work. Thanks for the tea and the shelter, Miss—"

"Della Miles."

She offered her hand and he took it.

"And I am John Ames Boughton," a version of himself which

only felt like a lie, called up by the tea and the china, and a certain exuberance at the fact that the afternoon had gone well enough. He had thought of forgetting the umbrella as a pretext for stopping by again, but she handed it to him. He would have to think of another ruse before he got rid of that suit.

He knew better. He would not be leaving books on her step with notes in them, brief but very clever, that would make her think of him for a minute or two every now and then. On one hand, if he did, it would give him a pleasant thing to be thinking about, working out the little messages in his mind, for weeks perhaps, and finding the right books to steal. On the other hand, people do that sort of thing when they imagine something might come of it. She couldn't be seen walking down the street with him without damage to her reputation, a risk a teacher can't take. The same would not be true for him, since he hardly had a reputation, properly so called. His old compulsion to do damage as chance offered had seen to that. If anything remained to him that might be called a good name, walking down a street with her would put an end to it. He felt the warm chill of impulse, actually frightened himself a little with the thought that he could do harm so easily, so innocently, really, except in the fact that he knew how grave and final the harm would be to her. A shudder of guilt passed through him, stirring other guilt, of course. There he was on a park bench in the morning sun, among the squawk and gabble and the church bells, to his inner eye naked as Adam to his own scrutiny. Stay away from her, fool. That's simple enough.

So the next day he went to the store, or whatever it was, where he had bought the dark suit, a room with harsh window light and festoons of flypaper and tables heaped with discards, and traded it, with his hat and umbrella, for another hat and a double-breasted brown tweed suit with the impersonal smell of cigarette smoke already infused in it and a small stain on the left lapel. He changed in a back room and emerged more or less himself. It was a relief to put all his pretensions down on the counter. The trade was not to his advantage, except in the sense that he had hoped to find something cheap and a little raffish. Fair warning, he thought. And he was somehow relieved that he was no longer wearing a black suit with brown shoes. The man at the counter said, "I always have things that would fit you here. The widows bring them in." Very funny.

He would not let his mood be dampened. He bought a newspaper and a pack of cigarettes at a dark little shop crowded with pipe racks and souvenir humidors and ashtrays and cans of tobacco and cigars that smelled something like tar and licorice. Somewhere in it all was a radio blaring a baseball game. The little man at the cash register watched him intently, as if theft were a card trick and he was going to catch him at it this time. The effect of the suit, he thought, since he was pretty sure he'd never been in that particular shop before. He startled the fellow with a dollar bill, slipped the change in his pocket, and went out to the street. The baseball game was close—it was the eighth inning—so he leaned against the wall in the sun to listen and folded the paper to the crossword puzzle. He pushed his hat back on his head, hung a smoke from his lip, and worked the puzzle, thinking that if anyone noticed him, he would seem to be playing the horses. Clothes do make the man.

He glanced up because he was thinking—six letters, the second one *d*—and there was Della. Flinch. That look in her eyes— surprise, realization, maybe rebuke. She was with another young woman. It seemed to him she paused for some part of a second,

long enough that the other woman glanced at him, a little mysti-
fied at the almost nothing that had passed between them. And
then they went on, arm in arm, heads together, laughing. Not at
him or about him, dear Jesus.

This was misery enough to justify a drink. A binge, in fact.
But for some reason he just spent most of the night lying on his
bed, feeling an elemental loneliness pour into his bones, that
coldness that inheres in things, left to themselves. When the
heart rests from its labors, for example, that excruciating push of
blood. What had happened was just what he had intended, but he
had not thought it would catch him off guard like that, all in one
instant, without a word to say for himself, though what that word
might have been he couldn't imagine. He had done her no harm
at all. One lie that was more her fault than his. No, it wasn't.
She had repaid his kindness with kindness. As she would not have
done if she had known who he was. What he was. When defects of
character *are* your character, you become a what. He had noticed
this. No one ever says, A liar is who you are, or Who you are is a
thief. He was a what, absolutely. He puts on one suit of clothes, a
fraud is what he is. He puts on another suit of clothes—a bum,
a grifter. A draft dodger was what he was. Even that was a lie.
His name was a lie, no matter who had dampened his brow with
it. Also his manners and the words he used and the immutable
habits of his mind. Sweet Jesus, there was no bottom to it, nothing he could say about himself finally. He was acquainted with
despair. The thought made him laugh. He had to admit that he
found it interesting, which was a mercy, and which made it
something less than despair, bad as it was.

I have been one acquainted with the night.
I have walked out in rain—and back in rain.

Much of the time this was his favorite poem. The second line seemed to him like very truth. It was on the basis of the slight and subtle encouragements offered by despair that he had discovered a new aspiration, harmlessness, which accorded well enough with his habits if not his disposition. Keeping his distance was a favor, a courtesy, to all those strangers who might, probably would, emerge somehow poorer for proximity to him. This was his de mon, an eye for the most trifling vulnerabilities. He was doing fairly well until he saw that umbrella. Not true. He had bought that suit to wear to his mother's funeral. His brother Teddy had found the rooming house where he had been staying and left an envelope of money and a note. This had put Jack to the bother of finding another rooming house. Teddy seemed to have contented himself that the man at the counter was not entirely dishonest and left money with him from time to time, enough so that the man could appropriate half of it and Jack would have something to get by on. Cash meant that Teddy had been there, had once more traveled whatever distance in whatever weather, at inter-vals that were long but regular enough that Jack could have been there, sitting on the steps, when that brown sedan pulled up. The embraces, the tears. Jack had thought about it, which did not mean he had considered it. In any case, there was the chance, the likelihood, that Teddy, ever the gentleman, was making himself easy to avoid. And he persisted, leaving money on the chance that Jack was alive and got some of the money, accepting the as-surances the desk clerk offered him.

For two years the clerk might not have known where Jack was or that he was alive, but he saved up half the money that Teddy left, which was notably honorable. When Jack appeared again, he handed him a note from his father that said, "Your dear mother is failing. She yearns to see you," and so on, and the note from his brother that said, "I can come for you. Or you can buy a bus ticket. At least try to come home in time for the funeral, which we expect will be soon." So, the dark suit. Half an intention, fought to a draw by a dozen considerations, the chief one being that he no doubt still had something of prison about him, sullen acquiescence and the rest. They might expect him to see his mother in her coffin, maybe with his father looking on, which would confront him with the meaning of his life, which had no meaning at all but was terrible in its consequences. He had learned to seem hardened against rebuke, and that would be unacceptable in the circumstances.

Terrible thoughts would get him out of bed, out into the weather where the trees and the people were, all, everything, indifferent to his sins and omissions. Why wash, why shave. He went to his bench by the bridge and dozed dreamlessly in the sun. Someone passed behind him and sat down at the other end of the bench. It was Della. He knew it before he had even opened his eyes, and he could hardly believe his eyes when he saw her, sitting there quietly, reading a book. Worse and worse. She glanced at his face, saw whatever she saw, and went back to her book.

He said, "I want to apologize."

And she said, "No need." It had to appear that they weren't there together, so she turned a little away from him. "I was rude."

A white couple passed arm in arm, talking together in those voices people use when they seem to want to be overheard. The woman—"I'll tell you what I think!" The man—"I think I already know!" Laughter.

Then Jack said, softly, "No. Not at all."

The bells struck up that great music of clash and clangor, and when they were done, she said, "I have to go." She put her book down on the bench, put a pen in her handbag, and walked away.

He waited a minute or two, then leaned across the bench to pick it up. It was hardly in his hand when a colored boy in a ball cap grabbed it away. "You were just going to steal that lady's book," he said, and ran after her to give it to her. He saw Della thank him, saw the boy wave off whatever she was offering him from her purse, saw her walk away without a backward glance.

He had to think this through. She had known where to look for him because he had mentioned that bridge. She had brought a book for him. He thought he could let himself believe this. So that he could knock on her door and say, I believe this is yours, Miss Miles? Or there was a note in it, or something circled or underlined. He wished he had seen just the title of the book. It was slender, mossy green, worn-looking. It might have been poetry, something someone had read again and again. She had come looking for him on a Sunday morning, which meant she knew now he wasn't the churchgoing type. It meant also that she might not be on time even for the last service at her own church. She had come a long way just to let him know that things were all right somehow, whatever "things" were, whatever "all right" could be. Since they could hardly manage a few words together. She would know he felt grief—that is what it was— at her disillusionment, since nothing less than grief would have made her come so far. To comfort him. That's what it amounted to. If there had been a note in the book that said, You are a despicable fraud, or words to that effect, even that would mean he had not ceased to exist for her when the idea she had of him perished. This was simply remarkable. Then she found him dozing on a bench like any bum, rumpled and disheveled, and she looked at his face so calmly, which in the circumstances meant kindly, and offered her apology and left her book. It was incredible that she would feel the need to apologize, but thank God she did, because what other pretext would have brought her there. Was it a pretext? Sweet Jesus, how he loved the thought.

What should happen next? Next. This was the language of consequence, lovely to him in this particular moment, because it meant there was an actual thread of connection between them. Knowing her in the particular way he did, he would also know how to answer her. What should he do next? This would take time, and thought, so he believed, but an answer began pressing itself on him immediately, because he had imagined something like it any number of times. He would ask her out to dinner. He had a dishwashing, floor-sweeping kind of familiarity with certain establishments, where mainly black people but a fair scattering of white people came for the fried chicken or the pork chops, and maybe for the piano player. Any of them might seem rambunctious to a Methodist lady. But she wouldn't mind! He knew that about her!

When he had once again collected Teddy's money and put himself in order, and the weather permitted, he went to a street near Della's house and loitered there, waiting for her to come home from school. When he saw her, he crossed the street and fell into step beside her. She only glanced at him, but she was smiling. He said, "Miss Miles, I'd like to take you out to dinner."

She laughed. "Well, there's a thought."

"Seriously. I know a place. There's always a mixed crowd. You might not go there for the food, particularly. But it could be, you know, a nice evening."

She shook her head.

He said, "I understand."

"You probably don't."

"I meant to say all right. No hard feelings."

She stopped and looked at him. "I'd meet you there. You shouldn't come here again. You'll have me on the train to Memphis if my family gets word."

"Yes," he said, "yes, I thought we should meet there. So I made a sort of map." He took the folded paper out of his pocket. "You see, on this side, all the streets, clearly marked. And on the other side"—he turned it over—"the place itself. From across the street." She laughed. "There are a few inaccuracies. I was mostly working from memory."

"I take it you added the angels."

"Angels, trumpets, harps. They are universal symbols of exceptional happiness. So I tossed them in. You can keep that if you like. Even if you don't accept."

She shook her head. "How can I say no?"

"A week night? Not so noisy as the weekend."

"All right. Thursday."

"Eight?"

"Seven. It's a school night."

"Fine. Till then."

"Yes. Go away now. If I'm not there, there's some reason why I can't be."

"Understood." He tipped his hat and walked on. It all went as he had hoped, knowing that his hopes, in the circumstances, had to allow for a certain reluctance, some caution. He thought, very briefly, about the risk to her they were always aware of, and then he put the thought aside. No doubt he would fall down a manhole or get hit by a streetcar before Thursday, before this unimaginable evening, fate intervening for her sake.

———

But there he was, Thursday evening, loitering a few doors away from the restaurant, watching the street. And then there she was, and wearing quite a pretty hat, considering that she was a Methodist and a schoolteacher, and very uneasy about drawing attention to herself.

He said, "Miss Miles," and she stopped and smiled, and he opened the door for her. The waiter, a black man, knew him, raised his eyebrows, but showed them to a table with a mock formality that was pleasant enough.

"Out on the town tonight, I guess. With a lovely lady, too. You better take good care of this nice lady." Jack tried to remember if this man had ever seen him sober. He hadn't given this aspect of things enough thought. The waiter laughed. "Don't mind me. I'm just here to say I hope you like pork chops, because tonight that's what we've got."

"Pork chops would be excellent."

They had the place almost to themselves. They could talk in the ordinary way of conversation, at least till later, when the piano started up and the crowd came. He had spent days in the library thinking about what he would say to her, drawing the map and the heavenly host on the flyleaf of a big travel book that had not been checked out for years, since before the war, and then only twice. The page pulled loose from its binding very cleanly. Whenever his father found one of his drawings, he'd say, "He's the clever one. He's going to surprise us all one day." He heard his mother say once, "I guess you're never going to give up on him." His father seemed to consider, and then he said, "I'm just not sure there would be any point in it." But the angels went well, they were fat and buoyant, cumulus. Della had to like them, he thought. And she did. Cleverness has a special piquancy when it blooms out of the fraying sleeve of failure. That was his experience, the magic trick he could usually play when he had to.

And here she was. He said, "New tie," when he realized he was smoothing it.

She smiled and said, "New hat."

He was in love with her. That did it. That hat brought out glints of rose in the warm dark of her skin. Women know that kind of thing. She, Della, wanted him, Jack, to see that particular loveliness in her. These thoughts interfered considerably with the efforts at conversation he should have been making.

She said, "That bridge you talk about really is handsome. Those huge stones. The walls of Troy must have looked like that."

"Yes. Herod's temple." Then he said, "Have you ever been to Bellefontaine?"

"The white cemetery? Why, no. I haven't had much occasion."

Of course. What a stupid question. He said, "I only ask because there is a tree there, a really huge old tree. I've probably walked by it a hundred times without noticing anything about it. But one time I happened to look back, and I saw blossoms all over it. Seriously. Big sort of golden-colored blossoms, each one upright, like it was floating on something. And I thought that was an amazing thing. The leaves hide them. But from a certain distance, there they are. I thought that was interesting." He didn't think it was even slightly interesting now, listening to himself tell her about it, although at the time it had seemed startlingly wonderful, one of those self-erasing, soul-freeing moments when you might actually say, "I get the joke!" He had felt the lack of someone to describe it to. This quiet, smiling woman had had that place in his thoughts for weeks. And now he was reminded that the places he went and the things he saw, few as they were, were nothing he had in common with her. That musty, unvisited corner of the library where he almost lived was a place he had imagined telling her about. And now he realized that it would be unkind to mention it—the refuge of his poverty and his idleness and whatever else it was about him that brought him to skulk among forgotten books, hoping that old lady had remembered him when she was packing her lunch. Dear Jesus, what a life! And this lovely woman, whose hat was no doubt actually new, wouldn't have the privilege of reading through all that pathos and pomposity and finding a line here and there worth reading to someone—she having been that someone in his thoughts for what seemed like forever.

She was looking at him calmly, kindly. She said, "It's probably a tulip tree. That's really what they're called. They're native to North America!" She laughed. "When I was a girl, one of my brothers gave me a book about trees. I knew everything about all of them for a while. Then he gave me a book about dogs."

"I have a brother. Actually, I have three brothers. But Teddy—he's a little younger than I am. We were close, I suppose. He's a doctor now."

"How often do you see him?"

"Never." Flinch. "Very seldom. It seems like never." If he wasn't careful, he might tell her the truth sometime.

She read his face, and then she said, "I've always heard that Bellefontaine is beautiful."

"If you like that sort of thing." The waiter put plates down in front of them. Pork chops, a mound of potatoes cratered with the back of a spoon and filled with that oddly species-less gravy. There are probably ten laws in Leviticus that forbid that gravy. He said, "There are some pretty amazing monuments in there, and whole little neighborhoods of Greek temples, probably accurate in every detail, I suppose. About the size of woodsheds. There is one that has a statue of the woman it belongs to lying there under a canopy. All marble, very elegant. The inscription on it says, 'She died for beauty.'"

"Really! How did she manage that?"

"Arsenic. A gardener told me. She took little dabs of it to make her skin very white, and once she took too much." Dear Jesus, what a story.

Della said, "The poor dear!" There wasn't just laughter in her eyes, he could see that. Affection, possibly.

Then he heard a voice he knew too well. There were some fellows, not always the same ones, who made a joke of shaking him down, collecting something he owed, they said, never quite enough to pay it off. He probably did owe something to somebody and was, in any case, usually too drunk to object. He glanced over his shoulder. Sure enough, two of them. Della looked at them.

He said, "Excuse me a moment, please," and left through the kitchen, glad he knew the place. It wasn't only the embarrassment, being taunted as a drunk and a deadbeat in front of Della, having to put his money on the table and then turn his pockets out. And having to do it sober. He would give in immediately, or he would attempt some sort of self-defense, which could only end badly, since there were two of them. In either case, the ruckus wouldn't end until they let it, and by then the cops might have come. There would be talk, and Della might be named—sneaky and spineless as it would have been under any other circumstances, often as he had done it under all kinds of circumstances, he was pretty sure this time he was doing the right thing.

It was a terrible thing. She would never forgive him. He had spared her having much better reasons for hating him than he had given her. What a life.

He loitered in that doorway, watching to see them leave, or her leave. Ah, Jesus, it was taking her such a long time to give up on him. But finally he saw her, walked her to her door, and left feeling less desolate than he had expected. He had been running their conversation through his mind. Not so bad, not so bad.

It was a mild night. He loosened his tie and folded his jacket over his arm. He took a shortcut down a side street, which he would never have done at night if he had been paying attention. And he heard that voice again, behind him. They were laughing. "Why, it's the professor! I been wanting a word with you, son. If you could just stop there a minute. The boss tells me you owe him. He wants his money. I guess you better empty those pockets."

Jack said, "What boss? Who's—"

And the other man hit him in the belly, a blow that startled him because it was so deft and mean. He almost said, Wait, this isn't the game! when he hit him again. He had to put his hand against a wall to keep from falling. He was carrying Teddy's money, all of it he hadn't spent on the tie and a shave. He took it out of his pocket and put it in the hand of the first man.

"This all?" the man said. "It better be." Jack actually checked, found a few coins, and gave them to him.

The man laughed. "Okay, I guess we're square for now."

Then the other man hit him again, in the face this time. He must have been wearing a ring. Jack felt a cut on his cheekbone, a gouge. He couldn't put his hand to it. Get blood on your hands and the next thing you know it's on everything. They were walking away, the one saying to the other, "I can't stand that guy. Something about him."

"I know what you mean," the other one said, and threw the change on the ground and shared out the bills.

His jacket was probably all right. He laid it down on a cellar door and put his hat beside it. In the dark he couldn't tell what was ruined already. He untucked his shirt to blot his face with his shirttail, then lay down beside his jacket and hat and waited till his breath was back and he had stopped bleeding. And the thought that came to him first, looking up at the narrow sky, was Now I can't go home, ever. He thought, I can't see Della again, I can't go to the library, I'll have to close my lapels over my shirt the way bums do, and that was all terrible. But the way his father would sorrow over this unconcealable wound was the thought he could not bear.

So he went to Bellefontaine. He had managed despite his ribs to pick up the coins that damn fellow threw on the ground. It was enough for a couple of Hershey bars, anyway. He would wait on a bench till the day began, the gates opened, the little shop across from the entrance that sold gum and cigarettes and candy came alive. He would wince back at the clerk who winced at his bloodiness, to let him know that comment was not necessary. Then he'd join any stream of people passing through the gates, walk on to some secluded place by the lake, take off his shirt and sink it in the water with a stone to keep it in place, close his lapels bum-wise, lie down on a grave, and eat some chocolate. Jesus, what a life. Water would not rinse out a bloodstain, but one does what one can. He would hang the shirt on a bush or a headstone, but only after dark, because it alarms people somehow to see laundry done in public places. Raskolnikov. He could pretend he was the villain, hiding the proof of terrible guilt. That would chase people away and give him a minute or two to consider his options, how to shelter that quivering nerve of pride, which was always ready to heighten the misery of any occasion. No, better, he would find a bouquet, lay it on his chest, and be very still. If someone came close, he would sit bolt upright and stare. The kind of thing a child would think of, but it would also be likely to give him a minute or two, and it would be less likely to involve the police. He crouched by the water and washed his face with his hands, like the first man who ever lived and died would have done, exactly. No one saw him. He was careful of that. People find attention to personal hygiene in public disturbing. He'd have to sneak back to his room for his comb and razor. People are reassured by combed hair. His effects wouldn't fill a paper bag. They might already be out on the curb.

The problem was to keep body and soul together until Teddy came with his stipend. That would be about a month, since winter was coming on, stirring his brother's solicitude, he supposed. He found a grave old enough that there was little chance of his actually terrifying survivors, and he fell asleep.

His luck had never failed him entirely to this point. A big fellow in a greenish coverall with a patch on the pocket that said *Bradshaw* nudged him awake with the toe of his boot and asked him if he was looking for work. It was well before dawn and the question was whispered, which should have raised suspicions. But Jack was absorbing the surprise of realizing he had been asleep and only thought of this later. Bradshaw, who was struggling out of the coverall, said he hated having to plant a million damn bulbs, hated the whole damn thing, but had to keep this job till he found another one. So he'd give Jack a few bucks to pass for Bradshaw. "This place gives me nightmares," he said. "I can earn better money on the docks any day. My brother-in-law got me this job, the son of a bitch. Steady work, he says. I could go nuts in here. I hate dead people." In the excitements of new resolve, he took out a roll of bills and handed Jack one of them.

Jack said, "I——" and Bradshaw said, "I don't have time for this," and handed him another one. He turned to look behind him. "Just wear this damn uniform for a few days! Is that so hard?" He gave Jack another bill. "And don't say nothing." He said, "Don't kill yourself over them bulbs, either. Dump 'em in a corner somewhere." And he strode away before Jack could think through his new situation. He had nothing against dead people or flower bulbs. He could put on the uniform of an honest workingman with that solid name, Bradshaw. He had money, three dollars, he supposed, though there wasn't light enough for him to see the denominations. If perfection ever stooped to consider the likes of Jack Boughton, to deal, so to speak, in such small coin, then he could call his surprising new circumstances perfect, or so he thought at the time.

He had fallen asleep thinking how to put an end to himself. There was the lake, and, in a virtual forest of low-hanging boughs, he had his necktie. Grotesque in either case. Sure to break his father's heart, once and for all, if word got back to him. He imagined Teddy there, somehow first to know, plumbing his gentle, practical wits for a way to make things seem other than they were. Then he woke up with that boot in his ribs, but on the undamaged side, and Bradshaw struggling out of his uniform and laying out a hectic plan for Jack's immediate future, which meant that that other decision could be postponed.

Perhaps. Jack put on the enormous overall, which fit over his jacket with room to spare, solving the problem of what to do with it, at least till the day warmed up. The cuffs dragged and the sleeves had to be rolled, but he was ready to give this Bradshaw business a try, in the absence of other options than those two he really hated to consider. Clothes make the man. He could see up the hill a big burlap sack. It did have bulbs in it. He found a spade lying in the grass nearby. Off to work.

Walking along a path, looking for a place where he might reasonably plant something, he passed a man who rather pointedly paused to read the patch on his pocket. The man said, "I'm surprised you'd even show your face around here!" His obvious disgust meant he would not take it well if Jack asked him to clarify.

So, something else to consider. What had Bradshaw been doing in the cemetery in his work clothes in the middle of the night? And he had been in too great a hurry to ask Jack why he was sleeping on a grave with a wilted bouquet on his chest. Other people spent nights in the cemetery, but the flowers would have given pause, under normal circumstances. Self-parody can be hard to explain. But no small talk, just that prodding boot. And the hasty handing over of money, to overwhelm possible reluctance, Jack thought. And the hurried exit into the near-night. That man had shed Bradshaw to make himself anonymous, with good reason, no doubt, and had left another Bradshaw behind for when the cops came.

Short of that, if the man had done something obnoxious and reprehensible by the code of the brotherhood of cemetery gardeners and punishable by their contempt and ostracism only, this would suit Jack's purposes, such as they were. He had thought at first that the man on the path was noting the mismatch of the name on the pocket and the battered face under the cap, and so he was relieved by the thought that, though the name might be locally notorious, the man it belonged to was a stranger somehow, successfully furtive. A remarkable thing in a giant, true. Worthy of emulation, and made easier in Jack's case by the repugnance Bradshaw had left in his wake.

Dear Jesus. Jack's mind ran over the very long list of possible offenses, saw himself accused and convicted, favored drowning as less judicial than hanging, as less likely to be seen as an implied confession, and wondered for the millionth time how he had trapped himself in such a ridiculous life. Harmlessness is not for the faint of heart.

If he had decided on drowning, it might be better to take care of it before he was embroiled in *l'affaire Bradshaw*. But if Bradshaw's transgressions were truly grievous, maybe he should wait around to defend himself, with all the futility that would involve, rather than seem to confess to it and let it cast whatever shadow it might over that rigorous pulpit, that upright house, that unoffending town, that earnest state—here he was sweating and trembling over an unspecified crime that might not have happened and that in any case was not his crime. He couldn't even think of Della.

But what if someone saw him pulling a bloodstained shirt out of the lake? Then again, what if he left it there to be found in the inevitable search of the area? Was it worse to be seen retrieving the shirt at night? Though night would diminish the chance that he would be seen doing it, which, of course, is what made doing anything at night presumptively incriminating. The thought occurred to him suddenly that he had not looked over these gabardines Bradshaw was so desperate to climb out of. Blood? Hair? So he also climbed out of them. There were a hundred stains, impossible to interpret. Dried sweat, of course, which could testify to the desperations of guilt and concealment. He was studying the cap when a man with an official air called to him, "Seen Bradshaw?"

Jack called back, "Not today," standing there with the flayed giant crumpled at his feet, implicating himself pointlessly in whatever it was, because that was just the kind of thing he did.

Why did he want that damn shirt, anyway? He imagined the cuffs floating up like some last supplication. A necktie on a bare neck looks ridiculous. Forget the damn necktie. A suit jacket over a bare chest looks ridiculous. He wasn't thinking clearly. Did he owe Bradshaw anything? Had there been some sort of agreement? A few bucks, or their equivalent in time spent abetting a crime. If the crime was truly grave, that time would have expired already in light of the risks involved. He had spent the morning as near guilt and humiliation if not death as an imaginative man could come without actually passing through them, and he had money in his pocket, which seemed fair. For one sick instant he thought he had put the money in the pocket of the uniform, and that he would have to go back and rifle its pockets in what was now broad daylight, workers everywhere, but no. He took the bills out and looked at them. Three twenties. More amazing still, they were absolutely new, the newest money he had ever seen in his life. This was exhausting. A bank heist, an armored car. Counterfeiting. This last would account for his readiness to pull bills off that roll he had, to silence objections Jack had been too sleepy to come up with. Suddenly he was thinking about cops again. Where did you get this money, pal? Somebody paid you? For what? In the dark? In the cemetery? The name Bradshaw mean anything to you?

He would go back to his room. Just two nights had passed. It was the endlessness of all recent experience that had made him sure he was late with his rent, but he wasn't. It was a relief to be out on the street. His razor and comb would be there on the dresser where he left them. He thought, I have been outside time and St. Louis, I have been in a dream, a Russian novel. And he decided to put the twenties in his shoes so that he could walk them into a state of wear that would make them less suspect. As an added benefit, should he be shaken down on the long walk home, he might get away with saying he had no money. A woman was waiting at the streetcar stop, watching him with that look people have when they're trying to make sense of something. He gave her a battered smile and she looked away. It occurred to him that Bradshaw might be getting his money's worth. The best thing about taking a punch or two in an alley is that, when they ask that witness what Bradshaw looks like, he'll say he had a terrible black eye, lots of swelling. That's all people notice. Jack would lie low, and Bradshaw was too big to get hit in the face, so pretty soon no one would match the description, or no one would if Jack remembered not to go down alleys.

The desk clerk glanced at him as he came in the door and said, "Ouch!"

Jack said, "The other guy looks worse."

The clerk laughed. "Then I guess the poor devil must have been born ugly."

Very funny.

He lay down on his bed and reflected on the night he had passed. Was there, or was there not, a Bradshaw? He was clearly a cosmic ruse, a means to an end, in fact a punch line, which was to put money in Jack's hands that he could not spend. Did he eat and sleep? Or was he conjured for just these few minutes, to rattle the jar in which Jack the specimen was trying to understand the transparent barrier between himself and ordinary life. The money was actually there, he had checked several times, twenty in the left, forty in the right. He did not know of a single establishment in walking distance whose till would not have been completely emptied by making change for a twenty-dollar bill. Nor was there a store where he could make reasonable use of twenty dollars to avoid the problem of change. Then he had a thought. He went down to the desk and said to the clerk, "I would like to pay a few weeks' rent in advance. With five dollars back."

The clerk said, "That will require money."

"Yes, I have money," but it was in his shoe, which might make the whole transaction less attractive, objectively speaking. He searched his pockets. "Oh, I left it upstairs." So he went upstairs, took a bill out of his right shoe, evening things up, he thought, and laughed, and went down to put the twenty on the counter. You would have to look very closely to see any sign that it was not brand-new.

The clerk took the bill to the window to see it in a better light. "Where did you get this?"

That dread question. Jack had no better option than the truth. "It's hush money."

The clerk laughed. "I guess that means you're not saying."

"Yes, I believe it was a mistake. I didn't actually witness a crime. I saw the fellow run off, probably from the scene of the crime, which I suppose is a crime in those circumstances. He gave me money and told me not to tell anybody anything. Which of course I won't."

The clerk shook his head, but he opened the till and put a five on the counter. "There's your change. But if this twenty is as phony as it looks, I'm calling the cops."

Jack actually thought about asking if he could have it back, but that would look like a confession. Well, at worst he had five dollars in his pocket. No, at worst he had passed counterfeit currency that he had received for abetting a crime. And at second worst, the clerk would forget to note that Jack had paid rent in advance and Jack would have no way to prove that he had, since the improbability of his having twenty dollars could only be countered by his producing another twenty dollars, which would raise and compound every suspicion. So, after an hour or two, he went back down to the desk and he said, "Pardon me. Could I have a receipt for that fifteen dollars I paid in advance? Or you could just write it down somewhere."

The clerk shrugged and said, "Maybe you gave me fifteen dollars, and maybe you didn't."

Exhausting. How could a man whose life amounted to absolutely nothing have so many things to worry about?

He went up to his room, lay down on his bed, and considered his choices. He could get dead drunk, let the world turn a few times, rouse himself with his face more like his face, his problems receded, even if that meant they were further from his grasp. It might be cops who woke him up, those heavy shoes on the stairs, and then those questions about whatever pernicious thing Bradshaw had been up to, about concealing evidence. He decided to stay sober, to give himself a chance, at least.

This was the world after Della. There were the hours in which he resigned himself, not for the first time, to the fact that he had nothing to give anyone, that his life was an intricate tangle of futility, sustained by the faithful brotherliness of Teddy, that impeccable human being, whose kindness shamed him because he could never reciprocate. He could have gone to his mother's funeral. How much of his reluctance had to do with a black suit and brown shoes? He laughed abysmally at the thought, the utterly damning triviality of it. It would have meant he could not

contrive to maintain himself as himself, and they would all notice and know what it meant. And prison, and that grudging sub-
missiveness to other people as authorities of some kind, which
made sense to him, since even that desk clerk had something
to do, and did it to some standard of sufficiency. Could I have
a receipt? Pardon me. Almost asking him to say no. People in
his family did not go to prison. They worked scrupulously, repro-
duced, and died in a good old age, as his father would say. It had
never seemed to him that this was so much to aspire to. He still
could not quite aspire to it, and yet any modest version of it was
so tauntingly unattainable by him. Taking a preacher's daughter
out for supper. How could this involve them both in humiliation?
Clearly harmlessness was more than he could aspire to.

On the other hand, he had tried from time to time to do something baldly self-interested, and not much came to mind. A few
minor thefts, that old habit, nothing acquisitive about it, since
the things he took were worthless to him if not to the people
he took them from. Moral scrutiny was invited by this habit of
his, he knew. He believed it might be an attempt on his part
to weave himself into the emotional fabric of another life. That
sounded right. It was a speculation of his father's, once when he
had found a shoebox half full of Jack's pilferings. "I think we
should talk about this," his father had said, and they had had a
good conversation, his father weighing his words so carefully. "I
know that you are most at ease by yourself. That's fine. But you
may be lonelier than you realize." He liked the thought that
he was weaving himself into the emotional fabric of another life.
And then he took the experiment much too far. "There was pure
malice in it," his father had said. "Surely you see that, Jack."
He saw it, he remembered it, the way you remember the mood
of a dream. With that impulse, when his thoughts centered on

fragility—fixed on it. No doubt also malice, always compounding itself by a logic of its own.

So, harmlessness. This really might be too much to hope for. He actually shuddered at the harm Della might have suffered, perhaps did suffer, from his stupidly hanging around her door. How could she have explained him to a principal, a board of some kind? He shuddered as if the thought had not occurred to him a thousand times before. And still he thought that he might sometime loiter near Sumner when school was letting out, just for a glimpse of her, to be sure that things were all right with her. This would not happen. He could not promise himself no harm would come of it.

Simplify, simplify. He had made a good beginning when he forbade himself the thought of Della. Once she was banished, he was freed of anticipation and regret, both of which were attended by calculation of a kind—how to have a glimpse of her, which became how to pass her on the street, and then what to say to her, what would make her smile. Or he would fall to thinking how to put something right, how to make something clear, for example that he avoided her for her sake and at some cost to himself, emotionally speaking. For a day or two he would take pleasure in the thought that her good life was unthreatened by his Jackness, Jackitude, Jackicity. How was it possible to be encumbered with slyness, so that his blundering always ended as shrewd harm? It was a shock to his metaphysics to discover that when he had forsworn malicious intent, the effects of his actions, his mere presence, were changed very little and not reliably for the better. What if Della read *Paterson* and was offended by it? He hadn't been to the library since he went there to draw that picture, chicken joint with angels. He had been, as the fellow said, ashamed to show his face, though he knew that the most respectable man in Missouri could be mugged if he happened to turn down the wrong alley. It was ridiculous to have believed that the circumstances of his life would not have touched him essentially so long as they left no visible scars. As if he could just walk into the old house and take his place at the dinner table. He usually banished that thought once or twice a day, but now he gave up on it for good. It was gone now, and all the sorrow he would surely have brought with him, like the wind he brought in at night when the house was warm and asleep. It was like a black cloak that swept around him, setting off disturbances among the crystals on the lampshades, leafing books left open, losing places in them. Scattering letters, half-written or half-read. He couldn't say he hadn't done any of these things. If they asked him why he had done them, he could not say, "I am at the center of a certain turbulence." That would sound flippant at best, a little deranged if they took him seriously.

He was inclined to believe that there were (a): energy, and (b): displacement. Any gesture was, whatever else, like freeing something from your hand, some living thing that would touch or settle wherever it happened to be carried on the surge of displacement. Rattle or fracture confirmed this. So as a living creature he was ill suited to the brittle, frangible world of things. It was as though planet Energy and planet Order had collided and merged, leaving displacement as the settling of the ruins. By extension, he thought, though he knew it was only by analogy, the small gesture of, say, recommending a book of poetry to someone became displacement that struck where it would, as it would, converting itself in midair into malice or stupidity. How did people live? His oldest question.

Nevertheless. But. Still. And. He went to the library, though his face was zombie lavender and zombie green, especially around his right eye, which looked a little reptilian with the swelling half gone. He hoped that kindly woman was not there, but she was, at the front desk, where she would be sure to see him. When he saw her there, he paused, thinking he might try another hour, another day, since there was certainly no urgency about this or anything else, but she glanced up at him just as he was stepping away. "Good morning," she said, which was kind in the circumstances, and then went back to sorting her cards, which was also kind. So he said, "Good morning," and smiled, insofar as he could manage a smile, and went off to the stacks, overtaken by that strange awkwardness that comes with feeling watched as you walk away. Shady intentions always make it worse.

He went to the place where he had hidden *Paterson*, behind *The Dream of the Rood and Other Early English Religious Poems*, the title he had memorized, and it wasn't there. It was not behind twenty books in either direction, above or below. He sat down at the table to think about this. Then he took down Robert Frost, so that he had something to look at while he absorbed his disappointment, which was really out of all proportion to the situation. He only meant to read the book over to resolve in his mind whether it would have offended Della or not. He hardly knew her—how could he be sure in any case? He could commit the whole thing to memory and be none the wiser. And she might have forgotten about it the minute he mentioned it.

He didn't look up when the librarian came into the room, but he could smell the bologna in the sandwich that, yes, she set on the table by his elbow.

"Frost is good," she said. "Williams is shelved in the *W*'s."

"Yes. Thank you." So he read some Frost out of loyalty to the pretense, then began to think that these poems might neutralize the effect of Williams if on another reading he decided *Paterson* might seem crude to her. The thought was a relief, even though nothing would come of it. He stayed long enough to have a reasonable hope the lady's shift had ended, but there she was, and there he was, with the two books tucked under his belt, a very insecure arrangement that could well embarrass him to actual death.

She didn't even look up. She said, "Remember to bring that back sometime." That, singular. So he had actually gotten away with the theft of one of them, and he took a kind of satisfaction in the thought. The other one she had in effect lent him, which is what librarians are paid to do. It bothered him that he didn't know which was which, but it didn't bother him much.

A week and two days had passed. He had run a thousand plans through his mind, thinking what he would do if the desk clerk at the rooming house decided to make an issue about whether he had been paid or not, whether that twenty was legal tender. He should have asked for more than a five back. He was afraid at the time that worse might come to worst and he would have to come up with five bucks at a minimum to even hope he could mollify the fellow. So he spent what money he had so unwillingly it was almost another form of not having any. When had he last thought of that word "mollify"? "Emollient." Association. Would he think differently if he thought in different words? He could dignify true nonsense, to his own satisfaction, in any case. A smaller vocabulary would keep him on a narrower path, no doubt limit these irksome divagations a little. Where did that one come from?

He had been as quiet as he could be for nine days, had gone downstairs only when very necessary, had read Robert Frost. Or he did until the clerk came upstairs, opened his door, and looked in at him there with his book. "Still alive," he said. There was a misleading raucousness in a rooming house, where, in fact, many a turbulent soul was, so to speak, silently coming to the end of his rope, or belt or electrical cord, or whatever. The clerk especially hated that kind of problem. It was best handled expeditiously. He had noticed the patch of silence in the thick of pandemonium and had come to check, confident enough of what he might find not to bother knocking.

Jack said, "Still alive."

The clerk laughed. "To tell the truth, I had a bet with a guy about whether you sleep with your hat on." And he went away.

Very funny. But the joke made him uncomfortably conscious that he did, in certain moods, sleep with his shoes on. When he dreamed of the return of Bradshaw. Or the police, always so eager to be confirmed in their suspicions, to bring the universal solvent of official attention to bear on every hapless thing until it was all just evidence, patently incriminating. But then, once he dreamed that the police did come and find him with the blanket over his head and his two shod feet sticking out at the bottom of the bed. His mattress was a few inches short, a fact to which he had, until then, been resigned. How better to pique that officious curiosity? The worst thing about the cops was when they couldn't help laughing. With judges it was even worse. He had to get some sort of control of his life.

Why? The point of all this was to stay alive as long as decency required. He thought it would be the considerate thing to minimize so far as possible the signs of struggle with futility and despair and that sort of thing, so that when Teddy and whoever else came to fetch him home they would be able to say, Yes, that is absolutely our brother Jack, that is just how he knotted his tie. There might be something to the idea of sleeping with his hat on, his shoes, for that matter. Then he would appear so lifelike, as they say, that their grief would be mingled with suspicion. Teddy would lay his cool, professional fingers on his throat, just to be sure. And Jack, which was a name he had for his soul, would even then be falling through uncanny voids and starry abysses toward perdition.

In the meantime, a man who stood six foot two in his socks could not sustain life on the occasional bologna sandwich. He did not want to fail at the one object he had set for himself, which was to stay alive until the next black-bordered envelope arrived, until Teddy pulled up in front of the wrong rooming house to offer him a ride home if he could find him.

Then he decided enough time had passed to make it worthwhile to check at the old rooming house, to see if Teddy had left money there for him. So he strolled the few blocks to the old place, and the man at the desk took an unsealed envelope from the cash drawer and handed it to him without a word, but with that old injured look that let Jack know he couldn't quite approve of the arrangement. He'd have had more respect for a thief, no doubt being one himself. Oh well. Jack put the money in his pocket, thanked the man with a cordiality meant to exasperate, and went off to buy himself a newer shirt.

It was feeling a little solvent and respectable that made him walk into a bar one night, to have one drink and listen to the piano. He had two drinks, waiting for the piano player to show up. Then he went over and started tinkering with the keys. Someone shouted "Tennessee Waltz!" so he sat down and played it, and someone shouted "Cool Water!" so he played that, and "I'll Be Seeing You," and "The Tennessee Waltz" again. Someone put a glass with change in it on the piano, then a glass of whiskey, and he played "My heart knows what the wild goose knows" and sang along. Then someone shouted "The Horst Wessel Song," which had been set to an old hymn tune his father liked, a perfectly good hymn, and out of drunken happiness at the coincidence, he fingered a few bars. There was a silence and then a blow to the back of his head that landed him on the floor somehow. He made the mistake of standing up temporarily, intending to explain, he was quite sure, but he was punched in the face before he could compose his thoughts. When his head cleared a little, he stepped into the kitchen and out through the door to the alley. The tumult inside went on without him. Just those few notes were incitement enough to make up for the lack of an antagonist. He had heard the glass with the money in it hit the floor and the coins scatter. Oh well. Here he was, alone in an alley, bleeding again. He would have to sacrifice his handkerchief to his necktie. What a ridiculous life.

A night or two later he pulled a flyleaf out of *Paterson* and wrote a note: *Mrs. B.—I have been away from work because I have not been well. Sincere regrets, J. A. Boughton (Slick).* He put it into the little basket hanging by the door, which was there to collect the bills and flyers that might otherwise have entered the establishment bringing threats and sad information. There was no chance she would find his note, but he would be able to find it if he needed proof he had been somewhat conscientious. But then, when he thought he might be presentable enough to show up for work and went to the shop, he saw the CLOSED sign, and a notice on the door, a piece of typewriter paper that said, matter-of-factly, *Going out of business, prices slashed, everything must go, all sales final, our loss is your gain.*

And still that pair of faded men's moccasins posed in the window. Why did it afflict him in some way that this starveling enterprise had suffered its final throes without his being there for the death watch? Well, a fragile strand of connection to ordinary life gone. What to do with the rest of the day. Beer, he thought. He could walk far enough to be out of the sphere of his acquaintance, beyond more than usual skepticism, and probably break a twenty. Worth a try. St. Louis is a German town, which made things a little unpredictable where the great issues were concerned. He would bear that in mind. But there was also beer with so much food value as to excuse his having it for breakfast. Then he could forget about lunch. And when it was evening, he would walk over to that place by the river, a sort of open-air plaza where there was a swing band and people danced. By then he would be too mellow to care that they were all young and that so many of them were soldiers or sailors, brought there to be scattered over the continent, back to the land of mom and dad. He was in general quiet when he drank. Anyway, he looked a little drunk when he was sober, a little sober when he was drunk, so his odds were always about even. He'd stand to the side and listen to the music, and no one would really mind, though everything about him said 4-F.

He found *schwarzbier* and *bockbier* in a shop that also sold very ripe cheese, white sausages, and giant pretzels. He felt a twinge of something like appetite. He left with a large, odoriferous bag in his arms and nearly sixteen dollars in his pocket. The man at the counter said, "You was never one of these soldiers," gesturing toward the street. "I can see that. They're rough some-times. I was not a soldier. I get along all right most of the time." And he made change like a gesture of subversive bonhomie and added an apple to the bag.

Jack walked down to the river and sat there in the sun with the bag sitting on the bench beside him, companionably. He smelled like cigarettes and cheap aftershave, and the bag smelled like cheese and pretzels, the two of them just being what they were, the cheese no doubt sweating a little in the sunlight, just as he was. Prolong the moment, he thought, and then he knocked the cap off a bottle against the edge of the bench. "Swig" is an odd word. Perfect, though. He knew he would go from being a little content to pretty content to despondent, each phase in his descent rewarding in its own way. No sober man could admit to mourn-ing the loss of the stupidest job imaginable. He would watch the river and consider the transiency of things for an hour or so, and then who knows. Whatever the virtues of food, it did blunt the effects of alcohol. If he ate the pretzel, he might never reach the state where he could put into words, and weep inwardly as he did it, that he would miss talking box scores with Mrs. Beverly. As a sober man he might maintain some sort of perspective, but once he was drunk, what mattered mattered. A trifling pleasure lost. He had nowhere to be, and he was really so sorry.

That done, he was any bum dozing on a bench, jobless and 4-F, steeped in beer and sunshine. Then the air cooled with eve-ning and the memory stirred in him that he had meant to go watch the dancing and hear the music. First home, to shave and pull himself together. No. He lifted his hat to run his fingers through his hair and straightened his tie and walked toward the sound of a piano.

It was a mixed crowd. More precisely, there were black soldiers on one side of the plaza, white on the other; black girls on one side, white on the other. All the shy business of pairing off for a dance or two, the awkwardness of teasing and roughhousing among the soldiers, like boys who have only a minute or two away from authority and order.

And there was Della, with two black men, one tall, the other taller, both in civilian clothes but with that martial bearing people talk about. Della was laughing, teasing and joking with a few black soldiers who stepped out of the crowd and gathered around them, shaking hands and clapping shoulders. He'd never seen this Della, had never imagined there could be such a Della. Well, of course. She was young and pretty, and he could never be standing with her like that in a public place, in a crowd, under a streetlamp. There was nothing at stake for him, no thread of connection to break, only the habit to rid himself of, of thinking about her, which he really had no right to do. He should have expected something like this. He had no reason to feel stunned by it, to be frozen in place by it, when he wanted so badly to leave.

Then she turned for some reason and looked right at him, and he just stood there, absorbing the fact. She spoke to the taller of the two men, who also looked at him. Jack touched the brim of his hat and smiled, just a glimpse of a rim of teeth and a look that meant, I have a certain acquaintance with your girlfriend. I have admired the lobe of her ear and have thought of tracing the curve of her cheek with my fingertip. Any number of times. It was so ridiculous he almost made himself laugh, even though he knew he was risking one of those dustups that never went well for him.

Della stepped away from the group and walked down the pavement to where he stood, he intent on lighting a cigarette so as not to lose face, whatever that might amount to.

She said, "I didn't expect to see you here."

He said, "Ditto," and flicked his cigarette.

"I'm here with my brothers. They have friends from the service who are passing through town." She said, "I'd like you to meet my brother Marcus."

Jack said, "Maybe another time. When I'm a little less drunk."

She nodded. "They came up from Memphis just for a couple of days. I don't know when there'll be another time."

He took a long drag on his cigarette. "Why do this, Miss Miles? What point is there in this?"

"Well," she said, "they've heard the rumors. About the white man."

He laughed. "So shaking my hand is supposed to make him feel better about that. I have my doubts. Sorry, lady. I've had a rough day. I don't want to meet your brother."

He was trying to put an end to absolutely everything, but she hung down her lovely head and he was covered with shame that he had been rude to her.

"I understand," she said. "Another time." But she didn't step away.

By then her brother was simply watching them, with his hands on his hips. And there was Jack, shivering in his stale shirt, with a pretzel in each pocket, which had earlier seemed a stabilizing arrangement but now seemed to sum up his whole life. He took a drag on his cigarette and did not look at her.

"I'm glad I know you," she said. "People act as though it's something to be ashamed of. I mean, that we're friends, that we talk sometimes. But I can't live that way. I can't just be ashamed because people say I should be." She said, "I have something to give you." She opened her purse—Good Christ, not a handout.

She said, "It's a poem. I'd like to know what you think of it. I've been carrying it around with me in case I might see you some-time. Don't read it now. Maybe I'll see you again and you can tell me then."

Jack said, "They're waiting for you." He didn't say, Please be gone. Let your brothers look after you. Don't associate yourself with some old white bum just to show the world that you're brave.

But she stood there with him, beside him, just long enough to make it clearly intentional, to her brothers and to him. Then she said, "You take care of yourself, Jack," and looked at him for emphasis, and walked away.

Mortal, can these bones live? O Lord God, you know.

He folded her poem to fit in his shirt pocket, not a place where those debt collectors would expect him to carry money. Then he ate a pretzel, which was a first step in rethinking his life.

The first thing to decide was whether it was kind or unkind of her to speak with him that way. To rekindle the thought of herself when he was ready to believe those ashes were cold. On the other hand, what could it matter? There were a thousand barriers between black Della and his indigent, disreputable self, and mere kindness could not lower any of them so much as an inch. Sometime he might have a chance to say, That poem of yours is very whatever, deep or something, and the world will clear its throat and scowl, seeing them together, and her brothers will be on the train to St. Louis. And he will skulk away, hop-ing to leave her life undamaged, her good name. He should have let her introduce Marcus, assuming he would have agreed to it. Furtiveness, evasiveness, would have encouraged the notion that impropriety figured somehow.

By the time he was back in his room he had decided that he might as well look at her poem. Clothed as he was in the garments of misfeasance and bewilderment, there lived in him a deeply arrogant man. How could this be true? But as he walked away from the miserable scene of his rudeness and drunkenness, having brought a beautiful thing to a bad end, he began to gloat a little in anticipation of the mediocrity, at best, of this attempt at poetry, for this purpose making himself believe that she was like most people. Maybe some third-rate magazine had held on to this scrap of martyred language long enough to have kindled hopes in her, pride even. It was a very good thing that he would never see her again. He would be spared the temptation of telling her, with unaccountable confidence, exactly what he thought of her poem. Of embarrassing her with a cutting assault on her illusions. That old, familiar qualm passed over him as he imagined himself giving in to his sense of her vulnerability. Jesus, what a good thing it was that he had utterly disgraced himself already.

He unfolded the paper. Below the poem it said, "Thomas Traherne." Oh. These two words deflated his condescension instantly. It seemed both deft and kind of her to put herself beyond the reach of even his fantasy of desolating criticism, though she could hardly have known when she wrote it out that he would have been driven to such a shift, that he would have hoped to smirk inwardly, to destroy his own illusions about her and to snuff out any hope that still lingered in him. At the bottom of the paper she had written *This is true.*

All right.

"For Man to Act as if his Soul did see
The very Brightness of Eternity;
For Man to Act as if his Love did burn
Above the Spheres, even while it's in its Urne."

Oh, too bad. "Urne" is a stretch. Plenty of words rhyme with "burn." This fellow was probably writing before some ideas were all worn out. Love does actually burn, to ashes, which is how it ends up in an urn, presumably. But no one could say that now. "Superannuated" was a word that came to mind. It would sound learned. Actually, she had made herself vulnerable. He could choose to dismiss her poem with a word like that. He found a disheartening comfort in the thought.

> For Man to Act even in the Wilderness,
> As if he did those Sovereign Joys possess,
> Which do at once confirm, stir up, enflame,
> And perfect Angels; having not the same!
> It doth increase the value of his Deeds,
> In this a Man a Seraphim exceeds.

This makes a kind of sense if the stress falls on the second syllable of "perfect," which would make it a verb. He would like to ask her what in this is true. "Sovereign Joys"—when he dared, he would think about that long night with her in Bellefontaine, the beautiful graveyard. So many angels in attendance, not one of them stirred up, enflamed, roused from the encumbrance of her stony flesh, not even the angel that reached toward a baby forever, day and night, and never held her. He laughed at the thought of all those angels ecstatically liberated, finally seeing the fulfillment of everything their presence had promised for so long. This had to be the dream behind all the statuary. The angels would open the caskets and lift up old Mrs. This and young Mr. That, making themselves, to their great joy, much less marvelous and interesting than the recently disinterred. Wings are fine, and a kind of luminosity would be very nice, but to hear a familiar laugh would be an almost unbearable joy, a human joy exceeding anything seraphim could feel, since angels cannot know death. So that much was true, granting his terms. In such a blast and glare of astonishment, what offenses could be remembered? Those who can't hope can still wish. He would not write Della a letter about this, with sketches of angels.

He spent that week offering to put his shoulder to the wheel of commerce and actually landed a stint in a dance studio. He got a haircut and a shoe shine and went back again to that dance pavilion where he had seen Della, and after an hour or two, there she was, with two young women this time. And this time he walked over to her, tipped his hat, and said, "Miss Miles," and her friends smiled at each other and him and stepped away. If she could be brave, given all she had to lose, certainly he could, too. He was glad he had nerved himself to read her poem, and avoided the embarrassments of dealing with the fact that estimable people—his sisters, specifically—could write very bad poems. Glory cried once. She was a little kid, for heaven's sake, and he had subjected her to fairly withering criticism. What a scoundrel he was, before he made a vocation of harmlessness. But people watch your reactions, and try as you might, they are rarely deceived. There was that fellow in prison. A left uppercut before Jack had even gotten to his main point.

And here was Della, standing beside him as if neither of them could ever be anywhere else. The crowd seemed indifferent to them, talking and joking around enough that they drifted to the edge of it, where they could hear each other if they decided to say anything.

Finally Jack said, "I thought Methodists didn't dance."

"Do Presbyterians?"

"This one does."

They drifted beyond the light, and they found that there were steps down to a shabby garden and picnic tables. By then he was holding her hand, her smooth, slender hand, more perfect in his than he ever imagined it would be. And she felt perfect in his arms.

"This is a waltz," he said.

She said, "I know."

They waltzed through four songs, two fast and two slow, and they waltzed in the time between songs and after the last one had ended. Then she said, "I have to find my friends. People *will* be talking!" When she was on the second step, she turned and lifted his hat and smoothed back his hair, kissed his brow, and replaced his hat. So he kissed her cheek. Chaste, chaste. The dourest angel in heaven could not find fault. They stood there together, not speaking, not touching. Then she ran up the steps. He followed, to make sure she was with her friends, and then he went down into the dark to sit at a picnic table and think.

He had a job, a very good thing in the circumstances. He would need to practice a few new steps, but that sort of thing came easily. His fox-trot was absolutely solid. He would be paid, and then he would consider his options. His option, more precisely, which was to bring Della upstairs to his room. There would be the smart remark as they passed the desk, then smirks and stares if other inmates of the place happened to be around, then his room with the door closed, his very orderly room with some kind of curtain thing on the window and two chairs he'd find somewhere. He could push the bed to one side to make room for the chairs and put the wobbly little table beside his bed between the chairs so that if he could think of something to offer her to eat or drink he could do that. It would mean moving the little Bible his father had given him when he found him sitting by the river early one Sunday morning and told him he might as well consider himself confirmed. "A full-fledged member of the invisible church," he said, and laughed, and shook his head. "God willing." He remembered the feeling of his father's hand on his shoulder. The day was calm and still, and his father was enjoying it, enjoying the silence, and Jack was, too. It was the Sabbath. The Reverend had to be elsewhere, but he could hardly bring himself to leave. "Well," he said finally, "dinner will be roast beef. To celebrate," hoping to lure him home. And he took the little book out of his jacket pocket and set it down on the rock beside him, not presuming even to put it in Jack's hand. He said, "The Lord bless you and keep you," to solemnize the moment a little, and then he went away. If Della saw that Bible, she'd know exactly what it was and how many years he had kept it. He had read in it when there was nothing else, which had given it a worn look. It would inevitably redound to his credit with a preacher's daughter. In his mind he put it away in a dresser drawer. He might let her see it sometime, when she knew him better.

Bringing Della upstairs to his room. So he could talk with her, show her whatever he could muster in the way of welcome and courtesy, which was so very little that, weighed against the jokes and insults they might expect, it hardly seemed worth the attempt. Still, he would look around for a radio.

The next day was a Sunday, enforced idleness just when he was filled with new resolve. So he made his bed and shaved and went out for a walk. The city was closed, but the doors of churches were open, releasing gusts of music and sociability, and incense and pot luck and perfume. The particular formal intimacy of reunion in these households, as his father called them. Pious obligation satisfied, pious expectation met. He could forget there were so many churches, opening on the cold pavement, then closing their doors for talk about absolute things in words particular and familiar to them, reminding themselves of their life together and the life to come, singing the old songs. Yes, households, where welcoming the stranger arose often as a subject, as if welcome were what every stranger wanted and strangerliness were without comforts of its own, habit, for example, and some others that were not coming to mind just then. He found himself stepping off the curb to keep apart from the intense little crowds that gathered at these doorways. Poe was exactly right—bells, bells, bells, bells, bells, bells, bells.

He felt a light, fluttering touch of some kind at the back of his neck and swatted at it with his hand. It was a thin strip of fabric, a part of the disintegrating lining of his hat. He took his hat off and was looking into its crown, an odd word for it, thinking whether it would be worth trying to mend the weary satin in some way or glue it down, or if he might as well just tear it out and be done with it. Then a dime dropped into it. He looked up to explain the misunderstanding, but whoever it was, a black man, waved him off, sparing him, as he must have thought, a word of gratitude. When he looked back, there were more nickels and dimes, and an old lady searching her handbag for change. "I was just looking at my hat," he said.

She said, "Of course you were, honey," and added a dime. She said, "You come on in. We're having a nice little dinner afterward. There's always plenty and to spare."

It was a black church, and he would feel like an intruder. That strange embarrassment. On the other hand, he was mortified that he had been taken for a beggar. Whatever depths he might sink to, he generally managed not to sink that far, at least while he was sober. So, to rescue what of himself he could from the ashes of humiliation, he would step into the church to find a place to put the money, a collection plate or something.

The congregation were all sorting themselves among the pews or seated, but there was a young man standing in the narthex, a fellow with the modest dignity of a minor office, a deacon, an usher. Jack held out his hat to him to show him its contents and said, "There was a misunderstanding. I was just looking at the lining of my hat." He couldn't bring himself to actually name the mistake.

"Yes, I see." The young man's tact made Jack aware of what a horrible exposure this was, a nest of satin much stained by use, in partial tatters, the tonic of every previous owner eating away at it. It looked like endless furtive disillusionment, like corrosive thoughts working their way through his skull, dampened a little by habits of embarrassment and regret. And then those pennies and dimes. He said, "I just wanted to give you this." The young man looked at him. So he said, "The money." It was pride as well as the thought of clarifying his meaning that made him take a dollar from his own pocket to add to the hat. "I see," the young man said, and took the hat in his hands, a little gingerly, and then, remembering his office, he said, "Please join us for worship. You're right welcome to join us," and walked off with his hat. It had cost Jack a dollar to lose his hat, a dollar plus considerable mortification. He had gone out for a walk, meaning no harm, and this had befallen him. These little cyphers in the arithmetic of cosmic justice must be as insoluble as the great questions, he supposed. If his error was to imagine that harmlessness was equivalent to insignificance, as if he could elude existence and its consequences by dint of sheer quietism, these thistles sprouted in his solitary path to remind him that meaning could have a decimal point with a thousand 0's before the cypher and still be what it is, could still permit certain conclusions that begin with There's no telling, or There's no escaping. He sat down on the last pew, a few feet from the nearest parishioner.

The preacher was a small man with a big, warm voice. "My dear friends," he said, "let us pray. Let us trust our whole hearts to the Father who knows us and loves us."

A hundred bowed heads. The thought came to Jack that someone here might know Della, a foolish thought. If the population of St. Louis was half black, that doubled the likelihood that any given black person might know her, but the chance would still be minute. This made no sense. It compared black people to an imaginary "people in general," to whom the words "white" or "colored" do not apply, and such people don't exist. Say there were two cities, one black, one white. This was and wasn't true, and was beside the point in any case. The people he was sitting among were Baptists of some kind, as their friends and kin probably were, too, and Della was a Methodist. People don't just know each other at random. But he, as a white man in the black city, felt conspicuous, that is, more likely to come up anecdotally somehow, so that this foolish episode would have an echo. Say he did not recover his hat but they kept the miserable thing in case he came back for it, ready on a table or a shelf so that someone could find it for him. Out of place, in other words. And people would say, Who does that old hat belong to? And the answer would be, You remember that skinny white man that was out begging in front of the church last week, last month, last year? And the story would live on and reach her finally.

He had tried, so far as this calculus of dread permitted attention to what was passing around him, to sway and sing and clap when they did, and to voice the occasional Amen. He was not failing to pass for a Baptist so much as experiencing the fact, whatever this could possibly mean in his case, that he really was a Presbyterian. He had experienced this, though not in so many words, when he realized he had to exchange the double-breasted suit for one that was a little shabbier but which carried no suggestion of bonhomie.

He was so preoccupied with his anxieties the realization came upon him suddenly that he was not far from Sumner, Della's school. He had been careful lately not to walk by it, or near it, but his old habit asserted itself when he seemed to be thinking of other things, more or less. A janitor or librarian might very well live in the neighborhood and come to this church. She would know everything. A surge of shame passed through his body. He felt for his handkerchief. Sweet Jesus, how sudden it was that he was daubing at his face, his eyes stinging, the man beside him watching him now with gentle concern.

Embarrassment overwhelmed him. The preacher had mentioned repentance from time to time without special emphasis. Still, everyone around him must have thought he, Jack, was in the throes of repentance, reconsidering his sullied life. And in fact, he was wondering why he should repent so bitterly when he had done nothing more disgraceful than stop on the pavement to consider the lining of his hat. If the Fall had made sinfulness pervasive and inescapable, then correction might be abrupt and arbitrary, to draw attention to itself as the assurance of an ultimate order without reference to specific wrongs, which, in a post-lapsarian world, must all more or less run together. These are the terms in which he made sense of most bad surprises. They were of little use except in retrospect, which had not arrived yet. And the same young man who had carried off his hat was coming down the aisle, taking the collection, so futile pride compelled Jack to drop his other dollar in the plate. His hat, his two dollars, his personal dignity, and quite possibly any hope he had of maintaining a jot of status in Della's eyes gone because he had decided to go out for a walk. No wonder he had a drinking problem.

He almost left the church without asking after his hat, but he loitered a few minutes, looking around for the young man. The lady who had invited him to come for lunch, dauntlessly cordial, took him by the crook of his arm and led him down some stairs to a basement, more specifically, a church basement, which resembles everything of its kind and nothing else in the world. His heart sank with nostalgia. Chairs and tables battered by merciless use, a frieze of child art on scriptural subjects. An upright piano. There was a kitchen, too, big pots on the stove and the smell of beans cooked with a ham bone, and corn bread. The lady said, "You sit here and I'll bring you a plate. Everybody gets in line and then they start visiting and forget why they're in line in the first place, and folks waiting behind them, getting hungry."

Jack said, "That's very kind of you, ma'am. I seem to have lost my hat." She said, "One thing at a time." And she did bring him beans and corn bread, with a promptness that seemed to suggest she saw him as an emergency. He knew it was his lean and hungry look that rallied old ladies, galvanizing their compassion, making him, in their eyes, a middle-aged orphan. The beans were wonderful, so he ate them even though this would encourage the notion that he was a beggar, not simply a gentleman betrayed by circumstance. The corn bread was also very fine.

She filled his plate again. All that nutrition settled his nerves. Surrounded by so much talking and laughter, he began to feel a little conversational, though he could not think of anything to say to anybody. He went to the piano and touched some keys. *I would be true, for there are those who trust me; / I would be pure, for there are those who care.* This came from the heavy heart of his nostalgia, the anthem of a childhood aspiration he did not himself share.

Somebody said, "Play the song!" So he played it from the beginning, with a few little flourishes. They clapped, and one or two said, "All right!" Then someone said, "Now you play something, Miss Jones. Show him how it's done!" That little woman shook her head, seemed to demur, then sat down and played a most spectacular "Rock of Ages."

"Your turn now, honey," she said.

"I can't do anything like that."

She laughed. "I doubt anybody expects you to."

So he played "The Old Rugged Cross," not quite as he had done for those convict funerals since he was in a church, but close enough. They clapped and said, "Now you, Miss Jones."

She shook her head. "I've got things to do. I've got to get home."

Jack said, "Yes, if I can find my hat, I'll be on my way. And thank you. Thank you very much."

"Well, you come back any time. I could teach you a few things!"

She was laughing, but he said, "That would be very kind."

"Here comes your hat."

The young man came down the steps carrying it upside

down on the tips of his fingers, a weightless vessel, the money still in it. He felt a shock of embarrassment when he saw it. He considered saying, This is a mistake. I was trying to give the money back, I'm not a beggar, but even the thought of the denial embarrassed him. He could hear the civilities through the thrum of blood in his ears—he should come back again, always a nice dinner, that piano doesn't get enough use. Yes, yes, he said, goodbye, certain he would never step through that door again, where everyone would think of him as the beggar out on the pavement, the stranger who wiped away tears at the mere mention of repentance. Where someone might know who he was and carry the piteous tale back to Della, none of it true, but all of it, he knew, entirely believable.

He came back the next Sunday for two reasons. Actually three. He could drop those coins into the collection plate, putting various things right even if no one noticed he had done it. A metaphysics is a great help in rationalizing scruple-driven behavior. Then there was dinner. And there was the fact that that whole week he had been feeling "Blessed Jesus" and "Sweet Hour of Prayer" and even "Holy, Holy, Holy" in his fingers. So he had thought he might as well go back the next Sunday and put himself in the way of some moral edification. He remembered glorious soprano voices rising out of the congregation to second the choir. He even liked the feeling that he stirred that tentative interest, that bated warmth, church people feel toward a stray in their midst.

Things were going well enough at the dance studio. The instructors came early to sprinkle a powdery wax on the floor and walk or waltz it slippery, playing at elegance in preparation for feigning it when customers appeared. They studied charts and followed them out till they could do the steps with a little ease and flair. He would repeat them all day long with his arms around perfumey women. *One* two three, *one* two three. It was an innocuous proof of the oddness of the world, and there was music. On his way home one evening, he bought a small geranium plant with a red blossom on it and set it on his windowsill. This was a first step toward improving the impression his room would make on Della, if he ever actually nerved himself to bring her into it. But the plant deeply changed his own impression of the room. He even dreamed one night that he heard those heavy shoes on the stairs, the police, but this time when they came through the door they were distracted by the sight of the geranium, as if it refuted suspicion, dispelling the mild aversion felt toward him and his kind by the constabulary. Assuming he had a kind. Its implications seemed so great to him, even by light of day, that leaving it where it was an actual decision. It had its effect when he set it on the dresser and on the bedside table.

Saturday came and he had a little money, so he went to a used bookstore, as he had often done lately, with the thought that he might find something to leave on Della's front step. Nothing was adequate, no *très riches heures*. Nothing quaint and curious, no gem of rarest ray serene, in that musty little cave walled with failed efforts of every literary kind, growing drabber together as the years passed. Still, the sheer mass of books and the smell of them always made him imagine the existence of the pure and perfect book, poetry no doubt, just barely translated from some ancient tongue, an earthy strangeness clinging to it. The owner of the place, a large, rumpled man, sat hunched uncomfortably on a high stool and watched him, clearly suspecting him of some legerdemain that would leave him poorer by some worthless tract or memoir. This became a part of Jack's sporadic inquiry into the nature of commerce. The man must value his time at less than nothing, because the world seemed to value his hoard of books at about exactly nothing, and the man was himself a cost, since he had to keep himself in sandwiches and chewing tobacco, not to mention all the odds and ends needed if one is to be even marginally presentable. Add to this the cost of keeping the lights on. Aside from a little sweeping, the man's chief occupation seemed to be watching Jack, who, so as not to disturb this strange equilibrium, never stole anything. It passed the time.

Then it was Sunday again. In preparation Jack had bought himself a newer hat. He retired the old one to a dresser drawer, a sacred object despite all, since Della had touched it. He walked to the church, walked through the door, returned the greeting of the young usher, who seemed glad to see him. He sat down in what he thought of as his pew, exchanging nods with the man who sat next to him.

After the benediction, he went down the stairs, a stream of children passing under his elbow, laughing, intent on some plan they had, all of one mind like a flock of birds. There was an empty table by a far wall and Jack made his way to it, past the smiles and nods and good mornings, which he acknowledged with nods. He sat down. No one joined him, which was the whole idea and embarrassing all the same, not least because they all read correctly his wish to be alone, but would no doubt have failed to notice the ambivalence of it. Miss Jones was nowhere in sight.

It made no sense to be sitting there, trying to seem relaxed and casual, legs crossed, arms crossed, twiddling a foot, nowhere to look. He thought, the heat that made him sweat was just heat, and the light that made him feel so exposed in that dim corner was just light, and if there were a time when everything dispersed through the universe gathered into its essence, this would be heat indeed, light indeed, rid of the dilutions that sometimes made them into warmth and illumination, those blandishments. This heat would be hot enough to burn in. Ergo the existence of hell was indisputable. If he could just see where the plates were stacked, he could step into the line without drawing so much attention to himself, without having to ask anybody. It seemed like a presumption to join the line, somehow much worse than theft. You can't actually steal food from a church supper. Too bad.

And sure enough, here came the minister, carrying two plates. He paused to speak with a family at another table. People always want to speak with the minister. They chatted and laughed a little, and then he came on to Jack's table and set a plate in front of him and another opposite, and said, "Please sit down," which made Jack realize he had stood up, though this man did not resemble his father. "I thought you might want a little something. Beans and rice. You know how it is. The churches have to squeeze every penny." This was to make Jack feel more like a guest, less like a mendicant. His father would have said the same kind of thing to some shabby exotic. "Yes," he would have said afterward, "an unusual fellow. He seemed bright enough. Maybe a little shifty." And the stranger would have stepped out of loneliness, moved by hope or nostalgia, then slipped back into loneliness, forgotten as soon as he was gone. Jack could see that the minister was taking his measure, so tactfully it was almost painless. There was the frayed cuff. He didn't cover it with his hand, but he could feel that slight, hard smile forming—I know what you see, I know what you think—and looked down to conceal it. The man was trying to decide how to speak to him. He said, "I'm the pastor here, Samuel Hutchins." He held out his hand across the table.

"John Ames," Jack said, for some reason, and shook his hand.

"You're a son of the church, I take it."

"Yes. Not really. My father is a minister. Was. He's still alive. The last I heard. He lost his church. My fault, I believe." He cleared his throat, which is a thing people do sometimes to sound reasonable when otherwise they might not.

"You certainly know the songs. I believe I heard you playing last Sunday."

He said, "They're hard to unlearn." Then, "I have great respect for my father. I didn't mean to suggest—"

"No, I understand that. It can be difficult, being a minister's son. I see that fairly often. Maybe the admiration is part of the problem."

"I'm not at all like him. I look like him. People used to say that. But I know age has been hard on him. Then my mother died. And I am"—he shrugged—"what I am."

The minister was watching him from that calm distance of kindly appraisal, probably because Jack was talking a little too fast, for one thing. He said, "Maybe you're looking for someone to tell you to go home and spend a little time with your father. I'd be happy to do that for you. Say the word." He said, "You look to me like you could use a little forgiving."

Jack said, "He's forgiven me every day of my life from the day I was born. Breech birth." He wished he could smoke. Where was all this candor coming from? He said, "Forgiveness scares me. It seems like a kind of antidote to regret, and there are things I haven't regretted sufficiently. And never will. I know that for a fact."

The minister removed his glasses, heavy lenses and gold wire frames that had settled into his face like one more feature. When he took them off, the skin around his eyes looked tender, like a

\private self. He rubbed his eyes with a finger and thumb and polished the lenses with the corner of a very large handkerchief—"I have to be ready for grief," Jack's father had said once. "You don't always see it coming." He was meticulously ironing, then folding, a dozen big handkerchiefs.

The minister put his glasses on again and smiled as if he were just back from a brief absence. He said, "Mr. Ames, if the Lord thinks you need punishing, you can trust Him to see to it. He knows where to find you. If He's showing you a little grace in the meantime, He probably won't mind if you enjoy it."

Jack said, "I'm not sure that's what's happening. It's not always clear to me how to tell grace from, you know, punishment. Granting your terms." If the thought of someone sweetened your life to the point of making it tolerable, even while you knew that just to be seen walking down the street with her might do her harm, which one was that? He said, "I don't actually believe in God. I'm sorry. That probably means I've been wasting your time."

"No, no." The minister said quietly, reflectively, "That's what it all comes down to, isn't it. The great question."

"I've never even understood the difference between faith and presumption. Never." He noticed a slightly aggressive urgency in his voice that he would not have expected to hear from himself.

The minister glanced at his watch. He said, "I have a meeting in three minutes. So I have three minutes to answer your question, or you can come back next Sunday, when I've had a week to think it over."

"Next week. I'll try to be here." Such a busy man.

"I'd take it as a kindness. I'm going to be thinking about this. Your word was 'presumption'? Don't get up."

But he did, and they shook hands. When he picked up his

plate, a young woman said, "Let me take care of that for you!" with that particular warm emphasis of a kindness that means more than itself—nobody cares how much you don't belong here, at least I don't. Jack nodded and went up the stairs before anyone else could speak to him. But there was the minister, coming back down. "I was looking for you, Mr. Ames. I just wanted another word or two, if you don't mind." He said, quietly, "You're all right?" A question without that irritating lilt.

"Yes. Fine."

The minister, half a head shorter than he and two steps above him, studied his face. "Well, I'm glad to hear that," he said. "Sometimes when people come to me with, you know, big questions, I find out that there's something else on their minds. Besides that question."

"What? Suicide? I can't do that. Not while he's alive. My father. So I'm all right." Jack saw a startled tenderness in the man's eyes and looked away. He thought, If I told the truth more often, I might be better at it.

The minister rested his hand lightly on Jack's shoulder. "Well, that's good to know. That you're all right," as if he had put his doubts aside. "That's good," he said. "You take care now," and Jack stepped past him into the foyer and out the door.

Once out on the pavement, he set his hat at a tilt that meant he was not the sort of man who would find himself in a church. Rakish. He lit a cigarette. He felt himself assuming himself again, and it was almost a relief. Those handkerchiefs, white, identical except for the tiny mending his mother made in them where the fabric might wear through. No telling which one had wiped sweat off the face of the woman dying in labor, which one had blotted an orphan's tears. When his father took a handkerchief from his pocket to wipe milk from Jack's chin, it felt like an induction into intolerable mysteries. He did not let himself inhale. This minister was polishing lenses that shone already with a corner of Lazarus's shroud, carefully laundered for its next use. These ministers were far too familiar with absolute things. Jack was startled when he heard the word "suicide," though he was the one who said it. Well, another thing to worry about.

Reverend Hutchins was a serious man, which placed Jack under a kind of obligation to be honest with him. This was the best interpretation he could make of his own behavior. He had heard himself telling, as if to his father, the very things he would never tell his father. Well, Hutchins did seem to be shaped by and for discretion. His vest was close, not tight, not new either, a sign of self-discipline persisted in for years. He was one of those people who look away when you speak to them, as if watching a story or an idea form under his gaze, ready to laugh or to add something or to ponder the sadness of a tale that was now as much his as it was the teller's. A respectful man. And Jack would go back the following Sunday to prove he was not dead, which seemed fair in the circumstances.

When he reached the rooming house and went upstairs to his room, he found the clerk and some friend of his looking at his geranium, fists on their hips, which means, more or less, What the hell?! The clerk turned to him. "A flower?"

"One. No harm in it."

"Nobody brings flowers in here."

"It's a geranium," Jack said, pointlessly.

"Who gives a damn what it is?"

Unanswerable.

"Anyway, it's too damn clean in here. Expecting company, I suppose. This is a respectable house, remember." It wasn't, but there was no point getting into that. Jack could feel the flush rising in his face that meant he would sweat. His whole miserable plan, already given the worst possible interpretation just because he'd put a blasted flower on a windowsill. He thought this as he also thought how ridiculous he'd look delving around in his pockets for his handkerchief, or wiping his face on his sleeve, or just standing there sweating. The clerk looked at him, almost smiling, and said to the other guy, "We've got work to get to," and they left. A joke, but a warning, too. I can humiliate you if I feel like it, with this company of yours here to watch.

Jack did not linger ten seconds over the thought of homicide. Suicide crossed his mind, but he really had forsworn it. That was true. There remained to comfort him an unformed plan to slip down the fire escape and abscond when the rent came due. He had thought through this plan a hundred times, or a thousand, as often as a man with no violent impulses might let himself dream of retaliation. If the bed where he lay was its center, then the area around it in which he might encounter the defrauded clerk on the street was the radius that determined the circumference within which he had better not find another room. Beyond lay all St. Louis and the world. There was the cemetery, but there was also a limit to how long he could stand to go without shaving. A day or two. He hated sleeping in his clothes. Neither would be practical for someone employed as a dance instructor, in any case. He spent an hour or two attempting to ponder how gross disproportion, incommensurability, could be a structural principle of Creation. Mighty hostility pitted against harmless fantasy. The cosmic disorder. The disorder of things. There were no books with these titles, so far as he could discover, and he had looked.

So here he was, buffeted like Satan, falling through the billowing voids. He could not stop himself from thinking that triviality added to triviality however many times should finally have some of the qualities of nothingness, nonbeing. But instead, a plan he would no doubt never act on, but which seemed somehow to consecrate his shabby life *ex nihilo*, a pleasant anticipation that seemed as real as daylight, could collapse into the nothing it always had been because somebody made a cheap joke. He and the clerk were alike in that neither of them mattered at all. Absent either of them, no one would look at the universe and say, Very nice, only one thing missing. This being the case, why could his mind create a demi-paradise, and the clerk destroy it, creating and de-creating like warring gods? At least this is how it seemed to him at the moment. Meaninglessness was no refuge. Giant miseries and giant hopes can carry on their wars in the merest cranny.

Then the door opened partway and the clerk tossed a small cat onto Jack's bed. "Dames like cats," he said, and closed the door. This was conciliatory. Jack could think of no other way to interpret it, though he was, of course, cautious. It was a passable cat. Gray with darker gray stripes. Or the other way around. It did not limp or cough. Eyes, ears, and tail were all intact. If there was a trick involving the cat, there was nothing obvious about it. It curled up against his side. When he touched it, it purred.

Whatever was pleasing about the plant was much enhanced by the cat. Here he was, again imagining Della stepping into his room, quietly, tentatively. She would glance around to see what kind of room it was, and be charmed by something, reassured. At first it was the stack of library books on his dresser, all of them poetry. Then it was the flower and the books. He put the little picture of the river on the dresser, too, then put it back in his suitcase, because if the clerk noticed it, he might steal it, literally or in effect. But the cat sleeping in the sunlight by the geranium—he would have to look at her face, the way it brightened and softened when she saw something that charmed her. And then he would ask her to sit down, but she would go to the window first and, say, touch a sleeping paw, make an ear flick.

Sardines ought to please a cat. He picked it up, hand under its belly, and carried it downstairs, alert but unresisting, an animal for which the world was no longer a matter of the somber urges and competences it had felt emerging in its sinews and bones, urges that sent it prowling among the unstartled sparrows and cold-eyed gulls scavenging at the same garbage cans it did. Jack slipped it into his pocket for the moments he spent buying a box of crackers and a tin of sardines.

He sat down on the stoop of the rooming house, rolled back the lid of the tin, and put one little fish on his palm. The cat ate it, propping itself with its paws, and scrubbed Jack's hand with its tongue. Another sardine. The third and fourth Jack put on a cracker for himself. Pleasant enough, a man and his cat. It leaped down into the bushes to do the meticulous business of scratching the ground and covering the place. Then it came back to him. He picked it up again, hand under its belly because he liked to feel its heart beating, and went inside.

The clerk said, "What do you think of the cat?"

"It seems decent enough."

"You don't like it?"

"I like it well enough."

"All right. Five bucks."

"What?"

"Three-fifty. I'll put it on your tab."

"You're trying to sell me a cat? It's just like every cat in every alley in St. Louis!"

"True. And there's a rule against cats in this house, anyway.

Dogs. And there's nothing particular about it, so there's no reason to pay me for it. That's true."

Jack had looked it over carefully. It had no distinguishing marks of any kind. It was too young to have any distinguishing behaviors. "This is ridiculous," he said, and put it back in his pocket. But this time it jumped out and ran. The clerk caught it up in his hand and chucked it out the door. "There are a million more just like it," he said. "Give me a few bucks every now and then to cover damages and I'll look the other way. If you decide you want a cat."

Jack stepped out the door. No cat in sight. He walked around a little, disgruntling pigeons, looking into garbage cans and around them with an interest that must have appeared fairly pitiful to passersby. Then he went to the shop where he had bought the sardines and got another tin. He was beginning to add up the expenses involving this cat. But he sat back down on the stoop with the open tin beside him. Two cats appeared, then a third, all gray with gray stripes, all half grown. Then a small, cautious fourth, gray with gray stripes. He held out a sardine to it on the fingers of one hand, grabbed it with the other, and left the oily tin on the stoop for the rest of them to fight over. As he walked in past the desk, the clerk looked up from his newspaper. He said, "That's not the same cat."

Jack said, "It'll do," feigning an indifference he could not actually feel. When he got to his room and closed the door, he examined the creature for any distinguishing features that would prove it was not his cat, but it had none, which proved absolutely nothing. How could this be? That part of his mind was off searching for equivalences again. Every defect is singular, but a perfect cat is indistinguishable from a million others, in theory, even though in fact there might be just one perfect cat. Well, he'd call this his cat and put a mark on it, a nick in an ear, a missing toe, so he would not be tricked into wasting sardines on a cat that had no claim on him. It disgusted him to think of marring the creature. So he patted aftershave on it, to distinguish it from the street cats if this was necessary again. It ran under the dresser and hissed at his shoe. He fetched it out and set it on the windowsill. It jumped down. He put it back again. It jumped down.

The clerk usually went wherever he went about nine o'clock and came back in forty minutes smelling of an unenviable supper. When Jack heard the front door close behind him, he reached under the dresser for the cat, doused it with aftershave, reasoning that it was very likely to attempt an escape, and bundled it into that brown V-neck sweater with the leather elbow patches and antique buttons Teddy had left for him, which was kindly intended certainly but which could only mean his earnest and loyal brother had, unbeknownst to himself, forgotten him. Through the loose fabric he felt the prickle of tiny fangs and still transparent claws far longer than he expected to, and then it fell asleep. He walked for miles. Never allowing himself a doubt about whether wisdom or decent manners should have intervened, he came to Della's house and sat down on her stoop. To sit there in the dark was his whole intention. What the hell, anyway. It would be his adieu. She would know this somehow. A reeking stray might cross her path, and she would think of Jack, suddenly, unaccountably. He almost laughed.

The porch light flicked on, then off, and the door opened. Della stepped out. "I thought it was you," she said, and she sat down beside him. Furry slippers, a puffy robe, hair in curlers tied up in a kerchief. Dear Lord, she was still warm from a bath. She said, "No one doesn't make any noise like you don't make any noise."

Wonderful. The sound of her voice was more than a relief to

him, quintessentially companionable, as if the two of them were together in the world, uniquely, like two strayed angels, despite anything and everything. He said, "I thought you might want a cat." He caught it before it could escape the bundled sweater and handed it to her, hissing. Why did he do that? He knew in the dark it was making a fiend of itself, bared teeth, flattened ears, slitted eyes, hind legs digging at her hand. "My landlord doesn't want me to keep it. Here, you'd better let me hold it."

It bit and struggled against her hands and fetched up wailing growls from its tiny body, but she pulled the sleeves of her robe down over her hands and kept hold of it. She began to laugh. "It smells like Old Spice," she said. "A *lot* of Old Spice."

"I can explain that," he said, though he'd rather die.

"Now I have to go in, smelling of aftershave! Aftershave all over me! I'll just say—what am I going to say? The house will smell like this for a month." There was laughter in her voice, thank God, because she had every reason to be mad at him. He should have thought this through, but he hadn't expected to actually see her.

"I didn't really expect to see you," he said.

"You were just going to sit here in the dark? You and your cat? You couldn't spare me a knock on the door?"

He said, "Della, I'm ridiculous. It never changes. Every day is a new proof. An entirely sufficient proof. This probably isn't even my cat. For example." No point getting into that. He said, "It would be like a curse, the everlastingness of it, except that it is so trifling, so meaningless. Half the time, when something happens, I'm thinking, Thank God Della didn't see that. I wanted to say goodbye to you. In my mind, anyway. And I knew it would calm me, just being here for a few minutes. One last time." He said, "'All losses are restored, and sorrows end.' One last time."

"I love that poem," she said softly. "'Dear friend.'"

"Yes."

They were quiet.

Then she said, "Is this the only time you've come here like this? Because there have been other times when I thought you were here, but when I looked, you weren't, and I thought you'd slipped away and I'd missed you. So here I am in my bathrobe with curlers in my hair, because I didn't want to miss you this time."

"Thank you."

"You're welcome."

"That means a great deal to me."

After a minute, she said, "It's real. That peace."

"'The peace that passes all understanding.' Sorry. I shouldn't joke—"

"No, it really does pass understanding. That has to mean something."

"Nothing has to mean something. So far as I can tell. Well, it does mean I'm much too happy to be where I shouldn't be. Which is here on your stoop. But that is its effect, which is not the same as its meaning, if it has one, I realize." The light from the streetlamp shone softly on her eyes, the planes of her face. She had taken to rubbing the cat's belly. Pensive.

After a while, she said, "If you make a sound it's just a sound, unless it belongs to a language, and then it's a word. It means something. It can't not mean something."

"'Day to day pours forth speech, / and night to night declares knowledge. / There is no speech, nor are there words; their voice is not heard; / Yet their voice goes out through all the earth, / and their words to the end of the world.' Is that what you mean? I used to memorize things. I was pretty good at it. I've forgotten

176

the rest. The sun, 'like a strong man runs its course with joy.' And so on." He said, "Did you just come up with that? The thing you were saying about words? It was pretty interesting."

"Oh no. I believe I came up with that about a week ago. You and I argue in my mind all the time. Often I win." She laughed. "I'm serious, though."

"So if I were to grant what I can't grant, everything would begin to make sense."

"Well, put it the other way. If, certain things being granted, the world began to make sense, that would be a reason to have some respect for the——hypothesis."

He truly did respect the hypothesis, and yet, feeling that old thrill of dread and compulsion, he knew circumstance had once again put him too close to a fragile thing. He said, "Look at the life we live, Della. I have to sneak over here in the dark just to steal a few words with you. Is that language, or is it noise?"

She said, "It's noise that you have to do it, and language that you do it, anyway." She said softly, "Maybe poetry."

Well, he would be thinking about that for a while, conjuring a memory of the flush of happiness that startled him at the time. Why should an emotion like that be as sudden as fear is? What use is it, when there's nothing to be done with it? The body imposes on itself a few seconds of pleasurable confusion, of vulnerability. Why? He stood up and stepped away from her, mainly just to look at her, her kerchiefed head and slender neck and that big robe falling around her. Chenille, sisterly and commonplace, probably pink, but so elegant in the faint light.

She stood up, too, abruptly. She said, "I have to keep this cat. He's my alibi." And she went up the steps to her door and went inside. He heard her speak to Lorraine, "I'm sorry if we kept you from sleeping. I know, Lorraine, I'm sorry." And the door closed.

But it didn't lock. So he took off his hat and he opened the door and stepped into that room, the little table by the window, the picture of Jesus on the piano, all of it so familiar, or at least so precisely remembered, that he almost felt as though he had some right to be there.

Lorraine said, "Now, what do you think you're doing in here, walking in like that. You go away. I'm about to start yelling."

But, what the hell, anyway, he went to Della and put his arms around her.

"Just a second," she said, and put the cat on the couch, and then she came back into his arms, and there they were.

Lorraine said, "They're going to be hearing about this in Memphis, I can tell you that for sure," and more to the same effect, but he held Della, and he kissed her lips. And she kissed his lips. It was entirely mutual, perfectly simultaneous, he was sure of it. There was no one to blame. He was about to say, I love you very much, thinking he might expect a reply of some kind. She said, "Goodbye" and stepped away from him, turned away from him.

And then he was out on the stoop, adjusting his hat. The door opened again wide enough for Lorraine to nudge the kitten out after him with the toe of her slipper. He leaned against a fence a few houses down and lit a cigarette. Della came out onto her stoop with a coat over her robe and in street shoes. She saw him, he smiled and lifted his hat, turned his back and walked away. He thought he might hear her following him, but she really did just let him walk away.

Sunday night. Everything was dark, everything was closed. He was walking just to be walking. Did he want to show up for work tomorrow to help a few ladies improve their mambo?

No. Would he? Yes. What a ridiculous life. But having a little money was good, and he got along with those ladies better than he usually did with people. Of course, sometimes they brought him a wedge of cake or half a batch of fudge. That was part of the economics of the universe. There were big freckled mirrors on the walls of the studio. Sometimes he could not avoid catching a glimpse of himself, seeing that strange excess of grace that looked like parody, and that now and then drew a cold glance from the manager of the place. Ah well. He might get an hour or two of sleep, pull himself together, and show up for work. The ladies would be glad to see him. They were flattered by his courtesy, somehow delighted when he made a joke of it—"You're looking unusually lovely today"—and her name, if he remembered it.

When payday came, he would spend the money drinking himself to death, more or less, and wake as wretched in mind and body as he already was in spirit. He would let himself think of Della, and rage and grieve from his very depths, and let himself feel his regret and embarrassment and his dreadful loneliness. After that, who knows. That one motive he had for going on was beginning to seem a little inadequate.

He lay on his bed without sleeping until almost dawn. Then he decided to rouse himself, to do some other kind of nothing until the sun was up. He put his feet on the floor and switched on the light, and then he saw a letter, which someone had apparently slid under the door. The envelope had the mark of a shoe print on it, no doubt his. So it had been there all night, maybe most of the previous day. The desk clerk let mail accumulate in a drawer until he had a better reason to come upstairs. Teddy seemed to accept the other rooming house as his address. His boss knew where he lived. Della knew. So he was probably being fired. He left it lying there. Reproof has its sting, no matter who has taken it upon himself to administer it. His boss had bow legs and no sense of rhythm. No one brought *him* cake. And *he* was the one who got to do the firing. The very smallness of it all loomed over Jack gigantically.

But, just in case, he did finally pick up the letter, and he saw the lucid script and the return address. This set off a storm of emotions he waited out flat on his back with his pillow over his face. When he sat up again and opened it, he saw the words *Dear Friend*. Sweet Jesus, when she saw him last night, she must have thought he had read her letter. "Dear friend," she had said. "While I think on thee." She had not said that. Still, how painful could any letter be that began with those two words? *On Monday I leave for Memphis.* Oh. That was painful.

> *My family is concerned that I might be losing my way. They think I may have forgotten who I am, and the hope they have placed in me. I regret all the worry I have caused them, of course. And truly, sometimes I do wonder who I am. I believe this is a question I must try to answer for myself. Not long ago I thought I had answered it, and so did they. I truly hope they will help me to feel that way again. I have such respect for them, and I hate the thought that they might lose respect for me. There is really nothing I fear more.*
>
> *You have been a gracious companion through this long night, and I will always be grateful.*
> *Della*

He was swooping his way through "The Tennessee Waltz," a little inattentive to the very small woman who was trying to keep up with him and growing winded from the effort, when he realized that he could talk things over with Reverend Hutchins. He had an idea that he thought might be worth acting on. He would go to Memphis, find Della's father's church, sit through a sermon, and on his way out the door, as they shook hands, he would say, "Reverend Miles, I want to assure you that my relationship with your daughter was entirely honorable." If he saw Della, he would do no more than nod to her. And he would nod to her brothers, unembarrassed by the fact that he had once appeared disreputable to them. It would be the humble act of a proud man, as it would have to be in order to be believed. The point of it all must be to seem capable of offering such an assurance for Della's sake, to defend her honor, as they say. The fact that what he would say was absolutely true was almost a problem. Being believed when disbelief is only reinforced by the effort to persuade, by the fear of failing to persuade, this is a problem he had encountered thousands of times. He could not calibrate his sincerity when he hoped to make an impression with it. Butter wouldn't melt in his mouth, they said or thought, when he was still young enough to have made the experiment and to have been relieved by the result.

He knew his awareness that a thousand things could go wrong made it certain that they would. There was no recovering that moment of purpose and optimism. But Reverend Hutchins might help him see things in a better light. This still seemed possible. So, once he was done with work, once he had led the last winded lady back to the bench where she had left her handbag, he was down the stairs and out the door and down the street on his way to Mount Zion Baptist Church.

It was a Tuesday. But he thought this plan would have its best effect if he carried it out promptly, before he lost the last of his resolve, before his motives began to shift into self-protectiveness—Your daughter and I were never close, nothing to worry about there, nothing at all—this with a worldly smile. He might have paused to light a cigarette. A hard man, probably not the type to trifle with a schoolteacher.

There was a light on in the church on the second floor, no doubt the minister's study. It was one of those big urban churches built in a spirit of optimism that passing years and eminent domain had failed to justify, a hulk trimmed with wooden fretwork losing its paint to the rain. He tried three doors before he found one that opened and stepped into the darker evening of a hallway and a stairway. There was a smell of recent popcorn in the air that aroused memories of youth, but the building was quiet now. He walked up the stairs, scuffing his shoes enough, he thought, to seem not at all furtive. Still, when he stepped through the half-open study door, the minister startled and dropped his book. Another plan he had not thought through.

But the minister was laughing. "Mr. Ames, isn't it? Come in, come in. I guess I was just lost in my reading." Convincing affability, and at the same time that tactful glance of appraisal, reasonable in the circumstances, since Jack could be deranged, for all he knew. "Take a seat," he said. "Please."

Jack the potential suicide. That was where matters had been left the previous Sunday. Sometimes his father would come back from some urgent conversation, plainly exasperated that someone's sanity or survival was thrust into his hands, suddenly a problem he should solve, comfort and assurance ready at the shortest possible notice. These attempts at rescue would keep him awake the whole night, thinking what he really should have said and how he might have been misinterpreted. "They keep *doing* it!" he said. That was the year a hailstorm stove the corn crop. But so much despair must have more than one cause. "If this was growing on him, he could at least have given some sort of warning!" Jack's mother would say, "He'll be down at the store, shooting the breeze with all the other suicides." And this was almost always true.

And here was this poor Hutchins, trying to figure out whom or what he was dealing with. The study was a small room, mustard yellow, furnished with the scantest odds and ends, no doubt in deference to a thousand higher claims on the church's resources. Books were stacked on the desk and floor. The room was lit by a single bulb hanging by its cord from the ceiling, the kind of light that brings out the full pallor of a pallid man and makes shadows of his eyes. I should leave, Jack thought, but his only hope of seeming rational was to muster a little conversation first. Short of that, he would be embarrassed to show up for beans and rice and "Nearer, My God, to Thee," though he knew he would do it, anyway.

"I'm sorry I've disturbed you, Reverend. I saw your light."

"Sit down, please, Mr. Ames. I have three grandbabies at my house just now, so I'm here for the quiet."

"I've disturbed you."

"No, that's all right. And since you're here, you might as well tell me what you have on your mind."

"Well, I'm not quite sure."

"All right. Think about it. There's no rush." After a minute spent fiddling with a pencil, he said, "You did mention a problem you have telling the difference between faith and presumption."

"Yes, I did. Mention that. I do have that problem."

"But that isn't why you came here this evening."

"No. In fact, sir, there's a woman." He had actually said it.

"I see."

"I hardly know her. We spent one night wandering around Bellefontaine. The cemetery. Just talking together. That was months ago. I have seen her a few times since then. It's very difficult."

Did the minister know that the lenses of his glasses were as opaque as two moons? A little backward tilt of his head and his eyes vanished. It was an odd thing to say, that they had passed a night in the cemetery. He almost said, "She's all right, she's fine," since the mention of the cemetery sounded sinister. That thing was happening again, when the cherished thought withers in the light of the slightest attention. "I should go," he said, and stood up. Then he said, "No matter what you might think of me, Reverend, you must understand that my relationship—friendship—with this woman was entirely honorable. Her family despise me, so I couldn't persuade them if I tried, but I worry that they might think less of her because of me. I'll never see her again. For her sake. But her family won't know how to interpret that. They'll think I didn't really care about her, when she may be the only thing I've ever cared about. So I was very careful, how I acted toward her. When I met her, I was just out of prison, which is, you know, a very emotional time, but it was much more— I've never told her I've been in prison. There are some other things she doesn't know—why frighten her?" Jack thought, Sweet Jesus, listen to me. I *am* crazy.

The minister nodded. "The way things stand, there wouldn't be much point. You said you're not planning to speak with her again, anyway."

Embarrassing. He never did quite remember that intention, that vow. It's true, the Old Gent was right, it helps to talk to someone sometimes, to keep your thinking straight. The minister leaned toward him, and his eyes appeared again, still tactfully appraising. He said, "It's an excellent thing to be able to say you have been honorable. If you leave things as they are, stop trying to see her, you will always be able to say that, for the rest of your life. You will know it, she will know it, the Lord will know it. So you can feel good about that. Her family—that's a problem that might get worse if you try to solve it."

Jack sat down again, assuming Hutchins had forgotten to ask him to. He said, "I've never said a word to anyone about this. Her name is Della." He laughed. "I've probably said it two or three times, to her, no one else. Della. She's been to college. She teaches high school. We like to talk." He shrugged. "It's amazing to me that any of it could have happened." He said, "That punishing grace we talked about. She's gone back to Memphis to try to put things right with her family. Her father's a minister there. A.M.E."

"Oh." The minister picked up his pencil again. "So we're talking about a colored lady here."

"Yes. That's part of the problem. I mean, part of what makes it so hard just to sit down with her and talk about something for a few minutes."

"Well, that might be for the best, don't you think? It might be best for her. She'll be wanting to make a life for herself."

"I know. It would have been kind of me to stay away from her completely. I tried a few times."

The minister said, "It would have been kind of her to encourage that. For your sake."

"She tried, a few times."

Hutchins seemed less cordial, now that he knew Della was black. He said, "A woman with her opportunities also has important obligations."

"She is aware of that. So am I."

"Well, then," he said, as if the conclusion to be drawn were too obvious to be put into words. As in fact it was.

"I really have no intention of trying to see her again. Her father is pastor of a big church. He'll be easy to find. I'll go there on a Sunday, tell him that, and leave. Because it does seem to me it might be a good thing for Della if he had a better opinion of me."

That appraising look again. "Possible," he said, in a tone that meant, Not possible. He said, "You should be prepared for the fact that he won't want a better opinion of you. I mean that, at best, he has no use for it. If you were the most impeccable white gentleman on earth, to him you would most likely just be trouble."

It surprised Jack to realize that, in some part of his mind, he aspired to being an impeccable white gentleman. On the one hand, there was jail time and destitution and a slightly battered face, and on the other, there were neckties and polished shoes and a number of lines of Milton. This might be a wholly groundless pretense, but he couldn't stop pretending. It was this or dissolution. He had abruptly confronted the fact that there was nothing to recommend him to anyone, which was a more profound concession than the situation actually asked of him. The minister sat quietly, fiddling with his pencil, seeing, apparently, that Jack needed a minute to recover himself.

Della's letter was in his pocket! "Look at this. She sent me this letter." Jack took it out and started to remove it from its envelope, then put it back in, so that Hutchins would see it really was addressed to him. Then he remembered he hadn't introduced himself by his actual name. But the minister didn't seem to notice. He took the letter from him, removed the slip of paper with pleasing care, and read it over.

He raised his eyebrows. "That's quite a letter!" he said, and handed it back to him. "'Dear friend, gracious companion.' She thinks a lot of you. I see that."

"Good behavior," Jack said. A little cynicism could damp down earnest conversation as needed. And why should he have let this stranger see her precious words? He had to try to get some distance. What might he do next?

"No, no," Hutchins said. "To be gracious is a gift. Lots of people can't manage it. You can be very proud of that. What she says there."

"Really? That sounds like a problem, theologically speaking."

"Well, then, let's just say I'd be proud that someone said those things to me."

Jack said, "It's gracious of you to sit here while I talk. A stranger. A bum, actually. Though at the moment I'm employed." Did Baptists approve of dancing? No point getting into that.

"It's been interesting. I'm not sure I've been entirely gracious in what I've been saying to you. I just wanted you to know that going to Memphis might be a disappointment for you. You could get hurt. Your feelings, I mean."

Jack laughed. "I'm really not fragile."

Hutchins shook his head. "Trust me, son. If I'm any judge of these things, you'd better take care. You'd better not be looking for ways to test yourself. Maybe you don't quite realize what you're living through already."

This summary of his situation struck Jack like a bolt of frozen grief. Those days to get through, those months, those years. Hutchins opened a desk drawer and handed him a handkerchief. Jack thought, I guess I'm crying. Nothing to be done about it.

After a few minutes, Hutchins said, "One last thing. Would this lady we're speaking about be a Miss Miles?"

"How did you know?"

"Well, her father is Bishop James Miles. He's much admired in certain circles. A very imposing man. I heard she was in town, at Sumner. I know her pastor."

Jack said, "Sweet Jesus! A bishop! She never told me that." And he laughed. "Sorry."

"So you'd be dealing with a very prominent family, very devoted to the betterment of the race—"

"—and in wanders Jack Boughton, a textbook case of human degeneracy!" He was laughing, painfully, and the minister was laughing a little, too.

"Jack Boughton?"

"Yes. My actual name. Who I really am."

Hutchins said, "As it happens, you *have* wandered in on the most respectable family on this round earth. *Everybody* is a little scared of them." He said, "I shouldn't be laughing. They're fine folks, all of them, their great-aunts and their third cousins, so I'm told. They'd make you quite a set of in-laws. They'd put you on the narrow path, for sure."

"If the police did not intervene in my choice of in-laws. And, theoretically, their choice of me."

"Well, yes, of course."

They were silent. Then Jack said, "I was just out of prison, still a little light-headed from the change. I was carrying an umbrella I stole from an old man dozing on a park bench, and I was wearing a black suit I bought with money my father sent me for my mother's funeral, which, as it happened, I did not attend." He looked at the minister for the expression of regret and disapproval, and there it was. He said, "It began to rain, to storm, really. I saw a young woman with an armful of books and papers, trying to pull a scarf up over her head. Some of the papers were slipping out of her arms and falling on the sidewalk, blowing down the street. So I crossed the street and gave her the umbrella and gathered up the papers for her. She said, 'Thank you, Reverend,' and invited me in for tea. We talked about poetry." He laughed. "It was very nice. I let her know I wasn't a minister, after a while. I mean, she found out. It didn't seem to matter too much."

Hutchins had been looking to the side, this tale of small gallantry unfolding before his mind's eye. "That's a nice story," he said. "All in all. I'm telling people all the time, take any chance you get to do a kindness. There's no telling what might come of it."

Jack was folding the handkerchief on his knee, fully intending to give it back. "There's a world of truth in that. In my case, I guess I know what came of it." He laughed, and the minister just shook his head. When he was almost out the door, he said, "So you're not going to try to save me."

"If you ever want me to, I might give it a try. Meantime, the ladies are putting together a dessert this Sunday. Somebody's birthday." He came to the door. He said, "You take care. That's the first thing."

He thought sometimes that he might tell Della just enough to let himself feel he had not been entirely dishonest with her. Two years—if that had been his sentence, and he would let her think it was, two years were almost nothing, at least in terms of the degree of criminality that would rouse society to such measured retaliation. It was almost an endorsement of his character. The terrible part was that, on the day of his arrest, he just happened to have been indulging that old thievish impulse, in imagination only, not to the point of acting on it. Palming some trifle, feeling thine dissolving into mine in the damp of his hand, was a familiar pleasure, one he could almost summon at will.

And there was the problem. It was as if his habit of guilt and guile, in the light of official suspicion, had conjured the small storm of larceny that had overwhelmed him, making nonsense of his protestations. To be fair, he was not entirely persuaded by them himself. Then prison, a simpler mystery than the outside world, clearer in its expectations, which were shouted and sometimes underscored with nightsticks. It was frightening that he took a very small comfort from the relative predictability of it all. What was the phrase? A sense of belonging.

What could this mean for the future? What hope of reform? If he was a thief to the marrow of his bones, essentially and, perhaps, everlastingly, what would keep further punishment, random yet condign, from embarrassing him every now and then for as long as he lived? He could never say, *I used to be a thief,* when any cop on a corner seemed to know otherwise. The plain truth, two years for crimes he did not commit, would be deception. Better to leave things as they were.

If he could get past the word "prison." "Penitentiary" was worse. He had not been guilty of theft that day, strictly speaking, though another day he might have been. One man's disorder was the next man's opportunity, and pawnshops were random assortments of things that might be there one day and gone the next, in any case. Would anyone even bother keeping track of the trifles he considered stealing? No theft was truly harmless, granted. Thou shalt not—a categorical prohibition. A violation of the courtesy we owe one another, his father said. Yet there were gray areas. In a pawnshop everything belonged to someone and was surrendered only conditionally and under duress, which meant anything could have a value far beyond ordinary estimation. A lonely man might be reminded of the intensities of life just by passing an odd few minutes in a pawnshop, gleaning this overplus. Then he would go out on the street with all that anonymous sentiment clinging to him, on which he had no more claim than theft could give him, feeling the vast distance between himself and the web of fraught lives that dealt among themselves in gifts and mementos. There would probably be a policeman across the street, alert to thievishness.

Jack had been leaning against a wall, reading a newspaper, aware of the policeman across the street, who was clearly aware of him. It was true that he had been browsing in a pawnshop, making a little practical use of an idle afternoon. It was true also that he had been curious to see whether the store was the chaos of minor valuables it appeared to be from the street, or whether there was a system behind it all that would draw attention to a minor theft. He wondered whether some of the items awaiting ransom, not the ones displayed in the window like trophies but the playing-card cases, the plated money clips, could be palmed or pocketed without much risk. Shops like this were an aspect of urban life, one thing that made Jack feel he really did belong in a city. These odds and ends could be intimate to the point of pathos, like the things he used to steal at home. There were brides and babies in ornate frames, crystal canisters etched with the dates of anniversaries. There was a long-handled shoehorn inlaid with rhinestones. All these things hovered between redemption by the wretches who had made hostages of them, or else abandonment into the traffic in preposterous things which must undergird the pawnbroking industry. And here they were, in their moment of poignant suspense. Jack had always felt a silent hum, like the nimbus of rubbed amber, around objects that had nothing else to recommend them. And here they were, as if some great thief moved by just the same impulse had found and hoarded them up. Two dozen clocks disputing the time. Chaos in another dimension.

"Just browsing," he had said to the clerk, though the better word would have been "casing." Then he sauntered out to the sidewalk, saw the cop, bought a newspaper from a stack on the street, folded it lengthwise, and read, with an eye on the cop. Here was the problem. He knew that, since he was aware of official attention, if he tried to walk away, he would appear to skulk. If he tried to look vigorous and purposeful, he would look as if he were leaving the scene, as they say. He had taken nothing. He was pretty sure no stray trinket had clung to his sleeve. So the wisest thing in ridiculous circumstances was simply to stand there and read about mounting tensions in Belgium. The cop would have to wander off sometime.

As it happened, however, a gentleman emerged from the pawnshop who clearly also saw the cop, bumped into Jack, begged pardon more sincerely than the situation seemed to require, and walked off, leaving Jack with a definite weight in his jacket pocket. Then another man came out, slapping his own pockets the way people do when they can't believe they have lost what they have lost. And there was law enforcement, just when needed, as was too often the case. The officer noticed and interpreted the citizen's distress, not remarkable considering the incredulous slapping, and he crossed the street. "My wallet!" the man said. The official gaze turned on Jack.

"Sir," the officer said.

Jack said, "A man just bumped into me. He must have put something in my pocket. To conceal evidence, I believe."

"Would you please show me what you have in your pocket, sir."

It was red morocco, hand-stitched, expensive but very lean. Jack should not have looked at it appraisingly. He handed it to the officer, who checked the name of the injured party against a business card that seemed to be the one thing in it. So, petty larceny. That was a relief.

But the policeman said, "Is there anything missing from your billfold, sir?"

"About five hundred dollars is missing! That's what's missing!" the citizen said, inflating his importance and making Jack a felon. The larceny was now grand.

Jack said, "If there was any money, the other man must have taken it."

"If there was any money! You calling me a liar?" said the citizen, shoving Jack against the wall in his indignation.

The cop said, "Calm down or I'll arrest you, too."

"Too." The word was a dagger in Jack's heart. And as he was pulling himself together, he realized that there was, again, a weight in his pocket. His amazement overwhelming his good sense, he slipped his fingers in and felt something round, metal, with a fine chain attached to it.

"Sir," the policeman said, "would you please empty your pockets." So out came a handkerchief, a quarter and a dime, and a necklace, maybe gold, set with what might have been precious stones. The policeman said, "Okay," and took it from him. It lay there in his hand, gleaming quietly, clearly valuable. The citizen gave Jack a look and shrugged almost imperceptibly, the gist being that he had a life that was incompatible with jail time.

Of course! That is the whole point of jail time! Jack said, "Officer, this fellow put that necklace in my pocket when he shoved me!"

"This happened to you twice in what? Five minutes?"

"Yes, Officer. It did."

"So the first fellow was a pickpocket who had robbed a thief."

"This appears to have been the case, Officer." His verb forms became exact under pressure.

"So now *I'm* the thief!" said the citizen.

"Calm down," said the policeman. "We'll step into the shop and see what the clerk has to say about this."

So Jack returned to that world that still seemed his somehow, even with a policeman at his shoulder. All the oddly deployed shine and detail, the kinds of things that reward prowlers for their trouble. There were the clocks, variously quartering the hour, time being one more dubious commodity. He was the suspect. The clerk, a stranger, glanced at him with bland hostility. Clearly this was a man practiced in negotiating desperation, nostalgia, the plain worth of a thing, haste, embarrassment, guilt, all of them leveraged against the naked hopes of the customer. This sly, cold arbiter of the fates of the bail-seeking and the creditor-pursued looked at Jack as if he were weary of him. "I wondered why this guy was hanging around in here," said the clerk to the officer. "Of course, I had my suspicions." He identified the wallet and the necklace.

"You see!" Jack said. "This fellow said the wallet was his! And in fact it was stolen!"

"No," the clerk said. "He paid for it."

"You have a bigger problem, anyway, sir," the officer said.

Meanwhile, the citizen, as if vindicated, took the wallet and left the store.

"Somebody took the tag off this necklace," said the clerk. "I'd get about three hundred for it."

Disaster. Jack was stunned. He went along quietly with the policeman, who looked very fit and could certainly outrun him.

So, jail until his day in court, which was over in about ten minutes. He had, in fact, no visible means of support, your honor. No ties to the community. "Unfortunate," the judge said. "And then the added misfortune that stolen items seem to materialize in your pockets." He shook his head at the pathos of it, banged his gavel, and said what sounded like "Five years," and something about the state penitentiary. Jack wanted to ask him to repeat what he had said. Shock had interfered somehow with his hearing. But the judge was on to other business.

Then after two years he was out on the street again without the courtesy of an explanation. He tried not to seem surprised. It was very likely a clerical error. If he mentioned it, it might be corrected, and the intoxicating privileges of wearing his own clothes and drifting and loitering as he saw fit would be snatched away. How he loved the sound of traffic, the smell of it. He went by the old rooming house to see if Teddy had been leaving money for him, and he had! There was the note about his mother, which grieved him, certainly, and made him glad that he would probably be able to find a dark suit he could afford. Grief and euphoria at the same time, with the looming expectation that he would behave appropriately in the gentle old home he had abandoned. He imagined his mother in a pretty dress receiving visitors in the parlor, she laid out in her coffin, all the talk in whispers, good old Reverend Ames there to provide a little wisdom on the subject of death and loss so the Reverend Boughton would not be expected to. And he there, Jack, not a mystery, which would make him interesting, but clearly a question, a distraction. Perhaps so much irritation, not to say resentment, had built up around him over the years that the decorum of the family would break under the stress of containing it. Everything would go smoothly, and then he would somehow give the slightest offense and their restraint would fail. They would tell him what they really thought of him and he would leave before the funeral, compounding every grievance. He thought he should take a little time to lose the habits of incarceration, sullen deference, and the rest. He should stop smoking cigarettes down till they singed his fingers, and should definitely stop saving the butts. There were no doubt other things he had not yet noticed about himself that marked him as a stranger in the ordinary world.

Seizing on this unanticipated freedom was probably a crime. If he was being rewarded for good behavior, it was the first he knew of it. In fact, he had acquired somehow a reputation for deft thievery, so whenever anything turned up missing, he and his cell were searched. And when nothing was found, this only added to his reputation for subtle criminality. They called him professor, even the guards. Who knows what the authorities would make of his escape, since that is no doubt what they would call it. The unease he had always felt at the mere sight of a policeman was almost infinitely compounded, and it had already been intense enough to have been the beginning of all these troubles. He had sometimes thought of turning himself in, to put an end to the suspense.

But prison was terrible. It reduced him to absolute Jack, no matter what anyone thought of him. His great problem, after himself, was other people. Prison was full of them. And they were all bleakly undistracted. He had once almost resented the anonymous city crowds, passersby who might seem to sum him up in a glance, if they saw him at all, taking whatever glyph of him into that vast convivium of strangers, adding some trifling datum to whatever humankind thinks of itself. But prison was immersion in a standing pool of strangers, day after day, in a twilight perfumed by mop water. The thing that saved him was the piano in the chapel. Once, when he was sweeping up, the chaplain came in, and Jack, who had thought this out over days, said, "If you ever want someone to play some music, I could do that."

The chaplain said, "Show me." So Jack sat down and played "Old Hundred."

"Pretty good. You know anything else?"

Jack played a few bars of "Holy, Holy, Holy," and a few more of "Immortal, Invisible."

The chaplain said, "'Shall We Gather at the River,'" and Jack played it. "I'm pretty rusty."

"You're all right."

"If I could practice——"

"'Sweet Hour of Prayer.'" Jack played it.

"See you Sunday," the chaplain said, and went away.

After that, Jack worked cautiously at enlarging little by little the time he could spend in the chapel, refining his repertoire. "What a Friend We Have in Jesus." From time to time there would be trouble——he was accused of cheating at cards because he was cheating at cards——but then it would be Sunday again and he would be playing a new variation on "The Old Rugged Cross" and feeling fine. Then one day he was called down through some gates to an office, given his clothes and shoes, walked through more gates, and put on a bus. He was afraid to ask.

Then something amazing happened. A few days after his talk with Hutchins, Jack went out walking, trying to get tired enough to sleep, staying sober, so that if he did jump in the river, he could feel that his demise had the dignity of a considered choice. This hope, that he might finally be weary enough, had already interfered with his tango, which really should not be done with vigor. He had felt the boss's eyes on him. When he did finally walk back to the rooming house, he saw the light on, late as it was, and the clerk standing at the counter playing checkers with that other guy, the friend. He nodded as he passed them and was all the way to the stairs when the clerk said, "Hey, Boughton, I've got something for you." So he went back and was handed a little book. H.D., *Tribute to the Angels.* "A colored gal dropped it by."

They were both watching him. He couldn't trust his voice. The clerk said, "I told her you should be back pretty soon. She could wait upstairs. She's still up there, for all I know. Probably a little tired of waiting for you." They were laughing. The clerk said, "Don't worry, I probably won't call the cops," and they kept laughing.

He went up to his room, and there she was, asleep on his bed, in her coat and her shoes, her handbag and hat beside her, her lovely head on his pillow. Just when he thought he knew something about the rest of his life, there she was.

The first problem was to be quiet enough. He moved the chair, picked it up, and set it down so that it blocked the door, and he tipped it back a little with the thought of resting, even nodding off until she woke up. He took off his jacket and put it over himself, arms folded, which was always oddly comforting, like pulling up a blanket. This was the most remarkable experience he had ever had in his life, when he considered the emotions it set off in him, joy and bewilderment and only a little dread, since, whatever else might be true, she had come to him. He could actually think of no way in which he could be at fault. The sense of guilt might be no more than habit. When she woke up, this would change, of course. There would be all the problems of helping her leave, of getting her down the stairs and out the door without exposing her to remarks and laughter. No hope of that. His palms dampened. A surge of imagined ferocity passed through him, putting an end to the thought of rest. Besides, there she was, quietly asleep, blessing his shabby bedclothes with her peacefulness, her soft breathing. Blessing the whole barren room with her amazing trust. There was dread, yes, but grace, too.

His dresser had a hat in one drawer and half a loaf of Wonder Bread in another, which was a little tainted by the cologne or pomade, whatever sad essence it was that imbued the drawers and cupboards of rented rooms. So he would have to figure out how to offer her an edible breakfast. This was a worry, one of those problems he could consider endlessly and never solve. He was protecting himself from the shock of this miracle—he allowed himself the word—with a dose of futility, a qualm or two, to remind himself who he was. He couldn't leave Della here to wake up alone, to suffer some rude intrusion, to deal with the police. Dear Jesus, not the police. He couldn't go out in the street with her. That would only multiply attention to them, especially since they would be up to something so flagrant as buying breakfast together. He should not feel shame about having to borrow money from her if they went out to the store, an extraneous misery since they obviously would do no such thing. She would be safer without him, and he could not leave her undefended. So many things made no sense to him at all, which is one reason he had kept to himself so many years. He regretted this as often as he realized he had learned next to nothing about the world.

He was inches into the shallows of despair when she stirred, opened her eyes, and looked at him. She whispered, "What time is it?"

"No idea."

She sat up. "This is really embarrassing. I just came by to let you know I'm back in town, then I spent too long waiting for you, till it was too dark to walk home. I decided you weren't coming, and I put my head down for a minute—"

"I was just out walking around. I didn't feel like sleeping."

"Well, you have to lie down now. You've been trying to sleep in that chair! Here, lie down." She stood up and gathered her hat and her purse. "I'm so sorry."

"No, it was very wonderful to find you here." But he did lie down without hesitation where she had been, where something remained of her warmth. Her perfume. He admitted this to himself, and he blushed. Where this lay along the continuum between honor and caddishness he simply did not know. He did believe it was harmless. "I can't tell you how wonderful," he said.

"I'd like to wait a little longer before I leave. Until daylight."

He said, "I wish you could stay for the rest of my life," and she laughed. "I do! That's about the truest thing I've ever said."

"Well, now you should get some sleep. You've got all those white ladies to dance with tomorrow."

"Yes, I do."

"I thought maybe you were out passing the evening with one of them tonight."

"Did you. And I thought you were probably in Memphis making plans with one of those handsome young preachers your father has lined up for you."

"I met a couple of them. They were fine. If they were the last men on earth, I might settle for one of them."

"I can't say the same for my white ladies."

"Poor things!"

"The indifference is entirely mutual."

"I suppose I believe that."

It was true. Despite the cupcakes, he knew he was only the least unlike Fred Astaire of the four or five men who showed up to trot them around the floor, a distinction that would not survive the sunlight of a slightly larger world, a city sidewalk. But she was teasing him with the notion that she could be jealous, which was objectively remarkable.

She said, "If you're awake, anyway, we could have breakfast. It must be almost morning. My mother always fills my bag with food for the train. I could have fed the whole coach." She picked up a carpetbag that had been sitting on the floor beside the dresser and opened it. A lovely fragrance reached him. She set its contents on the table. "Pecan bread, boiled eggs, apples. A bottle of orangeade, which I loved when I was ten, ham sandwiches, potato chips."

He lifted up the lamp so she could move the bed table away from the wall, then he propped it against the pillow. It shone on the food she was laying out, and on her dark hands, their rosy palms like a delicate secret. A bracelet he had not seen before. Her face was a little veiled by the shade of the lamp, and the walls were in shadow. She said, "The cat is in Memphis. I spent an hour hunting for it that night. Lorraine wouldn't have it in the house. It's taken a liking to my aunt Delia. At least she says it has. It's a terrible cat. She calls it Jack."

He laughed. "I'm not sure I know how to take that."

"She sort of liked you. We've always had some secrets, the two of us. She took me aside one day and asked if I'd seen you at all since she visited. She said she'd been so rude to you it worried her."

"She was actually very kind. That was the gentlest expulsion I have ever suffered. A fond memory, more or less." He watched her hands break the loaf, smooth the waxed paper.

She said, "You wouldn't have knives or forks or plates. Or cups."

"True. I don't really spend much time here. Except to sleep." He wanted to assure her that his life was solitary and ascetic, as it was, almost past bearing, relieved by the library, occasional drunkenness, and lately by lunch with the Baptists. But he knew how this would sound, either pathetic or, better, like lying.

She said, softly, "I had a terrible dream, that you needed me and I couldn't get to you. That you were so much alone, you were dying of it."

"Wait!" he said, and laughed. The tears were painfully abrupt, and he wiped his eyes with his hands.

She said, very softly, "I was dying, too. In the dream."

"I'm happy to know that, Della. I mean, it's kind of you to tell me that."

"But I was still glad you were longing for me."

"I was!"

"What a mess we're in, causing each other all this misery."

"And this is just the beginning."

"Promise?"

"Promise!"

She laughed. "Well, then, I guess we might as well have our breakfast. That's what people do."

"And you might as well come sit beside me, so I can put my arm around you. So you can put your head on my shoulder. People do that, too. A fellow told me that if the Lord gave this doomed soul a few minutes of grace, He wouldn't mind if I enjoyed it. If you're going to be doomed, too, you can join me in this moment of reprieve."

"You're not doomed. Neither am I. We've chosen a difficult life, that's all."

"You've chosen a difficult life, I'm doomed. But we have other things in common."

She did sit down next to him, actually against him, and he put his arm around her waist. She took his hand, turned it up, measured her hand against it, turned it over. She said, "This won't work. You're right-handed. We'll have to change sides so you won't have an excuse for not eating anything."

"Ah! But one of the little known wonders of my nature—I am ambidextrous! I use my right hand by preference, so that I'll seem ordinary to people."

She laughed. "That would do it."

"No, really. I have to keep my left hand in my pocket sometimes, to keep it from being too useful. I'm serious."

"Then eat something with it. I'll watch."

The pecan bread was very good. "See that?"

"Too easy. Can you peel an egg with one hand? I have an uncle who can."

"I like to keep some wonders in reserve."

"Meaning no."

"Meaning they're slippery little devils with the shells off. They can end up on the floor."

She peeled an egg and gave it to him. She said, "Isn't it strange?"

"Yes, it is. Very strange. I don't know what we're talking about, but I'm sure you're right."

After a minute he believed she had spent composing her thoughts, she said, "Isn't it strange that I could hardly wait to see you, and you were longing to see me, and here we are talking about hard-boiled eggs."

Oh. He had been thrown off guard by the surprise of it all, never mind the pleasure of it, and he had not paused to think what such a situation might demand of him, what might be expected. He said, "You brought it up," which sounded completely defensive, and a little cross. So he said, "Give me a chance here," which was worse, since it made clear that he was entirely at a loss.

"I just mean it's strange that there is nothing more I want from life. If I could imagine an eternity of sitting here with you talking nonsense, there'd be nothing more I would want from *death*. I mean it. And I'm a good Christian woman." Her voice was very calm, but there were tears on her cheeks. He touched them away.

She said, "Oh dear."

He said, "Yes." Further into trouble, past the last threshold where they could even imagine turning back. Should he mention to her that, if eternity existed, his eternity would be a very different thing from hers? He hated the thought of her waiting it out alone. People were always waiting, their oldest habit, and they would go on with it even though the end of all the waiting would be—never. He tossing in the fires of perdition, while she failed to attend as completely as she should to the gold and pearl and the hosannahs. His father, too, trying to find a calendar, sneaking a look at his watch, still hoping, in the perfect knowledge that the end of time made hope a nostalgia. Jack caught in the snares of loyalties he could only disappoint. Maybe this was hell. Hellfire is figurative, his father had said, in that tone of certainty that had nothing to do with his belief in what he was saying and everything to do with the certainty that it must be said. Still, what if it was true? No flames at all, just an eternity of disheartened self-awareness. Outer darkness. Wailing and gnashing of teeth.

She said, "What are you thinking about?"

"Perdition."

She laughed. "Of course. What else?"

"Our future."

"Really. You should tell me what you think about that. It's hard to imagine."

He said, "It will be made up entirely of stolen minutes and hours every now and then, for years and years and years, and we will pity all the people whose lives are diluted with time and habit and complacency and respectability until they can hardly savor the best pleasures—we will live for a month on just once passing in the street."

She said, softly, "You are the only man in the whole world who could promise me that!"

"Yes. And consider all the other advantages. You can meet your obligations, and I will remember to shave."

She put her head on his shoulder, toyed with his hand. "Now you're making me sad."

He said, "I can make you sad. That's wonderful, in a way." He noticed that the thought didn't really scare him.

"Before we begin on this future of ours, you should come to my house for dinner Friday. Lorraine is in Charleston. She has family there. School's out, so she'll be gone for a while."

"What about the neighbors?"

"They're sort of used to you. The thought of you. There's a rumor that you're worshipping at Mount Zion. That makes you a little interesting."

"'Worshipping.' You know that's an overstatement. They're

kind to me. I like the preacher. I like the choir." He didn't say, They give me lunch. That would not be interesting. A white stranger with a clerical manner is experiencing a religious stirring, the Spirit acting on his frozen soul here, now, among us. He could see the poetry in their misconception, could see why he might seem interesting to them. To Della. Despite certain attempts at reform, as far as he was concerned, truth versus poetry was really no contest. Yet here he was, being honest with himself, carrying on that endless, secret conversation that was himself, now making him wretchedly aware that, at best, he was allowing Della to be misled. Then he thought about the embarrassing business with the hat, and how that lady had hurried to feed him, as if she saw an extreme of neediness in him that alarmed her. Della might have heard about it all, though here she was, actually nestled against him, speaking so softly, toying with his hand. If she had not heard that story, she might hear it at any time. She would distance herself abruptly, and he would become as withdrawn and indifferent as he could manage without ending things irrevocably, until it was clear to him that that decision had been made. "Then." "Afterward." Two terrible words.

She said, "You're very quiet. You don't want to come to my house."

"You can't imagine how much I want to."

"Then will you?"

"I have one question. How can we do this without, possibly, ruining your life?"

"You'll arrive at six, sober, bringing flowers, and you will leave at eight, sober. And there won't be flowers or cats in the shrubbery to embarrass me once you're gone."

"You think it will be that simple."

"Not really. Who knows? At least Lorraine won't be there to

glower at us. In a week she'll be back. Sooner, if her cousins upset her somehow. That happens."

He said, "I should tell you that there is more, or less, to my visits to Mount Zion than you might realize. A long story; one that doesn't reflect well on me. If you don't know about that, maybe your neighbors do. Or they will. Their interest in me may not be entirely benign. I might not reflect well on you. To say the least."

"And my life will be ruined."

He nodded. "That's my point."

"I just can't quite seem to care. Things might go well enough, and after that I promise I'll be thinking about my life day and night. Lorraine will help me with that."

He said, "There's one more thing I want to make very clear. You might think I'm shiftless, in need of the love of a good woman, as my father used to say. But what you see here, this minimal existence, is actually the fruit of what can fairly be called earnest striving. I do not need to be converted to an ethic of work and frugality. I admire them heartily—I've aspired to them off and on for some time. And I've learned that I'm just not good at that sort of thing. I'm still more or less dependent on my brother. It's disgraceful. So you're involving yourself with a ne'er-do-well. You should think about that."

She said, "I have thought about it. I can't seem to care about that, either." She laughed. "I couldn't *wait* to see you. I was supposed to stay in Memphis the whole week, and I just couldn't do it. When my mother was putting all these things in my bag, she was too mad to talk to me. And my father! He wouldn't even come downstairs to tell me goodbye. They knew why I was coming back."

He nodded. "I'm ruining things. I do that. I try to keep to

myself, and it happens, anyway. The preacher at Zion said that if I were an honorable man I would leave you alone."

"Well, I guess I've made that difficult. You talked to him about me?"

"I'm sorry if I shouldn't have done that. He reminds me a little of my father. I guess I feel at home in a church. Not at ease, but at home." He said, "I thought we had ended it that night, and I suppose I was looking for comfort or something. Advice. A way to get by."

She nodded. "We did end it. You don't think I'd be outside in my bathrobe and curlers talking to a man I thought I'd ever see again. It just wouldn't stay ended." Her fingers were threaded through his. She picked up his hand and kissed it, a little absent-mindedly, and said, "I'll tell you my thinking."

"All right."

"We all have souls, true?"

He laughed. "Please go on."

"We do. We know this, but just because it's a habit to believe it, not because it is really visible to us most of the time. But once in a lifetime, maybe, you look at a stranger and you see a soul, a glorious presence out of place in the world. And if you love God, every choice is made for you. There is no turning away. You've seen the mystery—you've seen what life is about. What it's for. And a soul has no earthly qualities, no history among the things of this world, no guilt or injury or failure. No more than a flame would have. There is nothing to be said about it except that it is a holy human soul. And it is a miracle when you recognize it."

Her eyes were lovely with seriousness, he knew, though she didn't look at him. Still, he had to laugh. "Am I to understand that you are speaking here of one Jack Boughton?"

She nodded. "I learned this from you. From meeting you. It wasn't as immediate as I've made it sound, but I began to realize—"

"So I am immune from all judgment, on account of my celestial nature?"

"Other people are, too, or they should be. But since it's your soul I've seen, I know better than to think about you the way people do when they judge. The Lord says 'Judge not,' because when He looks at people, He just sees souls. That's all. I suppose I've seen a few others. Kids at school. Yours is the brightest."

"A mystic."

"Think what you like."

"I think the sun is coming up. And I am worried about the propriety of kissing you. I might singe your lips."

She laughed. "You very well might."

A fine, solid kiss, and another one. Then she said, "By six o'clock Friday. I don't mean twelve twenty-five. But it's all right if you're late. You don't have to bring flowers."

"I do have to be sober."

"I'd appreciate it." She stood up and began wrapping things in waxed paper to leave on the table for him. Light was leaking into the room around the edges of the window blind. She said, "I really should go now." He took her coat from her and helped her on with it and handed her her gloves. He watched her settle her hat in place expertly, by touch. "You don't have to be sober," she said.

He stepped away, to look at her face. "You don't really think I'll show up."

"You don't want to ruin my life. And I could ruin yours. You'll think of reasons not to come. You'll make reasons."

"I don't need to invent anything. If they decide we're cohabiting, we could both go to jail. You could go to jail."

"I know that. My father got a copy of the statute and made me read it to him. So he'd be sure I was paying attention."

"I found it in the library."

"I don't think they'd really do that, do you?"

"I'm pretty sure they'd really do that." He had dealt with law enforcement, though he still couldn't bring himself to tell her. "I do want to be honorable. Where you're concerned. The preacher said I should leave you alone. He's right. But I will come to your house Friday if you want me to. Unchaperoned. In broad daylight. With flowers. Neighbors be damned."

"I just want one ordinary evening. Before we start out on this lonely marriage of ours."

"To celebrate our lonely nuptials."

"Exactly."

"Whom God hath joined—"

"I'm serious."

He said, "Ah, Della, so am I."

She had a small suitcase and the carpetbag, which he carried for her down the stairs. The clerk was already at his desk, early as it was. He said, "Next time, I call the cops, Boughton. You can't start bringing colored gals in here." She took the bags from him; he opened the door for her and followed her a little way into the street. She said, "Go inside now."

"Friday," he said. Then he stood on the stoop and watched her out of sight. There were not many people on the sidewalks yet, but the ones likely to be there were not of the best sort or in the best state of mind, since daylight would have waked them out of oblivion into unassuageable surliness, into a small hell of watery eyes and personal squalor. He knew all this as well as he knew anything. It was perfectly possible that he had stepped out of an alley sometime to bother a passing woman for a dime or a little conversation, possible, too, that he had cursed at her back for shunning him. Della walked near the curb, away from the mouths of alleys and doorways, where taunting voices and reaching hands would be at some small distance from her. Drunkards could be especially serious about enforcing local standards—"What're you doing here! You got your own side of town!" She would be walking toward her side of town as quickly as she could, to escape the threat of insult or harm, to find safety, the blessed comfort of familiarity. He had not brought up with her an article he had seen in the newspaper announcing that the city had decided to demolish her side of town, churches and all, to replace it with something or other at some point in time, these decisions pending. She would know, no doubt, that she was hurrying toward a doomed refuge. And in this treacherous world he was the straw she grasped at. Unfathomable. He thought, Once again I am a person of consequence. I am able to do harm. I can only do harm. If I walk down her street tonight just to see if her lights are on, someone will see me, someone will talk. I'll be feeding the rumors that will sooner or later burst into scandal and break her father's heart. Ah, Jesus, get her home, keep her safe. Keep her safe from me.

Jack had gone to Chicago years before, just on the chance that he might come across that girl. He couldn't find her, strictly speaking, because he had no idea where to look for her. He had a little money he could give her, in an envelope with a letter of apology. Very difficult to write, a disappointing piece of work. But he knew, if he did find her, he might not actually say anything to her, or he might say something even more disappointing than the letter. The money was from his father, and the pretext was that he was buying that convertible—"For a while there we thought you might be coming back for it." The car wasn't exactly his, and it wasn't worth half the money the old man had sent. But that would be all right if he could send a note back to his father that said he'd found that girl, that he'd given her the money. And told him about whatever happened next. He might mention the apology.

When people have wearied of life in Gilead, when they want another life altogether, they mention Chicago. She had told him once that she would go to Chicago to see all the movies. She had the impression that movies all pre-existed in Chicago and were eked out to the provinces a few a year. Even for someone so young, it was amazing how little she knew and how much she believed. He blushed to remember. These jolts of realization stayed with him undiminished, try as he might to smother them, drown them, even conjure cynicism enough to attempt excuses or indifference.

He was getting used to St. Louis. Chicago couldn't be so different. One problem was that she had been young, and the last few years would inevitably have changed her. Even in those days her freckles were fading, little smudges half worn away. She could be tall now, or plump. Women dye their hair. She could be changed by the ways she might have managed to survive in a city alone. Jesus, don't let me think about that. He had almost told his father that she was not an innocent girl, when that would only have meant she was unsheltered, uncared for, and he was cad enough to make it all worse. When he remembered that he had almost said this, he could imagine he saw what he had never really seen, contempt in his father's eyes. Teddy had said, "What's wrong with you, Jack?" A real, sad question. And Jack took in the fact that his brother's unshakable loyalty to him was illusionless compassion, the kind he would see in prison chaplains, the Salvation Army. What is wrong with me?

A problem of finding that girl in Chicago was the near-certainty that he would not know her if he saw her. But she might recognize him. He believed that he had gone through certain things with her, but at such a remove they could hardly have changed him. Damned Glory, his sheltered and sanctimonious sister, had sent him photographs, which actually seemed to him to prove that his family were looking after the girl and her baby and nothing was needed from him. Then came the letters from his sister and his mother about the baby's death, his mother's distant and gentle, Glory's full of heartbroken wrath and exasperation. Once, she had sent him a baby picture of himself, pried from a locket, and one of his daughter at the same age, her point being that the two of them were for all purposes identical. Years later, after all that, he had put the two pictures in a cigarette case he had pocketed at a bar, a rather nice one with working hinges and a clasp, a little wear on the corners. He took it to Bellefontaine, to the monument of the infant and the angel, pried some turf away from its base, slipped the cigarette case into the space he had made, and tamped it down with his foot. He had no right to take any comfort from the sentimentality of the gesture, which in fact appalled him a little. But how better to be rid of these pictures? All the others he had sent back to Glory, without comment. He had hardly glanced at them.

Then he began thinking seriously about Chicago, even planning to go there. His father's money came, which felt like an affirmation, a fatherly nudge. He could buy a ticket, pay for a room, and still have something to give her, and the letter of apology, if he had the nerve to give her that. So sorry to have visited such utter grief on you, to have done you such terrible harm, before you had even lost your freckles. Words to that effect. Well, he'd get a haircut, shorter on the sides, and a very close shave. Painful as it was to remember, besides the convertible, the girl was much impressed with a sweater he took from Teddy's closet, bright gold with a big black *I* on the chest. Teddy was varsity. He had lettered in baseball. The girl thought it belonged to Jack and that it meant he was a college man. She wanted her cousins to see him in it, though he always talked her into long drives farther into the country. When Jack was packing to leave Gilead, after that talk with his father, Teddy came into his room with the sweater and stuffed it into his suitcase, and the corduroy slacks he wore with it. He did this without a word. Jack said nothing. Sometimes they understood each other perfectly.

He was glad he had kept the things for a while, because it occurred to him that she might notice him, wandering the streets in his Joe College attire. The sweater was absurdly bright. Teddy never wore it.

So he had taken the train to Chicago, carrying the sweater rolled up in a paper sack. At the station he put his jacket in a locker, pulled on the sweater, and walked into the men's room to comb his hair. Overhead lights. His pallor against that yellow was downright alarming. His face was thinner than he expected, and his hair. His closely shaved jaw was blue. Daylight might be even crueler. Oh well. He thought he had an idea. In the ranks of phone booths he found an empty one with a phone book in it, two things that were not often to be found together. He thought he might come across her name. What was it? Walker? Turner? Wheeler? Why didn't he remember? And that's another thing about women that changes, anyway. It was a very large directory. He had turned to *Boughton*, which made no sense at all. An inconsiderable lot, he noticed, so few of them in such a large city. He wasn't thinking clearly, so he went to a bench and sat down. A vast, echoing room, baronial, civic, neglected. Sparrows flying across the ceiling, pigeons burbling around his feet. The great male voice of Announcement moving the crowds, trains shaking the building. His cigarettes were in his jacket pocket. He checked to be sure he hadn't lost the locker key. Well, he shouldn't be sitting there, anyway. He had to make the most of his time. He went out into the bright street. Pavement, trolley tracks, beyond them cheap hotels.

He walked and walked, bought a hot dog from a cart, and walked some more, waiting for any sign of recognition. It was foolish, far worse than hopeless. He had failed to consider that Teddy's sweater might stir a sudden bitterness in that girl's mind, that woman's mind, since by now she would understand how cheap a fraud had been committed against her childishness. It was that turbulence he carried with him, that black wind. She might see his yellow sweater and suffer a sting of memory, and curse the thought of him for all the grief he had brought her. She would turn away from the sight of him, and he would never know he had been so close to her. Maybe it was really a hope of comforting his father that lay behind it all, so Jack could walk into the old house again, so much at home there that his father would hardly look up from his newspaper.

Since he had gone that far with the idea, he might as well go on with it. His darkest thoughts about what was liable to be the girl's present life would have led him down some dismal streets, and he did not look for her there, coward that he was. Another cause of regret. He'd certainly have been noticed in that sweater, which said in effect he had a life that allowed him to parade meaningless attainments, to expend effort just for the sake of a little sweat and sunshine on a grassy field, effort having nothing at all to do with shelter or food. Why did this thought make him more ashamed that it wasn't even his sweater?

When night came, he stepped into a bar and had a few drinks. He went to a hotel, got a room and a key, and went back to the bar. Then he realized that somebody had walked him out to the sidewalk and left him there, leaning against a wall. His wallet was missing and so was his room key. So was that letter. The name of the hotel was written on the tag thing they attach to hotel keys. There were a number of hotels nearby, and they all looked alike, in fact and because he had been drinking. If he happened into the right hotel, they'd probably put him back out again, anyway. His ticket home was safe in the pocket of his shirt. So at worst it was only a matter of waiting for morning. He curled up in a doorway and fell asleep, until a policeman prodded him with his nightstick and said, "Move along, college boy." He found another doorway near a streetlamp, but this time he couldn't sleep. The whole day he had been prey to his thoughts, but at least there were women around to distract him from them, to remind him of his purpose.

A small old black man with the look of a hardened insomniac stood at the doorway for a while, smoking and watching the night, as if there were anything to look at. He glanced at Jack, then he flicked a long ash off his cigarette and said, "What would your folks say, seeing you there like that." Then he strolled away, leaving Jack to think how steady his hand must be to have kept that ash from falling. Without twitch or tremor, a man of good conscience, he decided. Somewhere someone might have been laughing at that letter—Truly, I have no words to express—No way at all to make it right— It was a confession as much as it was an apology. That might always be true. Pointless in either case. He had felt as if the shame in the letter—it was really all about shame—was connected somehow with the perfervid, sulfurous yellow of the sweater, and he knew he would have thought the same thing sober. The locker key was in the shirt pocket with his ticket back to St. Louis. There was a logic in this he found reassuring, which proved that he was still essentially drunk.

A terrible day, wandering the streets, looking with unwelcome interest into the faces of women who might have any traits in any combination but who were still, good Lord, quite young. The use he had made of that sweater. Teddy's wholesome aspiring rewarded as it usually was, even while he put on Jack's tie and jacket, the one with cigarette burns on the lapel, sat in Jack's lectures, and took his exams. Surely the family knew—that B-plus in geology? They had to have known. But some morning Jack might wake up a new man. He might come into himself, as his father said, and find his life waiting for him, a creditable youth already half lived out, suiting him perfectly, though with certain options thoughtfully left open. He might step like Lazarus back into his own life, so familiar, so astonishing. This had never happened. He'd made sure it would not happen. Perhaps he might, for just a moment, have seen his father's contempt, an agony to his father, who would have sworn to himself a thousand times it would never come to that.

It was that night he was confronted with the indisputable truth that, all by himself in a strange city, he was in a situation and a condition that would indeed cause his mother sorrow and humiliation, send an icy pang into the warmest depths of her bosom. So with his brothers and sisters, after their fashion. Then it was that he had first realized what an exquisite thing harmlessness must be, what an absolute courtesy to things seen and unseen, to the bruised reed and the smoldering wick. If he could not achieve harmlessness, his very failures would give him much to consider. He would abandon all casuistry, surrender all thought of greater and lesser where transgressions were concerned, even drop the distinction between accident and intention. He was struggling in a web of interrelation, setting off consequences in every direction that he could not predict or control or even imagine with any hope of approaching the truth of a matter. He had no doubt read this somewhere. His brain was at least as sticky as his fingers. That old problem of mine and thine made his thinking a trove of unearned and unwilled pretentiousness, and this, he had learned on a number of occasions, was a thing some people took exception to. So that was another kind of offense to be aware of. He would speak only when necessary.

And so he had lived, more or less, until he met Della. A little thievery when the opportunity was too patent to be ignored, or too interesting. A drinking bout for some reason or no reason. A stint in prison. Then an occasion for him to try out his manners, so long of no use to him, put away with his necktie and his shoe-laces. Running after her papers as they blew down the street, then "Thank you, Reverend," and tea in her parlor with Jesus looking on. She so lovely besides, and a woman of some learning. What more could fate have done to stamp her in his mind as the angel waiting at the door of his tomb? No wonder he could hardly go an hour without thinking about her. And since it was always true of him, truer since prison, that his thoughts were the idle companions of his idleness, his isolation, and were never meant to govern his behavior any more than practicality or ambition could do, he really had believed she was safe in his thoughts, and aloof from him, too, for good measure.

And here he was married to her. Granting that the marriage was only an agreement between them—not "only," as if it were diminished by secrecy and illegality and the rest. Those were the things that made it pure, or proved that it was pure. He did take a kind of comfort from the fact that there seemed to be little more than loyalty involved, which might come very easily to him in this case. And as for her, if sometime she decided she wanted another kind of life, he would forgive her on account of her youth and love her, anyway, at the same sanctified distance they had agreed to. That moment could come at any time. She would go back to her family and her life with his blessing, with no new experience of sorrow or guilt, uninjured in his care. He would never have imagined that harmlessness could be so sweet and so protective of them both, or that solitude could be the proof and seal of marriage. A few old songs came to mind—Every road I walk along I walked along with you—which had never been true of them and never would be. Something to regret, of course, but they would understand that being apart was the pact they had made, and the sadness they felt would be the secret they shared, always tenderly alive as even shared memories would not be. All this seemed possible, he believed.

That was a Wednesday, or it became a Wednesday as he washed and dressed and buffed his shoes, and walked out into a world oddly untransformed. Miracles leave no trace. He had decided, hearing his father preach on the subject, that they happened once as a sort of commentary on the blandness and inadequacy of the reality they break in on, and then vanish, leaving a world behind that refutes the very idea that such a thing could have happened. He left the bright day behind for the twilight of the big upstairs room with its mirror ball and its smell of wood and wax. First to arrive, an effect of his resolve to embrace conscientiousness in every circumstance, he sat down on a bench with his hat beside him and thought what it might be like if the miraculous became the natural order of things. Loaves and fishes in inexhaustible supply. Troops of Lazaruses putting off their cerements. Infinite hours where Della was always waiting for him, and he was always somehow not a disappointment.

The boss walked in and pulled the chain that started the mirror ball, and tawdry spangles swept the room. First there were the ladies who came in after lunch, and then a few high-school girls who stood at the door laughing among themselves, perhaps at the fact that his jitterbug was brisk and exact and his hair was thinning. On the street they might have avoided him, hid their laughter behind their hands if he smiled at them. Then there was the unaccountable Della. While I think on thee, dear friend. How could anyone promise to be loyal to anyone? Loyalty is fragile. A change would come over her face and she would never look at him that way again, with that sweet trust he had done nothing to deserve and could lose in a moment of ill-considered honesty.

By Thursday he had begun telling himself that there wouldn't be any harm in a drink or two, so he went to the library, found a book on orchids and a fussy little volume of poetry whose flyleaf had mellowed to cream through its many years of deserved neglect. It tore out nicely. He copied an especially flamboyant blossom, enhancing it a little, with all due respect to the Creator or evolution or some combination of the two. His hand was still clever. He could still please himself with a sense of the sketch answering back to him, a pretty line, shading that did look like shadow. This would be the flower he brought her, and she would laugh and put it aside somewhere to keep it safe, and then she would go look at it again. It occurred to him to wonder how long ago this seraphic bloom had been translated into the ghost of itself, an unusually slight change. Thy eternal summer shall not fade. He wondered if he might love Della less if that look of gentle trust passed out of her eyes. One way to find out. No one would ever see it again. There would always be a shadow, her memory of him. When he was a kid, he used to know if there was something he was going to steal or break. He resisted just enough so that there was a certain relief in actually doing it. Ah, Jesus, not this time.

But when Friday came, he took the day off work, did as much as scrubbing and shaving and brushing and buffing could do for his appearance and self-respect, then did it all over again. He wished there were such a thing as a warm and manly scent, and that he had a bottle of it. Don't let me get arrested, don't let me get drunk.

He knocked on Della's door at six. She kissed him before he had even put down his hat. So there he was, with Della in his arms, on time and sober. She had roasted a chicken. She had made biscuits. The table was set, with candles and what he supposed was a vase for flowers. Everything else was exactly the way it always was, but perfect. He knew there was no mote of dust in that room. There was no slightest sign of rumple or displacement in the couch cushions. "Here," he said, taking the page from his pocket, "this is what I have for flowers. Sorry." And she unfolded the page and said "Oh!" and then she said, "Another angel!" which pleased him, because seraphic was his thought as he made the drawing.

He stood beside her in the warm little kitchen while she finished the gravy, carried their plates to the table, watched the effects of candlelight on her hair and her eyes while they talked about something wonderful, to judge by the laughter and then the silence that came over them when he reached across the table to stroke her hand. Eight o'clock came and went. In fact, he woke up the next morning with her cheek against his shoulder and her arm across his chest.

He went to work that afternoon to make up for missing Friday. So Saturday passed, and on Sunday he went to church. He sat in his pew next to that man, whose name was Arnold and who said good morning to him. The pulpit was a fair distance away, but of course the minister saw him, noticed him, was clearly aware of him. There was no hint of cordiality in his expression.

Singing and praying. Then the preacher stepped into the pulpit. He said, "This morning I'm going to speak my mind. That's my job. Maybe sometimes I let you all forget what you are paying me to do. So today I'm going to remind you. I'm going to talk to you about your debts. I'm not talking about money you owe. Nothing like that. I'm talking about the debts you rack up when you lie, when you make promises you don't mean to keep, when you disturb a peaceful home." Jack had not felt so targeted by a sermon in years. Of course he hadn't been to church in years. Still, Jack Boughton seemed to be as fruitful a sermon text as the Lost Sheep, the Prodigal Son, the Unfaithful Steward. When he was young, the feeling had made him smile. Now it made him sweat.

"If you are honorable people," the preacher said, "you will know that other people's lives are fragile and precious and important to everybody who loves them, and that means precious to our Lord Jesus Christ. Do you think you can do harm to the least of his brothers and sisters and He will not feel it as an insult to himself? Then you better read your Bible. If you think your sins are just going to vanish away like they never happened because Jesus loves you—well, I've got news. Jesus loves lots of people. He loves the man you cheated and the woman you made fun of behind her back. Little sins, you say. Little wounds in the heart of Christ. Think about it. He wants his own to have abundance of life, and you steal from that abundance—maybe not money or goods, but the peace and trust and love that are theirs by right. You see women, we all see this, women putting up with everything, forgiving everybody. They're saints! Everybody says it. Sister Smith, Sister Jones, she's a saint on earth! That could well be the truth. And how do we treat these saints? I borrow a little something from her, well, she'll never ask for it back. She's a saint! I see her hopes valued at nothing. I see her loving heart fixed on some unworthy fool who will just turn away from her, abandon her. She'll forgive, she's a saint. And what do we learn in Matthew 25? That Christ our Lord is a judge. A judge. And He is also the injured party! Look at the text. Do you think He does not feel the hunger of loneliness, the nakedness of abandonment, the prison of faithfulness that is not answered with faithfulness? Is He not sick at heart, together with a mother, or a father, whose child makes nothing of his life but a shame and a sorrow?"

Arnold was slumped in the pew, hand over his eyes, possibly weeping. Wonderful! That could mean that the sermon was meant for him! There was comfort in the slenderest possibility. So he went downstairs to lunch, took his place in line to have his plate filled, and thought about what he would say to the preacher if he had a chance to speak to him.

People were quiet, subdued, no doubt dealing variously with this rebuke, turning over in their minds whom it had been meant for and what had provoked it. Some of the women seemed to Jack to be smiling to themselves, pleased that sainthood was mentioned, to justify the grudges they held against an unappreciative world. Or what he sensed might have been a discreet satisfaction at hearing the preacher give that white man a good talking-to. Who knows what might be known or believed among them, up to and including the plain truth. It might be appropriate to show a few signs of shame, to concede the point without surrendering too much dignity. He could have grabbed his hat and ducked out into daylight and left them to talk it all out. It was not only because there were beans on his plate by the time he decided he probably should have left. It was also because Della had said, before he left her that Saturday morning, "Now you're a married man! You have a wife!," straightening his collar, which he had always been careful to keep straight, and tightening the knot of his tie, a half-Windsor. But he knew what these gestures meant—You don't face the world alone, you have a wife who invests care and pride in letting the world know you aren't just wandering around on your own, mattering to nobody, killing time, maybe cadging a little small talk here and there. A married man! A higher order of loneliness altogether! If it were not for the criminal code of the state of Missouri, he could very reasonably have shouted it from the rooftops. He found it all difficult to believe, except for the criminal code.

The minister came down to lunch, put his plate on another table, and involved himself in talk with the people there, never casting a glance at Jack, as if he knew Jack hoped to catch his eye. Finally, Jack carried his plate to the kitchen and walked over to the minister's table. He said, "Reverend, if you could spare a few minutes, I'd like to speak to you." There was a pause, felt and understood around the table, and then the preacher said, "Why, Mr. Ames! Or is it Boughton today. You're in luck. I can spare a few minutes." He stood up. "Here or in my study?"

"The study, if that's all right. I don't want to interrupt—"

"I'm sure you don't," he said. "You know where to find my study." And he stayed behind a little to shake hands and send good wishes to relatives and so on, prolonging the time Jack stood waiting in the study, even after he had delayed awhile in coming up the stairs. The minister finally came into the room, gestured to a chair, and sat down at his desk.

Jack said, "Boughton. That is my actual name."

The minister nodded. "So we've settled that. Now, what is on your mind today, Mr. Boughton?"

Jack cleared his throat. "I believe your sermon this morning may have been directed at me. In some part."

"You'd be the best judge of that. There are entirely too many people who might feel that way. That makes it worth preaching about."

"Yes. Well, I intend to reform my life. There have been other attempts, not well grounded, I believe. Not quite serious, though I didn't really realize this at the time. I lack moorings, somehow. What you said this morning will be a great help, I feel quite sure."

The preacher nodded. "I know I've said this before, but you probably need to go home and talk to your father."

"I will, at some point. When I can tell him I've reformed, at least enough to look him in the eye while I say it." The preacher smiled, and Jack said, "That's a problem I have."

"Yes, I see."

There was a silence long enough that Jack half expected the preacher to push back his chair and check his watch and wish Jack success in his efforts at self-betterment or something. Finally he said, "Can I take it that you're seeking me out again because the advice I gave you last time we spoke has been useful to you?"

"Yes, sir. Very useful."

"You have followed it, then."

"No, sir. I can't really say I have. But it has given me a lot to think about."

"Wonderful," the preacher said, by which he did not mean wonderful. Then, "I happened to speak to Miss Miles's pastor

225

about her the other day. Not about you, just her. He thinks the world of her, of course. Her accomplishments, and also her Christian character."

Jack had noticed many times that anyone with any sort of place in life became, at some point, the exasperated authority. What have you done, Boughton? Why did you do it? He had found he could accept reproof from anybody who was not dead drunk and be no better for it, unless the discomfort involved was actually payment against outstanding debt. This thought may actually have comforted him, since debt can be reduced, unless it involves interest of some kind, which would be a way of understanding the steady accumulation of lesser errors and transgressions also to be atoned for, if there was merit in this view of things. Those fellows who said they were debt collectors, making him turn out his pockets every week or two, he hadn't seen them for a while. So he had sought out a man of the cloth, he thought, perhaps looking for another version of the same experience.

Jack said, "I'm sure I couldn't break off our relationship without causing her a great deal of sadness. Grief. I truly believe this."

The minister shrugged. "People recover, generally speaking. They can look back on their sorrows, sooner or later, and be grateful for whatever caused them. Impossible as it may seem at the time."

"And she would be grateful. She'd have a better life."

"I believe in time she would be grateful."

Jack nodded. "Still."

The minister leaned back in his chair. "Mr. Boughton, I will be very frank with you. I think I understand what I'm asking you to give up. You strike me as an intensely lonely man, someone for whom life has not gone well. And suddenly a fine young woman has decided she is in love with you. Her life up to this point has been sheltered enough that she doesn't really know the kinds of things that can happen when laws are violated. And what can you do for her? You can be loyal to her. That's worse than useless in the circumstances, unless you decide the loyal thing would be to leave her alone."

Jack said, "To me it feels like disloyalty even to be thinking about leaving her alone. I believe it would feel that way to her. I know it would."

"Well, if you don't want my advice, why are you here?"

Jack said, "I'm sorry," and stood up. "I've imposed on your time."

"Redeem the time, son! You can pay me back by telling me what you came here for."

"It doesn't matter. A sort of blessing, I suppose."

"What? No! Did I hear you right? A blessing? No! Nothing about any of this has my blessing! Surely I have made that clear!"

"Yes, sir, you have. But you asked me why I had come in the first place. I guess I didn't realize then that your position was quite so final. I wouldn't have bothered you if I'd known."

"Did you think I would put a little sprinkle of holiness on this arrangement of yours, maybe help you convince that good woman that it really is some kind of marriage?"

"No, sir. She doesn't need to be convinced. The blessing would have been for me. As I said, I'm trying to reform, but I lack— moorings. I used that word before. I can't think of a better one."

"And you want to reform for her sake."

"I have a wonderful wife, and I want to be very good to her."

"We're speaking of Miss Miles."

"Of course. Yes."

"She isn't your wife."

"There are varying definitions of marriage. In Scripture—"

227

"I know all that. And will there be children of this union? Yes, there will. That's clear enough. You'd better give some thought to how many people you're making trouble for."

Jack nodded. "I do think about that. I'm not an innocent man, obviously. I've done a lot of damage in my life. I'd like to get some control of certain of my impulses. It would be a good thing if I could do that, in any case, married or not. So I thought I'd ask your help."

"Well, I suppose you can see that you're causing trouble right now. And you don't intend to stop. I don't know how a blessing's going to help. How I'm going to help."

Jack nodded. "It was just a thought. Thanks for your time."

He stepped to the door, but the preacher said, "Mr. Boughton, I can spare a few more minutes, if you want to tell me a little about these impulses you mention."

"All right, I'll tell you. I'm a gifted thief. I lie fluently, often for no reason. I'm a bad but confirmed drunk. I have no talent for friendship. What talents I do have I make no use of. I am aware instantly and almost obsessively of anything fragile, with the thought that I must and will break it. This has been true of me my whole life. I isolate myself as a way of limiting the harm I can do. And here I am with a wife! Of whom I know more good than you have any hint of, to whom I could do a thousand kinds of harm, never meaning to, or meaning to."

The minister said, "Good Lord."

"Yes. So I hoped you might help me. You're supposed to be a sort of last resort, aren't you? Who else could I say this to? I don't even know anybody."

"Well, yes, Mr. Boughton. I understand your concern, I do. I've wondered why you've been coming here, to Zion, when there are plenty of white churches you could go to. But now I see they'd have less sympathy for your situation than I do, little as that is."

"It's like I'm in hell. A destructive man in a world where everything can be ruined or broken—whole avalanches of bitter consequence ready to be set off, my very wife jailed, if things go too wrong, as they do."

"Well, yes. Please sit down, Mr. Boughton. Let's see if we can put some of this in a better light. Sit down for a minute."

He did. "I had no particular reason for coming to this church. Some people were kind." He didn't mention the business about retrieving his hat.

"I'm glad to hear it. And of course you're welcome to come."

"I can be calculating, but in this case I was not. Just to clarify." He did not mention lunch, or that piano.

"I'm sorry if I seemed to imply that you were."

"It's all right."

The minister said, "It might be worth remembering that responsibility for this doesn't rest on you entirely. I have the impression that Miss Miles has gone along with it."

Jack laughed. "We are altogether of one mind. We are conspirators. This is the most wonderful feeling I have ever had in my life. I get no comfort at all from the thought of lightening my burden by reminding myself of her 'responsibility.'"

"No, of course not. But to put the matter another way, she must see something in you, since she loves you, apparently."

"She has a high opinion of my soul. The first time we met, she thought *I* was a preacher. I don't know how she could have thought so. I was wearing a black suit, with brown shoes."

The preacher said, "It can happen to the best of us." He was making a study of his pen.

"No, I mean, I must have been putting special effort into my respectability, to distract her, or to compensate." He said, "Her kindness meant a great deal to me at the time. I did not wish to——complicate it. I mean, after I had first let her call me reverend, I couldn't set it right without explaining myself, which at that time would have been exceptionally difficult."

"But you did tell her."

"She found out."

"And it didn't matter. She is still impressed with your soul."

"Yes, my battered, atheist soul. I've been honest about that. Also, she's an English teacher. I like poetry." He laughed. "I have no explanation. I don't think there is one. I'm going to be loyal to her. She has my worse-than-useless fidelity, death do us part. If I am disloyal sometime, because it's my nature or because I'm persuaded by the soundest, holiest reasons in the world, that will end me, which might be a relief."

"Well," the preacher said, "if I can be any help to you, or if you just feel like talking, I'm usually here. I'm still thinking about that first question you asked me, how to tell faith from presumption, as I recall. An interesting problem." Then he said, "You should remember that the part of you that makes you try to avoid doing harm is as much yourself as any of these impulses are. Maybe you should try calling them 'temptations.'"

"Yes. There's a thought." They shook hands, and Jack went down the stairs and out the door into the bright heat of afternoon. He saw a woman passing on the other side of the street. It couldn't be Della. If she had come looking for him, how could she have waited for him so long without the risk, the certainty, of drawing attention, stirring gossip? He crossed and followed the woman for a few blocks; then she went into a house, letting herself in with a key. Not Della. Nothing like Della. She glanced at him, he tipped his hat, she stepped through the door and closed it behind her.

Here was his first thought. He would write the Old Gent a letter. It might be preparation for a visit home. His father would certainly write back, which would give Jack some sense of what he might expect, beyond the usual fondness and pardon and groundless hope. There would be a check, too, which Jack would not cash for ten or twelve days as a way of assuring his father that his straits were not especially dire. It was true of his good father that he allowed himself only virtuous words and behavior, which meant virtue in some form must be put to every use, even those best served by barbs and edges. This was not Jack's impression only. Teddy would smile and shrug, almost imperceptibly, when a crack seemed about to open in their father's determined patience—"If you could help me understand your reasoning here, Jack"—parsing some youthful dereliction that obviously made no sense at all, gently acquainting Jack with the fact that he wandered an inward terrain that was without pole or polaris, to put entirely too fine a point on the matter. And after the truth had sunk in, that Jack was as confounded by himself as his father was by him, Teddy would say, "Want to play a little catch?" or "It rained this morning. Let's see if the fish are biting." "Jack is with Teddy"— To the Boughtons, Jack, too, this meant Jack is all right, and the neighbors' setting hens and pumpkin patches are all right, together with whatever other movables his attention might have drawn him to.

Jack would say, "You always worried that I was alone. So you will be pleased to know that I consult from time to time with a pastor. He is not unkind, though he is sometimes remarkably candid, and of course this can be disturbing, the pain involved overriding the benefit I take from it only if, for example, I get drunk, which I cannot do because it is Sunday, a fact which also prevents me from buying a pad of stationery and a pen, also no doubt for the best in my present state of mind. I just might find myself writing to him."

"Dearest Della, my life, my love. The thought of you brings peace to my unquiet spirit." He could write letters to her at long intervals, weeks rather than days, since mailmen are not always perfectly discreet. But he would use the time to make the letters very fine. He'd include sketches in them, and poems. He could write out musical notes, and they would be like a code. *I don't want to set the world on fire. / I just want to start a flame in your heart.* She would laugh. He imagined her touching out the notes on Lorraine's piano. He might make a tasteful display of his intellect if he had read a good book lately. He would read only very good books.

"Dear Reverend Hutchins, I am writing to tell you that I resent your word 'arrangement' and all that it implies. A Presbyterian by birth and rearing, I respect candor, even when I find it patronizing, stinging, as in this case. My reverend father often said that the kind of emphasis given the sacrament of baptism in your denomination tends to elevate the minister toward a status he called priestly, by which he meant, fairly or not, that some random Reverend Hutchins might feel himself to be invested with a degree of authority relative to a fellow Christian that the covenant honored among Presbyterians would not countenance, to the point, it seems, of denying a man a simple blessing. So presumably I must forgive you for assuming authority over me as you did in intruding so bluntly into my personal life, of which you know almost nothing. An intensely lonely man for whom life has not gone well—I believe that was your language. And how has life gone for you? I have read about eminent domain, a yet higher authority. A wrecking ball will break in on your parish, Reverend Sir, and the sheep will be scattered!"

Terrible, desperate malice, which, sweet Jesus, arose in him only after any rhetorical use could be made of it, leaving him grateful for the near-miss. He was shamed nevertheless that he had entertained such thoughts, less for their meanness than for their blatant desperation. They arose just before the passions of embarrassment passed and the foolishness of his wrath became overwhelmingly clear to him. Presbyterian, indeed. His father would be mortified to know that, even in imagination, his son would send a wrecking ball against a house of prayer. True, being Jack, there was that in him that had to wonder how it would look to demolish a steeple. Closing the world down once a week to frustrate some percentage of bad impulses was Moses' best gift to humankind.

Wyoming doesn't rhyme with anything, but it would make a good title. Della told him at their wedding supper that when she was a child there was an old man in her father's church who had retired from the railroad. She asked him if he had ever been to Wyoming. He nodded. "Nothing there," he'd said. "Just a bunch of half-wild white folks doing whatever they damn well please. No need to leave Memphis to see that. You got no business with Wyoming." She said, "Well, it's part of America," because she'd read about it in school. He said, "It is. You ain't."

She'd gone to her father, crying, and he had said comforting things to her. She had so much to be thankful for, the Lord wouldn't want her to be crying over Wyoming, of all things, which might as well be another planet for all it had to do with her life. Then he went off to talk to that man about what it was useful or appropriate to say to children, what it was kind to say to them.

"I couldn't stop thinking about it," she told Jack, her eyes mild in the candlelight. "My Wyoming was all wind in the grass and mountains off in the distance and nobody to say, You don't belong here. It was like stepping off this world, the way I dreamed of it."

He almost said, That's a little like Iowa. No mountains, of course. He had often thought of walking with her among those fields, undulant as dunes, and the vast, reaching oaks, and the flickering cottonwoods shadowing the rivers. A modest, open, sunny place, at peace with itself. So many bird songs, such a thrum of crickets. It could be that no one would put those hard questions, that no great eye of custom and expectation would find the two of them on some nameless road through endless country and ask, even silently, Why are they here? Should they be walking along together, arm in arm? He couldn't tell her he had dreams of Iowa, that shining star. People might say, Did you hear about what Jack Boughton has done now? About the wife he brought home to his poor old father? Always up to no good. He had a history, nothing to be done about it.

He walked and walked, and ended up at Eads Bridge. He had dressed for church that morning, but tilt his hat a little, hang a cigarette from his lip and he was Slick. Who was he kidding, he was always Slick. He could lean against the wall and smile too wide if some pretty colored woman passed, maybe tip his hat to get a laugh. The usual effrontery nobody noticed. He thought of her seeing him there, fossils constellated around him in those great stones, the lore of the place a secret between them. And then it was evening and he walked back to the rooming house, back to his room.

———

The next day a note arrived from Della. "Come by my house tomorrow evening. My sister is here for a visit. She wants to meet you. She isn't as nice as Aunt Delia, but it should be all right. It has to happen sooner or later, anyway, and it will give me a chance to see your dear face. (I haven't mentioned anything to her about marriage. So—discretion.)" He actually checked his shaving mirror to see what about his face, its off-center aquilinity, its blue jaw, might be called dear. He attempted a smile. Then he thanked the Lord for the eye of the beholder, that perjured witness. His existence had begun to take on some qualities of a life. This is a well-known effect of marriage, not the most attractive feature of it. He could be very nice to the sister-in-law, who was not herself very nice. He would put the little volume of Frost in his pocket—"I have been one acquainted with the night. / I have walked out in rain—and back in rain." An honest account of himself, yet somehow romantic. Poetry does that, another perjured witness. Maybe he liked poetry because it also could not help lying. Oh well. There would be that moment when he stepped through her door, when he would study her face, if he let himself, to see how welcome he was, preparing always for some sad shock. He would not conclude anything from her formality and distance. Memphis has sent a chaperone, an informant. He would not watch for signs that she had been half persuaded of the foolishness of putting so much at risk for mere him. If he did see a sign, he would leave. There would be no recovery if she once began to doubt.

On the way to work he bought a pad of stationery, some envelopes, and a pencil. He spent the afternoon waltzing abstractedly, forgetting to accommodate his long stride to a short lady until she began gasping a little. Aside from that, his employment was far from his thoughts. His boss glanced at him twice at least, as if to remind him that there are such things as expectations. Point taken. He waltzed the last lady to the bench where she had left her purse, sat down with the pad of stationery on his knee, and wrote, "Dear Reverend Hutchins, Thank you again for your time and insight, and your candor. Sincerely, John A. Boughton (Jack)," and slipped it into an envelope. This was a pretext for going by the church, saving himself a stamp, giving himself a chance to lay the flat of his hand against a shingled wall of the place to feel its solidity. The paint was parched, and some of it would come away on his hand, but there would be no tremors yet, no colossal impact of metal against old wood, no splintering yet. Sweet savors, of popcorn, baked beans, peach cobbler, could still rise to the heavens from that corner for a little while, or a long while, condemnation idling in another street, coming when it would.

There were times in his youth when his imaginations of destruction were so powerful that the deed itself seemed as bad as done. So he did it. It was as if the force of the idea were strong enough that his collaboration in it was trivial. These impulses—they were not temptations—had quieted over the years. But the realization startled him when he recognized the fantasy he had allowed himself was actually identical with the desolation intended for this swath of city. He was a man of no influence, and he took comfort from the fact. But what if the particulars of his life were only flotsam, so to speak, drowned necktie, drowned wing tips, and he was sunk in that dark flood of unstoppable harm, somehow adding to its appalling weight, lost in it, even while its great shoulder pressed into the age-brittled side of that old sanctuary, that tabernacle raised to the glory of God Almighty, for heaven's sake? Some thoughts scared him more than others. He might have awakened to the explanation for many things, arrived abruptly at that insight into his own character and motives his father had urged on him, as if any good could come from it.

He had made an outcast of himself, yet he now knew he was not only a part of society, he was its essence, its epitome. If you could just explain your reasoning here—why you destroy and destroy, why you steal. He felt suddenly worse than ominous, the first buzzard to arrive at the scene of heartbreak. What a lovely home you have, Miss Miles! Jesus is looking especially well this evening. Then, crash! Your gentle self in jail, all love anyone ever felt for you an agony, all hope ever placed in you dissipated like smoke. I am the Prince of Darkness. I believe I may have mentioned that. For me, jail is a second home. Something I think I have not mentioned.

He went by the church, and there was Hutchins, sitting on the front steps, reading a newspaper. When he saw Jack, he laughed and flourished a cigarette. "At least I'm not hypocritical about it," he said. "Good to see you, Mr. Boughton Ames."

"Yes. I wanted to give you this. It's nothing. A thank-you note. Really nothing."

"It's kind of you to go to the trouble."

"No trouble at all." This was not the plan. There was no way to explain that he had somehow promised himself he would lay a hand on that hulking building. He'd have had to step into shrubbery. God forbid he should mention any of the thoughts that made him crave this momentary assurance. He would have walked away, but Hutchins said, "I've given some thought to the things we talked about. I know you will do as well as you can in the circumstances, by your lights, which is all I can ask, all you can do. I know the gravity of the situation is clear to you."

"Yes, very clear! Thank you." He walked away before the man could say more. Once, when he was a boy, he had asked his father if the devil could feel regret. His father said, "Well, you know, the devil might be no more than a figure of speech." Satan is Hebrew for adversary, and so on. So Jack didn't ask the next question, whether the devil had nightmares. The abysmal has no place in polite conversation.

By your lights, said the preacher to the man wailing in outer darkness. If Della were less splendid, less burdened with others' hopes, there might be less shame in his sidling up to her, pestiferous or combustible, or something of the kind, disguised as a social reject so that he could be the perfect agent of society's malice. These Baptists, dropping their dimes into his hat, sharing their supper, dreaming no harm, probably. And he would make a miserable return on their kindness. He had dabbled in shame as a youth, and he had learned from the experiment that shame had qualities in common with very lofty things, infinity, eternity. Like them it could not be divided or multiplied. Time-bound creature that he still was, he could not say for certain that there was no end to shame. He had suspected for a long time that it had at least that much to do with hell—also probably figurative, his father had assured him, tears in his eyes as there often were when he had to curtail another part of the great explanatory system his theology once was, to spare himself the implications it might have for his son. Jack had dabbled in shame, and it still coursed through him, malarial, waking him up to sweat and pace until, unsoothed, unrationalized, unshriven, it secreted itself again in his bones, and at the base of his skull, and was latent except for the occasional leering strangeness of his dreams. An ordinary man would not grieve forever over the sins of his youth, he was fairly sure. And an ordinary man would not dread this great, blind impulse of destruction prophesied at officious length in any newspaper. Then there was Della. Abstractly considered, a man who could threaten her as Jack did, if he felt no more guilt about it than he could live with, would be an utter scoundrel. This meant the dark storms of bewilderment would deepen and Jack would have no refuge except, of course, in Della's sweet calm. He took comfort so quickly at the thought of her that he felt a shudder of calm pass through his body, a thing he had never even heard of. He had to surrender his refuge in order to avoid the most desperate need of it. An hour or two tomorrow evening and then he would tell her goodbye and he would mean it. Try to mean it.

He knocked. The sister opened the door.

"John Boughton," he said.

And she said, "I know."

Della came into the room, quietly. He could not remember if he had been told the sister's name. He seemed to have interrupted something, no doubt a conversation so intense that a moment passed before they adjusted to the fact that anything else could matter.

He had left work early to make himself presentable. A barbershop shave, matching socks, a carefully brushed jacket that had begun to show the wear of brushing. His clothes were too old to be relied upon. A pants pocket had failed at work a week before, and a handful of coins had spilled down his leg. It was funny, he couldn't blame the ladies for laughing. He had gone to the five-and-dime for a packet of needles and three spools of thread, and he had mended, darned, reinforced with all the discretion he could manage, knowing these shifts might be seen as poignant, that the repair might be more conspicuous than the fray. In fact, standing there in Della's parlor, the object of weighty silence and pure, blank scrutiny, he felt every mend as if it were a scar on his person. Cicatrix. Strange words came to him at strange times.

He said, "I'm sorry if I'm late." Then, "Sorry if I'm early." He made a gesture with his hat, which reminded him it was still in his hand. No one had taken it, which, he realized, was the omission of a conventional sign of welcome. Don't interpret.

The sister said, "You're fine," in that tone of familiarity that is neither wholly dismissive nor, in a word, respectful. Not that he looked for any sign of respect, but he'd have been happy to find one.

Della came across the room, took his hat, took his arm, and rested her cheek against his shoulder. Reprieve. It brought tears to his eyes.

"Oh, Lord!" the sister said. "I'm not staying around for this. I've got a letter to mail. I think I saw a mailbox about ten blocks from here. About halfway to Illinois. You two need some time to talk things over. You'd better do that, Della." She didn't slam the door behind her when she left, she only closed it very firmly.

Jack said, "That was sort of decent of her."

"She meant well."

They sat on the couch. He decided it would be best not to put his arm around her. She pulled the book out of his coat pocket. "Robert Frost."

"In case there was a lull in the conversation."

She nodded. "I think we can expect a few of those." She said, "Thank you for being here. I needed to see you."

This was something he could have said to her any hour of any day, if she meant that a sort of need or craving was always awake in her that the sight of him could nearly quiet. Hunger increased by what it fed upon. Words to that effect. But she might only mean that she had something to sort out with him, a knot or kink in reality to be dealt with. It could never mean both at once, which was interesting. Of course, he and Della were entirely beset by problems, as many obstacles as the combined efforts of Missouri and Tennessee could contrive for them, if she chose to take that view of things. He could not imagine a sober conversation about their relationship that would not end with him out on the stoop, adjusting his hat. But if she said such a conversation was necessary, then it was.

Clearly he was not there to meet the sister. He still didn't know her name. His mind was reducing the simplest things to riddles, an evasive tactic that set in when it did him the least possible good. He actually thought of kissing the lobe of Della's ear before the last opportunity had passed. So deep were his fears. She took his hand in both her hands, closed her eyes, and said nothing. This might mean that she was feeling something like that peace she had mentioned once, or else that she was finding a way to say, as kindly as possible, something very difficult to say. He knew that things were not where he had left them, even where they were when she sent her summons.

After a few minutes, the sister came back. She said, twice, before she had opened the door much more than a crack, "It's me. I'm just here for a minute. I forgot the letter I was going to mail. I'll just come in for a minute. Have you told him? You have to do that, Della."

"I'll tell him. First I just want to enjoy the fact that he's sitting here beside me."

The sister said, to Jack, "The principal of her school came here, right to her house, to tell her that there was talk, that there was some question about whether she was setting a good moral example. He just left an hour ago. You could have come while he was still here!"

Della said, "He told me he didn't believe the rumors. He was just letting me know that I should be careful of appearances."

"And I suppose that's what you're doing right now," the sister said. "Being careful!"

Della stood up, went to the window that looked out onto the street, parted the curtain, and raised the shade. She said, "I'm tired to death of worrying about appearances." Jack went into the kitchen, undercutting her bold gesture by ducking out, a little humiliated, even though he was doing it for her sake. The back door was at the end of the hall, if he should need it. The sister was saying, "You are not thinking clearly! You're throwing your life away! Della, I'm closing this blind! And it's going to stay closed! It'll be the landlady bothering you next," and then, raising her voice a little, "You can come out of the kitchen now, Jack." Her tone was mildly derisive, of course.

"Thanks—"

"Julia."

"Thank you, Julia."

She said to Della, "Even he knows I'm right!" He had sided against Della. He had always assumed that sooner or later society might put a word in, some stark prohibition too codified and predictable to note the particulars of their situation, their austere and lovely marriage, except as an offense, a provocation. Surely Della knew this as well as he did. She could be careless because she was the one with something to lose. And he would have to be cautious, his least impressive, most wearisome quality in any case, let alone now that his loyalty was being tested, because every risk he took was a threat to her. She might come to his room, where the principal would not know to look for her and the desk clerk would smirk and mutter something about the cops, but where at least no one would be looking to them for a moral example. The long walks there and back at very odd hours—her problem, a threat to her. He thought of the two of them whispering under the covers on that narrow bed, laughing as quietly as they could, talking about Wyoming and the end of the world, he with his arms around her dear body. This would not be perfectly wonderful, it would be very imperfectly wonderful. What anyone at all might say or think would hover around them, a very real threat. To her.

He said, "I shouldn't be here. I should leave."

"Now or an hour from now. It won't really make any difference. I'd like it if you'd stay a little while." She said, "My sister can sit here with us, so she'll have some impressions to share with the people in Memphis. They might as well start getting used to us, the two of us."

Julia said, "I'm not here to carry tales back to Memphis. I'm here to tell you that you're causing a whole lot of unhappiness to your family. And I'm telling you, myself, what I think about that. I think it's a pure disgrace. When I heard about what was going on here, I couldn't believe it. I thought I knew you better than that." She glanced at Jack. "I don't mean to be rude. But you keep him sitting there. So he's just going to hear what I have to say."

"I've gone over this in my mind a thousand times. You know I would have done that, Julia. I am sorry that I've disappointed you."

"Not just me."

"I know."

"All of us."

"I know."

"We deserve better."

"I'm not so sure about deserving. I mean, there are some things you just can't owe to other people."

"*Some* things! You're ruining everything! You've got your boss worrying about your *morals*, for heaven's sake!"

"He suspects me of sleeping with my husband. Which I have done."

"Oh, don't talk to me like that!"

"You know it, anyway. So does my boss. We are one flesh. The cops have nothing to say about that. Whom God has joined, let no man put asunder. Scripture. The only time I feel immoral is when I'm lying about it."

"What do you even know about this—Jack?" A dreadful question. "How many women is he one flesh with? You've never even asked him, have you? I bet you wouldn't dare. Just *look* at him!"

The naked man in his clothes was suddenly, starkly exposed. Slick was no longer a refuge. He was an indictment, a false but telling testimony against himself, an attempt to look hard because he was not, wise in the ways of the streets because he was not, dissolute because this could not be helped, anyway. There was no John Ames Boughton to step out of this disguise, this carapace. There was hardly even a Jack Boughton. He offered that name to people sometimes as if it opened him to some kind of familiarity, but he was familiar with no one, not even Della, he thought, who did not look at him though she held firmly to his hand.

"Don't you leave!" she said to him softly, forbidding what anyone on earth would have wanted to do in the circumstances.

He found enough voice to say, "I won't," and wiped his brow with his free hand and wiped his hand on his pant leg, and thought he had felt wretched before but never, never like this. If Della had turned against him, taking as true the worst her sister was implying, he would have felt the betrayal as a kindness, on balance. It would be a cruel change, terrible to remember, impossible to forget, but so welcome in that moment that he could almost feel the calm of the evening air and accept the finality of the door closed behind him.

"You want him to be the father of your children?"

Della's hand in his tightened a little. "Yes," she said, "I do."

What a question. What an answer.

"You've lost your mind. There's no use talking with you."

Della said, "I'm pretty sure I told you that two days ago. Just after you got off the train."

Julia said, "I'm going outside for a minute. If I don't cool down, I'm going to start saying things I'll regret."

"You've done that already, Julia. So you might as well tell me the rest."

But by then Julia was crying. She sat down again and covered her face with her hands. Jack had Reverend Hutchins's handkerchief in his pocket, despite his fairly explicit intentions, and he stood and offered it to her. It was so immaculate and ample it was like a credential of some kind, to certify him as someone prepared to show compassion or gallantry whenever occasion arose. Julia took it and buried her face in it, and she said, "Thank you."

When he sat down beside Della again, she smiled at him and took his hand in both of hers, as if every good thing she might think of him had been confirmed. There was no end to deception. He had meant well enough, presumably. But he had stolen not only the handkerchief but the act it allowed him, that intimate courtesy to another soul despite anger or injury or estrangement. "You're welcome," he said, in a tone of tactful solicitude that reminded him of his father—this while the mention of his fathering Della's children brought back to him the thought of the worst he had not told her, the worst he had done. Julia was saying, "They shouldn't have asked me to do this. They thought I could talk to you because we used to be close. But that just makes it harder."

"We can still be close."

"I can't see how. You don't realize how upset they are with you, Della. Papa won't speak your name. He won't *hear* it. If I take your side, he'll never forgive me. I really believe that."

"Well, maybe with time—"

"Don't tell yourself that, Della. If you think time is going to end this, then you don't understand the situation!" She searched her sister's face. Della was calm under her scrutiny. "Well, I'm done. I've said what I have to say." Julia stood up and went to the hallway and the back door, blotting tears with that handkerchief he himself had wept into at the words "intensely lonely" and "life has not gone well." His mind was at work on this concatenation. Concatenation. There he was, destroying Della's world just by being who he was, where he was. Look at him! Guilt in his bearing, fraudulence in his attempts to seem like a fairly ordinary man. All this apparent to anyone, as he knew without any Julia, any Hutchins, to tell him. Still, Della held his hand.

That was something. What a relief to be out on the street. Della clearly did feel sure that she loved him. When her sister was out of the room, she turned to him, smiling, face shining, proud of her loyalty, at having withstood the onslaught. It was rare, even in his experience, to hear exactly what someone thinks of you. No point brooding over it. Still, that triumphant look of Della's meant she thought she knew the worst and was loyal all the same. The actual worst would be still another test. Obviously she had found this one hard enough to let her think the final trial of her loyalty had been made. He might as well let her think that. "Just look at him!" She did not look at him. If she had, she'd have seen him paralyzed with unease, like a criminal watching a search of his dresser drawers, his dirty clothes, waiting to see which of his paltry effects could at least seem to testify against him. His scar had begun to itch. Would it be the knots in his shoelace that gave him away? The thinning of his hair? Or was it that the disreputable pointlessness of his life had put its mark on him. Sometimes, when he had nothing better to do, he lit a cigarette, slouched against a wall, and watched people. He had found that passersby were less offended by cheek than by simple curiosity, so he adopted a wry and knowing air, smiled a little. From these studies he had concluded that the hardest faces were set in the moment of worst surprise—So that's how it is! These hard faces were a pitiless exposure of old damage. Innocence isn't lost, he thought, it is obviously, terribly, injured. And it abides as a gauge of the injury. He had no claim to being a veteran of these wars. No one had done him any real harm, except himself. He knew there was an old home always waiting for him. His fine, loyal family was the most presentable thing about him. Still, Look at him! the sister had said. That was a shrewd blow. No need for her to say more.

On the other hand, a wonderful woman loved him. He owed her some feelings of happiness on this account, a spring in his step and so on. But he could not put it out of his mind entirely that her father would not speak her name. His own father would embrace him weeping if given the chance, he was fairly sure. This thought was the thread his life had hung by. It was why he had to give a little thought to his own well-being. But now there was the fact of a colored wife, nothing that had arisen as an issue in Gilead, so far as he knew. His father had never said a word in his hearing about the mingling of races. It might be that his father would turn away from him, dear Jesus, a miserable thing to imagine. He would tell Della once more to consider what she was doing. These men of high principle made him feel pretty harmless, from time to time.

What he had in mind was not so much a plan as an interesting possibility which had presented itself unexpectedly, a kind of reward for his attempts at being conscientious and unoffending with the thought of keeping his job. He had been early to work a number of days in a row. There were few ways for him to ingratiate himself. This one, fairly useless in itself, signaled good intent but did not oblige conversation. The boss had decided that if Jack was going to be hanging around, anyway, he might as well be inside sweeping up, choosing records for the Victrola, allowing the boss himself to make a dignified entrance. His boss had given him the keys to the front door of the building and to the dance studio on the second floor, a big room with the scars and stains of other use showing through the midnight-blue paint on the walls, and in the dents in the oak floor, which was sanded and polished, and still darkly marred as if by weighty machinery. They danced with feigned grace across this scene of forgotten productivity, avoiding the bad places as they could. The windows were things of great dignity, tall and arched, framed inexplicably in heavy ornamental woodwork. They were hidden behind blinds and drapes to suggest night and to heighten the effect of the mirror ball, since the swooping and swirling in this ballroom occurred during business hours only.

Jack's sudden sense of the possible must have been as readable as were his boss's second thoughts, though possibility was as undefined in that moment as the boss's suspicions would have been. A pause, a glance of unspecific reproof, and then the keys were in his hand. "Don't—" the fellow said, and walked away. Jack put the keys in his jacket pocket, the two on one fob. All his conniving was mainly just an exercise of imagination, half of it daydreams about stealing time with Della. But he was open to suggestion. What interesting violations of trust had the boss imagined in the second before he handed over those keys? Downstairs were a barbershop, a failed lawyer's office, a dentist's office, the office of an accountant. Jack knew, because he knew such things, that there was hardly anything worth stealing. The dance studio was an empty room, in which even determined malice could hardly be up to much. There was a big, open elevator at the far end of it, for raising and lowering very heavy things from or to an alley. If it had worked, it would have been perfect for bringing up a piano. A lot of the futility of the instructing that went on there came with the problem many of them had really hearing the music, and from the fact that Jack heard it in his head and forgot to make allowances. This was not a problem. The slower their progress, within limits, the longer the ladies came back. Selling shoes, waiting tables, waltzing strangers— there is a craving for courtesy, even when it draws attention to itself as a sort of shared joke. Courtesy was one thing he still did fairly well, especially sober.

If he stole the Victrola, he would have to change his address and find another way to survive. The interval would no doubt involve selling the cumbersome thing in a back street for a pittance. Or trying to pawn it. Then desperation would prompt one of those shifts that bring jail time. His father called this "thinking things through." Such considerations had grown tedious because he was still a thief and endlessly obliged to rehearse them to stay on the narrow path. That pious demon Consequence had much diminished his interest in life.

His actual plan was simply to bring Della there, to the studio, to spend a few hours with her. They could play the Victrola and talk about whatever they wanted to and let the night take its course. Just stealing a few hours together could expose them to much more indignation than would any actual theft. There was a terrible vision that sometimes crossed his mind, of Della led away by police, not speaking, not crying, not looking back, proud as a martyr. And he, back in jail, having no way to find out what had become of her. Dear Jesus, what was he doing? This was not what he had promised himself. This was not harmlessness. He was sure he had no right to involve her in so much potential misery. How often had he thought this? But she had the right to involve herself, or had claimed the right, holding his hand the way she had. She was young, the daughter of a protective family. She might have no idea yet that embarrassment, relentless, punitive scorn, can wear away at a soul until it recedes into wordless loneliness. Maybe apophatic loneliness. God in the silence. In the deep darkness. The highest privilege, his father said. He was usually speaking of death, of course. The congregant's soul had entered the Holy of Holies. Jack sometimes called this life he had lived prevenient death. He had learned that for all its comforts and discomforts, its stark silence first of all, there was clearly no reprieve from doing harm.

Because there was a logic in the tendency of his thinking that made the idea seem reasonable, he decided to spend a night by himself in that building, that room, to make sure there was nothing about it to especially alarm Della. Then he would send his note. Please come by yourself through the unlighted, hostile, judgmental streets to an empty building where the Prince of Darkness will be watching for you, ready to die of shame if it all goes wrong. As if his shame were worth anything to her or anyone else. What would he say to her father? To his own father, for that matter, since he was now amplifying dread by imagining conversations that would never happen.

But staying there by himself was a mistake. The very first night he had the keys, as soon as it was late enough that the streets were empty, he rolled up his blanket, walked out past the bemused glance of the desk clerk, through the streets, pausing only to buy a hot dog from a malodorous cart still open for business in the hope of selling that last sausage. Jack had never learned to share the local love of sauerkraut, but it was free, as were mustard and ketchup. He was relieved to have stepped into the deeper darkness of the entry and to have turned the key in the lock without attracting any attention, so far as he knew.

Buildings dream at night, and their dreams have a particular character. Or perhaps at night they awaken. There is nothing cordial or accommodating about buildings, whatever they might let people believe. The stresses of simply standing there, preposterous constructions, Euclidian like nothing in nature, the ground heaving under them, rain seeping in while their joints go slack with rot. They speak disgruntlement, creaks and groans, and less nameable sounds that suggest presence of the kind that is conjured only by emptiness. Grudges, plaints, and threats, an interior conversation, not meant to be heard, that would startle anyone. Jack had never realized before that the city, the parts he knew of it, might despise its human infestation. He went up the stairs nevertheless and into the studio, as they called it, as it was listed in the yellow pages. It was vast in the absolute darkness. It smelled like Chicago.

The memory of that wretched pilgrimage, that frustrating, humiliating experience of drunkenness, of course made him crave a drink. He was suddenly sure that one small whiskey would give fluency to his thoughts and clarity, as well. How he could find himself persuaded of this again and again, despite all evidence to the contrary, he could not imagine, but so it was. Considered choice seemed suspect by comparison. He could wander the streets till he came upon some dive furtively alight and astir, where he could squander his pocket money, the whole of his worldly wealth, on a few watered drinks. Then those debt collectors would probably find him and pound him a few times for having nothing to give them, and he would congratulate himself inwardly on having spent it all before they found him, which would make sense to him because he was drunk. He had thought this through, and still he craved, still he was tempted.

He did find his way to a bench. It was actually his shin that found it. He sat down, then lay down, with the blanket roll under his head. He closed his eyes, then he put his hat over his face to make the darkness smaller. Then he took it off his face to feel less defenseless against sounds that were for all the world like stealthy approach. This was becoming a test of his conscience, to give him a sense of how much he had to dread. It wasn't theology that told him this, it was experience. Theology simply rationalized those nights he spent walking the streets, exhausted and glassily alert, a dull weight in his chest, thinking, Macbeth does murder sleep, or I have been one acquainted with the night, which was better suited to his situation. Why should a man with no other expectation of an afterlife than adding his bit of clay to verdant Iowa experience dread? His father told him once that the more scrupulous a conscience is, the heavier the burden it carries. He had decided at the time that Jack had a low estimation of himself because his conscience was so delicate it seemed to truly condemn him in his own eyes. Its stores were not so remarkable, after all, and if he could realize this, he could stop, so to speak, touching the wound. He worked this into a sermon, apologizing for the mixed metaphor and generalizing the thought to describe the whole of humankind. No one was deceived. And not so long afterward, Jack had mooted this comforting argument by adding a burden to his conscience that his gentleman father could never call unremarkable. Common is somehow indeed the opposite of unremarkable. *Hamlet.*

Being there alone was a bad idea. For one thing, he realized instantly that the big freckled mirrors would be reflecting that darkness, and he could not tell if he could see any difference between the reflected darkness and the darkness itself. Those unapproachable spaces beyond this bewildering emptiness. It would be altogether different if Della were there. If he imagined her sitting across the room from him, taken up with some thought that had nothing to do with him, the silence would be so gentle, so replete, that courtesy would oblige him to lie still. While I think on thee, dear friend. It might be infidelity of a kind to wonder how it was that his heart, as they say, had settled on Della, absolutely and exclusively, before he really knew her at all. He could have wondered to what extent she was the creature of his imagination, but he didn't, because the thought would be disloyal and because she was Della, far beyond the reach of his imagination. As a proof of some kind, they two seemed more and more to "mix irradiance," like the angels in *Paradise Lost.* He had used that phrase once to make an English teacher blush, and again to confound his father, a straitlaced man if one ever lived. "Easier than air with air, if Spirits embrace, / Total they mix." He must have been fourteen. His father, who knew his Milton, had looked at him, a serious, inward question apparent in his face, What does this child know? Jack had come into the world trailing clouds, certainly, which must have had another origin than glory, one that would account for a grating precocity uncannily predicting a jaded adulthood. So, at least, he construed his father's sad gentleness, the allowance always made for behavior that would have sent any other child Boughton to bed without supper. This anxious indulgence had scared Jack half to death. Now it seemed to him that he and Della were mixing irradiance whenever they were in the same room. Intimacy at a distance. So he was glad the grand poet and the irksome boy had supplied him with the phrase.

He imagined her sitting across the room beside the Victrola, all drawn into herself, still with dreaming, and at the thought of her, the darkness became an atmosphere he could breathe. He was a creature at home in its element, more or less. The thought of a benign presence takes the curse off loneliness, for some reason that is as natural as loneliness, a necessary mediation that made the human situation less an embarrassment. A snatch of vapor between earth and that raging star. The inward privilege of belief that a kindly intent had not forsaken him, and would not. It could not be altogether different if the presence were Jesus. His father could make something of this, a theological proof. Intending no disrespect by the thought, he said inwardly, to Della. Jonah was exceeding glad of the gourd, the plant that grew up overnight to shade him. Even his father used to laugh at that. Jack was exceeding glad of that hand holding his, an unaccountable loyalty, while those searing words were said out loud that were always in his mind. Just look at him.

After a while, light will reveal itself in a very dark room, not quite as a mist, as something more particulate, as if the slightest breath had lifted the finest dust into the stillest air. Then he could see the place where Della was not sitting, and where the walls must be. This bench reminded him of other benches, so he sat up. He might as well leave. Everything was about as he might have expected. Cars and trucks passed at long intervals, sending thin streaks of light across the ceiling. This was why he could not risk any light inside the room. There were a few voices in the street, then there were none.

But one mind by itself can fill a room. In such a large space there were no strategies of concealment, neither of him from his thoughts nor of his thoughts from his unguarded awareness of them. So there they were, that girl and the child. Glory had seen them playing in the river together, and told him so in one of those terrible little notes he had hardly glanced at. That one had made him wish he had been a third child, harmlessly there with them. Kneeling in the river, barefoot, soaking his dungarees to the pockets, he would rear up on his knees to throw a rock and be pleased at how far away it hit the water. He would ask, "You live around here?" The formalities of child acquaintance, tentative, oblique, shy. "I've caught some catfish just down by that bend. Pretty good-sized." She would say, "I just call her Baby. Seems like I can't make up my mind." And the baby kept stooping into the water, trying to pick up stones for him to throw. She never gave them to him. He never saw her face.

No, he was a college man, trying his hand at cynicism. He had the use of a convertible and a letter sweater. Ah, Jesus. "Give me a cig, Jackie. Just 'cause you puked the first time don't mean I will." He hated that fellow, always had. Thief, liar, worse, defrauding his father of every ordinary hope. And what was he doing now after so many years of penitential attrition? He was, day by day, depriving his father of his last hope. He knew exactly how the water and stones and silt felt in that baby's hands, under her feet. The West Nishnabotna was the river that circled Eden. He thought sometime he might get off the bus a stop early and walk to it, and kneel and wash his face in it, and then he would feel ready to go home.

But for now, here he was, entrusted again, by whatever it is that does the entrusting, with another human soul. He had not even bothered to promise himself this would not happen, since every single thing about his life had made it impossible. When the Lord shows you a little grace, the man said, he won't mind if you enjoy it. She had looked up at him that day, tiny droplets of rain in the puffs of hair that had escaped her hat. Then they were laughing, like girl and boy enjoying the accidental flirtatiousness of escaping the rain together. Tea from that chipped pot. Tea! It brought tears to his eyes. A moment of grace, truly, that ended with his slipping her book into his pocket, the one signed by the poet, and the slim *Hamlet* in the other pocket, so that the first one would not have so much effect on the hang of his coat. When she realized what he had done, she would never want to see him again, which would have likely been true in any case. He was just introducing himself—I am Jack Boughton, thief. He meant to leave the books on her step with a rose or something when he was done with them.

He had long recognized in himself a nagging urge to confess, which he sometimes indulged. To be forthright about his dishonesty, for one thing, could be a relief. To speak about his impulse to harm was much harder. So it should not have surprised him that the darkness had conjured that girl, so strongly that he was afraid to think what he might say to Della if she were there, what confession he might make to her. Della fallen silent in the dark, he unable to see her face, not daring to take her hand. Receding from him, while the river slid through its shallows, braiding and pooling.

He had to be gone from that room. He felt a kind of pressure of attention, something watching him closely when he could not see himself. Himself being the wretch that lived in his clothes. Look at him. But he did find his way to the door, found the doorknob. Then he remembered he had brought his blanket, so he had to try to find where he had been when he had it, groping along the benches, increasingly upset that he could be so wrong, that his sense of things could itself be a complication, a snare. He'd have risked turning on the lights just for a second, to orient himself, if he could have found the switch. It wasn't much of a blanket, but the difference between a blanket, however thin and short, and no blanket is absolute. In the morning the miserable thing would be there, anomalous as anything a windstorm leaves behind. If he left it there and came back early, he could find a place to stash it, surely, and if not, he could disclaim it. If he said it wasn't his, that would mean someone else had been there while he, Jack, had the keys. So not only would the lie be obvious, but the thing itself would be incriminating—why, after all, would he have a blanket there if not because he meant to bring in a lady friend? Jack might say, My wife, actually. And the boss would smile at the ridiculous transparency of the lie and fire him, anyway.

The scheme was so trivial it made him feel how overwhelming the darkness was. Whenever he did something he thought might be ordinary, marrying for example, it was as if he'd bought a ticket and a box of popcorn for an event everybody was going to, streaming in, the quick and the dead. And then the curtain would go up and it was the Last Judgment. What was he supposed to do with that ticket? He'd try to slip it in his pocket, to conceal an embarrassing misunderstanding no one else shared, and there would be no pocket, only his bare side, his bare leg. It was ridiculous that he still had his hat on. A terrible occasion he hadn't really remembered to prepare for. His astonishment would damn him all by itself.

He had stood still to think these thoughts, and then he began groping along the benches until he found the blanket, then along the benches in the direction he had come, then along the wall to the door. It couldn't be hard to find a door he had just left, but the distance from one thing to the next kept seeming wrong.

His entire life was an engrossing confusion, very small change cosmically speaking, and still anything at all could loom up like a great foreshadowing and accuse him. A baffled struggle in a dark place. A veritable Jabbok. Some laming involved. True enough. Point taken. When his pocket had given out the other day and his money had spilled on the floor, coins rolling in various directions—what genius decided that coins should be round?—he kept looking for that last penny because he knew he had five of them. Two quarters, two dimes, and five pennies. Four bought four hard candies, but five bought a chocolate bar. The petty dramas of his earthly pilgrimage. And still these overwhelming, Balthazarian revelations were visited upon him. Reprobate in any case, he tried to make it a point of pride to ignore them, insofar as they seemed only to point to his human vulnerability, of which he was wholly aware, thank you very much. So they became less nuanced, even blunt. The debt collectors began using their fists, for one thing. He hadn't told Della about that problem. He imagined himself with Della on his arm, showing her the city by night, when they appear, suddenly, anywhere, and he turns out his mended pockets and they punch him, anyway, for laughs, and what about Della? A miserable thought, bright as a dream. He might have a knife in his pocket, a switchblade, and then: Surprise! You didn't expect that, did you? There would be four of them, at most. If they got the knife away from him, who knows what might happen. They were always meaner. What about Della? She wouldn't run away. She might be all right if she were a white woman. Ah, Jesus!

He took off his jacket and hung it on the doorknob because his shirt was wet. He tried to wipe the sweat away from his eyes with his damp sleeve. Then he took off his shirt and spread it out on the floor as well as he could. The air was so still in that room, it would never dry, but he would have to put it on again as soon as he could stand to, to be out of there, out on the street.

The point was familiar enough. He was guilty of exposing this wonderful woman to risks—no, call them dangers—that he could not protect her from. It was as if he were being forced to see his whole life under an unbearably bright light. Was. The experience was not at all subjunctive. He had always been drawn to vulnerability, to doing damage where it was possible, because it was possible. Della was an educated woman firmly ensconced in a good life. He was nothing, a mere unshielded nerve, a pang mollified by a drink or two, a shine on his shoes. He had let himself be deceived by whatever it is that does the deceiving. He should have realized. No, he had to have known, somewhere in that dark brain of his that knew the word "uncountenanced" before it knew the state capitals. So he had committed himself to harmlessness, and it was his harmlessness that made a joke of their stealing from him, he even pretending they had some claim on him, some debt to be settled, to keep the transactions simple and brief, so he thought. It was his harmlessness that would make a joke of God knows what humiliation of him with God knows what consequences for his colored gal. He was still sweating, fanning himself with his hat. It was so clear, so obvious.

An honorable man would never have let things go this far. But she could still go back to Memphis. Her family might be angry at her, but they would protect her. Her family would see to it that she was safe. He could not. He would tell her he had reached a decision. The thought calmed him, though he would like to ask that preacher how he could enjoy a moment of grace and refuse it at the same time, a fair question, the kind preachers take seriously.

It was so late it would be early sooner or later. Night to morning turned like an hourglass, darkness divided arbitrarily. One of those mysteries sustained by nearly universal consent. Clearly prowlers and insomniacs were never consulted. In any case, he could go sit on Della's steps until the sun was well up, and then he would knock at the door. If the sister answered, no matter, because the speech he was composing in his mind would be just what she wanted to hear from him. Then she would know something about him that she could not tell by looking at him: he could be honorable. She would tell Della's father how candid and well-meaning he had been in his farewell, and how deeply he seemed to feel the loss to which he was nevertheless resigned. The whole business would be done within ten minutes. He could see past it already. He could draw his breath, almost light-headed with relief. "I have to give you up because I love you." She would see his point. He would have to nerve himself to glance at her face, but he could do that. It shouldn't seem too easy, since he believed that would hurt her. He knew how badly calculated his attempts at charm could be. Slick. But at worst that would make things final, which was the whole idea. She would think she had finally seen him for what he was, and honor would be served, at some cost in regret, which would involve him in fantasies of making things right to relieve the misery now and then. He went down the stairs to the street.

He had rolled up his sleeves, left his collar unbuttoned, tipped back his hat. A breeze chilled him. He was carrying his jacket slung over his shoulder and the blanket under his arm. A black couple, out late, dressed up, arguing pleasantly—"No, I didn't," "Why yes, you did!"—smiled and said hello. He felt like part of the neighborhood sometimes, his familiarity made interesting by his stealthiness. He said, "Good evening." At night the streets looked calm, solid, darkness hiding the decrepitude brought on by Eminent Domain, the giant that would fell forty churches. "Condemned" is the word they used. Bedamned. Steeples and sanctuaries bedamned. Even the very poor churches had managed a peaked window or two, or some lesser elegance that meant here we sing, here we pray, here we tell our children who they are. And all that life was condemned for the ground under it. He sat down on a stoop.

Della's church would be gone, and the house she lived in gone, too, condemnation certain, though every other part of the great plan was still being weighed. His own church would be gone, where he had known he could always go for a plate of beans and a little painful candor. Surely the Baptists would remove that rather bad painting of Christ ascending that hung behind the choir, put it away somewhere before a wrecking ball exposed it to the street, where its awkwardness, desacralized, ungraced, would make a joke of it. It was the earnest sign of solemn hope. It was a gloss on a beautiful text in the form of a clumsy image, which, he sometimes thought, if no other provision was made for it, he would steal and carry away to his room. It was hard to get a sense of its scale from the last pew, but he thought it would probably fit through his door edgewise. After that, decisions would be made. To stand upright it would have to be tilted, which would take up some part of a small space, from the floorboard to the foot of his bed. He'd have to move the dresser. This big, vivid, floating man did not square precisely with his own Presbyterian notion of Christ, but respect was owed. It might do him good to sleep under those blessing hands. If the desk clerk was astounded by a geranium, what would he make of this? The whole idea was ridiculous. The pastor probably knew the painter's name and where he lived and how he fared or where he was buried. He might have six cousins in the choir. This Jesus was family, and he would be seen to.

Exposure was a particular nightmare of Jack's even when he was not reminded of it by walking through these streets. He imagined all the papered walls, too pretty or too bright, the shadows of vanished furniture showing that they had once been prettier and brighter. Gaping doorframes, the ghosts of stairways. The rooming house he lived in would be excellent material for demolition. The apparent pathos of its bared interior would align with reality exactly. But his side of town was under no threat. Why should he feel guilty about this? Perhaps because, an adult male from a fine family with a plausible claim to a little education, he had absolutely no influence of any kind. He was not dust in the scales. This was a condition to which he had once aspired, which he could no longer think of as exonerating. He could watch with a certain joy a wrecking ball making splinters of that oversized hovel he called home, since Jack the Cat was safe in Memphis and the desk clerk would have been warned ahead of time. But this was no part of any plan. The shadow of Civic Improvement would pass over his house, and there would be no more weeping and gnashing of teeth in it than usual.

If he was going to spend the night on a stoop, it might as well be Della's. He put on his jacket and tied his tie. The sister could be the first one to open the door. It wasn't as if he had much to lose, as if her opinion of him could suffer any decline. Or it would be Della who opened the door, in which case he would rather not seem too hapless. He imagined himself making a dignified exit from her life, insofar as possible. He almost succeeded in persuading himself it would be better to go back to his room, to talk with Della in a clean shirt, with a fresh shave. He walked a block in that direction before he admitted to himself that he was very likely to lose his resolve. This was the kind of struggle he had often found himself sleeping off on a bench somewhere. And why assume her last impression of him would have a special importance? She had seen him drunk, as phony clergyman and roué; she had seen him as well turned out as circumstance permitted. She could be angry or scornful or wistful or embarrassed, and her memory would choose from the range of Jacks, narrow as it was, to suit her state of mind. He knew he would definitely have a place in her memory, for the misfortune he had been to her, and would continue to be, as long as she felt his effects on her good name and her father's hopes. Ah, Jesus. Was he talking himself into or out of that final conversation? Having done so much harm, was it really the honorable thing to walk away from it all? He had done that once, so long ago, and there were still leaden guilt, merciless dreams.

Ducking out was different from acknowledging the impossibility of going on together when the whole world has made and kept this infernal compact, making transgression and crime of something innocent, if anything could be called innocent, a marriage of true minds. Yes. Exacting from them a precious thing it had no right to and no use for. He could say this to Della, to be sure she would realize that he was saying goodbye because they were caught in a great web that made every choice impossible. He would be telling her something she knew much better than he did. There is always a risk in that. He must resist the temptation to lament to her as if the sorrow were his, when the whole brunt of trouble was already coming to bear on her. He had the distance between where he stood and where she might find him to decide if lamenting was a good idea, not simply an overwhelming impulse. Her composure was among the things that were beautiful about her. He might disrupt the courage and discipline and pride that sustained her. He could simply say, "I know you understand my decision. Of course you do. I thought this is what you might want to say to me. If you had, I'd have understood entirely."

When he came within sight of Della's house, he could see she was sitting there on the porch steps in the dark, bent over as if she were reading, though she could not be reading. There she was. It was because he had spent so long nerving himself for this conversation that he was a little bewildered when he saw that it would not unfold as he had imagined it would. He had not anticipated the privilege of this long moment when he had not yet said what he had come to say. He took off his hat.

When he saw that she had looked up at him, he said, "It's Jack," so she wouldn't be alarmed. She laughed. "I was beginning to think you weren't going to show up, Jack Boughton." She stood up and came to him and took his arm.

"I'm sorry. I didn't know I was expected. It's not the sort of thing I would forget—"

"I prayed you would come."

"And here I am."

"And here you are."

"This is very interesting. I thought I was engaged in a grim struggle with a decision, whether to come here or not, when there was no decision to be made. I was cosmically ensnared."

She nodded. "I plan to do this often. I get tired of sitting around waiting for the mail." They were walking arm in arm away from her house, toward the darker streets. She was happy to be with him, resting her cheek on his shoulder. She said, "I'm thinking how this could work. I could make you eat a few square meals. I could snuff out all your nightmares—"

"Thanks. You know, I might not be Jack without my nightmares. That's all right with me. It's just that I've never figured out the source of my appeal. So you might want to remember that random benevolence has risks. I do appreciate the thought."

She nodded. "I was drunk with power. I was about to give you a raise."

"Very kind."

"I know you'd just spend it on neckties."

He laughed, but he didn't really feel like laughing. Dear Lord, he had never considered what he actually knew, which was that she considered this marriage real and thought of their dear friendship as ongoing, abiding, perpetual. These were not words he had ever found much use for. It was no doubt literally true that she had in fact prayed that he would come by her house, which struck him as extremely remarkable. There is a difference in kind between what you want or wish for and what you pray for. It would require some thought to figure out the ways in which this is true, but it is true. And into this moment he came with his goodbye, which he had told himself she would surely understand. What a stupid thing that would have been to say to her. He felt himself blush.

She said, "You're quiet."

"Della," he said, "I've had a strange night. My boss gave me keys to the studio, the place where I work. So I can come early and open it up. That plan I mentioned—I thought if you met me there we could have a couple hours away from the world. I decided I'd try it out before I wrote to you about it. It was actually a very bad experience. Not that anything happened. I was just there by myself. An hour alone with my own worst enemy. I really roughed me up. You probably think I should be used to that. I thought I was."

"So you came to me! And I was waiting for you." She said, "I was really hoping you'd come because I've been having some troubles myself. Trouble sleeping, for one thing."

"Is your sister still here?"

"Yes, she is. She's been almost living in that phone booth by the corner. Now she's saying my brothers might come to St. Louis, at least two of them. Apparently they've persuaded my father to talk with me one more time. I'll go home for a few days. I'll have to do that. I love my father."

"Of course."

"All this scheming going on, all about me, and I'm just watching it happen. Every now and then Julia remembers to give me a little information. My mother is in on it, too, of course, planning everybody's favorite dinners so we'll all be in a good state of mind."

"Sounds painful."

"I'll just have to live through it. The hard part is that there's no use in it. I'm going to disappoint them." She said, "You'll be praying for me this time. That they'll let me come back here, first of all. I know this is not some kind of abduction, but—keep me in your prayers."

This would be the time to say something about understanding entirely if she decided to go back to her family, about how he would completely respect that decision. Then again, if she did stay in Memphis, he might be less miserable if he didn't remember helping her find the words, didn't see them in the letter she would surely send him. She stopped where she was, and he put his arm around her. He said, "You know, I plan to try to find a real job. That might make things better."

She shook her head. "He doesn't believe in marriage between the races. I probably don't either."

"Is that a fact! Then I have a confession to make."

"You're white? That's one of the first things I noticed about you!" She laughed. "I thought, If that man is ever hit by a sunbeam, somebody better call an ambulance."

"Nocturnal habits."

"You really could use a little color. If you're ever out in daylight, you might take off your hat."

"You don't know what you are asking."

She laughed. "I have a general idea." She said, "Let's go to that studio of yours. We could still have the place to ourselves for an hour or so."

"All right. Be warned. It's a void, a sepulcher."

"I fell in love with you in a cemetery."

"Is that true? I fell in love with you when you asked me in for tea."

"That memorable day."

"I suppose you're thinking about those books I stole. You know, that was a kind of confession, a clarification. You thought too well of me."

"You took care of that."

"I'm not sure I did. I mean, here you are."

"True."

As they walked, Jack kept an eye on doorways, the mouths

of alleys. The few black men they saw on the street paid them no particular mind. They watched them, of course, and one of them roused himself to step toward them and say, "Where you taking that girl?" But he was small and old and too drunk to be threatening, only trying to threaten because he was drunk. Jack realized he had imagined the impact of his harmless fist against an elderly jaw. Well, of course he was vigilant. Della was on his arm.

She had fallen silent. The two of them walked on like any unoffending couple, but faster, a little less inclined to look up at the people they passed than a couple would be who could actually be sure they would give no offense. They passed quite abruptly into the other side of town, where there were more streetlights to expose them, where those dreadful encounters always happened that sometimes inclined him to drink so that the pain would be dulled in anticipation and he could feel that in fact he had humiliated himself, their laughter and hard fists and taunting thieveries being purely adventitious. What a life.

It is impossible to walk naturally when you really want to run, but they walked quickly and quietly to the corner where the building stood, huddled in the dark of the entryway while he put the right key into the lock the right way, hurried up the stairs to the door of the studio, closed that door and locked it. And then they embraced, and what an embrace it was, as if they two had survived flood and fire, as if they had solved loneliness. Such an embrace.

After a while, Della said, "We have to think about some things."

"Yes. We do. I agree."

They were quiet. Then Della said, "There's something my father made us say. Whenever we quarreled with each other or told a lie or cried over something that didn't matter, or got a bad grade, my father made us say, 'I'm a Negro, because my God created me to be what I am, and as I am, so will I return to my God, for He knows just why He created me as he did.' Marcus Garvey, of course. Teaching us to respect ourselves. To live up to ourselves. I will say it to my children, and they will say it to their children and their grandchildren. They'll be Negroes and they'll live Negro lives. And you won't have any effect on that at all. Does that bother you?"

"No. A little. I haven't given it much thought, really." This was probably not true. When he walked through black St. Louis, he felt conspicuous and awkward. He felt no less conspicuous and awkward when he walked through white St. Louis. But he had begun to imagine a child walking with him, to whom he could tell things, which would seem impressive enough until the child, the boy, began to realize that the fragments of world his father had shown him or told him about failed to cohere. Eads's great bridge and its fossils, Gilead and its forgotten heroics, baseball. How to catch a fish or sew on a button. Psalms and sonnets.

A child is like anyone else. It needs food, clothes, a hand to hold, a place to be out of the dark and the weather. Jack might sometime try his luck with another cat. The child would be six or seven, and they would go out hunting together for a gray kitten with gray stripes, tins of sardines in their pockets. They could sneak into Mount Zion to play chopsticks if the place was somehow still standing. Hutchins would laugh if he caught them at it. Jack had often noticed that children are very ready to laugh. Merriment would be a pleasant addition to his life. He was an unserious man, but that is no fault at all in the eyes of a child. There were two reasons why his thinking on the subject of fatherhood did not go any further than this. It brought to mind that other one, whose laughter entered the world and left it while he tried out cynicism in the big city. His pleasure in the thought of a possible child felt like a slight on the actual, lost child, though it was not clear to him how this could be true, that is, how that child or her mother could feel the slight. And then there was the fact that Della's child would be colored, and if the two of them went anywhere as father and son, there would be no more to say. Dead to rights. What a phrase. The country had set up this whole crude order to thwart the creation of sons like his. He would see the boy when he saw his mother, by stealth, under cover of night. He would always be half a stranger to him, a puzzle to the child, an embarrassment to the boy, then an object of resentment to the man, very likely. His mother had unaccountably taken up with some old white bum. What gifts could he bring them, what comfort could he give them that would make him remember that man, if not fondly, at least kindly? Jack might try to pass himself off as casually interested, his mind on worldly things, his time spent on a shadowy, masculine elsewhere, except maybe on Christmas Eve, when he'd come by late with some trifle. Slick. The defense of his pride would be a thing he owed his son, however shabby the pretense involved. Ah, Jesus, the loneliness of it all.

"Yes," he said, "I know there would be problems."

By then they were sitting side by side, their backs against the wall, their knees drawn up, sharing his blanket and her coat. She said, "I do want children, though. Not right away, of course."

"You'll lose your job. You've got a good job."

"That's happening already. It's all right. There must be something else I can do. Maybe I could work for a newspaper. You know, one of the colored papers."

"And I'll be looking around."

"Yes."

None of this sounded like optimism. It sounded like two people saying the kind of thing they thought they should say, though they were too comfortable to rouse themselves to any serious intention. All losses are restored and sorrows end. What more could be needed. Then there were voices in the street. He lit a match so she could see her watch, they pulled themselves together, kissed in the darkness, and he watched her walk away down the street in the near-dawn, close to the curb, away from doorways and the mouths of alleys.

So Della went back to Memphis, to the embrace of her family, to dinners made sentimental by favorite dishes and old stories and smiles of abiding love. She will be an impostor of sorts, to all appearances herself and inwardly a stranger to them all, patient with their insistent kindness, waiting to be gone. She will come back to her unmarriage to her unhusband and live as she can, her vocation lost to what they will call turpitude. Eminent Domain will make rubble of the house she lives in, rubble of her church. The world around her falling away, she will still be gracious, her voice still soft. It was almost a habit with him to imagine her loveliness, the same through every change, rarefied, not vanishing, the very idea of loveliness. While I think of thee, dear friend, my heart breaks.

He went to church that Sunday, took his place in the last pew, listened to the hymns, listened to the prayers, heard out the sermon, left before the benediction. The topic had been "the least of these." Three infants were named and blessed, to applause and rejoicing. Then the minister said, "We all know these verses in the Gospel of Matthew, in the Parable of the Great Judgment.

The Lord says that every kindness you do to 'the least of these,' you do to the Lord Himself. So these babies give us a thousand chances to wipe away holy tears, and also to hear holy laughter, and to see those creeping things that creep on the face of the earth as the wonders they were on the day the Lord called them good. Yes. Jesus wasn't speaking of children particularly. We get old and ugly and maybe disappointed, and we don't see much of the Lord in ourselves or in our brothers and sisters. But the Lord does. This is something we always have to remember. The world can make you feel so small, the very least among society, humanity. And it is just then that the Lord is with you, loving you, saying, 'I know your heart just as well as I know my own! Stranger, prisoner, I know your heart!' Just think of that!

"But today I'm going to talk about these little ones we just welcomed into our church and into our life. We know that they will need special care. We know they will need the best teaching we can give them, to make good lives in a world that can be hard and cold, a world made difficult in order—in order—to keep them at a distance. We know they won't learn much we don't teach them, here in the church and in the schools we have struggled to provide for them. Not many are teachers, the Apostle says. Teaching is a sacred vocation, right up there with preaching and prophesying, according to the Apostle. This would have been true for the early church, when any sort of heathen might have wandered in just looking for a plate of beans, a kind word or two. In need of teaching. And it is still true for us. It wasn't so long ago that a man had to anchor a raft in the middle of the Mississippi River to teach our children at the high-school level, because it was illegal to do that in Missouri and in Illinois. That was a sacred work he did. Now we have Sumner High School, where this very sacred work goes on today. It is a rare thing among us to enjoy a real education, and it is a heavy burden on us that schooling is what we lack. So those among us who are teachers are like pearls and rubies, the best help we can find for our children. Our teachers must be honored and assisted in this sacred work—"

It was actually at this point that Jack stood up and slipped out the door and out into the street. No one had glanced at him. Hutchins kept his eyes on the front pews. Arnold seemed to be studying his hymnal. A discipline of kindness had set in that made Jack as self-conscious, almost, as if he were sweltering under a collective stare.

Of course, of course. His errors were so obvious when realization dawned. Did the preacher tell him anything he didn't already know? And yet it was as if a great light had found him in a guilty act, one of those deeds of darkness that seemed so much less nefarious in the dark. Here was consequence again, a gigantic, censorious presence showing him diminished lives, children robbed in their cradles by one Jack Boughton. He had been a little afraid to wonder why he felt implicated in the imminent destruction, and now he knew. If he were an honorable man, he'd have left her alone.

He had one twenty left. He went by the old rooming house to see if Teddy had left money for him lately, and an envelope was there waiting. He went back to his room and put Teddy's two tens into his pillow with the twenty through a gap in the seam which he closed with a few stitches to keep feathers from floating out and defeating his stealth. Then he began work on a letter.

> *Dear Della, I have left St. Louis. I can't stop thinking of you, so I have to go away, too far away to find myself sitting on your stoop again, longing to hear your voice one more time. I know I am not worth the loss you will*

be to your students if you can't go on teaching. It is
really very simple. I'm ashamed to think of the harm I
already have done. I actually in a sense pray that there
is still time for things to be all right, for the scandal
to end when I am no longer here to be the cause of it.
Please understand and believe that I am doing this in
deep love and respect. Jack.

It really was simple, adequately dealt with in a few words. He did not mention their marriage, since she should feel completely free to make other choices. He was careful not to make the letter emotional, because then it would be at odds with his purpose in writing it, with the finality of his intentions. He knew that if he got himself a bottle of something to get through the day and the night, his resolve would dissipate or in any case lose itself in the bogs of dissipation. Better to do all this sober. He would turn up at work just to hand back those keys, a responsible ending to the old life. Then he would go off to the dead men's shoppe to see if some gentleman had departed without his valise. He would leave a note for Teddy at the old rooming house, telling him he was no longer in St. Louis and thanks for everything. He had no intention of sending him a new address when he had one. He was cutting a lifeline. Teddy would interpret. Teddy would grieve. He might not think, That son of a bitch, but he would know he had the right to think it.

Here he was, trying to change his life for an excellent reason and oppressed by that old feeling that he was enmeshed in a web of potential damage that became actual in one way or another if he so much as breathed. All right then, he would keep his eye on the object, protecting Della and her sacred work. Whatever else burned or shattered as he did this one thing he would simply ignore. Little had ever mattered more to him than the loyalty of his brother Teddy, for example, which he had tested severely and had never shaken. Here he was depriving that good man of the possibility of doing further kindness to him, which, loyalty being what it is, was cruel. But he had nothing to tell his brother about where he would be, and he had to spare him the bother and the expense of future trips to St. Louis. If he ever got on his feet, he might begin to pay Teddy back. He imagined re-entering Teddy's life with a costly gift, a gold watch, say. And Teddy would accept it in that bemused and tentative way he had always accepted gifts he thought were probably stolen.

But painful as it was, this was a minor problem. He had written the letter to Della. Now how was he to get it to her? He did not know her family's address. It would be best if she were with her sister or her mother when she read it. She hadn't planned to stay in Memphis long. She could be on her way back already. Then she might come to his rooming house from the station, as she did that other time, and learn he was gone from the desk clerk. That lout as witness to her surprise and hurt. The thought was intolerable. He would have to stay in St. Louis until she came back and give her the letter himself, and wait with her while she read it.

The letter was a problem. If he spoke to her, he could choose his words very carefully, so that he could live with the sorrow he would see in her proud, gentle face. This was clearly his only choice. He tore the letter into very small pieces.

It was still Sunday, a very long day. He thought she might not have left Memphis on the Sabbath when, if things were going well at all, there would be a big dinner, maybe with guests and relatives. So he went out for a walk. To her house, as it happened. Just in case she might have come home and he could speak to her while that sermon was still ringing in his mind. He knew that if he saw her his resolve might dissolve—nerves—but at worst he would see her. Then, as he approached her house, he saw a notice of some kind in the window. It said FOR RENT. There were no lights on. He knocked and there was no answer. He had to sit down on the stoop to get his breath. People passed as he sat there. It was early for him to be haunting their street. What the hell. He stepped off the stoop into the bushes and cupped his hands against the window glass so he could look into the room. No piano. Crates in the middle of the floor. His emotions, unnameable as they were, would be seen and interpreted by any number of passersby. He had to pull himself together and leave with whatever dignity he could manage.

There had to be a letter from her. The desk clerk might or might not mention that mail had come for any of them, as it did so rarely that they never bothered to ask. As soon as Jack was out of the neighborhood where anything would be made of it, he actually ran back to the rooming house, burst through the door, and demanded the letter.

The desk clerk took note of his agitation. "What letter? I mean, which letter?"

"Hand it over."

"The one that says, Get out of my life, or the one that says, We can still be friends. They both came the same day, so I couldn't tell which order you should read them in."

"Hand them over."

The clerk opened a drawer and took out a stack of envelopes and slips of paper. He removed one letter and gave it to him. It was sealed. He said, "You've got to learn to take a joke, Boughton."

"You said there were two."

He shrugged. "Kidding."

"When did this come?"

"The other day."

He went up to his room to look at it. The postmark said Memphis. She must have mailed it as soon as she arrived there. Still, she had hardly been gone long enough to have given in to the pleas of her family. She might have written the letter before she left, or on the train. So whatever it said had been decided by her even while they were together that night. There was no return address, which seemed ominous. Why was it so hard for him to catch his breath? At worst, she was writing to tell him more or less what he had decided to tell her, which would be a blow, but also a relief. At best, it was some sort of love note, which would be a disaster, since he could tell by the event it was to hold the letter in his hand that his resolve would not survive the sight of one fond word from her.

To expend some emotion, probably, he went halfway down the stairs and said to the desk clerk, "Somebody's going to kill you one day."

He didn't look up, still sorting through the stack of mail. "Maybe so, but it won't be you."

True enough.

"By the way, here's the other one." He put a letter down on the counter. "You might want to read it first." The envelope was sealed, there was no return address, the postmark said Memphis.

The desk clerk could not know what was in the letters. The envelopes were clearly intact. Still, it probably did matter which order he read them in. He used a key to tear open both envelopes, then took the letter from one of them. It began: *Dear Mr. Boughton.* So he glanced at the signature. *Julia Miles.* No need to read that one. The second began: *Dear Mr. Boughton* and was signed *Delia Highfield.* Why had he assumed they came from Della? The delicate female handwriting. He might have noticed differences if he had thought to look for them. As far as he was concerned, their case was made. He had relinquished his wife to them, for heaven's sake, granting certain difficulties, for instance Della's refusal to be relinquished. Neither sister nor aunt had done him the minor courtesy of providing a return address. So he could not tell Della that he would be gone from St. Louis. She might come to this damned flophouse asking after him and the clerk would tell her he was gone and then watch her dear face while she tried to compose herself. Jack could leave a letter for her, but clearly he could not be sure the clerk would give it to her.

He went down the stairs. The clerk glanced up from his newspaper. He said, "Boughton, you're alarming me," and went back to his newspaper. Jack walked around the desk, opened the drawer where mail accumulated, and grabbed the stack of letters, cards, scrawled scraps of paper, and took it all up to his room. Why? But there it was, scattered on his bed. First he sorted through to see if any of it was addressed to him, reasonably enough. There was an IOU he seemed to have signed, with no amount written in. There was a card that said, "Please! Please! Forgive me!" without an address or signature, and one that said, "I will die soon. I blame you."

These were thoughts of the kind that more or less hung in the air in that establishment. He should have left there years ago. He might have been a different man if he had passed those years in a different atmosphere. That he had to remind himself that his adult life had not been purgatorial by accident was already a sign of progress. The thought of leaving that room was bracing. He was startled to realize that he felt less dread than anticipation. He would send a letter to what had been Della's house, hoping someone would get it to her if she did not find it herself. He would leave a note with the desk clerk in the hope of comforting her a little if need be, assuming he would actually give her the note.

So, two notes to Della, one to Teddy. He tore the IOU to atoms. Then he undressed for bed, negotiated what he could in the way of comfort with the scanty blanket and thin pillow he had once shared with Della, his wife. She still felt a little bit present with him. That would end. He was doing right by her, her whole family would tell her that, or some version of it. He had not felt so morally certain, as his father would say, since he left college for St. Louis to spare his brother the perils of cheating for him. Now Teddy was a doctor and Della might still be a teacher, despite his pernicious influence. The best thing he could do in either case was to disappear.

It was also the worst thing. A chilling thought. He got up, got dressed except for his shoes, and lay down again. More than once he had heard his father say, "That little fellow just refused to be born. Ames and I were on our knees for days!" He didn't say, "That little fellow almost killed his mother." One bad act in the closing hours of his pre-existence, then who knows what. Her soul enfolding forever her little assassin. When he heard the story of his birth, the doctor down with pneumonia and the vet, smelling sweetly of carbolic acid, rocking those hours away on the front porch just in case, he sometimes wished he could have been left unborn. But that had been decided for him. His refusing birth, or attempting to refuse it, might have meant he suffered the kind of foreknowledge the unborn lose as they pass into the world. He had read about that somewhere and it seemed plausible to him. In any case, his mother lived to grieve over him, which was the better outcome, since her other children flourished and cherished her and altogether exceeded any mother's hopes. His father would say of his fiercely recalcitrant son, He grew up as tall and fine as the rest of them. It was true, Teddy was his virtual twin. Their father would say, "These hands are not more like!" And once Teddy had asked, "Which one is the ghost?" That was when he was still showing up to Jack's classes in Jack's clothes, when he was learning to hang back, to smile almost sardonically, to loiter where anyone else would simply stay or wait, as if he had no good reason to be anywhere. It was frightening to watch. Next he would be lying or stealing, not just making hash of the honor code. Teddy should have been living his own estimable life. Jack was right to have vanished into St. Louis. Of course, there were all the other things that made it wrong.

Morning would never come.

But it did, and Jack set himself to preparing his departure. He went to Chez les Morts, where he did in fact find a valise, worn at the seams but respectable, and a newer shirt. He went back to his room and stuffed his earthly possessions into the bag. When he went to the studio to turn back the keys, he found the boss so shorthanded that he stayed and danced around for a few hours, which meant his trip was delayed to the next day. But the boss gave him a couple of dollars and several ladies kissed him goodbye, and that lightened his mood.

Another night, then the long trudge to the bus station. As he was leaving, the desk clerk said, "It's going to be pretty dull around here." This made no sense at all. Jack was quite sure he had never even screamed in his sleep, though that would have been perfectly acceptable behavior. He knew he had never assaulted another tenant despite provocations enough. He had never once been arrested in the entire time he had lived there. In general, he had been careful to add no interest at all to their collective life. He took pride in the thought.

He said, "You'll manage."

The clerk shrugged. "So far so good," which wasn't true either. No one under that rotten roof, no one in that heartbroken street, could say those words and mean them. Jack paused in the doorway to consider a reply. The clerk half smiled the way he did when he knew he'd gotten under Jack's skin. So he left, done with all that.

He bought a one-way ticket to Chicago. None of his associations with the place were positive, but at least he had been there before. Youth in Gilead, Iowa, had not exactly made a worldling of him, and since then he had kept his expectations low enough to assure himself a very simple life. He had no reasons to prefer Chicago to Indianapolis or Minneapolis except for his slight, unhappy acquaintance with it. That was at least something.

He took a seat toward the rear of the bus, by a window. In the waiting room he had noticed a young woman struggling to quiet a child who appeared to be restless with fever. Sure enough, they took the seat next to his. The woman was wearily apologetic. Jack said, "I know how it is, don't give it a thought," implying that he knew something about children in order to lessen her embarrassment. In fact, he was surprised by the strength of the creature, the weight of its lolling head, the impact of those hard little shoes kicking against his leg. The woman tried to hold the little girl's legs and set off an eruption of shifting and striving that Jack, a patient man, thought might make the trip unendurable. He could get off at the next stop and hope for better luck whenever he had the price of another ticket. But the buses were still crowded with the effects of repatriation. He was lucky, in a manner of speaking, to get the seat he had.

The woman said, "I'm Margaret. She's Lucy."

"John," he said.

Lucy bucked against her mother's embrace and cried loudly. "This just started yesterday. She was fine before that. I wouldn't have left home if I'd known this was going to happen." The baby lolled her big head, wet face, damp hair, and looked appealingly at Jack, as if there were anything he could do for her. She reached out a wet hand toward him.

Margaret tried again to bundle the child against her. "So you have kids?"

"Yes. A girl. And a boy." Why not? He was only elaborating on the first lie, which was innocent, kindly meant.

"How old?" How long ago was she born? Or how old was she when she died?

"Two and a half," he said. "The girl. The boy is seven."

"So he can help his mama keep an eye on her. Lucy's two and a half. She runs me ragged."

He was trapped in this conversation, hearing himself lie for no reason, really, except that he couldn't see how any harm could come from it, which never meant harm didn't lurk. The woman stood up to adjust the hold she had on the baby, who whimpered and squirmed and, when they sat down, thrust out her legs against Jack's thigh. He said, "You have to get her to a doctor."

"Doctors cost money. Besides, she's just coming down with a cold or something. She'll be fine."

"I have money!"

She leaned forward to look at his face. "So do I," she said. "Because I don't spend it when there's no need."

He said, "You don't know. An infection can take hold very quickly." Words his mother had written, regretful that they had not reached him earlier so he could have come home in time. As if he'd have done that. He said, "We could get off at the next town. I could help you find a doctor."

She said, "You just relax, mister. I can take care of my baby." Then, after a few minutes, she said, "You lost your own little girl, didn't you? I am so sorry!"

He set his hat over his eyes and leaned back. He could feel the embarrassed restlessness of the woman beside him, a compassionating gaze with nowhere to rest, no one to see it. Like what? Like that letter from his mother.

He got off at the next stop, bought a bottle of orange pop, and brought it back. "I thought she might like this," he said.

"You're real kind."

He leaned back, hat over his eyes, and pretended to sleep. In a while the fussing and pummeling stopped. The baby was asleep on the breast of her sleeping mother. He actually touched the baby's plump, sticky cheek, just to be sure. It was cool. The baby murmured and turned away from his touch. They two had spent any number of hours wrestling each other and now they were lovingly asleep. There wasn't light enough for him to read. He could hardly stir without waking this Margaret and Lucy, whose quiet was a great relief to him. Towns and farms and rail yards. Once at a stop he contrived with much care and long-leggedness to extricate himself, to walk out into the chanting night for a smoke, then to insinuate himself again. So far so good.

He would have left the bus that morning in the fringe of the city that was clearly hospitable to low expectations, but the woman and baby were still asleep; the baby's head was pillowed on his arm. Two more stops and Margaret woke up. The shops now had a flourishing look, the hotels a certain polish, a certain urbanity. Supposing things could only get worse, that is, more genteel and expensive, Jack took down his valise. When he stepped into the aisle, Margaret said, "Wait! My aunt has a boardinghouse not too far from here. I can give you her address."

He gave her a book he had meant to return, Robert Frost, and she wrote an address on the inside cover and a note. *Dear Auntie, this gentleman has been very kind and helpful to me! Margaret.*

He thanked her, stepped off the bus, and noticed a café and a bookstore. First a roll and coffee, then, unshaven and weary of his clothes, he nevertheless stepped into the bookstore just for the familiarity of shelved books, some of which, in shabbier versions of themselves, he had spent stray or furtive hours with, engrossed from time to time despite the comeuppance or plain maleficence that stalked his contracted world. It was a beautiful bookstore with high ceilings and fine old books in glass cases. All the classics were there, robust ranks of them. There were books in French and German, books of poetry and history. There was the smell of books. To calm himself he took down good old *Leaves of Grass*, and stood in the aisle reading until he almost forgot where he was. When the clerk spoke to him, he quickly checked his memory to assure himself he had not slipped anything into his pocket, took off his hat, and smiled.

She was a young woman with a pleasing face, smiling at him.

She said, "Can I help you find anything?"

"Hart Crane," he said, to impress her. "He's difficult. I thought I might give him another look." He'd checked. There was nothing by Hart Crane. He wouldn't have to talk his way out of buying anything. He touched his shadowed jaw. "I've been traveling all night. I should find a hotel. But this is such a beautiful store, I had to look in."

"We're proud of it," she said. "I see you found Walt Whitman."

"Yes, an old friend. I knew he wouldn't mind if I'm a little rumpled, a little weary." His reluctance to shelve the book was unfeigned, but with this pleasant little woman standing there, there was nothing else to do with it.

"Not so many people come here asking for Hart Crane. For poetry, really." She asked, "Are you a writer? You sort of look like one."

"From time to time I try my hand. I don't think that counts. A nice thought, though." Even dishevelment seemed to be working in his favor.

"Well, if you're new in town, we have an opening here. My father is always looking for someone who knows the merchandise, he says. If you come by late morning tomorrow, he'll be here."

"Yes. Late morning. Thanks." He backed out the door, gesturing ceremoniously with his hat, and she laughed. It was a joke. It wasn't nerves.

This was all very strange. Here he was with the prospect of a position that would be both suitable and desirable. Then he remembered that the address of the boardinghouse was in a book in the valise he had left in the store. He stepped back in, and the young woman was waiting there to give it to him. Another flourish of the hat, very pleasant laughter, and he was in the street again, thinking, to his surprise, he'd have to find a way to mention that he was married.

He found the boardinghouse, not so far away. It was surrounded by commerce of various kinds, low-lying buildings with signs over their doors and parking in front of them. But the boardinghouse was a holdout from another time, with gardens in front of it and a wrought-iron gate. It looked like the very idea of a comfortable old home, curtains in the windows, rockers on the porch. Nevertheless, he went up to the door and knocked. This time it was a pleasant old woman who asked if she could help him, then smiled and said, "Oh, yes! My niece telephoned. She said you were very kind. Yes, I have a nice room all ready for you." He followed her up the stairs, and she opened the door on what indeed was a very nice room. The bed was fat with pillows and blankets, there was an overstuffed armchair, a big, polished dresser. Oh, for heaven's sake, a trouser press with a shoe brush. Decent prints of old paintings. Bathroom next door.

He said, "It's very nice. My wife will love it. I believe I will have a job soon—"

"Good for you. You get some rest now. I put out a little light meal at seven in the evening. Then there's breakfast. You're on your own for lunch."

What was the joke? He tried not to be too obviously amazed, too effusive. But there was an enormous porcelain tub in the bathroom. Tile everywhere, all intact, shining. The lavender in the air was about half as sharp as smelling salts, a purgation all by itself. Stacks of white towels. He would scrub that scrawny devil, Jack Boughton, within an inch of his life, shave him to perfection, lay him down on that fat bed and drowse until it was time for the light supper. He could not stop wondering when he would make the fatal misstep, when the trapdoor would open. Everything was going far too well. At very worst, though, he would face ridicule or denunciation clean and shaved. The light meal was sliced beef, warm brown bread, potato salad. The four other boarders nodded but showed no interest in him or in one another. Wonderful.

The next morning, after ham and eggs and a stiff black coffee, he strolled in the direction of the bookstore. He worried a little about being too early or too late, but then he noticed that ahead of him there was a doughty old church with a clock in its steeple which was just then confirmed by a peal of bells telling the hour. Eight o'clock, they said, as if they had heard him wonder. Uncanny. He had left the bus two stops late and found himself—here. If Teddy somehow tracked him down, Jack could show him an acceptable life. For how long? If he got a job, and if he could pay his room and board. In the meantime, he would consider it all unusually satisfying theft. The distance wasn't so far from his window to the ground.

Five minutes before the church bells would ring ten, Jack walked into the bookstore. He was Teddy for the moment, calm and forthright. The father was there and so was the daughter, both, it seemed, pleased to see him. "John Boughton," he said, and they shook hands. In just a few minutes he was employed at a decent salary, expected to keep up more or less with the new books coming in, though a wider familiarity with their stock would be a good thing. He would actually be paid for this, for standing around looking as though he belonged there, with a book in his hand. He had left university without a degree— this was very true—then knocked around awhile—also true, though he shrugged and smiled when he said it, to suggest that his scarred face had a raffish tale or two behind it. He did not mention his stint as a dance instructor, which seemed even more inelegant in retrospect, and of course dishwashing and the rest were so firmly unmentioned that he almost forgot them himself, together with the time in prison. He had really never considered that there could in fact be a place in life suited to Jack Boughton. The boardinghouse had a parlor with a piano. It had a washroom and a porch for hanging laundry. And his rent was just a little higher than the rent he paid on that bleak room in St. Louis. Still, he was always writing letters in his mind—If only you could be here, too, dear wife. Dear friend, the loneliness might kill me. He would save up some money and go looking for her.

What would be the point? All this misery was meant to send her back to her good life. Weighing one thing against another, say, for instance, that she was sad, embarrassed, disillusioned, she was also young, full of life, charming. It wasn't in the nature of things that she would be alone any longer than she chose to be. He might show up sometime, just to say he regretted the way things had ended, and she would say, "I thought *I* was the one who ended it," and laugh. She might say, "You're looking very well," to make the point that their separation had been good for him, which would imply that he had his own reasons for putting an end to the endless awkwardness they called their marriage. He might sense anger in a remark like that, knowing she would never admit to anger. He would be making a kind of demand on her pride that was never welcome, making her eyes tear or her voice fail or break, when this was the last thing she would want to have happen. Then he would know he had hurt her once by leaving, then hurt her again by disrupting the calm she had induced in herself to hide her shock, her sadness. He thought sometimes that he should give up the constant bathing and shaving, the suppers if not the breakfasts, because he had noticed he did look better. Flourishing seemed wrong in a man so disheartened as he was. He thought of sleeping on the floor. Then again, if Della saw him looking trim and fit, she might not wonder how she had ever felt an attraction to him. If he took reasonable care of himself, her first thought might not be that he was old. Years could have passed before he saw her again.

He would buy a suit. In St. Louis he used to wonder how many of the best suits went into the ground with their owners, as if their clothes could recommend them to that Dread Tribunal which, as Jack read the Text, would have found merit in a second-best suit, the better one left behind as a courtesy to the necessitous shopper. So many of earth's grievances could be soothed by a little consideration. These were the thoughts of a man settling into a life of comfort, more or less. He found sheet music for Chopin's *Etudes* in the piano bench, and he studied them, softly exploring them on the parlor upright to the inexpressible delight of the landlady. His manners were not too refined for any occasion, as far as she was concerned, at least. Nor was his grammar too precise. He gave the place a certain tone, clearly, frayed cuffs notwithstanding. Still, he needed a new suit like a snake needs a new skin. There was a kind of itching involved.

At work he mastered the cash register. He was very much an adept at dealing with change. That old courtesy that had stood him in good stead as a shoe salesman and dance instructor had to be tempered a little, made slightly conversational, but he did well enough. He forgot customers' names but remembered their interests, which flattered them. He got a raise. On quiet days he stepped out to lunch with the boss's daughter. He had not yet found the moment to tell her that he was married, though he was always imagining that he would show Della this pleasant life he had wandered into. He imagined her sitting in that overstuffed chair in the evening lamplight, reading while he read, listening while he told her how long the days would be if he did not almost believe she was with him there. "This is our marriage," she would say. "This is what we promised each other."

On Sundays he would walk to black neighborhoods. He had looked in the phone book for the streets where their churches clustered, A.M.E., Baptist, Pentecostal. There were people in the streets on Sundays, dressed up, convivial. The idea was to find, to hear, even a word that reminded him of her voice, a timbre that he now and then did hear, that confirmed his memory. He could not summon it in his mind the way he could almost hear notes of a song, but he heard the unlikeness of other voices, the likeness of a rare few voices, there and gone in a phrase. She *had* to have sent him a letter. Her gentleness would have compelled her to.

Until further notice he was a married man. He found the idea bracing, stabilizing. The savings that had accumulated in a dresser drawer would go first toward a suit, but this was part of a larger intention. He had learned the practical value of a reputable life, not only its health benefits, but also the presumptively good opinion that came with expecting to be well thought of. A rope of sand. The trick was simply to think about the rope and forget the sand.

Having erased the last marks of pathos and distress from his appearance and manner, he would go to Memphis, to that A.M.E. church, and speak to Della's father. He would bring a letter, carefully thought out, addressed to him. He hadn't thought it out yet, but it would take a little time to make himself as presentable as he ought to be, so there was no urgency. If that went well, if her father accepted the letter, he would ask if he, Jack, might be put in touch with her, understanding, of course, that she might not want any contact with him. He would basically repeat the contents of the letter, but this was not to be avoided, since her father might refuse to speak with him and the letter would be one last chance, hope, really, to get all this said. Once, he had imagined telling her father that his relationship with Della had been entirely honorable. Now, while this was still absolutely true, it was no longer true in the sense he had meant it then or that her father would understand it now. We are married. No, you are not married. Both true, both false. I have been honorable. He could imagine himself sweating, wincing, under her father's contempt. He was a liar, but not at that moment.

Just the same, he adhered strictly to his plan. No drinking, no cigarettes. So he had a little something to add to his savings every week. He did not steal anything, no matter how negligible it was, no matter how thoughtlessly it had been abandoned to the whims of the light-fingered. He did buy a sketch pad and some pencils, thinking he would try to draw her face from memory and expecting to fail at it. Memory would be less engrossing if it were more sufficient. He spent an evening making drawings that looked nothing like her, no matter the care he took over the curve of her cheek, her brow, the set of her eyes. The landlady came in with an arm full of fresh bedding and saw the pages he had left on the dresser. "An artist, too!" she said, and stopped to admire them. "She looks like a Negro woman."

He said, "That's what she is." He watched her leafing through the pages. She said, "I like this one the best," holding up what happened to be a fair likeness. "It's very realistic. You know, you could make money drawing pictures of people."

"Lots of people don't want to know what they look like." Another truth he had learned in prison. "They think they do, till they see the picture." Then you might get your fingers busted. This amounted only to a minor sprain and a very alarming threat, but it had persuaded him that there might be little profit in portraiture.

"Well, you're a man of many talents," she said.

Not all of them strictly legal. The petty thievery was surprisingly hard to give up. "Thank you." He could not help being aware of the drawers full of silverware. Some vagrant spoon might yet be his undoing. He knew the landlady trusted him, not on the basis of any presumed insight into his individual character, but as a being of a higher order, too devoted to books and music to check the back of a fork for a sterling mark. The old impulse was still there to remind him that he was Jack, after all, defrauding people of their good opinion, if nothing else. A new suit would help, since the material benefits of respectability were made so clear to him every day. Enhanced, they would no doubt overwhelm temptation, offering inducements far more lucrative, though he was not sure calculations of this kind had any significant part in determining his actions. His father had observed, even dwelt on, the fact that the laws of Moses actually treated theft as debt. No hanging, no branding, only, in effect, a very steep rate of interest—steal one sheep, restore two. That was the Old Dispensation. Under the New Dispensation, debt was to be forgiven, as every Christian knew. Jack would stand by his father at the church door to see the pointedly blank expression of whatever parishioner he, Jack, had trespassed against recently, and whom his father, with homiletical legerdemain, had relieved of the right even to grumble. From boyhood he had schooled his poor father, staunch and doctrinal as he was by nature, in a kind of metaphysics of inversion and dissolution. The distinction "mine and thine" collapsed altogether, at least in his sermons. Even "good and evil" were held up to scrutiny. It had seemed to Jack that his father proposed a sort of Promised Land where troublesome categories did not apply. "Night shall be no more; they need no light of lamp or sun, for the Lord God will be their light." Those words nullified a very primary distinction. "God separated the light from the darkness," in the very first moments of creation. Verse 4. Then how was anyone to believe that any distinction was absolute, not secondary to a more absolute intention, the luminous reality concealed behind the veil of experience? He thought he should write this down, to show it to Della, maybe to her father. He and Della had been there, in that luminous absence of distinctions, in that radiant night.

He found a shop that sold ready-made suits with cuffs unfinished, to be tailored to fit the purchaser. Wonderful. Jack excused himself from lunch with the boss's daughter twice to stand in a shadow of chalk dust and basting threads while a man with a mouth full of pins made and unmade minute adjustments. The pant leg should touch the shoe and break a little. The sleeve should allow for a quarter inch of shirt cuff to show. It was a very muted tweed, gray blue, a good choice for his coloring, the man said, with the suspect objectivity that always complicates decisions of this kind. It was a fine suit, inexpensive, but tasteful in a way that concealed the fact. Jack had put a deposit on it, the balance due when this maddeningly meticulous tailor actually finished it. Meanwhile, he found the *Moonlight* Sonata in a stack of sheet music the landlady brought down from the attic and tried his hand at parts of it that looked possible. People had started calling him professor again, this time without any sign of malice.

It might not end! There might be no joke, no trapdoor, no banana peel. He had found himself in a highly congenial life that broke no laws. It took him a minute or two to remember the last time he had been seriously embarrassed. Then, to top it off, the landlady came to his door and told him that the young couple who had stayed in the largest room were leaving. It was in effect two rooms with sliding doors between them and a little balcony. She was beaming. "You could bring your wife here!" she said, gesturing at the flounces on the vanity, the cushion on the rocking chair. "You see, there's a writing desk in the alcove." She opened the desk to show him its hidden drawers and the tiny key that locked them. "It's a little too dainty for a man. Perfect for a lady."

"I'm not sure I could afford it," he said.

"Oh, nonsense! Another dollar a week." The landlady was in

love with him, in some sense of those words. To her mind the absent wife was the elegant consort he deserved, and her face glowed with the thought of their happiness. He certainly could imagine Della in these rooms, their bridal excesses a tribute to female loveliness. He would add a geranium. Fool that he was, or wasn't, since he knew that in this world there are limits to reasonable expectation, he said, "My wife is a colored lady."

She said, "That isn't possible. It's against the law." She turned her back to him. She said, "Just when you think you know somebody!"

So, just like that, it had ended. He knew there was no appeal to be made. But he said, "She's a wonderful, gentle woman. She's educated. She's a minister's daughter, an English teacher."

"She's a Negro. I don't want her coming around here."

"Well then, I'm leaving!" he said, as if this were a threat. So much had he come to assume.

She turned and looked at him, eyes bright with wrath. "You damn well bet you're leaving! Now! I took you for a decent man!"

Dear Jesus, don't let me lay a hand on this woman! He waited for the outrage that flooded him to recede enough to allow him to move or speak, but it was clearly apparent to her, and she was alarmed.

She said, "I'm going to call the cops!"

He stepped aside to let her leave the room, to ease her panic. This meant she could get to the telephone, with what consequences he could hardly bear to think. He went to his room and grabbed everything he could stuff into his valise, including certain cautious purchases that meant the catch wouldn't close. He did remember his hat and what remained of his money. As for anything else, hell with it.

He had money enough for a bus ticket to Memphis or to

St. Louis. St. Louis was where it seemed Della would be, but in Memphis he might find out where she really was. Out on the street again, he felt a sharp yearning for the meager comforts of the old room in the old flophouse, only a long walk away from what used to be Della's house. That would be capitulation. He would just be looking for memories. So he would go to Memphis, where she might not be, and then he would have the trouble and expense of following her, if they told him where she was, and in any case of getting himself back to St. Louis. While I think on thee, dear friend. It was the thought of her that made all this tolerable, the hope of finding her, just seeing her. He would sleep on a bench, sitting upright with his arms around his valise to protect it, buy his ticket, hope for a tolerable seat, and let himself be delivered to Memphis, stale, rumpled, and unshaven. His new suit, half paid for, would hang forever where he saw it last, and he would present himself to Della's father exactly the old white bum of that man's deepest fears. All losses are restored, and sorrows end. So long as he thought of her, and it was somehow really her he thought of. He knew that with use even memories wear.

He arrived on a Sunday, found the address of the church in a phone book, was pointed in its direction by a porter, and walked. Churches everywhere; chatty crowds at open doors, perfume, wafts of organ music, bells. The great Sabbath and its festivals. He walked on into the black city. By then doors were closing for the hour or two the worshippers variously pondered life and its implications. The church he was looking for finally came into sight. It was a big stone building with an urban, prosperous look, two squared-off towers with a stained-glass window between them. The wide doors at the base of each tower were still closed, so he loitered in a doorway across the street, wishing, pointlessly, that he had shaved and that there was anything he could spare, to abandon in some corner so the valise, which was a decent enough thing in itself, would close. But he couldn't risk being seen rummaging in it. If he didn't stop trying to force it, the catch would break. This felt inevitable. He wished he had a cigarette. Then the doors opened to a robust postlude and the bishop came out and took his place, ready to greet his congregation. He was a large man, attired in that episcopal finery Jack's father, in the black weeds of true Protestantism, sometimes took a moment to deplore. A wind stirred his vestments. Good Christ, he was imposing.

There was nothing else to do—he had spent his last dime getting there—so Jack began to saunter, a little obliquely, toward the edge of the crowd that mingled on the broad steps and on the sidewalk. The bishop looked up and saw him. It was a look like a rifle shot, aimed at him precisely. Jack stopped where he was. He decided to remove his hat. The bishop excused himself to the gathering and crossed the street, stopping at a distance from him of several feet.

"John Boughton," Jack said.

"Yes." The man was studying his face the way people do when they're about to say, How could you! Then he said, "You can wait inside," and walked off briskly toward the big stone house beside the church, the parsonage. Jack took this to mean he should follow, uneasy at the thought that he might have misunderstood, that something else was meant by "inside" and he was tagging along for no reason. But he followed him up the steps and into a big room with a public feeling about it. There were two pictures of Jesus, the one in Della's apartment but larger, and on another wall the one where He is holding a lamb in His arms. There was an upright piano and a chalkboard on an easel. The minister gestured at a chair, said, "I'll be back in a few minutes," and went away. And Jack sat there, thinking he would be much more comfortable on one of the couches but loath to presume. How had Della's father known who he was? He could not have been expected. Surely if Della described him she would not have described him as he was then, exhausted and so visibly out of luck. He was being treated like the embarrassing relative, to whom something both minimal and absolute is owed, respect having no part in it. Well, at least that would put him within the family circle. There might be some frayed version of those mystical bonds that attach relatives, if magazine poetry speaks true. This impressive man, he thought, is in some way or degree my father-in-law. He had to be careful what he thought. It might affect what he said. He had to laugh at the horrible possibility of his seeming in any way familiar.

The bishop was gone a good deal longer than a few minutes. Jack's carnal self had learned to expect breakfast. Chicago seemed more and more like an episode in *Pilgrim's Progress*, an enchanting byway where the hero's soul is imperiled by excesses of sound sleep and personal hygiene. What would John the Baptist have to say about all that? Jesus Himself, for that matter, before He was translated into the figure in the calming portraits. Jack had his hunger and the rest in common with the primitive church, who would stream into this room, impressed by the mismatched lamps and the wilted doilies, clamoring for some explanation of Methodist Episcopal, while his own reverend father stood by, hoping to offer a few words on the meaning of Presbyterian. He was falling asleep on that comfortless chair. He began to wonder if the delay meant that he should take offense and leave. And go where? And do what? He would be lurking around the next day, having come so far, having spent his last dime. The cops would get him for loitering and keep him for seeming deranged. This was life at its lowest ebb. But Julia brought him a tuna-fish sand-wich with sweet pickle along the edge of the plate, a napkin, and a newspaper. These little attentions were an almost unbearable relief, though all she said to him was "I'll bring you some coffee" and "He'll be back soon."

When he did come back soon, Della was with him. Her father shook his head, absorbing a difficult fact, and said, "She's been waiting for you. I hoped you might not come, but here you are."

Della came and stood beside him in that way she had, some-how affirming every vow he could ask of her, as if every promise was as good as kept before it was ever made. Forsaking all others, remarkably enough. Her father walked out of the room. Della sat down on a couch and patted the place next to her. She said, "I meant to just come here for a visit. But then after a few days I started feeling bad in the mornings. And my mother knew what that was." She smoothed the lap of her dress with both hands.

"Oh," he said.

"Yes."

He was glad she did not look at him. Shame and embarrass-ment overwhelmed him before he had time to think, and he was ashamed and embarrassed to realize that this was true. His wife was expecting a child. This was a blessing, pure and simple. But shame was a very old habit with him. He had long considered it penitential, payment extracted in the form of steady, tolerable misery, against a debt he would never settle. He was even a little loyal to it, as if it assured him there was justice in the universe. Shame stirred in him when he felt disapproval, like an ache in bad weather, and here he was, the center of scandal, and of out-rage pent up on grounds of religion and good manners. That big room they sat in was conspicuously empty. All the wear of endless, impersonal hospitality meant emptiness, as if someone had shouted "Fire!" Word had gone out. This good family would be spared at least the crudest effects of scandal. He took Della's hand and she leaned against him. Well, that was wonderful.

"What now?" she said.

"I've been thinking about St. Louis."

She nodded. "I think about it all the time."

"I tried Chicago. It didn't work out. Neither did St. Louis, I suppose."

They laughed. "We had some good times there, though," she said. "We did."

Julia came into the room, all tact, to head off a dozen adolescents who had gathered at the front door. A confirmation class, no doubt. She spoke to them and they went away adolescent fashion, jumping from the top step to the sidewalk two or three times, laughing, bickering companionably, scuffling a little, expending energy that came with being released from expectation. That part of life wasn't a bad thing to give someone.

Julia said, "I'm going to go find Auntie. She's probably still at the church," and she left.

After a few minutes, the brother Marcus stepped into the doorway. "I have an appointment," he said. "I'll see you later, Della. Tell them not to wait dinner for me."

She said, "Marcus, you don't have an appointment. At dinnertime on Sunday?"

He shrugged. "I was just trying to be polite," he said, and he put on his hat and left.

Jack had stood when Della's father came back with her, of course, and both times Julia came in, and again when Marcus had stood there in the doorway. He was beginning to feel ridiculous, thrown back on that punctilious courtesy that struck more than a few people as sardonic. He could never find just the right degree of deference. There were things other people seemed to be born knowing. He could hear voices in other rooms, some of them sounding heated. Whoever appeared, in whatever emotional state, he had only courtesy to defend himself. He had stood there, hat in hand figuratively speaking, while Marcus paused in the doorway, barely glancing at him, and excused himself from any acquaintance with him. Why were there an infinite number of ways to feel awkward? He believed this was a theological question having to do with man's place in the universe. But when he felt the true force of the question, he was always in the middle of an embarrassing emergency of some kind that paralyzed reflection.

But each time he sat down again Della took his hand. He had pondered at some length the very great comfort there was in the touch of that hand. Another theological question, how one human being can mean so much to another human being in terms of peace and assurance, as if loyalty were as real as gravity. His father said it had to be that real, because the Lord is loyal. Jack was just then feeling the force of the idea.

Julia came in, smiling, with smiling Aunt Delia, who offered a hand in a lavender glove and said, "Mr. Boughton!" in a tone that acknowledged old acquaintance. "It's good to see you!" A favorite aunt with the kind of charm that came with a good heart. Della kissed her. Jack could have kissed her. She was pretty and enjoyed the fact. She was the ally anyone could wish for and enjoyed that, too. "I've been recruited to help with dinner," she said, and laughed. "So I guess I have some work to do!" Julia looked on, pleased, and then they went away.

Jack said, "I should go. I mean, I shouldn't be hanging around. Maybe I could see you tomorrow."

Della said, "Don't leave. Nothing will be better tomorrow. At least today we still have the advantage of surprise." She said,

"It's not so pleasant for me here, either. No one has been unkind, really, but everything is different. My fault."

"Mine, too. We're in this together."

She nodded. "That's the good part," she said.

He did not put his arm around Della, his wife, or kiss her. That could easily inflame the situation. "I do have something to give you." He had, in the last furious moment, jammed the pictures he had made of her into the valise, since, disappointing as they were, they might be the only likeness he would ever have of her. "I was trying to remember your face," he said. "Please don't be offended."

Della looked them over. "You think I'm pretty."

"Yes, but the expression of the eyes is wrong. Look at me." He studied her face. She studied his.

Then Della's mother came into the room, arm in arm with Aunt Delia. Jack stood. Her mother said, breathily, "Mr. Boughton, I hope you can stay for dinner. It will just be the family. You'll be very welcome."

Jack said, "Thank you. That's very kind. But I really should be going."

Della said, "Thank you, Mama. He'll stay."

And Delia said, "Of course he will stay!"

Sweet savors. His father said the essence of the thing was that fragrance ascending. Who would suppose some flustered, crotchety old chicken could yield up such perfumes? Grace upon grace. The Old Gent had blessed their dinner in just these terms, sometimes having skipped breakfast to appreciate it properly. Jack felt a pang of longing to be in his father's house. He was thinking, I could pray your prayers, I could sing your hymns, I could bless your dinner. I shouldn't be such a stranger here. Or in my father's house, for that matter. Why do these embarrassments always feel new?

Della said, "It will be all right." And then she said, "If it isn't, what will it matter?" True enough. No real problem would be solved at best, or made worse if it all went wrong, and dinner would be a good thing in any case.

He said, softly, "I know a man in St. Louis who might help us out a little." This was Hutchins. There was a fundamental kindness behind his disapproval that, who knows, might prevail in the circumstances. Which should not have arisen, as he would say, and Jack would not grant. But there must be some ladies in the church who would love to help bring a baby into the world. That desk clerk at the old place might not mind too much if Della stayed there for a while, discreetly, of course, until they found other arrangements. For all his threats he never did call the cops. Maybe Teddy had gone on leaving money at the other place. That fellow might not have seen his way clear to give Teddy the note, and if he had put maybe half of the money aside like he did while Jack was in prison, it would have added up. Jack was not in the habit of mustering hopes, since they invited disappointment, a possibility that aroused anxieties in him that actually seemed to summon disappointment.

Della said, "Jack?" wanting his attention, and he realized that her mother had come to ask them to sit down for dinner. Della showed him where he could wash his hands and his face, and then he came into the dining room. It was set with ten places, six of them empty. Della's father was not in the room.

"Julia," her mother said, "go find your brothers."

Julia was gone and came back and whispered something to

her mother. "Yes, they will come to dinner!" her mother whispered loudly. "This minute!"

Jack stood up, about to excuse himself, and the lady of the house said, "You just sit down!" as if she'd forgotten he wasn't one of hers, a pleasant thought. And then, "Where's Delia now? Where's she off to?" and she left the room to answer her own question while the handsome dinner cooled.

Delia came in with two tall boys, teenagers, who glanced at him and shared looks, drew their chairs out noisily and slouched in them, kidding around with each other a little, as if furtively. Then Marcus came into the room with Julia, and stood behind his chair as though he could not make the final concession and sit down in it. His mother said, "We won't start without your father," so Marcus left and Julia followed him, then Delia. Their mother said, out loud to herself, "Everything's going to be stone cold."

One of the teenagers turned to him and said, "Hi there, Jack."

The other one said, "How's it going, Jack?" Then he said, "No, wait a minute. Jack's dead!"

"Yeah! Didn't he choke to death on a chicken bone?" They laughed uproariously.

Della said, "Jack the cat. Sorry."

Their mother shook her head. "What have I done to deserve such children!"

The older boy said, "We're not minding our manners. Isn't somebody going to send us to our room?"

"Yeah! Put your foot down, Mama!"

"If you keep on this way, you're going to be sitting in those chairs till your beards are gray. We have company!"

"Oh, sorry, we didn't realize he was company. He just kind of showed up, didn't he?"

"Yeah, like a stray cat." They laughed and laughed. "Now do we have to go to our room?"

Their mother said, "I am so ashamed of you. I didn't know you could be so rude."

"Well, where's Papa? Where's Marcus?"

"Yeah?"

"Never you mind. Sit up straight and act your age!"

Jack stood up. "Yes, well, thank you, Mrs. Miles, but I have to go." He realized he had put his hand to his face, hiding that damn scar. But the bishop walked in, with Delia and Julia and Marcus and another brother whose name he didn't know. The older man stood at the head of the table and said, "Heavenly Father—" Then everyone stood up. Jack couldn't very well walk out during grace. Then Della put her arm through his and said, "This man is my husband. If he leaves, I go with him." No one wanted that, Jack least of all. Go where? Do what? And with a wife to think about! It was brilliant. Her mother was saying, "Please stay!" And the boys were saying, "We're sorry, Della! We didn't mean it." And her father was saying, "We should all calm down and enjoy this fine meal together!" The thing that would have been Jack's fiercely guarded secret if it were not obvious to everyone, that he was a hungry man with no money in his pockets, was certainly a consideration for all of them, for Jack definitely. After he had filled his plate, with proud restraint to spare himself that appearance of mendicancy he so often had reason to dread, Della filled it again twice. It was all very good. Marcus attempted conversation—"I understand you're a country boy." This rankled Jack a little, because it was probably true.

"Small town," he said.

"Right," Marcus said, as if acknowledging a distinction.

"I did do a lot of fishing. Played lots of baseball." Lied a lot, stole a lot. Blue eye, tan cheek, larcenous habits, a Child Slick somehow rusticated. Not what anyone means by the words "country boy." The dinner was exhausting, and when he was tired, Jack had to watch out for bouts of candor.

The bishop said, "This is a pretty full house, as you can see, but we do have a couple of cots in a back room for unexpected visitors."

"Thank you. That's very kind." He hated how often he had to say those words. When Della's mother told the boys that they would be doing the dishes all by themselves for the rest of their lives, Jack caught himself before he could say he had useful experience in that line, or he was living proof that you really could end up doing dishes for the rest of your life. It wasn't even dark out, and the thought of sleep almost made his knees buckle.

"First, though, I hope we can have a few words, Mr. Boughton," the bishop said.

"Of course." Of course. Jack followed him into his study. Big books drab with age and use, a picture of Jesus preaching.

"Mr. Boughton," he said.

"Jack."

He nodded. "Mr. Boughton. My family and many of our friends have devoted ourselves to a certain way of life, one meant to develop self-sufficiency in the Negro race by the practice of separatism, so far as this is possible in society as it exists now. I know there are white people who are offended by separatism, but the alternatives also offend them. I'm not asking your opinion about this. My point is that my objection is not to you as an individual."

Jack said, "You don't know me very well."

"Maybe I don't. I think I have gleaned a few things. But we won't get into that."

"Thanks. You're very kind."

"Kinder than I want to be sometimes."

Jack said, "I understand. My father was a clergyman."

He smiled. "Yes, Della has mentioned that." After a moment, he said, "You can never be welcome here. I want you to understand that. Della and any children can come here if they want to, or need to, so long as they come without you. You have disrupted our lives, but not our intentions. The situation of black people must change. They must have the opportunity to decide what form the change will take and how it will be achieved. I regret that my daughter does not choose to have a part in this. For the time being, at least."

Jack said, "Della is loyal to me and I'm loyal to her. I never intended things to work out this way. I couldn't have imagined it. Neither of us meant any harm, I promise you."

"So she says." He took up an envelope from his desk. "Money," he said. "Enough for bus fare to St. Louis. I want you to go away."

"Then both of us will go."

"Maybe so. We'll see."

Jack would have refused the money on principle if he were not in fact desperate to leave and at a loss for another way to manage it. "Thank you" seemed wrong in the circumstances, so Jack said, "Christian of you." This may have sounded a little sardonic, since the bishop said, "You should be very grateful that I am a Christian man."

The fact was that Jack saw his point. In simple truth, society was a great collaboration devoted to making everything difficult and painful to no good end, a curse on the life of his good Della and her unborn child. True loyalty to them might have been to step away and let this man go about his necessary work undistracted by worry about his daughter, by fear for her. But if Jack did that, if he left her, even her father might think, might say, "Well, what did you expect?"

Jack said to this formidable man, "I'm really very tired."

"Yes. I'll show you to your room."

It was a bare room with three cots in it, two closed up and one with a pillow, sheets, and a blanket. Jack almost made a joke about handing over his belt and shoelaces, which would actually have seemed prudent in his current state of mind. It felt very good to take off his tie and jacket and his shoes. There was a knock at the door, Julia with his valise and a paper bag that smelled like sandwiches. "Della is leaving tomorrow, too," she said, and went away.

When the light was out, he sank into a despondency that had many of the effects of sleep. He was immobilized and his thoughts were strange, unstable as water. Then it was sleep, the same except that from time to time he woke out of it. Well before dawn began, he pulled himself together as well as he could and sat on the bed wishing the light was good enough to let him read. He had that small old Bible in his valise. After a while there was a knock at the door, Julia again. She said, "Della's in the kitchen making coffee." So he went to find her, and there she was, in that warm, enclosing light that blackens windows and delays morning, that most domestic light. Of course he put his arms around her. For a minute or two they had the world to themselves.

Della said, "Are you ready to go?"

"Absolutely, utterly, passionately."

"I'm sorry it's been so awful. They're really wonderful people."

"I'll take your word for that."

"Hurt feelings," she said.

He said, "Let's not think about it. It's done. We'll think about it later. Forever, probably."

"You know, we don't have to wait around here if you really want to leave. But at least we can be together here." Out in the city everything was Colored or White.

"I really don't want to stay here for the goodbyes. But you should."

"Yes. I will."

"Give my thanks to Aunt Delia and your mother. Tell your little brothers I hold grudges."

"Marcus?"

"Nothing comes to mind. Though I have drawn up a list of my strengths and virtues for him to share with your father, with a tastefully gilded account of my prospects."

"You made a copy for me, I suppose. With angels."

"Yes, and one for myself, to help me through life's bleaker passages."

They heard stirrings, voices. Jack said, "I'm getting out of here. I'm about to skedaddle. Goodbye, Julia. *Au revoir*, my love." He kissed her. "Give me your suitcase. I can carry it for you. That's the sort of thing a gentleman does, I believe."

So, with her bag and his gaping valise he made the long walk back to the bus station. He got his ticket and took a seat where he could watch the door and see a part of the colored section of the waiting room. It was almost time for the bus to leave when Della finally came in, bought her ticket, and walked through the waiting room to the sidewalk where the bus was panting and reeking like an overexcited beast. Jack got on and took a seat at the back of the white section. It appeared to him that the colored seats were nearly all taken. From the window he saw his lovely Della pleading and cajoling, trying to talk a very old woman out of taking the last seat. Finally a young man, with the abruptness of contained exasperation, got off the bus, and the two of them boarded. So she was with him. She would tell him that she had been delayed by her mother's grief and her father's alarm. Jack's visit had done not one thing to reassure them. Della would say, "I have been disowned," and Jack would say, "That's just how it is for some people." They were together, after their fashion, and the world was all before them, such as it was.

And this was his grandest larceny by far, this sly theft of happiness from the very clutches of prohibition. True, it was also the theft of a beloved daughter from her proud family, with the damage this involved to their honorable hopes, and with a secondary though much greater damage that would come with the diminishing of those hopes. This might be felt for generations. It would touch his own child, too. Then there was the theft of every good effect she would have felt from her education. Over time she might decide that she was not in possession of her happiness as she might have believed, even, dear Jesus, of her own self-love. How would she live with that divine anger of hers when mere he, so far as he could, and not her father, stood between her and the insults and abrasions of the world?

The knowledge of good. That half of the primal catastrophe received too little attention. Guilt and grace met together in the phrase despite all that. He could think of himself as a thief sneaking off with an inestimable wealth of meaning and trust, all of it offended and damaged beyond use, except to remind him of the nature of the crime. Or he could consider the sweet marriage that made her a conspirator with him in it, the loyalty that always restored them both, just like grace.